Empire's Ashes

Ashes

Blood on the Stars XV

Jay Allan

system 7
publishing

Books by Jay Allan

Flames of Rebellion Series
(Published by Harper Voyager)
Flames of Rebellion
Rebellion's Fury

The Crimson Worlds Series
Marines
The Cost of Victory
A Little Rebellion
The First Imperium
The Line Must Hold
To Hell's Heart
The Shadow Legions
Even Legends Die
The Fall

Crimson Worlds Refugees Series
Into the Darkness
Shadows of the Gods
Revenge of the Ancients
Winds of Vengeance
Storm of Vengeance

Crimson Worlds Successors Trilogy
MERCS
The Prisoner of Eldaron
The Black Flag

Crimson Worlds Prequels
Tombstone
Bitter Glory
The Gates of Hell

Red Team Alpha
(A New Crimson Worlds Novel)

Join my email list
at www.jayallanbooks.com

List members get publication announcements and special bonuses throughout the year (email addresses are never shared or used for any other purpose). Please feel free to email me with any questions at jayallanwrites@gmail.com. I answer all reader emails

For all things Sci-Fi,
join my interactive Reader Group here:

facebook.com/groups/JayAllanReaders

Follow me on Twitter @jayallanwrites

Follow my blog at www.jayallanwrites.com

www.jayallanbooks.com
www.crimsonworlds.com

Books by Jay Allan

Blood on the Stars Series
Duel in the Dark
Call to Arms
Ruins of Empire
Echoes of Glory
Cauldron of Fire
Dauntless
The White Fleet
Black Dawn
Invasion
Nightfall
The Grand Alliance
The Colossus
The Others
The Last Stand
Empire's Ashes

Andromeda Chronicles
(Blood on the Stars Adventure Series)
Andromeda Rising
Wings of Pegasus

The Far Stars Series
Shadow of Empire
Enemy in the Dark
Funeral Games

Far Stars Legends Series
Blackhawk
The Wolf's Claw

Portal Wars Trilogy
Gehenna Dawn
The Ten Thousand
Homefront

Also by Jay Allan – The Dragon's Banner

Chapter One

Forward Outpost Seven
Delta Orion System
Year 327 AC (After the Cataclysm)

"Commander, we're picking up energy readings from the transit point." The officer's words were tentative, his tone edgy. There were any number of things that could cause a transit point's emissions to spike, most of which were benign, but Outpost Seven was positioned along the line of systems that formed the tentative border between Hegemony systems still controlled by the Pact, and those in the Occupied Zone. It was the front line of a war that had been largely silent for three and a half years, but which no one expected to remain so indefinitely.

"Full scan, Lieutenant. Get the AI on it as soon as we have more data." Commander St. James shared a bit of the scanner officer's tension, but it was weaker, more controlled. St. James had commanded Outpost Seven for almost two years, and in that time there had been at least a dozen alerts and causes for concern, all of which had proven to be nothing.

Still, it had been almost four years since the Battle of Calpharon. No one had expected the lull in the fighting to last so long, and St. James's hope that the Highborn had decided to cease their invasion warred with a growing sense that a renewal in hostilities was 'due.'

"Yes, Commander. All scanners retargeted. We should have updated readings in...four minutes, thirty seconds."

St. James just nodded. He was anxious, more so, he realized, than he'd thought at first. He'd told himself it was just an asteroid or a concentration of particulate matter coming through. Or even one of the completely unexplained pulses that sometimes spewed forth occasionally from the mysterious points that allowed humanity to travel from system to system.

But he had a bad feeling this time, one that grew with each passing second.

He glanced at the chronometer. Four minutes wasn't a long time by any reasonable measure, but it could *feel* long, especially in situations like the current one. There was nothing to be done, no order he could issue that would change the fact that the automated scanner stations monitoring the point were four and a half light minutes from the outpost. That was a speed limit imposed by the universe, one that had held firm, despite the advancement of human science. Only the transit points themselves offered a way around that constraint, and St. James had taken the word of the physicists that moving through the point did not actually involve exceeding lightspeed, but rather altering the distance between systems via alternate space. It was all very confusing, and he wasn't sure the experts knew as much as they claimed to. Still, the points worked, that much he'd seen hundreds of time through personal experience.

He would just have to wait four minutes—down to more like two and a half as he looked again at the display—to get the report from the focused scans. He turned toward the tactical station, intending for a moment to put the outpost on alert, even to launch the fighter squadrons. But he held back. He'd put his people on battlestations the first three times the scanners had picked up dust clouds and meteors coming through the point, and he'd long since decided to show some restraint. One day, enemy ships could very well pour through the point, and he wanted his people sharp and ready when that happened, not jaded and dulled by too many false alarms.

Not that any of it matters…not if the Highborn ever come through in force.

The outposts were placed along the entire disputed border, every one of the seventeen systems that connected to space controlled by the enemy. But they watched that frontier more than defended it. Their true purpose was one upon which St. James didn't much like to dwell. The most important systems on the outpost were not weapons, but communications drones, the ones St. James would send off when and if Highborn vessels every *did* stream through the point. The drones would race to the system's only other transit point, and they would take back the warning, the news every Confederation, Hegemony, and Alliance warrior had been expecting—and dreading—for more than three years.

And then, St. James and his people would die. They would fight, of course, extract whatever price their batteries and squadrons could on the enemy. But the outposts had been built as warning stations, not fortresses…and Thomas St. James was enough of a veteran to understand just what it would mean for his small command when the Highborn did come through that point.

"Enhanced data coming in, Commander. The AI is working on…" A pause, and then the officer turned, the essence of his report clear in his eyes. "Highborn ships, Commander. Six confirmed…and continued energy readings at the point."

St. James had been waiting for those words for two years, wondering how he would respond to his moment of truth. And very likely, his own death warrant. Now that it was actually happening, he felt strangely cold about it all, almost clinical. He was afraid, he supposed, but it felt odd, distant, almost unrelated to his actions.

"All squadrons are to scramble for immediate launch. The AI is to download all scanner data into the drones." He would command his people in battle, see that they did everything possible to inflict as much damage as possible on whatever was coming through the point. But he knew his most important task was seeing that the drones escaped the system. The longer he waited, the more data he could send back to Admiral Barron.

But if he waited too long, the enemy might intercept the drones.

He turned back toward the display, realizing he hadn't been listening to the scanning officer's continued reports. He'd imagined the very circumstance then unfolding around him since he'd first arrived on Outpost Seven. Now, he knew he was living it, that it had arrived.

That he and his people likely had only hours to live.

*   *   *

"Alright, let's keep those formations tight, all of you. We've run enough exercises, practiced this again and again. It should be secondhand to all of you by now." Commander Susan Contrall sat in her cockpit, knowing all she said was pure truth, but also that it was irrelevant. Her people were mostly rookies, new trainees rushed through the Academy and shipped to the front lines along with all the new Lightnings Confederation industry had been able to produce. Training and practice were useful, essential even, but no amount of preparation could truly ready a pilot to face the enemy.

She had six veterans in the entire wing, to command and steady ninety-one pilots who'd never fired a shot in anger. It seemed strange, at first, that the contingents posted along the most forward borders were so heavy with new pilots, but she'd understood quickly. It came down to a single word, one that concisely expressed the grimness and brutality of war.

Expendability.

Her squadrons were valued, of course. The Pact needed every ship it could get, every spacer, every bit of combat power. She knew Admiral Barron cared for every man and woman in his command, that he took no life for granted. But he had no choice in many of his decisions, no more than she did. Fighting the enemy would be a costly endeavor, and she'd always known that her people would be among the first to die if it turned out that their outpost was along the Highborn's chosen invasion route.

That, at least, was still undecided. The force that had emerged from the point was substantial, but not overpowering. It *might* be an advance guard, the leading edge of a massive invasion…or just some kind of scouting effort.

She would know soon enough, when the new arrivals stopped, and she could see just how many ships had come.

She stared at the display, quickly analyzing the enemy formation, developing a plan of attack. There were still ships transiting, and uncertainty about the scope of the incursion meant any plan she developed would be risky, based on guesswork as much as tactical expertise. She only had a single wing, and she decided to strike as hard as possible against the forces already deployed in the system. If she *was* watching the lead elements of a massive invasion, she didn't have the strength to defend against it anyway.

"Green Dragons, you've got the lead. Steel Gators, Dark Storm, you're both on the starboard flank. Push forward, and get in position for a flank run." Contrall watched as her pilots executed her commands, and she felt some faint optimism as she saw the tightness of their formations. They were well trained, if mostly unblooded by combat. They were flying with commendable precision, and skillfully executing complex flight plans. Facing an enemy firing back at them would be a rude awakening, no doubt, but the years of practice and preparation were at showing in their flying as they approached.

Contrall *had* faced the enemy in battle. She had been at Calpharon, seen the enemy missile volleys, and she knew just how deadly a danger they really were. She'd commanded Outpost Seven's wings for a little over a year and a half, and she'd developed an attachment to her people unscarred by the constant losses of active combat. For a veteran like herself, that had felt like a luxury, a real chance to bond with her pilots, to get to know them, and to mold them into a special team.

That respite, she realized was over. She didn't realize just *how* over it was, though, not until a moment later.

"Commander, we're picking up some strange readings from the enemy ships." Contrall had already noticed that the Highborn vessels—and she was still only *assuming* it was the Highborn coming through the point—were different from any of the previously encountered classes. They were larger than the normal, cruiser-sized units, but smaller than the heavy battleships that had fought at Calpharon.

She flipped her scanner array to full power, directing it toward the cluster of enemy ships ahead, even as she leaned toward the comm and said, "All units, direct scans toward the enemy ships. Relay all data back to Outpost Seven command." Information on new enemy ship classes was vital intel…and despite her pride in her squadrons and their still unproven combat capability, she still realized the major purpose of the outpost line was to warn the main fleet, and to provide as much data as possible on whatever was coming through.

That included new Highborn ships.

"Commander, we're in missile range…but I haven't detected any launches yet."

"Me either."

"None here."

Her lead squadrons commanders were all telling the same story. They were at least ten thousand kilometers past the range that had normally prompted enemy missile volleys.

Contrall looked down at her own screens. Nothing. The bulk of missiles launched at Calpharon had come from the enemy battleships, and the force in front of her squadrons had none of the heavy battlewagons, at least not yet. But the vessels her people faced were substantially larger than the enemy cruisers. Large enough, she would have guessed, to mount missile launchers. Especially when those weapons had been so effective against the Rim bombers, and almost four years seemed like more than enough to install the systems in the mid-sized vessels.

"Wait, Commander, I *am* picking something up. Might be a missile launch…"

Contrall felt her insides tighten a bit. She wasn't surprised the enemy had missiles, but she realized she'd let optimism get the best of her for a moment.

"Alright, you all know what to do. We practiced those evasive routines a hundred times." *Yes, they know what to do…but you know they are still rookies, at least in terms of facing the enemy.*

She'd seen the casualty lists from too many fights, analyzed the ratios a hundred different ways. It was an inescapable conclusion. New pilots died in far greater numbers than veterans, often at six or eight times the rate. Her pilots knew what to do when the enemy missiles came for them…but that didn't mean some of them weren't going to die.

A lot of them.

She angled her own controls, brought her thrust vector around and upped her engine output. She'd been holding back, waiting to see what sector of the formation saw the heaviest action. But if her people were going to face a missile attack, she was going to be up there with them. She wasn't sure her example would do much to pull her rookies through the ordeal, but it wasn't going to hurt.

Besides, they deserved to have their commander up there with them, and it was the only place she knew to be in a fight. She'd mourned the loss of Jake Stockton as fervently as anyone in the fighter corps had done, even the entire Confederation as a whole, but she also honored his memory, by remembering his teachings, and the creed he had instilled in every pilot he'd commanded, and even more, in every commander he placed in charge of others. Lead from the front.

She adjusted her course again, moving toward the center of her small formation. Once, ninety-odd bombers would have been considered a substantial force, but the scope of battle had escalated enormously over the past twenty years. Great battles were fought by thousands of fighters, and in a struggle like Calpharon, her ninety-seven ships would be little more than one unit out of dozens.

She looked down at the screen again, ready to track the incoming missiles.

But there were no missiles. No clusters of the great weapons moving toward her ships, no sign of any incoming volleys.

There was something, however.

Her eyes fixed on each of the three closest enemy ships. The contacts weren't missiles, she was sure of that, but there was *something* going on around each of the Highborn ships, a hazy glow around each of the reddish symbols at first, and then, as more data came in, a grouping of small white dots on the black screen.

It took her a moment to realize what she was seeing. Then she felt as though her blood had frozen solid.

The enemy ships were launching small craft of some kind. Her squadrons were still too far out to get detailed readings, but she didn't need them. The coldness in her gut told her what she was seeing.

Highborn fighters.

Chapter Two

Forward Base Striker
Vasa Denaris System
Year 327 AC (After the Cataclysm)

The child threw a small red rubber ball across the room, knocking over a pile of data chips on the desk in the process...and then she laughed wildly. She was tall for a girl of four and a half, and her long, light brown hair was almost an exact copy of Andi's. Cassie reminded Tyler of her mother in many more ways than one, including a few that tied his stomach into knots with concerns about her future. Andi Lafarge was smart, capable, resilient, reliable...and sometimes gut-wrenchingly reckless. There was no guarantee, of course, that Cassie would dive into things as aggressively as her mother was wont to do, but he could see enough foreshadowing to fuel worry. Tyler had some years to go before his daughter would have the chance to put him through the wringer as her mother had, diving wildly into one dangerous situation after another, but part of him still dreaded it.

A different part of him was terrified she would never get the chance to follow in her mother's footsteps, that the universe that had produced Andi and him would be fundamentally changed, that defeat in the war would reduce

Cassie, and billions of others, to little more than the slaves of a race of self-proclaimed gods. It was that thought, and others like it, that drove him through sixteen hours days, that fueled the near-monster he'd become, driving his people forward without the slightest hint of mercy or leniency. The Pact had gotten a longer respite than he'd dared to hope they would, but he knew the struggle he'd dreaded every day would come upon them, likely sooner rather than later. He wasn't sure be believed his forces had a real chance of victory, but he was damned certain they would be ready, and that they would fight with everything they had...technology, tactics...and the blood and guts of dedicated men and women behind it all.

Tyler Barron had lived the last three and a half years amid fear and desperation, surrounded on all sides by construction and preparation so intense, it had almost overwhelmed him, even as he demanded more from those around under his command. He had lived under the shadow of death for forty-four Megaran months, working at a pace that seemed destined to drive anyone mad...and he had never been happier.

His dead spacers were there, as always, their ranks greatly expanded by the horrific carnage at Calpharon. His outlook was bleak as well, and for all the ships that had poured forth from the Confederation's shipyards, for all the enhanced weaponry Hegemony technology had given the Confederation, for all his undiminished confidence in his officers and spacers, he still didn't *really* believe victory was possible. His people had been building, preparing, fortifying for nearly four years, but he knew the enemy had not been idle in all that time. He knew what he'd done with the time, but all he could do was guess at what the Highborn had accomplished in more than three and a half years.

Still, none of that had dampened his happiness at almost four years with Andi and Cassiopeia. His quarters on Base Striker, the half dozen rooms he shared with his family, were adequate enough, if far from plush. His schedule was grueling, and it reduced the amount of time he'd had to spend with those he loved. That time was further ravaged by Andi's equally demanding commitment to researching old imperial records, combing every known artifact for any further clues about the Highborn…how they were created, and how they were seemingly driven out of the empire before the final fall. But even when he was stuck in some conference room or out inspecting new ships, Andi was just a few decks above or below, pawing through old records…not hundreds of lightyears away, out of reach.

At least when he was elsewhere in the system or the fleet, he knew they were close. His daughter had been almost a year old before he'd seen her, and he'd gone even longer without seeing Andi. He could feel the shadow of desperation and despair that hung just beyond the edge of his thoughts. But none of it, not the Highborn threat, nor the dark clouds of renewed battle on the horizon, nor the desperate struggles to prepare, to find a way to meet the enemy, to survive and attain victory, could take away from what he felt when he held his daughter, or when he and Andi had some time together, stolen moments that they may be.

He leaned down and picked up the ball, smiling as he tossed it back in Cassie's direction. He threw it softly, and it bounced off the floor about a meter in front of her, unleashing another burst of giggles as she lunged to pick it up.

"You can throw harder than that," she said, staring at him for an instant with a mischievous look that almost seemed to make Andi's face morph over hers, before she scooped up the ball and threw it back, with considerably more energy behind it.

It bounced off Barron's thigh and flew off across the room. "I guess I'm tired, sweetheart. And I've got a lot of work to do right now."

"Okay…fine…" Cassie stood there, looking as though she was caught between wandering off and amusing herself…or ratcheting up the guilt, and trying to lure Tyler from his work. Finally, she just smiled and said, "You can work for a while, I guess." Then she turned and walked off into the next room.

Barron smiled for a moment, his eyes fixed on the door his daughter had just slipped through. He felt happiness, mixed almost inextricably with sadness. He loved Cassie, but he wished the reality surrounding her birth, and the life she'd so far led, had been one of peace, and not blanketed by the shadow of deadly danger never far from thought. Cassie didn't know much about the Highborn, or at least what she knew was limited.

At least you think she doesn't. Fatherly pride notwithstanding, Cassie's intellect was clearly a sharp one, and he wondered if the child was more aware of the situation than he liked to believe. He didn't like the idea of trying to deceive her in any way, but she was too young to face the harsh reality of what was coming.

He'd almost sent her back to Megara a dozen times, and he knew on some level he'd kept her on Striker out of selfishness, because he so desperately wanted her near him. There was something deeper, too, he realized. He believed deep down that the day he put Andi on Cassie on a ship heading back to Megara would be the last time he would ever see them. He put on a brave face for his spacers, but his gut told him he'd finally found the war that would claim him. Having his family there, for another day, another week, another month…it was priceless to him.

Very possibly the only chance he would ever have.

He pulled his thoughts back from his wife and daughter, to the work that still demanded most of his time. Gary Holsten had made the long trip back and forth from Megara half a dozen times, spending much of his time in space so he could alternate between meetings with Barron and keeping the Senate under control. Barron had managed to get the politicians more or less onboard with all he needed, through a combination of Holsten's looming presence…and the stone cold fear that had come from realization of what the Rim was truly facing. Still, he couldn't take anything for granted. He'd had too much trouble from politicians before, and he knew just what a drain the massive war effort had been on the Confederation's resources. The massively accelerated ship research and construction program had been monumental in scale, and still, it diminished almost to irrelevancy next to the construction of the Confederation's first antimatter production facility.

Antimatter was the fuel for the most advanced systems, and the most potent weapon known. It also took monstrous amounts of energy to produce even small amounts of the amazing substance. Confederation science had possessed the skills to produce antimatter for almost a century, but the lack of a means to produce the concentrated energy required for mass production restricted its use to scientific experiments requiring minute quantities.

Until the Pact had made Hegemony technology available to the Confederation, along with the schematics to turn an entire planet into a vast production facility. The system utilized geothermal energies, nuclear fusion, massive solar power, weather…every method known to modern technology to produce the required energy to create antimatter in quantities measured in the tons instead of micrograms.

Hegemony technology made the construction of such a facility *possible*, but it did nothing to blunt the ruinous cost. At more than twice the size of the Confederation, the Hegemony had only managed to build two such production facilities in a century and a half, and one of those had now been destroyed, its remains captured by the enemy.

The Hegemony had spent twenty years constructing each of their production centers. Tyler Barron had insisted the

Confederation do it in four, and he'd sent Gary Holsten to make sure the Senate was cooperative, and Anya Fritz, his longtime engineering master, to oversee the construction. It was an impossible task, he knew, and yet Fritz's latest report suggested antimatter production could begin in as little as six months. That was cause for optimism, or he tried to make it so, but his mind was still focused on the enemy, on their technology…and on a notion he couldn't shake that the Highborn themselves were simply *better* than he and all his people.

Barron had been repelled by the Hegemony's genetic rating hierarchy, but he'd also recognized the advantages behind it, even the justifications. He'd seen too many fools in position of power causing unspeakable damage, too many important jobs left to men and women incapable of completing them. The Highborn were something else entirely, not just the Hegemony's selection of those pegged to be the best of any current generation, but a true effort to push the entire species forward. Their genes had been manipulated, enhanced. They were larger, stronger, smarter. As far as his intel went, it seemed they were immune to most illnesses…and the Firstborn, at least those of that initial group of five hundred specimens not killed by violence, were alive nearly four centuries after their 'births.' There was no argument, no intelligent one. They *were* better in many ways.

It disgusted him to think that way, but he had to fight them, and underestimating the enemy was the surest road to defeat. He even understood why the Highborn's creators had done what they had done. Their imperial society had been decaying, the drive that pushed people forward almost gone from a decadent society. If the Highborn had behaved as expected, as teachers and leaders instead of would be gods consumed by arrogance and ambition, the program might very well have save the empire…and all humanity.

Instead of leading to the Cataclysm, and creating the

deadliest enemy every known.

He looked at the small screen on his desk, at the starmap displayed there. *What are you doing out there? Why have you waited so long? When are you coming?*

He had precious little heard intel on just what was happening on the worlds the enemy had occupied, and what shreds he did possess had been bought with rivers of his scouts' blood. But one thing was clear. The Highborn had harnessed Hegemony industry and populations in a massive way, and they were turning out a constant stream of new ships…weapons of war he knew would eventually be turned on his forces, and those of his allies.

He'd imagined fighting a war against an enemy coming from unknown space, but now he realized, every step backward, every system left to the enemy, strengthen them, and weakened the Pact. He'd considered trading space for time, and he'd almost brought it up with Chronos, simply to test the waters. But now he realized there could be no more retreats, no more systems given to the enemy.

They had to be stopped when they finally came. They *had* to be stopped…

Somehow.

* * *

"Our research has expanded our knowledge of the Highborn considerably, however those efforts have recently ground to a virtual halt. We have extracted all the information possible from the data chips in Folio One." Andi realized the name she'd given to the binder she'd retrieved from her storage unit was less than imaginative, but it served. "Our audit of previously discovered imperial artifacts and records has yielded a number of additional data sources as well, references to the Highborn that had previously been unclear without the greater context we now possess. Our newest and most recent efforts have involved recruiting crews previously engaged in Badlands prospecting." Andi paused, shifting on her feet for a moment. She had been a Badlands prospector, and a damned good one if she did say so herself. But she'd also been an outlaw of sorts, and every expedition she'd undertaken had been in violation of the pointless treaties the Confederation had signed, and which only it had ever taken even semi-seriously. Andi was firmly entrenched among the highest levels of the Confederation's military, but she still remembered what it felt like making a run for it from more than one naval ship. Wherever she had gone, however she had grown, her roots were still there, and she knew she would never forget the realities of life as a Badlands explorer.

She still carried a little resentment for it all, too.

She wasn't the only one. It had been her idea to seek out the old prospecting teams, to organize them to conduct a comprehensive exploration effort in the Badlands. More than a few had told her to get lost, that they'd rot in hell before they'd cooperate with the naval forces that had hunted them down for so long as criminals. She'd argued that the fight against the Highborn was a struggle for all of them to survive, but Badlands prospectors were a hard breed, and more than a few possessed stubbornness that overruled their good sense, even their survival instincts. But she'd managed to convince more than a dozen teams to get back together, mostly after she'd enhanced the puny payouts the Senate had authorized with her own funds. There was some patriotism mixed in with the resentment among the prospectors, but money had always been the surest way to motivate them.

She'd also agreed that after any information was extracted, any artifacts would be theirs to sell in addition to their bonuses. The Senate had expressly forbidden that, of course, but she already had a plan on how to deal with it.

She'd always wanted to stand up on the main podium in

the Senate and tell them all to go…well, she had a few versions of that thought, one progressively harsher and dirtier than the last.

The prospecting efforts had shown some success in the year or more they'd been underway, but overall, Andi was disappointed. She'd hoped more records would have been found, that such things had been overlooked by teams hunting for electronics and other, more valuable finds. There had been a few new discoveries, bits and pieces of information that referred, peripherally at least, to the empire's struggle with the Highborn. But nothing comprehensive…and nothing that held any real clues to a way to defeat the genetically-engineered enemy. The Badlands were coreward of what the Confederation considered to be the Rim, but it had all been part of that backwater periphery during imperial times. She'd come to believe the information she needed, that the entire Pact needed, was deeper coreward.

Into the areas occupied by the enemy, and even beyond.

"To summarize, the Highborn were created by a fringe group in the empire, who intended for their genetically engineered and enhanced specimens to serve as inspiration, even as leaders, to push humanity forward in a nurturing way. The program was a response to the decay and decadence that gripped the later empire, and hastened its decline. Unfortunately, this group lost control over its creations, who came to view themselves as gods, and sought to take their place as mankind's masters and not its partners or mentors. Our information on the later stages of the resulting conflict is admittedly sparse, but we can be fairly certain that the Highborn wielded considerable power for a number of years, and controlled a significant portion of the imperial armed forces at their peak. They very well may have come very close to ultimate success. What is far less clear was how they were defeated…and it seems clear that they *were* at least held off and driven from imperial space. That was a victory without lasting value, however. The empire's wounds proved to be mortal, and the final collapse was not long delayed." Andi paused. The next bit of information was vital, at least as she saw it. "But there appears to be little question that the Highborn were indeed driven from imperial space *before* the last stages of the Cataclysm."

"Is it possible that was the result of a strictly military victory, a defeat of the arms supporting the Highborn by the loyal imperial forces? Imperial technology was quite advanced, and its military immensely strong. We know that much." Clint Winters sat along the right side of the table, opposite Tyler, and even as he spoke, it was clear to Andi he'd already answered his own question internally.

"Of course, we cannot be sure what role the force of arms played in the defeat of the Highborn, save to say that it seems extremely unlikely the enemy was driven away by a pure military victory. At their peak, the Highborn controlled thirty to thirty-five percent of the imperial fleet, per our best calculations, and with the loyal imperial units far less concentrated, an overwhelming military victory seems unlikely. Further, as the Highborn controlled hundreds of systems, even in the wake of a crushing military defeat, they would have been able to dig in, hold on in well-fortified systems, for years, decades even. Yet, every analysis we have been able to conduct suggests that one moment they were in the empire, fighting for control, even on the verge of total success…and then almost immediately they were gone, fled across the imperial borders with their followers. They left the empire mortally wounded…but they *did* leave it, and some years before the final stages of the Cataclysm."

"So, there was some kind of weapon, some way to hurt them. The imperials found a way to defeat the Highborn…and we have no idea how. Correct?"

"That is essentially correct." Andi suppressed a smile. Winters was relentless, and his analysis almost always carried a negative tone. He was someone who saw the problems first, the dark side before the light.

That's what she liked about him.

Many found his way off-putting, but Andi was cut from the same cloth, and she counted Winters among her closest friends, and one of the few whose opinions she truly respected.

Clint Winters was also Tyler Barron's second in command, and an officer almost as revered by the fleet's spacers as her husband. He was gruff, hard, known by those he commanded as the 'Sledgehammer.' Andi knew a different side of the often-terrifying officer though, the loyal friend, the rational strategist…and the soft touch that Cassiopeia wrapped around her finger with inexplicable ease. Andi's daughter was four and a half years old, and she held court on Base Striker like some kind of tiny queen, pulling the strings of those who pulled the Confederation's. Clint Winters, Gary Holsten, Anya Fritz…the Rim's greatest heroes, and some of its toughest screws, were her virtual supplicants, and they shamelessly indulged the young girl. Andi had struggled with guilt about keeping her daughter in a place like Striker, but the truth was, Cassie loved the place. And it seemed perfectly normal to the child that men and women who commanded thousands, who had fought apocalyptic battles, would bend to her every whim.

Above them all loomed Cassie's father, who, in Andi's rough calculation, refused the child exactly nothing. She'd worked harder than she ever had in the last years, driven herself to outright exhaustion. But for the first time in her life, she had a family, and for the moment at least, they were all together.

And in that, she could feel the seeds of new and deeper guilt. The three of them would almost certainly be separated again at some point…but the realization had been growing in her mind that she would have to be the one who left first. She had some idea of the pain that would accompany that necessity, and she'd done all she could to push it from her mind, to enjoy what she had while she could.

Chapter Three

120 Million Kilometers from Outpost Seven
Delta Orion System
Year 327 AC (After the Cataclysm)

"All squadrons…break. Prepare to engage enemy fighters." Contrall was nauseous as her hands moved over her controls, adjusting her course yet again, and confirming what her unsettled gut had already told her.

The Highborn ships *were* launching fighters. A lot of fighters.

There were over a hundred in space already, and they were still pouring out of the forward vessels. And more of the mysterious enemy ships were moving up from the transit points.

Carriers…those things are carriers…

She told herself she'd had no way to know, no cause to expect the Highborn might have fighter squadrons.

Then she told herself that was bullshit.

You tore them apart at Calpharon, even in defeat. If it hadn't been for the squadrons, the war would already be over. Why wouldn't they copy that? They've had over three years, almost four, and their tech is half a century ahead of ours, at least. It would have been surprising if they hadn't done this.

That last part echoed in her brain. The Highborn tech was well ahead of the Hegemony-Rim coalition's, and that meant those fighters forming up in front of hers were probably more advanced than her own.

That's   okay…longer   ranges,   bigger   guns, whatever…fighter combat is about pilot skill and training.

That was true, to a point. And the Pact forces would have that edge, she was sure of it. Whatever the enemy had done analyzing bits and pieces of wreckage and petabytes of scanner data, perhaps even improving on the design of the Lightning craft, they didn't have the Rim's history and tradition of small craft tactics. Their rookie pilots could never match the Rim fighters, and especially not the veterans waiting back at Striker with the main fleets.

Her people were in trouble, though. For most of its history, Confederation fighter tactics had been mostly about dogfighting, the bulk of squadrons launching as interceptors, with smaller contingents equipped for bombing runs. Then, the war with the Hegemony changed everything. The wings faced an enemy with no small craft of its own…and dogfighting almost vanished from the squadrons' arsenal.

The struggle with the Highborn had only continued that trend.

Until now.

Contrall faced a stark reality. She had just under a hundred pilots, rookies facing their first combat, and every one of them was in a Lightning fitted out with a cumbersome bombing kit. Worse, they were double loaded with torpedoes.

"All squadrons…jettison torpedo loads. Prepare for fighter to fighter action." The words blurted out, driven more by instinct that considered thought. Dropping the payloads was a painful decision. It eliminated any chance of damaging the incoming carriers. But her people weren't going to get to the carriers, not if they tried to get past the now more than one hundred fifty enemy fighters standing in their way.

Fighters she could tell from their flight profiles were outfitted as interceptors. Every one of them.

The bombing kits reduced maneuverability, and dropping the torpedoes would only restore a portion of it. Her people would be at a decided disadvantage in the coming fight, no matter what she did. If they'd been more experienced...veterans of long enough service to remember dogfights with Union squadrons, they might have made up for that. But there weren't too many pilots with that kind of experience left in the entire fleet, not with the casualty levels of the last ten years of war.

"Okay, listen up...all of you. You've been trained in fighter vs. fighter combat, so you all know what to expect." That was technically true, but less so in a practical sense than she wished. The Academy program had steadily deemphasized dogfighting in favor of bombing tactics as the Confederation faced enemies without their own fighters, and unescorted attack runs against fleet units became the preeminent role for the wings.

"Those things...whatever they are, they're outfitted as interceptors, which means they're probably going to be faster and more maneuverable than we are." She paused. The more she thought about the situation, the darker it became. Especially since the second wave of enemy ships appeared to be launching fighters as well. Not many of her people were likely to survive the next hour or two, but any chance they had depended on maintaining some level of morale, some fighting spirit.

Some hope. Even if it was false.

"The enemy can copy our fighters, build ships just like ours..." *Or better.* "...but they can't match us. Fighter combat is about more than just hardware. You're all part of a long and proud tradition, an honored corps that has fought wars against the Union, the Hegemony, and now, the Highborn. You are part of that, and the spirits of those who came before are with you now. Stay sharp, remember you probably have a maneuverability disadvantage...but you've got lasers, and those pilots have to be unfamiliar with their craft, poorly trained. It's time to show the Highborn it takes more than technology and factories to produce fighter squadrons!"

She smiled for a moment. Her words had come out better than she'd hoped, and she believed they would help her people, keep up their courage, allow them to do their very best to strike at whatever the enemy was sending at them.

Her little speech hadn't been good enough, though, to fool herself, and the grin quickly faded from her face. She reached out, exhaling hard as she flipped a series of switches, activating her comm and linking it directly with the outpost command. She was still trying to tell herself some of her people would make it through, but it was proving to be a hard sell. At least she could get a nonstop feed of information to the outpost. Giving Admiral Barron as much information on the new enemy fighters would accomplish more for the war effort than anything her doomed squadrons did in the next few hours.

Commander St. James would see the scanner data got back to fleet command...before he died too.

*   *   *

"Definitely fighters, Commander. Over three hundred so far. And there are still enemy units coming through the point."

St. James leaned back in his chair, trying to look like anything but a man who'd just been punched in the gut. Trying, but not necessarily succeeding.

The scanner profile of the enemy incursion didn't suggest a massive invasion, at least not according to the AI, which assigned a ninety-one percent probability to its analysis. That was good news, at least in the greater scheme of things. Though, it was still possible a massive invasion fleet was simply waiting in the next system.

The bad news was more abundant. Major invasion or not, the enemy force already in the system was more than powerful enough to blast Outpost Seven to plasma, along with every ship in the small support fleet posted to aid in its defense. It wasn't even going to be close, not if any of those Highborn ships packed the weaponry he'd seen at Calpharon.

The strange thing was, his own imminent destruction and that of all his people wasn't the worst news. The Highborn had fighters. That was the shock, the deadly surprise that meant, not only would he and his people die in the fight just beginning, but they would do it knowing whatever chances the Pact had of defeating the enemy had just dropped through the floor. Most of the tactical doctrine developed for the war was based on fighter-bomber operations. But the Pact had just lost its monopoly...and it remained to be seen how many fighters the Highborn had managed to build.

And how good they were.

He'd get an answer to that question, at least, before the enemy reached the station. Commander Contrall's people were about to engage. *Or be engaged?* He wasn't sure which was the correct terminology. Save for a few encounters with Hegemony squadrons late in the war between those powers, it had been a decade since the Confederation wings had fought any major battles against opposing small craft.

"I want all weapons systems checked and rechecked, Lieutenant. And feed all scanner data to the gunnery stations. I want targeting updated in real time as those ships approach." That assumed the outpost would even get off any shots before it was destroyed. There were all kinds of rumors flying around about new systems, weapons in development to increase the fleet's combat strength—including shadowy whispers of a new superbattleship class under development somewhere in the Iron Belt. But the outposts had been hastily assembled, and their technology levels, save for some upgraded scanning and comm systems, were pretty much prewar Confed norms.

Which meant the Highborn ships could stop well out of St. James's range and blast the outpost to scrap.

He watched as the two fighter wings closed on each other. He felt a few bursts of excitement, a sense of rooting for his people, almost willing them to teach the enemy a lesson, to show them what flying really looked like. But Contrall's people were outnumbered three to one, and they were stuck in clumsy bombers.

And the enemy wings looked awfully good as they approached, their formations crisp and ordered. He wanted to assume the lack of enemy experience would be a huge factor in the coming fight, but he knew very little about the Highborn, and even less about those who manned their ships. Thralls, he'd heard they were called.

He'd also heard they were humans who served the Highborn, and even worshipping them as gods. He didn't want to believe that, but some part of him whispered deep in his mind that it was likely the truth.

"We're getting a comm beam from Commander Contrall, sir. No message as of yet."

St. James understood immediately. Contrall was a veteran, and a courageous warrior. She understood just how important it would be to get any information on the enemy fighters back to Admiral Barron.

And she also understands how likely it is that none of her people are going to make it back to provide those reports directly.

"Hold the last two pairs of drones, Lieutenant. Download any transmissions from Commander Control

directly into the comm units' memory banks." He didn't
even need to see it himself. If he somehow survived what
was coming, he would analyze every aspect of just what the
Pact was about to face.

But that was tomorrow's problem, assuming there was a
tomorrow. Just then, something else was on his mind,
something pressing, a dire need coming from the deepest
depths of his consciousness.

Hurting the enemy. Killing as many of the bastards as he
could before his people all died in the ruins of the outpost.

*   *   *

Contrall squeezed her fingers on the firing stud, her face
twisted into an angry, vengeful grimace. She barely had half
her people left. The enemy fighters had been armed with
ship to ship missiles, much like the ones Confederation
interceptors carried. Her bombers had none, and that meant
they had to endure the preliminary attack, doing the best
they could to evade the incoming death with their bulky and
unresponsive craft.

Some of her pilots had managed to evade, and two had
actually taken out approaching missiles with their lasers,
good shooting by any measure. But they had drawn no
blood in exchange for their losses, and an enemy advantage
of three to one was now one of six to one.

She tried to ignore that fact. At some point, it didn't
matter. If she'd had veterans, pilots with some dogfighting
experience, she might have held off a raw enemy force three
times the size of her own, but six to one was another matter.
Besides, her pilots weren't veterans, they were rookies too,
and even more so when it came to battling enemy fighters.

She realized as she stared at her screen that she had not
conducted one exercise on dogfighting since taking
command of the wing. That had made sense at the time, but
as she sat there, bringing her clunky bomber around, trying

to lock on one of the Highborn fighters, she felt fury rising inside her. Rage at the enemy, of course, but even more, at herself. The Hegemony had copied Confederation fighters, and if that had come too late in the war between the two now-allied powers, it should have been a lesson, a warning. But it hadn't even occurred to her. All she'd been able to think about was honing her raw pilots into a force that could deliver devastating bomber strikes to Highborn vessels.

Now, she realized, the Confederation, which had once mastered the art of dogfighting, was going to have to relearn that legacy.

Quickly.

She brought her ship around, nudging the controls, redirecting her thrust in a combination of evasive maneuver and honing in on her target. She was an experienced pilot, with years of combat under her belt, but truth be told, she had the same zero kills as every pilot under her command. She'd seen service in the final battles of the Union war, but she hadn't managed to take down an enemy fighter. And she hadn't flown an interceptor in ten years.

She remembered the final engagement of the Union War, the astonishing display of Jake Stockton leading his pilot into the fight. Raptor had scored six kills that day, almost rewriting the book on dogfighting in front of his astonished and worshipful squadrons.

But Stockton was gone, just one more grievous loss the fleet had faced. Raptor's death had almost cut the heart out of the fighter corps, and if it hadn't been for Reg Griffin, and for an almost insatiable craving to avenge their lost leader, Contrall doubted the squadrons' morale could ever have recovered. They would never forget their legendary commander…but they would go on as he would have wanted. They would fight in his honor, and they would extract a vengeance on the enemy that defied imagining.

And that will start here…

She tightened her finger again, and she watched as the laser pulses flashed across her screen...and her target vanished.

She was stunned, staring in a state of near shock, and it took her a few seconds to realize what had happened. She'd destroyed an enemy fighter. She had a kill.

She turned her head abruptly, a startled expression on her face as she jerked her hand to the side and watched as a lance of laser energy ripped by...right through the space her ship had occupied an instant before.

There were enemy fighters everywhere, their formation expanding, coming around on both sides in a flanking maneuver. The Highborn pilots were far better than she'd expected. There was still some sluggishness, at least in the intricacies of close combat, but the order of the enemy ranks, the way they were deployed along the line of attack...it was almost inexplicable, as though the Highborn knew not only how the Confederation squadrons attacked their capital ships, but also how they had fought against Union fighters in their past wars.

She wondered if they could have found some kind of old Confederation footage, data files on dogfighting tactics or something of the sort. But there was no way. The battle lines hadn't come anywhere near Confederation space, not yet at least. And, save for a few engagements with Hegemony fighters, it had been more than a decade since Confed wings had fought major battles against enemy squadrons.

But how then? How could they have learned such complex tactics?

She moved her arm again, increasing the frequency of her evasion efforts. Even as she did, three of her ships blinked off her screen in rapid succession. She took a deep breath, willing herself to focus, to fight off the grimness trying to consume her. She was more certain than ever that her squadrons were doomed, that Outpost Seven was as good as finished.

But she was just as sure she was going to take down as many enemy fighters as she could before they got her. She might die in Delta Orion, but if she did, she was determined to set an example for the thousands of pilots who would face the new Highborn threat. She would take down five of the enemy ships.

She would die as an ace.

Chapter Four

Reconstructed Hall of the People
Liberte City
Planet Montmirail, Ghassara IV
Union Year 231 (327 AC)

"It is good to see you, Admiral. You have done well, better than I could have hoped. You are a hero of the Union, and I will see that you are rewarded with the honors you so richly deserve." Sandrine Ciara was meticulously dressed, looking in every way, the calm, rational head of state.

"It is my pleasure, First Citizen. We meet in far better circumstances than prevailed the last time we were together. Though, even then, we had much cause for optimism. But, please, do not heap your praise on me. It is my privilege to lead our forces, and it is they who deserve recognition, the men and women in the Union's uniform, those serving in our victorious fleets...and those lost."

"Of course, Admiral...and we will see to it that all those who have fought are well and truly recognized for their patriotism." Ciara paused and then added, "And we will make certain the families of those killed in our noble struggle are cared for." There was a slight change in tone, and Denisov felt as though he was being humored, managed. He wasn't naïve enough to imagine Ciara gave a shit about the families of those who had died fighting for her, but he still fancied that he would retain enough influence to see that she followed through.

His eyes darted up and down, noticing the fineness of her clothes, and even more the clearly expensive jewelry she wore. He had last seen Ciara in her drab worker's garb, and the grim fatigues of a revolutionary soldier in the field. Clearly, she had decided such masquerades were no longer necessary.

They're no longer necessary because the fleet has prevailed, because Gaston Villieneuve is trapped, the small cluster of systems he controls virtually surrounded and cut off. They're not necessary because you have almost rid her of the threat of her deadly enemy. Have you fought, as you told yourself you were doing, to free the Union, or at least to move it somewhat in that direction, or have you simply replaced one brutal tyrant with another?

Denisov wasn't sure of that answer, not yet. Ciara had cut back on some particularly oppressive regulations of the Villieneuve-era, but she still retained a firm hand on the wheels of government…and the lives of the people. And she's cut through Sector Nine like a tsunami, eliminating anyone even suspected of lingering loyalties to her deposed predecessor and replacing them with her own creatures. But she'd taken no steps toward dismantling the notorious intelligence agency.

"I almost sent one of my commanders back to report, First Citizen, so I could remain with the fleet. I will feel considerably better when Gaston Villieneuve is dead." Denisov wasn't usually so blunt, but there was no point in prancing around the realities of the civil war drawing to its close. There was no way Villieneuve could be allowed to live. The blood of billions cried out for his execution, and Denisov had privately decided to spare the Union the pain of a trial or anything that might appear like a government-ordered murder. So much better if Villieneuve died in battle, fighting to the last against the legitimate forces of the Union.

Even if he 'died in battle' with his hands in the air, pleading for his life.

Denisov wasn't a vengeful man by nature, but his hatred for Villieneuve was both fully earned and intense. And he wouldn't rest until his enemy was utterly defeated.

"You did the right thing, Admiral. It is important we discuss…what happens after the final push. We must chart a course forward for the Union, and you should be part of that."

Denisov wasn't sure if Ciara was serious, or if she was managing him. Or a bit of each.

"I agree on the importance of that, of course…but until Gaston Villieneuve's forces are completely defeated, the war is still the top priority." A pause. "How are relations with the Confederation?" Denisov's primary demand in return for his support had been a normalization of relations with the Confederation. And he was determined to hold Ciara to her promise. He'd served alongside Tyler Barron and his spacers, fought together with them against the Hegemony. He would have been with them even then, facing the new enemy threatening the Rim, if he hadn't been called back home to help set the Union to rights. He had no intention of facilitating a renewal of tension and struggle with his recent allies.

"Everything is fine. The Confederation is quite distracted, I am afraid. The war beyond the Badlands does not go well, it seems. I have sent Admiral Kerevsky back to Megara, along with a delegation to work out a new treaty."

"You sent Kerevsky back?" Denisov was surprised. The Confederation admiral—and spy—had been Ciara's steadfast ally, and her lover, too.

"Yes…Alexander has been a great help to us, but I thought it was…wise…to remove him from Montmirail as we prepare to conclude our change of government. The

Confeds will be good neighbors, even allies, but eliminating Gaston Villieneuve's influence has required…direct…measures. Admiral Kerevsky was an ideal choice to accompany our new diplomatic mission back to Megara." A pause. "No doubt, he understood what had to be done here. But there were things I suspect he did not wish to see."

Denisov shifted on his feet. There were things he was uncomfortable hearing as well, and he wondered if Ciara was about to unleash some sort of reign of terror on Montmirail. Then he wondered if there was any other way. The capital had likely been infested with Villieneuve's operatives—was likely still full of them—and unpleasant or not, there was only one way to clean house in a place like Montmirail.

He could only hope that's where it would end. He was committed, and the thought of what Gaston Villieneuve would do if he ever regained power was almost unimaginable. He could support things he considered morally repugnant, at least to the end of eliminating Villieneuve's influence. But if Ciara pushed it farther, if she started targeting her own political rivals…he would have to cross that bridge if it came.

"I cannot stay long, First Citizen. Much of the fleet was in need of repair, and the spacers were exhausted from the continuous campaigning. Villieneuve is trapped. He has some productive capacity in the systems he controls, but his only open supply line extends out into the Periphery. When I return, the fleet will move to close even that, and then we will begin the final phase…and the dark reign of Gaston Villieneuve will truly be at an end."

Ciara smiled. "That will be a glorious day, Admiral. And I can think of no one more trustworthy or better suited to take on that burden. Stay for a few days, allow me to show you some of the steps I have taken here. You will see I have taken the promises I made to you seriously. Then go back and finish your task, lead your victorious spacers to final victory."

Denisov nodded, and he managed a smile. He wasn't sure he believed Ciara, and he almost certainly did not in everything she had said. But she had sounded convincing, and while he knew she was an impressive liar when she wished to be, he decided he had no choice but to trust her. For the time being.

Nothing was more important than ridding the Union, and the universe, of Gaston Villieneuve's foul stench.

*   *   *

"I would have returned sooner, Gaston, but your enemies have closed off almost all approaches to this remaining pocket of space you occupy. The route around the Hegemony and the areas of what you call the Badlands close to Confederation space, is a long and arduous one, even for vessels with the thrust capacities of ours." The Highborn stood in front of Villieneuve, towering the better part of a meter over the ousted head of the Union. Percelax was not only Highborn, but also one of the Firstborn. That was a rank that perhaps slipped by Villieneuve's understanding, but it signified the priority level Tesserax and the Colony had assigned to employing the Union to distract and damage the Confederation. Percelax had some difficulty accepting that such efforts were useful, much less necessary, but the limited intelligence available on Confederation production *had* painted an alarming picture. The war to unite the Rim under Highborn rule wasn't being fought by all the forces available. Most of those were tied down on the primary front. The newly founded Colony had been thrown largely on its own captured resources to sustain the war.

Tesserax had worked wonders harnessing captured Hegemony technology, and upgrading and expanding it, but if it was possible to slip a blade into the weak side of the Pact, it was well worth the effort.

"Lord Percelax, I am most pleased to see you again. I am anxious to hear what resources you have brought." Villieneuve was clearly trying to hide his fear, but it was obvious enough he was on the precipice of total defeat. That would have made him a poor choice for an ally, of course, at least in most circumstances. But the Union forces facing his own depleted fleet were also battered and worn. The Union's economy was on the verge of total collapse, and most active shipyard capacity was committed to repair operations. That was mostly based on Villieneuve's intel, of course, and Percelax would normally have placed little faith in it, save for the fact that it made perfect sense and correlated almost perfectly with his own computer models.

"I have brought enough, Gaston…enough to defeat your enemies and to restore you to unchallenged rule of the Union. When that is achieved, you will receive further shipments to prepare your forces to satisfy their obligations under our agreement."

"I will do as I have promised, Lord Percelax…with great pleasure. First, we must deal with these rebels, and I must be restored to my position on Montmirail. Then, I will repay my debt to you. The Confederation has been my enemy for as long as I have conscious memory. It is well past time to give them what they deserve."

"Very well, Gaston. I suggest you assemble a group of your most reliable naval officers. I have brought a number of warships to supplement your forces, as well as weapons and other equipment to enhance your remaining vessels. Based on the intelligence you have provided, it appears you have roughly four to five of your months before your enemies are ready to resume their offensive, an effort they no doubt view as the final attack. Ideally, you will strike them while they are still mobilizing and organizing.

Assuming they do not have active intelligence assets on your occupied worlds…"

"They do not."

Percelax paused for a moment, struggling somewhat to defuse his anger at Villieneuve's interruption. He found it quite exhausting dealing with the human on a level that even appeared remotely as equals, but it served his purpose for the time being. Once the Union Civil War was ended, and its enhanced forces were deployed against the Confederation, there would be time to put Gaston Villieneuve in his place.

"Assuming that is the case, they will almost certainly proceed as we have projected, giving us an opportunity to strike before they are fully prepared, with a vastly stronger force than they are expecting to encounter. We will obliterate their main fleet, and then, with the engine enhancements to your vessels, we will move on the capital before they are able to respond in any meaningful way. Your enemies will be destroyed in one swift stroke…assuming your engineering crews are able to work quickly enough. We have three months, perhaps even four…after that, there is risk the enemy will move first."

"My people will do what has to be done, Lord Percelax, and they will do it in the allotted time. I can assure you of that."

Percelax didn't much like Gaston Villieneuve. He found most humans to be at best annoying, but the deposed Union leader was particularly loathsome. He was, however, just what was needed, the perfect proxy to carry out the mission, a man so blinded by lust for power and revenge, he would be easily influenced. He was a tool only, of course, and Percelax scoffed at whatever fantasies the human harbored about sharing power. He and the forces remaining under his control were resources to be used—and expended if need be—and nothing more.

"Very well, Gaston. Three months. In three of your months, the attack will commence. I will rely upon you to…motivate…your people to see that all the required preparations are complete."

Chapter Five

Forward Outpost Seven
Delta Orion System
Year 327 AC (After the Cataclysm)

"Enemy fighters, coming in on attack vector."

St. James listened to the report, but he just nodded in response. There was nothing to say, no orders to give. The outpost line had been a hurried project, and the resources available had been poured into areas that had been deemed most vital. That didn't—hadn't at least—included defense against small craft attacks.

Outpost Seven, along with its sixteen brethren in the other border systems, didn't mount so much as a point defense turret to direct against the incoming squadrons. The enemy was fresh, their formations perfect. The first three hundred fighters launched by the Highborn fleet had engaged Commander Contrall's squadrons, and were still in the process of hunting down her last few survivors. The force approaching the station was also three hundred strong, launched by the last enemy ships to transit into the system.

That, at least, has stopped...

It had been almost two hours since a ship had come through, but St. James knew that was of little relevance, at least to his people's vanishing hopes for survival. The forces in the system were strong enough to destroy Outpost Seven a dozen times over.

At least it's not a true invasion force.

Not yet. But who knows what is waiting beyond that point…

St. James heard the sound of the outpost's laser batteries opening fire. They weren't designed for targeting maneuverable small craft like fighters, but they were what his people had. His gunners might take out a handful of enemy bogies, especially since the attackers *had* to be inexperienced and new to small craft operations. Still, even that was eating away at him. There was something not quite right. The enemy pilots were good. *Too good.* He'd seen the first Hegemony formations, witnessed the skill and dedication in their performance, but also their greenness. That didn't matter much for the outpost's chances, perhaps, but he could feel his apprehension rising for his comrades, those he would very likely leave behind shortly, those who were facing a war even more unwinnable than they'd imagined.

Highborn fighters…we should have expected this…

He was frustrated, angry with himself for not being more ready for what he was facing. The Confederation had watched as the Hegemony developed small craft in response to the success the squadrons had achieved in the last war. As he watched the deadly swarm closing, it seemed downright careless and stupid that the possibility the Highborn would do the same had been ignored.

He'd known just what his duty would be if the enemy appeared on his watch, and the Highborn squadrons had just upped the stakes on that. He *had* to get word back to Admiral Barron, along with as much data as he could on the fighters…and on the apparent and inexplicable skill of the pilots flying them.

* * *

Contrall's back ached, pain radiating out from her shoulders and just under her neck. She was curled forward in her cockpit, every centimeter of her body wracked by tension. She was afraid, scared to death in fact. But she was also consumed with battle lust, with the need to strike back at the enemy for the deaths of so many of her people.

Most of them...

And for her own death, which she knew could not long be delayed.

She had six pilots left in action, at least that's what her scanners told her. The others were all dead, save perhaps for a few floating in space in their survival pods with no hope of rescue. *Dead too, just not officially yet...*

And those remaining, herself included, had lifespans measured in minutes. She'd considered giving the order to try to break off, to flee back to the outpost. But aside from the remote chance that any of her people could escape the faster enemy fighters, there was no point. Another strike force had launched, bypassing her beleaguered wing and moving around the flank on the outpost. The station was already under attack even as the enemy hunted down the last of her fighters. She knew the end was near, for the outpost as well as for herself and her survivors, and her mind was focused on all she had left...fighting to the last, hurting the enemy as much as she could.

Scoring her fifth kill. She'd taken down four of the enemy fighters in the swirling combat, and she needed one more. It was pointless, of course utterly without meaning in any conventional sense. Her AI's recordings would be destroyed with her ship. Not even a posthumous record would remain that listed her as an ace pilot. Another kill wasn't going to save her, make her less dead. But she *wanted* it. It was all that was left to her.

She brought her ship around, blasting wildly along different vectors to evade the fire of at least half a dozen pursuers. She had an enemy ship in her sights, just ahead.

The pilot had almost shaken her three times, but she'd managed to hang on.

A pair of laser blasts ripped by, coming within a hundred meters of her ship. She could feel death stalking her, and she knew every second that passed could be her last. Her eyes were fixed on her own display, trying to get a lock on her target even as she used every trick she knew to buy a few more seconds of survival, perhaps a minute. She'd lived her whole life, and she knew she was at the end. *Just a few more seconds…*

There was hopelessness weighing down of course, for herself certainly, but also for her comrades, for Admiral Barron and the fleet…and the entire Rim. The enemy was too strong, and now they had fighters. Worse, those small craft were flown by well-trained pilots, perhaps even a match for the fleet's bombing-focused squadrons. That seemed inexplicable, impossible even. Technology was one thing, but the Highborn hadn't even seen Rim squadrons battling other fighters. Such combats had become vanishingly rare in the last decade. How had they developed such advanced tactics, trained their pilots so well?

She didn't have an answer…and she knew she would never would.

Another shot flashed by, even closer than the last two. She fired as well, missing her target by two hundred meters. The Highborn pilots were not only well drilled in formations and flying, but they had clearly been trained to evade pursuing fighters. If she'd had an interceptor kit, and a pair of ship to ship missiles, she would have fared better, but she was still pleased with herself at managing four kills, at least to the extent such feelings could push through desperation and terror. None of her people had come close to that total, though a few had distinguished themselves before death caught up with them.

She'd imagined her own death many times. That was the curse of the fighter pilot. She'd held her breath as she'd closed on enemy ships, evading point defense fire, and those deadly missiles the Highborn ships mounted, feeling the cold shadow all around her…but she'd never been in a situation as hopeless as the current one, never before been *sure* she was about to die.

Her life's wishes' desires, all she'd hoped to achieve, to see, to do…it was all gone, all save the burning need to kill the pilot in front of her before the pack behind finished her.

She fired again, and then again. Two more misses, both close. But not close enough. The enemy ships on her tail were closing, her time was running out. The Highborn fighters had stronger thrust levels even than the new Lightning IIIs. The fire was getting heavier, and the group pursuing her had grown to eight or nine. The fire was constant, a pulse of deadly energy ripping by every few seconds. One of them would get her, it was almost a mathematical certainty. Whatever evasive routines she executed, however well she flew, sooner or later, she would guess wrong.

Her eyes narrowed, focusing on the blip in front of her. The target she'd been pursuing with relentless determination. The last goal in her life, the one thing she wanted, needed, before death took her. She fired again, and she missed.

Damn…

She was running out of time. She started forward, punching coordinates into a small keypad on her console, nudging her targeting screen. She was going to hit with the next shot. If effort, determination, pure stubbornness had any say in the matter, she was going to hit.

But she never got that final shot off.

Her fighter suddenly lurched hard, and then it flipped over, spinning end to end in a vicious roll. She knew she'd been hit, and she reached out, trying to grab the throttle, to regain control of her fighter. Her eyes moved to the side, trying to get a read on the damage her ship had suffered.

She was still there, still alive, and she still had at least some power. But she could tell almost immediately her control circuits were fried.

She sat still for an indeterminate time, probably no more than a few seconds, but seeming like much longer. She was dead, in every way except the final blow. She had no control over her ship, and that meant her vector was fixed. Her ship might be spinning and rolling all around, but it was following an unchanging course in space...and that reduced targeting to a simple set of equations.

A microsecond's effort by an AI, and then...

She looked ahead, ignoring her screens, her gaze fixed on the black velvet of space before her, trying to focus on its beauty, on anything except the thought echoing through her head...the realization that she would die with four kills, not an ace, just a pilot who had come close. A commander who had lost her entire force.

She could feel the tears filling her eyes, streaming down her cheeks. And then, suddenly, her ship shook hard again, and she could feel the thing splitting apart, the cockpit shattering, the breath being ripped from her lungs...and the unimaginably frigid cold...of space, and of the death that took her.

* * *

Sparks flew across the control room. Metal creaked and twisted, and a few seconds later, an entire section of the structure collapsed from above with a sickening crash. Outpost Seven was dying. The attacking fighters were tearing it apart section by section, one laser blast after another ripping into its lightly armored hull.

The fighters were interceptors, their only ordnance a pair of wing mounted lasers. They'd loosed their ship to ship missiles on their first run, and that barrage had virtually crippled the outpost's defenses. Now, they were picking it apart piece by piece in an extended orgy of destruction.

The energy output of their lasers was a bit higher than that of the comparable weapons on the Lightnings, a reflection of generally higher enemy technology. It hadn't made any sense to St. James, not at first. Why send in fighters ill-suited to take on the station when the Highborn ships could have positioned themselves out of the range of return fire and blasted the structure to atoms in a matter of minutes.

Then he understood. The enemy was making a point, showing the defenders just what they faced. Perhaps they were even giving their own squadrons combat experience…before any truly climactic battles were fought.

St. James had dispatched all the comm drones, but the station's battered transmitters were still sending data to the ones that hadn't yet transited. He knew he had to get as much information on the enemy fighters as possible back to Admiral Barron…but it pissed him off as it occurred to him that was just what the enemy wanted as well.

He understood, or at least he thought he did. *They want to crush our morale. They think they can break us, that we'll surrender when we realize the fight is hopeless…that we will worship them.*

Never!

St. James felt an instant of rage, of defiance, but it quickly faded, buried under the realization that whatever resistance the warriors of the Pact offered, however hard they fought, he wouldn't be part of it. His role in the war was almost finished. It would end right there, in the collapsing wreckage of his outpost.

Almost as if to reinforce that realization, the station shook hard, and he could see on the single screen that remained functional that a large lower section had been blown apart. It hadn't been the reactor. If it had been, he wouldn't still be there staring at the display. But a series of secondary explosions had definitely torn through the structure.

His eyes moved to the comm panel, unmanned at present. He'd expected the enemy to demand surrender, to offer him a chance to plea for his people's survival. The Highborn were brutal, willing to kill as many as they had to, but they weren't genocidal. If the research done over the last four years had gotten anything right, the enemy wanted to conquer humanity, rule over it. Not destroy it.

But it seemed a tactical decision had been made to destroy Outpost Seven. Perhaps there was a large invasion force just beyond the point, waiting to come through. Possibly, taking a few prisoners was just too much trouble.

More likely, the Highborn wanted to send a message to the Pact forces, of the futility of resistance.

St. James was grateful in some ways the surrender demand had not come. He was full of fury and resistance, but the fear was growing as well. Cold terror at the approach of death. He wanted to believe he would spurn any demand that he yield, but he wasn't sure his will was strong enough. His image of himself was of a man fighting to the very end, but there was something else inside, and he feared what he might do to survive, wondered if he would beg for life, bow down as the enemy demanded rather than face a death he saw as honorable.

The station lurched again, and he could hear a series of explosions closer than the last. The air had turned acrid and it burned his eyes. The smell of electrical fires was everywhere. There were three officers left on the bridge. The rest had been killed or wounded, or he'd sent them elsewhere, to reinforce hard hit sections of the outpost.

'Lucky Seven,' as he'd come to call it in his tenure as commander, was almost out of action…but not completely. There was a single gun still in the fight, and enough power to fire it—though he wasn't sure exactly how. He'd ordered the reactor shut down after a series of hits had pushed it to edge of a containment breach. That was standard practice, but it had left the station with nothing but battery power.

He knew that wasn't going to keep the laser firing much longer. He was stunned it had lasted as long as it had.

His decision to issue the shutdown order had also denied the crew's survivors the fast and somewhat merciful death of uncontrolled nuclear fusion.

He took a deep breath, a reflex action that backfired badly as he coughed wildly, and spat out a spray of blood. He wasn't sure what had gotten into the air, what caustic and toxic chemicals were loose in the outpost's atmosphere, but between that, and the explosions and wild shaking, he knew the end was close.

He could feel death's breath on his neck, the coldness spreading over his body.

He caught one last glance of the screen before it went black like all the others, and he saw the line of Highborn ships, waiting just outside range as their fighters picked the outpost apart one chunk at a time. That had been a tedious operation for the pilots involved, no doubt, but it was nearly at its end.

St. James was thrown forward suddenly, his harness holding him back, and nearly breaking his ribs in the process. His hands moved about wildly, trying to unhook the thing, to escape from his chair. He had done all he could to push back the fear, to take hold of himself and face his end as he'd always imagined he would.

Among other things, that meant, on his feet.

He finally unhooked the heavy straps and threw them aside, leaping up to a standing position…and then stumbling forward, landing hard on his knees with a painful grunt.

The fight was almost over. Everything was almost over. He hadn't heard the whine of the laser in some time, and now he could hear a hissing sound growing louder. The shattered hulk of the outpost was losing pressurization, bleeding out the acrid haze that passed for its air. St. James wondered if there would be an explosion, if he would die quickly. Or if his end would come with him on his knees, coughing up bloody chunks of his lungs.

No…not on my knees…

A strange will hardened inside him. He had no hope of escape, nor of survival. All that mattered now was that he die standing, staring back at the enemy with the defiance he believed would see his comrades through to victory.

He managed to get back on his feet, holding on to the edge of his chair as the station shook again and again. He could hear the screeching sound of metal twisting and fracturing.

The end had come.

He stood where he was in his final few seconds, and at the very end, he screamed with all the volume his bloody throat could muster. "Avenge us, Admiral Barron…avenge those who died here for…"

Chapter Six

Planet Elestra
Site of Quasar Project
Epsilon Demarest System

"I want every micron of those magnetic conduits checked and rechecked, and I do mean *checked*. This is damned ticklish stuff we're playing with here, and one microscopic failure, anywhere in the system, and almost four years of work, the fruit of nearly twenty percent of Confederation GDP, vanishes in an instant. Along with all of us." Anya Fritz had always been a brutal taskmaster. Her reputation as the best engineer in the fleet—hell, in the entire Confederation—had been built to some extent on the effort and work she'd squeezed out of her subordinates. But there was something different now, something even harder and more resolute than Anya Fritz in her normal role with the fleet, in battle.

She was a straightforward sort, and she didn't sugarcoat things, not for others, and least of all for herself. And she had to admit…antimatter got under her skin.

She was cold, in relationships and in the face of danger. She'd crawled around fusion plants, channeled massive energies, often at flow rates well past safety levels, even sanity levels. She'd faced death a hundred times, and she'd never let it interfere with her work, her duty, but the antimatter had gotten to her in a way nothing ever had before. She'd never had so much difficultly dealing with edginess and tension, and she knew she was unloading that on her people.

Antimatter wasn't like any other substance. The reactions inside fusion plants were monstrously powerful, and the magnetic bottles containing them held temperatures inside in the millions of degrees. But a fusion reaction could be terminated almost immediately. Warships scragged their power plants all the time, shutting down the deadly reactions inside if a containment breach seemed imminent, even for routine maintenance. But antimatter couldn't be turned off. The slightest loss of containment, any contact at all with regular matter, and an apocalyptic explosion was inevitable…and instantaneous.

She was precise by nature, but tackling a system where the slightest failure, even for a microsecond, would cause utter and complete disaster, was almost too much, even for her. The plans the Hegemony had provided detailed numerous and repetitive backup systems, half a dozen lines of defense to prevent cataclysm if a system failed. She had added more to these…new monitors, auxiliary control stations, extra reserve power sources. Still, she felt a cold chill down her spine every time she walked down the endless corridors of the enormous complex.

"The crews are checking, Admiral Fritz, as per your previous orders. The systems have been tested twice already. The current effort is the third."

"And I just ordered you to conduct a fourth, didn't I? Was I somehow unclear? I'm not repeating my previous order…I take it as a given that will be followed and completed. I want those systems checked *again*. And I don't' expect to have to give the order another time." She knew the stress was affecting her behavior, and she felt guilty for being so hard on them. But she didn't stop.

It's for their own good, too. Most of them will die in a nanosecond if any part of this system fails...

That was true, of course, and she knew it. But she also knew there was a line, a limit to just how hard someone could be pushed before they fell apart, before the whole thing became counterproductive. And she was close to it.

Even for herself.

She rubbed her face, pushing back against the fatigue. She felt the impulse to take another stim, but she remembered she'd taken one less than two hours before. She was addicted to the things, she realized that on some level. She told herself once Quasar was up and running, she'd be able to stop.

Then she told herself addicts had been saying that kind of thing for centuries.

Still, she had to get some sleep. She'd grabbed about three hours, two days before.

Or was it three days?

She couldn't remember.

"Let's go, all of you. We've got a major test run tomorrow, and we've got to be green in all respects if we're going to make our production deadline." And I promised Admiral Barron I would have this place generating antimatter in quantity by then. I've never broken a pledge to him yet, and I'm damned not going to start now."

"Yes, Admiral."

"Advise all teams we'll be working through the night. If everything gets done, if the test run goes as planned...then everybody gets a hot meal and a night's sleep. Until then, it's nutra-bars and work, so let's pick up the pace around here."

The last part had been louder, intended for all in earshot to hear. If Barron and the Pact's other top commanders were going to find a way to defeat the Highborn, one thing was damned sure.

They were going to need more antimatter than one overtaxed and vulnerable Hegemony facility could provide.

And she was going to see that they got it.

*   *   *

"Mr. Holsten, it's a pleasure to see you, as always." Emmit Flandry was a seasoned politician, the Speaker of the Confederation's Senate, and skilled at both of his primary trades, negotiation and lying. But he still couldn't disguise the fact that he was about as glad to see Holsten as he would have been a recurrence of Crellian Firerash.

Holsten and Flandry had worked well together in the past, and Flandry had learned to shove his normal political urges to the side and focus on striving to give Admiral Barron all he needed to win the war. It felt unnatural to the Speaker to ignore political gain, to set aside his usual agendas and truly serve the Confederation's interests. But Holsten had won him over, in no small part with a gentle and somewhat inappropriate touch of hand brushing across the back of his neck...along with a vague description of something called a 'Collar' Holsten had described in excruciating detail his experiences watching the thing extracted from a recovered enemy body, and the last time he'd been on Megara, he'd explained with some degree of relish, the experts' best guess on how the thing was implanted.

"I am as pleased to see you as you are me, Speaker."

Touché.

Flandry just nodded. "So, what brings you back so soon, Mr. Holsten? Surely you do not believe we are going to find more resources somewhere for your war projects?" Flandry might have said something similar at any point in his career, though in the past, he might have conspired to devote more of his efforts to personal political aims, like bribing and rewarding allies. This time, he really didn't know where to look to find more production. Every factory, every shipyard, every mine in the Confederation was working at full capacity, even beyond. Safety regulations had been suspended, workplace accidents had increased measurably, and mandatory overtime requirements had been in effect for over two years. The Confederation's economy had been pushed to the brink, and on more than one planet, Flandry feared outright rebellion, even mass starvation if things didn't change soon. It had been a longstanding economic exercise to estimate what the Confederation could produce if it poured every resource into something with single-minded dedication.

It wasn't an exercise anymore. It was reality.

"I am back to check on the progress of Project Quasar…and on our other efforts, especially *Excalibur*. The admiral knows all resources have already been committed, and that you have done all you have promised, all you can do. He just wanted to be sure that no one on Megara—or elsewhere—was beginning to think the lull in hostilities was reason to believe the war was over. We have limited intelligence from beyond the border, but what we do possess suggests that the enemy is building as quickly as we are, perhaps even more so."

"No, Mr. Holsten…I, at least, am not of such an opinion. Though I will confess, the lack of combat has made it difficult to keep the Senate united. Many are indeed beginning to wonder if the threat was exaggerated, if perhaps this is a Hegemony problem and not one that need concern us."

"You mean, assuming we hadn't signed the Pact and taken all their technology, of course."

"Yes…ah…of course." Flandry wondered sometimes if Tyler Barron and his group of comrades were really as earnest as they seemed at times…or if they were better politicians than even he and the other senior Senators. He knew Holsten, at least, was no stranger to crawling in the mud when it served his purposes. The head of Confederation Intelligence had quite the file of Senators' secrets and even crimes, including a few of Flandry's own, and Holsten had never shown the slightest hesitation to resort to blackmail when it was the most efficient route to accomplishing his goals.

"That is immaterial in any event. We have committed to the Pact, and the Hegemony has honored their obligations to the letter. And, if it helps, if honor and honesty and doing as they promised to do are not enough for you colleagues, it is very clear the enemy is massing some kind of very large force. The Hegemony is immense, and the Highborn occupy almost half of it. That's a lot of industry turned to their uses, assuming they have been as effective at controlling the native populations as we expect. They will attack, Speaker, that is a virtual certainty. And when they do, we will need every ship under construction, every weapon in production…and we will most definitely need Quasar."

Flandry nodded. "I believe I can keep the Senate under control for another six months, perhaps close to a year. Fear is a powerful motivator, and I will use it freely, but it also fades quickly when an expected threat does not materialize."

"Do your best, Speaker." Holsten paused, and then he continued, a sinister tone slipping into his voice. "And I will do mine."

* * *

"You will have to report to the Senate. Indeed, I suspect a summons is already on the way. But I wanted to speak with you first. I need to know exactly what is happening in the Union. We've got almost everything deployed out on the border with the Highborn. If our old enemy becomes a problem, we're in big trouble." Holsten stared at Kerevsky, trying to evaluate the admiral turned spy. He'd lost some of his trust in his operative, and he was trying to decide if Kerevsky had simply become too involved, blundered on his tradecraft…or if he'd actually shifted his loyalties.

"When I left Montmirail, Admiral Denisov was due back to make preparations for the final assault on Villieneuve's positions. Denisov's forces have followed up their victory four years ago with a series of campaigns against systems loyal to Villieneuve. They have largely achieved success, though it has proven to be a slow process."

"And…*First Citizen* Ciara? Are her overtures legitimate? Does she really intend to sign a long term peace treaty and end Confederation-Union animosity?" Holsten was skeptical. In his experience, things rarely worked out that well on their own.

"I believe she is entirely sincere. She has promised me that her first order of business after Villieneuve is defeated will be to send a new diplomatic mission to Megara to begin work on a new treaty."

Holsten was watching intently, his eyes focused on Kerevsky's, and on the spy's body language. He'd never discouraged his field operatives from using sex as one of their tools, but he wondered how much farther than that it had gone with Kerevsky. He was reasonably sure the admiral was being honest as they stood there…but he also knew that if Ciara went back on her word, if she posed a threat to an overextended Confederation almost defenseless on the Union border, he would only have one way to try to stop her. He would need other resources for that, and even as he stood there, faces and names rolled by in his thoughts.

If it came to an assassination attempt, Kerevsky would know nothing about it. Holsten wasn't going to test his subordinate's loyalty with that much force.

"Are you scheduled to return to Montmirail after you have made your reports?"

Kerevsky paused uncomfortably. "No, Mr. Holsten, not in the near future. I hope to return to see to the establishment of normal relations, but First Citizen Ciara thought it would be…better…if I remained here for a while.

Ah...she plans to clean house Union-style. That's both a good sign and a bad one...

Still, despite his concern over Ciara's willingness to employ brutal force, there were hopeful aspects. First, the fact that she didn't want Kerevsky there to witness her consolidation of power suggested she didn't want the Confederation to see any more dirty laundry than necessary. That implied some level of sincerity in her diplomatic overtures.

And second, Holsten was damned sure Montmirail did, in fact, need a good cleansing, and he knew there was only one, very untidy, way to wash away the stench of Gaston Villieneuve and the tentacles he still likely controlled throughout the Union capital.

*   *   *

"She is magnificent. Unlike anything I've ever seen before." Captain Cliff Wellington stood behind the floor to ceiling hyper-polycarbonate wall of the observation deck, looking out over the vast ship floating before him. His statement wasn't exactly true. He'd seen *Colossus* in action, and that imperial relic was even larger and more powerful than the ship in front of him. But *Excalibur* was the largest warship the Confederation had ever built, by a considerable margin. She was bigger than anything the Hegemony had as well, and she was the first great example of Hegemony technology meeting Confederation industry.

"She will be ready to launch in three months, Captain. And her first three sisters will be completed just under a year from now." A pause. "Assuming we are able to prevent any further labor...difficulties."

Wellington knew some of the worlds of the Iron Belt had a poor history of mistreating their workers...but he also knew the Confederation was fighting for its life, even if it didn't seem that way back home. He'd washed the blood of close comrades and friends from his uniform, and while he might have sympathized with the workers in another situation, he was completely ready to send in the Marines if that's what it took to keep the building program moving. He had the needed force at hand…and he had Tyler Barron's permission to do *whatever was necessary* to get those ships, and the hundreds more in the shipyards, into space and out to the frontlines.

That was a duty he would gratefully hand over to others when *Excalibur* was launched. The admiral had placed him in command of the massive new vessel, with orders to bring her forward as soon as she completed an accelerated shakedown cruise. The ship, being called a super-battleship, colloquially if not officially, mounted a fearsome array of weapons, but perhaps most importantly, it carried four magnetic deflector field generators. The experimental system wasn't likely to match the enemy Sigma-9 emitters for effectiveness at interfering with targeting, but there was a good chance they would make a considerable difference. And every one of the Highborn beams diverted, any hit turned into a near miss, was one more building block to victory.

"*Fully* operational in three months?" Wellington was doubtful, but he wanted to believe the shipyard master's statement.

"Yes…well, probably. You know normal procedure would be for a test cruise with shipyard staff aboard and then a maintenance session to address any issues before formal commissioning. We're working on an expedited schedule, as you are aware. She's even commissioned already. Technically, *Excalibur* is already an active ship under your command…though until we get those new drives activated, she won't take you very far.

"Make sure that three months holds." Wellington's tone wasn't threatening, exactly, but there was urgency in it. Tyler Barron had entrusted him with the command of the

Confederation's newest warship, along with two dozen other vessels that would be accompanying *Excalibur* to the front lines. He was honored by that, grateful, and a little overwhelmed.

And he'd be damned if he was going to arrive late.

Chapter Seven

Forward Base Striker
Vasa Denaris System
Year 327 AC (After the Cataclysm)

Tyler looked across the table at Andi. They'd been sitting there for over an hour, but neither of them had touched anything on their plates. Cassie had devoured her dinner, as usually, and she was off watching vids, apparently ignorant of the dark cloud hanging over her parents.

The drones from Outpost Seventeen had reached Striker ten hours before, and Barron had finally torn himself away from the endless meetings that followed to have dinner with his family. He'd had a vague feeling he should be working, that it was wrong for him to carve out personal time at such a moment, but there had been nothing he could do about any of it, not until the level nine encryptions in the drones were fully decoded...and probably not until he could send a scouting mission to track any subsequent Highborn moves.

Besides, he felt somewhat of a renewed imperative to spend time with the two people closest to him in the galaxy...especially since the newly arrived news placed an ominous countdown on their time together. He'd realized as he considered the prospect of renewed warfare, just how accustomed he'd allowed himself to become to quiet time with his family…and how difficult it would be to tear himself away from that.

"It doesn't mean they're launching a renewed invasion immediately…and we've got fortified positions between there and here. Even if they're coming, they won't get to Striker for some time." A pause. "Still, I think we need to be ready."

"Ready?" Andi looked back at him from across the table, the sadness in her eyes clear to see, and something else, a deep thoughtfulness that twisted his stomach into knots. She knew exactly what he was talking about. Why was she acting strangely?

"For you and Cassie to go back to Megara. Or at least back from what is likely to become the new frontline." It broke Barron's heart to send his family away, and the pain was almost unbearable. The only thing worse would be to expose them to danger, to risk their lives. That he would never do.

"Cassie certainly. Lita can take her back." Andi was clearly trying to retain her composure, but Barron could see the pain she was feeling, and he felt a deep sense of foreboding. What did she have in mind?

"I can't go with her, Tyler. And I think you know why."

Barron shook his head, an instinctive response, despite the fact that he was beginning to realize just what she was talking about.

"No." He shook his head, and he could feel his hands tightening into fists. "No," he said again.

"There is no choice, Tyler…and you know it. If it was anyone but me here discussing this with you, you would agree. But you know what the fleet will be up against. You have an idea, at least. We need something else. We need to know how the empire drove the Highborn out. And I finally have some idea where that trail leads."

"Into the Occupied Zone? Beyond even? It's a suicide mission, Andi. I'd do everything possible to avoid sending *anyone* on such an impossible quest. Anyone. But you…"

"No one has a better chance than I do. Is there anyone on Striker, anyone in the fleet, who knows his way around imperial ruins better than me?" He could hear the insistence in her tone, struggling with her efforts to control it. Barron didn't doubt that Andi was as reluctant as he was to risk tarnishing what could be one of their final times together.

"No one is going to argue that you don't know your imperial artifacts—or that you aren't capable and handy in a fight, God knows—but how can we send anyone into the Occupied Zone? We have no idea of enemy security and patrols. We take risks in battle, but we don't walk right into certain death." Partially true. He tried not to send anyone into no win situations, but he *had* done it. And he was very afraid he'd do it again.

Just not with Andi.

"Tyler, I understand that you're worried about me. Hell, *I'm* worried. You don't think the idea of trying sneak past the Highborn scares the hell out of me?" She paused, and her voice wavered a bit. "Don't you think I'm scared to death when you're with the fleet? When you're in battle?"

Her words were like a fencing master's rapier finding a weak spot in an opponent's defenses. He'd been in almost all of the largest and most terrible battles fought in and near the Rim, and she had never complained or tried to prevent him from doing his duty.

A voice screamed inside his head, insisting it was different. But he knew it wasn't. Andi was the best candidate to search for imperial records on combating the Highborn, he couldn't deny that. And while he had some doubts the secret to defeating the enemy lay in old imperial scraps and records, he was no more optimistic about achieving a purely military victory.

He looked at Andi, trying to resist the moisture he felt building in his eyes. The thought of letting her take off again, to try to sneak behind enemy lines and prowl through ancient ruins, cut off and beyond the reach of any help was unimaginable. The very idea of it terrified him. He felt the urge to stop her, somehow. She wouldn't listen to an order, regardless of his official authority over everyone on Striker. He knew her far too well to even hope *that* would work. He could lock her up, he supposed…though he'd have to send a heavier than usual detachment of Marines. Andi was his wife, and he loved her more than anything…but sometimes he forgot what a deadly fighter she was. What a stone cold killer.

Cassie.

His daughter. That was the one thing that might work. Andi was right, Cassie's future depended on finding a way to stop the Highborn. But maybe if he hit her hard enough over sending the child away with neither parent, threw as much guilt at her as he could…

No, he couldn't do that. Not to Andi. And he couldn't use his daughter as a weapon. Especially not when he knew Andi was right. If anyone was going to find the lost secrets of the empire's struggle with the Highborn, it was Andromeda Lafarge, the scourge of the Badlands.

But how could he let her go?

* * *

"It looks like we're going to see some action soon, Reg. The enemy has attacked and destroyed Outposts seven *and* Nine. They may be planning to come along two axes of advance, which means splitting the fleet if we want to fight them before Striker." The Pact's main base was well located, its system a choke point in the transit network heading toward the Badlands and then on to the Rim. It wasn't a perfect bottleneck. The Highborn could bypass it several ways, but each required at least eight additional jumps, and even if they were willing to undertake the longer route, they could never leave something as powerful as Striker and the main

Pact fleet in their rear. No, Barron knew any Highborn invasion plan would have to come at his fortified position sooner or later.

And that would be a bloody day.

"Two outposts? I hadn't heard about number nine."

"We just got the word this morning. I haven't released it yet. We don't need to help the enemy by allowing idle speculation to begin eroding morale. Once we have a better idea of what happened, we'll figure out how to proceed. Meanwhile, the data from Outpost Nine confirms everything we got from number seven. The Highborn *do* appear to have fighters. It is unclear whether they're modular like ours or simply dedicated interceptors, but I'm sure you understand the implications for your wings."

Reg nodded, but it was the almost despondent look on her face that confirmed she completely understood. "It means we'd better dust off our dogfighting tactics."

Barron sighed softly. He liked Reg Griffin. He respected her, both as an officer and certainly as a pilot. She'd done a remarkable job pulling the wings from their despair, training them and honing their skills for more than three years. But the shade of Jake Stockton cast its shadow over everything she did. And Barron couldn't help but think how much he missed his friend every time he met with Stockton's replacement.

"With regard to that…you know I have the utmost confidence in you, Reg. You earned the commodore's star Jake gave you…and the admiral's insignia I added to it. So, I don't want you to feel that I believe any less in you, but…" Barron paused. "I sent for some help for you. I've sent word calling Olya Federov and Dirk Timmons back to the wings."

Griffin was silent, nodding immediately, but with an uncertain look on her face.

"You will still be in command, of course. Olya and Dirk will be here in an advisory capacity to help train your forces for fighter to fighter combat, not to interfere with your authority." Barron hesitated for a second. "You have my word, Reg. You are Jake's chosen successor, and you have my every confidence, but you're going to need help getting your people ready to face interceptors...and Timmons and Federov are probably the two best dogfighting experts we've got left."

The two pilots were the last of Stockton's Four Horsemen, the legendary team of officers who'd led the wings through the Hegemony War, two men and two women who'd fought at Raptor's side in one bloody battle after another. Now, he was gone, and two of them were as well.

Johannes Trent had died in *Renown's* fighter bay, trying to land his mauled ship, and Alicia Covington was still classified as missing in action...though after so long, that was just a technicality.

Timmons, long Stockton's bitter rival before the two became friends and close comrades, was widely considered to be the second best pilot in Confederation history. At least he had been, before age and repeated wounds—including the loss of his legs—had worn him down. He was still extremely capable in a cockpit, his prosthetics functioning well enough, but he wasn't quite what he had been, and for the last five years he'd been someplace where he could impart his skills and do the most good...serving as commandant at the Academy.

Olya Federov had also been desperately wounded in battle, and she'd spent more than two years recovering from her injuries. She'd been retired since, no doubt trying to heal mentally and emotionally from her traumas, but Barron knew she wouldn't refuse his call to return.

Reg had been silent for a few seconds, but then she nodded and said, "Thank you, Admiral. I am sure their help will be invaluable."

Barron was about to say something else—he wasn't quite

sure what—to reassure Griffin, but before he could come up with something, his portable comm unit buzzed.

"Yes?" he said as he tapped the unit.

"Admiral…I need you up in the control room. As soon as possible." It was Clint Winters, and it was clear something was very wrong.

"I'm on my way." Barron turned toward Griffin. "You'd better come too, Reg. Whatever is happening, I'm sure your people are going to be neck deep in it."

*   *   *

"Two more sets of drones have transited into the system, Admiral. From Outpost Three and Outpost Sixteen. Initial data transmissions indicate both have been attacked and destroyed."

Barron sat silently as he listened to Winters's report. It might as easily have been him on the bridge an hour earlier, when the new drones began to arrive. That was just the mandate of the schedule, a bit of randomness that had placed Clint Winters in the control center at that moment.

"There's more as well. There was a resupply convoy on the way to Outpost One. It found the station under attack after it transited, so they turned around and came back to report. They just transited, so my guess is One's drones won't be far behind. That's five of the outposts, all attacked…and likely all completely destroyed. Almost simultaneously."

Barron inhaled deeply. "I think we'd better send scouts to the other outposts to check on their status." A pause. "Perhaps we should even order them abandoned. The automated systems can send warning of any additional Highborn attacks. We're asking our people to throw away their lives if we keep them there." Barron phrased his thought as a question, but he knew it was his call. Vian Tulus would support any decision he made, he was sure of that. And he doubted Chronos would object, especially since the construction and manning of the outpost line had been a Confederation responsibility. The men and women up there alone, in those lightly-armored stations, were Barron's.

"I agree, Admiral." Winters nodded. "If it's not already too late."

"You think they're going to hit more of the outposts, Clint? Or that they already have?"

"Two might have been a sign of a split attack, but five? I doubt they're going to divide their forces that much. Perhaps they're trying to throw us off, keep us guessing where the main attack with come. I don't know, but is it going to surprise you if another series of drones limps into the system from one of the others?"

"No, it's not. Let's see to that evacuation order now...if it's not already too late." He turned toward the officer sitting next to him. "Commander Carlisle, see the order is issued at once. Send a courier ship to every remaining outpost with orders to prepare for evacuation. Then arrange for transport to follow up and pull the crews out of there."

"Yes, Admiral." The officer stood up and saluted, then he strode briskly out of the room to carry out Barron's command.

Barron had come to lean on Tilson Carlisle more and more over the past three and a half years. He looked across the table at Atara Travis. Travis had been his chief aide in one way or another almost since he'd taken his first command. She had followed him around the fleet, and up the chain of command, and now she wore her own admiral's stars. But she hadn't been the same, not since she'd been wounded at Calpharon. She'd survived, something that had seemed unlikely at first, mostly because of Chronos's intervention and the application of superior Hegemony medical technology. She looked much the same as she ever had, though Barron knew about three kilometers of her body weight now consisted of bionic bits and pieces, as well as three metal alloy bone segments. The treatments had been painful, the recovery slow and grueling. But she *had* recovered. Physically at least.

Barron wasn't so sure about emotionally. He was worried about his friend, and that had caused him to rely more heavily on his junior aide…which was probably just making things worse. He'd started by trying to ease her workload, give her time to fully recover. He'd intended to give her time, but recently he'd been concerned he might have given her the impression he'd lost confidence in her. Perhaps his efforts to help her had turned counterproductive. He had to sit down with her and have a long talk, but he'd been putting it off. That was something else that had slipped away. Once, he'd have spoken comfortably with Atara about almost anything.

But seeing her so badly hurt, watching her fight on the edge of death…he wondered if *he* wasn't part of the problem, if seeing his oldest friend suffer so badly had affected how he perceived her, dealt with her.

Barron had been grateful at first for the respite from action, but he'd come to wonder if that hadn't been harmful to Atara. She had been wounded before, just as he had been, and both had always returned to action as soon as they were up and around. Perhaps an extended rest was counterproductive. Four years was a long time to think about things, to dwell on what had happened, how close she had come to death. Sometimes, he knew, the voices inside, and the rambling of one's own thoughts, were the deadliest enemy.

"Very well…that is decided." He looked across at Atara, giving her a passing smile. She returned it with one of her own, but there was just something in her eyes that troubled him. His friend needed help, and he wasn't sure how to give it.

He hated to think that answer was combat, that returning

to battle would restore Atara's confidence, that she needed to prove to herself she could be as effective as she had once been, and battle was the only way that could happen. He hated the thought…but he realized he had come to believe just that.

"Now, if the enemy does launch an invasion soon, before we're able to do any serious reorganization and training of the wings…" He glanced over at Reg. "…how do we respond to these Highborn fighter squadrons. The easy answer is to outfit all our wings as interceptors, in spite of the lack of dogfighting experience among the pilots. But we don't have enough ordnance for that. Interceptor kits have not been a production priority for more than ten years. We might put a thousand ships in space right now, at most. And our ability to resupply those with missiles or to repair damaged ships will be extremely limited. I have already dispatched a message to Gary Holsten, one that expresses our urgent need for more ship to ship missiles and interceptor gear…but we all know it will take close to two months for that communique even to reach him. It will likely be a year, perhaps more, before we are able to massively increase our supplies of interceptor kits."

"We have some production capacity, Tyler…left over from…" The words, 'when we were fighting each other' seemed to echo off the walls and ceiling, though Chronos hadn't actually said them. He'd let his voice drift off to silence for a few seconds instead. "It's not enough to provide what is needed, and we will have to rework much of it to fit your Lightning fighters, but I believe we can get at least some equipment and ordnance flowing to your squadrons before you can hope to begin receiving shipments from the Confederation.

"Thank you, Chronos. Anything you are able to do in that regard will be most helpful. Of course, you will have to retain enough unaltered production to supply your own wings. Your pilots were trained from the start for fighter versus fighter actions. They may actually be among the best suited right now to face the enemy squadrons." He turned to look over at Vian Tulus. "The Palatian wings, at least, are well-supplied with interceptor ordnance." Barron barely managed to suppress a laugh. Dogfighting fit the Palatian warrior ideal far better than coordinated bombing runs, but he still found it amusing that the Alliance had shipped large quantities of the materials all the way across the Confederation, the Badlands, and into the Hegemony…when there had been little reason to expect any of it was necessary. For all the thought and strategy and tactical debates that had failed to create readiness, pure Palatian pride and stubbornness had won the day.

"I will order all of our squadrons configured for interceptor operations at once." The eagerness in Tulus's voice was clear to Barron. For all the imperator's tactical wisdom, he was still a Palatian warrior at heart, and it was clear he was anxious to see his squadrons take on the enemy wings. "At least until we are able to get more of your ships so equipped…and we decide on the appropriate force breakdowns to face the enemy in the future."

"Thank you, Vian…that will be most helpful. With the Palatian and Hegemony squadrons configured as interceptors, plus the portion of Confederation forces we can currently so equip, we will have a substantial force available to screen our bombers and meet the enemy fighters." He turned and looked down the table. "We will have to give some thought to the ideal allocations once supply constraints are no longer making our decisions for us. We can't convert all the wings to anti-fighter operations. I think we can all agree, the fleet has no chance at all against the Highborn forces without bomber support. We've…hopefully…improved our targeting and scanner locks over the past few years, but I think it would be extremely unrealistic to assume that alone will be sufficient. And yet, if we have too few interceptors, the enemy squadrons will obliterate our unprotected bombers."

The room was silent. Barron wasn't surprised. He had no idea how many fighters the Highborn had, or what numbers his mostly-inexperienced wings would need to combat them. He wasn't surprised no one else did either.

"Okay, we'll table that until we have more data. Or until we run out of time. It's possible a closer review of the scanner data from the destroyed outposts will give us at least a start. And, on that topic, there is one more thing we should discuss. What we have analyzed suggests a level of cohesion and order in the Highborn squadrons that greatly exceeds what we might expect from a force so new to small craft operations." He looked one way and then the other, panning his eyes over the officers present. "Does anybody have any thoughts on how *that* is possible?"

Chapter Eight

"You have done well, Thrall-Commander Stockton. Very well indeed. Your pilots have exceeded all expectations and parameters, and their kill ratios have been excellent."

Jake Stockton knelt in front of Tesserax, waiting for the Highborn to give him permission to rise. He'd resisted prostrating himself, at least in the small part of his brain that was still his. That was still *him*. But as always, he'd had no control. He retained only enough consciousness of his own to feel remorse and self-hatred at what he'd been forced to watch himself do for more than three years.

"Thank you, Highborn. I exist to serve." The words, too, came from part of his mind he couldn't control. Stockton would have put a gun in his mouth before he'd have uttered such obsequious drivel to an enemy. He'd longed for death, begged the forces of the universe to let him die, stared with longing at guns, knives, vertical drops, anything that promised the sweet relief of oblivion...but all to no avail.

His brutal fate, the cold destiny that had claimed him, denied him the escape of death. He'd imagined his end a thousand times, but never in his darkest nightmares had he imagined the hell that had consumed him.

His body simply wouldn't respond to his commands, no more than it had the vast number of times he'd tried to attack his captors or end his own life. The Collar controlled him, his every move, even his mental activities. He was unable to refuse orders from the Highborn, incapable of trying to escape. He'd told the Highborn everything he knew about the Confederation forces, spewed out information in a torrent, each word a profound betrayal of those he'd left behind. He'd tirelessly trained thousands of Thrall pilots, too, teaching them every dogfighting tactic he knew.

Preparing them to kill his comrades. His friends.

Jake Stockton had been a Confederation legend, the supreme commander over thousands of loyal pilots, and a hero celebrated from one Confed planet to another. And now, at least to the sensibilities he retained, he was the foulest, most vile traitor in history.

" We will soon face the human forces, Thrall-Commander, and you will be a central figure in our victory. You will serve us well, Jake Stockton, and secure a place for yourself among the very highest of the Thralls."

I will live to see you choking to death on your own blood…if there is any justice in the universe.

But Stockton didn't believe there was justice or fairness. They were fairy tales, invented to brainwash children.

"Thank you, Highborn. Your words do me honor." More words he couldn't stop…and more self-loathing.

"You still have some time to complete your training operations, Commander. We have destroyed all seventeen of the enemy outposts along the border, each of them with your fighter squadrons. The primary assault, however will not commence at once. Our goal is to break the morale of the humans, to destroy their will to fight. They will be shaken when they realized that all of their forward positions have been extinguished simultaneously. They will debate and argue as they try to decide from where our attack will commence. They will review scanner footage, watch the skill of your fighter wings, the sharpness of their maneuver…and then they will realize that six hundred of the small craft attacked each of seventeen outposts. They will know we can deploy over ten thousand fighters…and they will quake with fear."

Stockton felt as though his body was quivering with rage, but he knew he was still kneeling perfectly still in front of Tesserax. The Highborn had not given yet him leave to rise, no doubt a way of making a point to the scrap of Jake Stockton that remained under the Collar's crushing power.

He'd expected the orders for the offensive to come immediately, and he felt relief at the apparent delay. He understood the Highborn plan. It even made sense to him, save for one thing. It didn't account for the will of his colleagues. It didn't matter what force the Highborn paraded before the scanners. Clint Winters would never yield. Stara Sinclair, Reg Griffin, even Chronos and his top Hegemony commanders…they would never give way.

And Tyler Barron, his friend, his mentor, his commander for almost all of his illustrious career, Tyler Barron, the Confederation's hero, the very embodiment of his famous grandfather…Tyler Barron would never surrender, no matter what force, what deadly danger the enemy threw at him.

His certainty in that was the first sense of relief he'd felt since the day he'd been captured.

*   *   *

"You have done well, Keremax, beyond even the high expectations I had for you." Tesserax stood next to the other Highborn, looking out from what had once been the Council's Hall on Calpharon. The Hegemony capital had put up a short but nasty fight, and the Kriegeri's resistance had caused considerable damage. But much of the planet's industry had been captured nearly intact, and the repairs that were needed had been combined with upgrades and modifications to meet Highborn standards. Production had commenced less than six months after the occupation, and Calpharon's factories, and its orbital shipyards had been producing weapons, supplies, and ships at a breakneck pace ever since. The same was true on almost a hundred other planets, but Calpharon had been in every way the powerhouse of Hegemony industry and power. That was why Tesserax had proclaimed it the capital of the Colony, and the center of Highborn rule in the Rimward sectors of the old empire. One day it would be revered as a sacred world by hundreds of billions of humans, and they would look to its star from their home worlds and know that is where the gods dwelled.

"You do me honor, Commander. We did face some challenges, at least before we were able to begin local production of Collars. But more than half the population here is now encollared, and the reduced need for conventional security had enabled us to increase production more rapidly. In another year, every human on Calpharon will wear the Collar."

"See that we achieve that goal in six months, Keremax, even if you are required to terminate surplus segments of the population to do so. The humans breed rapidly, and any damage done to long term productivity by unanticipated population losses will soon be repaired. We are to begin the final phase of the reduction of the humans remaining in arms against our sacred rule…and I would risk no distractions from uncontrolled populations in the occupied areas."

"I will see it done, Commander. I believe we can increase Collar production, perhaps not enough to fully encollar the population in the specified time, but I am confident we can keep the surplus down to perhaps one hundred million. The terminations of such a small population segment will hardly affect productivity, especially since the Hegemony was thoughtful enough to maintain detailed genetic records on its population. We can quite easily target those remaining of moderate to high capability to be given the Collar, and ensure that any groups eliminated will be among the lowest rated, those with little measurable value to our efforts going forward."

"Excellent, Keremax. I leave such details in your capable hands." Tesserax was pleased with his subordinate's efforts, and he considered Keremax one of the most valuable members of his team. Still, he felt a prejudice of sorts, a sense of superiority that had little to do with achievement or accomplishment. Tesserax was of the Firstborn, the initial quickening of the Highborn, and a group that had become a sort of royalty among the others, rulers over the gods in a manner of speaking. Keremax was of the second group of Highborn, placing him near the top of the second and middle level, which consisted of those quickened before the exodus from the empire. The Highborn created in the centuries since the departure from imperial space were the lowest of the three groupings, gods still, in relation to the humans, but a decidedly lower order in the minds of those quickened earlier.

Tesserax might have considered, for all the superiority of the Highborn mind and the millennia of genetic advancement they represented, the foolishness of such pointless claims to rank and prestige. The thoughts existed, no doubt, somewhere deep in his vast mind, but they were far from his consciousness. To the speaking, thinking, acting being he was, his superiority as one of the Firstborn was self-evident, and he never imagined it as something subject to question or doubt.

Tesserax turned and looked out again over the broad street below. Hundreds of humans were visible, moving in neat lines, coming to and from the factories and other places of work. All he could see exhibited the orderly and pleasing crispness of motion common to encollared humans. The Collar had been an enormously successful invention, one that had unfortunately come too late for use in the early struggles to control and save the empire. The Collar didn't eliminate a human's memories, nor even his personality. It simply directed all mental efforts, focused energies on the subject's true obligations…and restricted action initiated by wrong-minded thoughts. Encollared humans were obedient, worshipful, hard-working…in every way the ideal subjects for the Highborn to rule.

"I see the church construction program is also well underway." Tesserax had been with the fleet for much of the past six months, and before that he'd returned to the Highborn capital to report his progress to Ellerax, the First of the Highborn. The churches were a paramount part of the long-term plan to rule over and control the humans, and to facilitate their worship of the Highborn. But in the shorter term, they had been subordinated to the need to put the industrial facilities back into production.

"Yes, I wish we could have begun sooner, but Calpharon is a heavily industrialized world, and it took considerable effort to get the factories and such back at full operation. Now, the humans will truly learn their place. They will worship us, and to serve. And when the Rim is completely subdued, they will labor to support the true war effort, doing their part, and setting aside the folly that so often consumes them when they are bereft of our guidance. They will produce and build strength, and they will know there is a greater power above them."

"Indeed, Keremax. Indeed."

Tesserax nodded and smiled as he looked out again over the former Hegemony capital. The Colony, the name Ellerax had given to the sections of the Rim and the Near Rim the Highborn controlled, was already vast. Over one hundred billion Hegemony citizens were now under

Highborn rule, and if only a minority of that total had yet been properly conditioned as yet, that process was well underway. The Church enforcers were out among the people, and those who proved overly resistant were expedited on the schedule of Collar implantation…or simply terminated. Tesserax hadn't expected the process to be complete overnight, but he had no doubt those living on the Colony's current worlds, and those yet to be conquered and added to the mix, would one day be docile and obedient, hardworking and respectful of the Highborn who ruled over them. That would be a joyous day.

The project that had begun almost four centuries before would finally reach its successful conclusion…and the Highborn, and their rightful flock of humans, could focus their full attention and resources on the true fight, on winning the war that had plagued the Highborn almost since they had fled the empire so long ago.

It is nearly time. They will come soon. They will answer our beckon call, and they will advance to their destruction.

And when they come, it will be time to unleash the forces we have massed on the stubborn and disobedient humans. Time to put them in their rightful place, for now, and for all time to come.

If a few billion more had to die to achieve that state of divine righteousness, that was of little consequence with creatures that bred as quickly as humans. It was a small price to pay for a great step forward for Highborn rule over the cosmos.

Chapter Nine

Forward Base Striker
Vasa Denaris System
Year 327 AC (After the Cataclysm)

Yes…that's the same reference. Another mention, from a completely different source. That's confirmation…at least enough to justify following up…

Andi Lafarge was bent over her desk, ignoring the throbbing pain in her hunched back as she scanned what seemed like endless files. Most of what she had were snippets, bits and pieces of previously meaningless information drawn from various imperial artifacts, now made suddenly relevant by context that hadn't existed before.

Badlands prospectors were a rugged and a focused group. They had combed ancient and ruined imperial worlds seeking items they could sell, valuable ancient electronics and the like, all the while dodging the dangers of hostile planets, partially operable security systems, Sector Nine kill teams, and Confederation naval patrols. Such men and women had little use or patience for less useful items, things without easily definable worth, and they had often cast such finds aside, or sold them for pittances. Andi had thought to herself a number of times, just how arbitrary her own retention of the folio that started her research had been. She'd kept, it certainly, not thrown it away or sold it for drinking and carousing money as so many others would have. But she'd tossed it in a storage facility and almost forgotten about it for more than a decade.

She cringed at just how much priceless history had been tossed out the airlock by grim-faced Badlands rogues, uninterested in damaged old data chips and history and philosophy texts. She wondered how much information about the Highborn had been cast aside, whether even, if the key to defeating humanity's enemy had been found, and then simply thrown out by some ship captain heading to a black market rendezvous with a box of old computer parts and no concern for the historical record.

Still, despite those realities, Andi had managed to collect a fair amount of such things that had survived. She'd done it through a variety of means. Offering large sums to old prospectors for any trinkets of the sort they might have saved, calling in every scholar of imperial history, even sending Marines to virtually ransack museums on a dozen worlds, armed with Senatorial orders to confiscate any imperial informational artifacts the institutions possessed.

She'd set up an impressive operation on Striker, over two hundred people, historians, data experts, engineers…a far cry from the days when she and Sy Merrick sat alone, painstakingly pawing through the battered but mostly-salvageable chips. Her team had been working together now for three years, coaxing information from damaged data units and translating various dialects of old imperial searching for any mention of the events of the final years of the empire…and especially of the Highborn, who seemed to have gone by several different names in those days.

Now, she'd found a second mention of a still-unnamed project, one that had been developed to combat the deadly threat…and appeared to have succeeded in driving the Highborn from the empire. The references were tangential, noting only that the Highborn had indeed been expelled. But both spoke of a planet, a place well coreward of the present day Hegemony, that had been connected to the project.

A world that had also served as the empire's first capital...if such things could be believed.

This new source included additional navigational information. Andi didn't know all the nav points the data referenced, and it was far from something as simple as a map leading directly there. But she had spent most of her adult life sniffing out imperial worlds, and she believed she could find this one.

Assuming we can slip by the Highborn without getting fried...

She pushed that thought away. The less she considered the enemy the better, especially since it had become increasingly clear her road led through the Highborn-occupied zones of the Hegemony and beyond. She would have enough of a challenge forcing herself to leave Tyler and Cassie, she didn't need to stoke her fear of the enemy as well.

But she knew what she had to do. Leaving the two people who mattered most to her, going off on what she knew looked for all the world like a suicide mission, would be the hardest thing she had ever done. It just might be the thing that saved both of them, too. She wanted to hold her child, as though her arms could protect Cassie from the harshness of the universe. But she knew she couldn't save her child with her arms or hands, or even with every weapons she possessed...any more than her own mother had been able to shield her from the realities of the Gut.

She couldn't turn back the invader with her strength...and nor, she was almost certain, could Tyler, with the entire fleet behind him. No, if the Highborn were to be defeated, she and her comrades were going to need something more. She had to go. She had to find the secrets of how the empire had driven the Highborn out...and she

had to bring that, whatever it was—weapon, tactic, trick?—
back to Striker, so it could be used again. So the Pact could
repeat what the empire had apparently achieved more than
three centuries before.

So it could defeat the Highborn.

*   *   *

"All of them. Seventeen. Every one. Every outpost along
the frontier destroyed utterly, with no survivors. And, as
best we can ascertain, almost simultaneously." Tyler Barron
sat at his desk, speaking to Clint Winters. The two were
alone. Barron had almost called Atara into the meeting, but
he'd held back. He knew his friend was struggling, and he'd
been trying to give her some time to fight off her demons.
Besides, Chronos was in the outer system inspecting a
portion of the Hegemony fleet, and wouldn't be back until
early the next morning. Vian Tulus was consumed with
some Palatian spiritual ceremony, and couldn't be reached
for—Barron looked at his chronometer—eleven hours and
seven minutes.

He'd come to respect the Palatians, and to think of Tulus
as his brother, but the warrior race that ruled the Alliance
had its strange aspects, and he still struggled a bit to truly
understand them.

The war council would meet the next day, and he would
update Atara then, along with all the others. But he'd
needed one person to serve as his sounding board before
then, to help him make sense of the mountain of data that
had streamed in over the past week.

"And no sign of invasion yet? Along any of these axes?"

"No, nothing. Not even in the systems where the
outposts were destroyed. It appears that the enemy forces
that struck those stations pulled back almost immediately
after."

"That *is* strange. Maybe they want us guessing where

their attack will come. Destroying all the outposts prevents us from fixing on their intended approach. They could come through anywhere on the line now."

"That is true…but I've dispatched scouts to all those frontline systems, and they will provide the same warning the outposts would have. So, I'm not sure what they've really gained simply destroying the outpost or outposts in the way of their planned invasion route. If they'd hit all the outposts and come on immediately, before we were able to reestablish some kind of monitoring, maybe they could have achieved some surprise. But they sacrificed anything they gained by giving us time to restore some level of reconnaissance along the border."

Winters didn't respond. He just nodded, and he put his hand under his face, adopting a thoughtful pose.

"There is one additional bit of information we've gleaned, Clint, and it's not good news." Barron looked right at Winters. "The scanner data suggests that each station was struck by an identical task force, every one of which included six hundred fighters. We've confirmed this for ten of the stations, and while we're still going over the rest of the data, my guess is the results will show the same thing. Assuming the remaining seven are the same, that means over ten thousand fighters were deployed…and we're fairly certain the attacks were synchronized, or close to it. That means none of these squadrons were in two of the attack forces. I'm jumping the gun a little here, but it seems very likely the Highborn not only possess fighters…they have at least ten thousand of them in active service right now, and every one of their pilots appears to be trained to a skill level far beyond anything we might have expected."

Barron hesitated, trying to keep his thoughts focused. The news he'd just given Winters was indeed bad. So bad, he was still struggling to comprehend the implications himself. "We've built up to almost ten thousand as well, including the wings based on Striker, but we still have to maintain some kind of bombing potential…and almost none of our pilots have meaningful dogfighting experience. We're also limited, at least for now by supplies of interceptor equipment and ship to ship missiles, but once we can correct that, how do we divided our forces? We need enough interceptors to deal with the enemy fighters, or our bombers will get blasted to atoms before they get anywhere close to launch range. But we also need our strike wings powerful enough to get past Highborn point defense and missile barrages, and do some damage to those ships before the lines engage."

Barron looked intently at his friend. "I'm going to confess right now, Clint…I've got no idea, no answers to those questions, and a boatload of others…and I'd be damned grateful if you had some wisdom to offer right now."

* * *

"I know you have to go…but I still can't reconcile with it. I want to order you to stay, to post Marines at the door, to have *Pegasus*'s engines sabotaged…even to use Cassie to try to guilt you into staying." Barron's tone was taut, his ragged emotions apparent in every struggled word he uttered. "But you know I can't do any of that to you."

"Cassie is the biggest reason I have to go, Tyler." Andi was a tough screw, a Badlands rogue at heart, and she rarely held back when unloading on someone, or making her point. But she sounded as fragile as Barron, as close to losing the control she proudly wore almost everywhere she went. "My mother, too. I owe it to her. I want to stay with Cassie, I want to sit and watch her sleep, read with her…just touch her, feel the warmth of her skin. I'm sure my mother wanted the same thing. But she died in the squalor of the Gut, doing what she had to do to protect me. I *want* all the peaceful parts of motherhood, Tyler, more than I could ever have imagined I would have. But what is more a mother's need than to protect her child? I'd never even thought about having a child before…" She stepped toward him and placed her hand on his chest. "…or someone like you. You know I love you, more than anything. Both of you. But if we don't discover a way to defeat the enemy, I'm going to lose you both. We're all going to die, and I can't allow that. Not when there's a chance I can do some good."

"Do you really believe you can track down this phantom imperial weapon, whatever they used to expel the Highborn?" Barron sound doubtful. "It doesn't seem like a lot to go on."

Andi sighed softly. "I can't lie to you, Tyler. I don't know. The data we have is vague, far from conclusive…but I don't doubt the empire *did* find a way to drive them out. The records are much stronger on that, and I think we can call it fact. The Highborn were gone…before the final stages of the Cataclysm. They may be responsible for hastening the final fall, but they were *not* there when it happened. And that means *something* forced them to withdraw. Whatever that was, we need to find it, use it. Otherwise, at best we're looking at war without end, an eternal meatgrinder consuming billions in an effort to hold the line. And at worst, abject slavery under beings that expect us to worship them. You know what that means for us, Tyler. I will kneel down to no conqueror, no more than you. Nor would I see my daughter reduced to such a level. No, Tyler my love, for us, this is truly a fight to the death. And I can do more in space, searching for the secret that might lead to victory, than I can here. More for our cause, for the Confederation. More for you."

She sniffled a bit, pushing back on the tears she could feel trying to come out. "More for Cassie."

Barron stood silently. Andi could feel the struggle inside him. She'd resented his efforts to hold her back from danger in the past, even as she'd understood them. She'd lived her life for a very long time as the sole arbiter of what she did. Her crew, her friends, even the laws of the Confederation…none of them had ever prevented her from doing what she'd felt she had to do. But she realized she wasn't alone anymore. She understood how much it hurt Tyler to let her go, and she knew the pain Cassie would feel if she never came back. Staying would be the easy choice. All it would require of her was to pretend everything would be okay.

Until the day Tyler died in front of her. The moment she fell protecting Cassie, knowing in her final seconds that her daughter would die right after her…or live a life in servile bondage. No, she didn't have a choice, even though she knew she would thrust a dagger in Tyler's heart when she left.

As he had done many times to her, with no more choice or malice than she had now.

"I will be fine, Tyler." She felt guilt immediately. She knew it was a lie, or at least a promise she very well might not be able to keep. He knew it as well, she was sure of that. But the mind was a strange thing, and she imagined her words would come back to him, and on some level, he would believe them.

He would believe them because he wanted to, because he needed to…and that would make his ordeal just a bit easier to endure.

"I want that ship of yours checked out from bow to stern, and especially that stealth unit. We don't even know if those will work against Highborn scanners, but I'm damned sure going to be positive its functioning at one hundred percent."

She nodded, and she could feel a single tear escape, rolling down her cheek. She could feel the pain in Tyler's voice, and she knew the depth of his feeling for her. He was trusting her, too, showing his confidence in her abilities.

And it was nearly killing him to do it.

"And I want you to take some Marines with you. I don't suppose you can fit more than half a dozen on *Pegasus*, but I want you to have some real muscle when you're wandering around some imperial ruin."

Andi didn't say anything. She just stood where she was for a few seconds, and then she stepped forward and put her arms around Tyler. She pulled him close to her, and for a fleeting few seconds, she gave in to delusion, and told herself she would never let go.

Chapter Ten

Around Forward Base Striker
Vasa Denaris System
Year 327 AC (After the Cataclysm)

"No, no, no...I've told you a hundred times. Interceptors are a whole different animal. If you go up against the Highborn squadrons the way you'd run at the point defense of the capital ships, you'll get blasted to scrap." Reg Griffin was shouting into her comm, her voice hoarse from hours of haranguing her people. She knew she was being unfair to them. She had hundreds of ships out there, not one of them holding a pilot who'd ever flown an interceptor outside an Academy exercise. Now, they were up against every old line veteran in the fleet, every pilot she'd been able to find with actual dogfighting experience...and that picked force was being led by two legends, names that carried almost the level of magic Jake Stockton's had held in the wings. Olya Federov and Dirk Timmons. Known in their combat days—and once again—as Lynx and Warrior.

The two veterans, the last remaining of the five revered pilots who'd led the fight against the Hegemony, commanded about three hundred fighters, in every way, the handpicked elite of the squadrons, men and women who had all survived longer than pilots were supposed to, through multiple wars and endless battles. Reg had thrown over a thousand of her people at them, including many hardened in the fighting at Calpharon. They had better than three to one odds, and every one of them flew a fully-equipped interceptor, with missiles and enhanced battle computers.

And they'd been slaughtered. At least in a simulated way.

Timmons had the most AI-allocated 'kills' at eleven, besting 'Lynx' Fedorov by a single one. It was a friendly rivalry, and one Reg imagined would continue, but her mind was mired deep in fake casualties, and in loss ratios that threatened her resolve. Half her people were dead, if only in the memory banks of the computers running the wargames, and fewer than forty of Timmons's and Federov's pilots had suffered similar make believe deaths.

That was worse than a ten to one ratio. She knew, intellectually at least, that however inexplicably well-trained the enemy pilots were, they wouldn't be match for the very best of the Confederation fighter corps, led by two certifiable legends. But it wasn't going to take anything like ten to one ratios to doom her forces, and the entire fleet. They had to do better. A lot better.

And fast.

Admiral Barron had been excruciatingly clear. There wouldn't be enough ordnance to arm all her ships as interceptors, not anytime soon. And even if there had been adequate supplies on hand, the fleet still needed a powerful bombing force to have any chance against the enemy battle line.

That meant, whatever force she threw against the Highborn fighters, it was going to be outnumbered. Badly outnumbered.

She looked at her display, her fingers punching at the controls, replaying the last segments of the simulated engagement. She was looking for errors, mistakes in her formations. But there weren't any, at least none that explained the fictional loss rates. Her people just didn't fly that well, not when they were engaging small craft. They had almost no experience battling other fighters, and it was showing with glaring clarity against pilots who had.

At least the enemy doesn't have any either. They might have found some way to train their pilots well, but they still don't have any experience in actual fighter combats. They can't possibly.

Her people would do better against the Highborn than they had in the encounters with Timmons and Federov and their veterans. But how much better?

Not enough. Not yet. But she was going to get them there, whatever it took.

They would improve given time, she was sure of that. The big question was, how long would she have?

"Alright, we've got enough fuel for one more run. Attack forces, get ready to come in again. Defenders, do better this time." That probably hadn't been the most helpful thing she could say, but it was all she had. She'd instructed them, harangued them, showed them endless recorded battles from the Union War. They knew what to do. They just weren't good enough at it, not yet.

They will be good enough…or I'll kill them trying to get there…

* * *

"I don't think there is any other way, Admiral. I know it's risky, perhaps it even seems reckless, but wargames and training aren't going to get us there. We need to find some enemy formations and fight it out with them. The pilots need to know they can do it, that they can defeat the enemy. The Highborn haven't invaded, and it's been months since the outposts were destroyed. They probably don't have large forces deployed forward, not unless they're ready to launch their invasion. That would be a supply and logistics nightmare. And if there *is* a huge fleet massed just behind the border, then this mission will let us know about it, which alone *has* to be worth the risk. If I'm right, if there aren't any major forces positioned forward, it means we can probably find some small task force somewhere...and see just how our squadrons match up with theirs."

Barron nodded, his head moving only a few centimeters as he did. He agreed with Griffin, at least that the squadrons needed real combat experience against enemy fighters. *He* needed them to have it. He had to know what he could expect, what they could do. It was the only way he could plan a battle when it finally came. But pushing forward past the line of destroyed outposts and into Occupied Space...it seemed wildly risky.

Still, there was something about it, a gravitational pull of sorts, drawing him in. Barron would be happy if the enemy came forward and threw its forces into the teeth of his defenses, but he'd begun to doubt they would be so accommodating. He didn't know what they would do, but half a year of inaction following the attack on the outposts suggested a level of planning far beyond a direct lunge forward. He felt as though he had surrendered the initiative, and that feeling was becoming more and more uncomfortable. Sending a small force into Occupied Space would at least be doing something.

And sending a larger fleet would be doing more.

The thought flooded into Barron's mind, and almost as quickly his defenses flew into action. *No, it's too dangerous, too reckless...*

But you can't just sit here, allow them to dictate the course of the war...

"Admiral?"

"I'm sorry, Reg, my mind...wandered." Barron hesitated, taking a deep breath. "I was just thinking...perhaps we could..."

Barron's voice hesitated, and another chimed in. "You want to launch a major operation...or at least that's what you're thinking." Clint Winters had been silent while Barron and Reg had been discussing targeted incursions into the Occupied Zone. But the prospect of a full scale assault past the outpost line had drawn him into the mix.

"I was thinking about it. I know all you're going to say, Clint. But we've been sitting here, waiting for the enemy to come to us. How long before the Senate falters, before we're faced with a struggle at home to maintain the support levels we need? What would we do if dire warnings and Gary Holsten's threats and machinations prove to be inadequate six months from now, or a year? There are already multiple reports of unrest in the Iron Belt. Are you ready to lead a fleet home, and keep the Senate in line at gunpoint...or land Marines to fire on striking workers?" Barron hesitated for an instant. The thought that Clint Winters might be willing to do just those things passed through his mind. But not even the Sledgehammer would easily unleash such power against his own people. Determination was one thing, but brutality and treason were quite another.

Barron kept his eyes fixed on Winter's. "Do you have any idea what the Highborn are up to, why they haven't come yet? I don't suspect you doubt their ability to take us on and win any time they want to. So, what's the delay? Are they plotting a different course, a route around the edge of the Hegemony and the Badlands? Will they emerge one day in our rear, astride our lines of communication? Or will word come one day that a fleet as emerged at Dannith? Perhaps the destruction of the outposts was simply a way to keep us focused on what they know *we* perceive as the front lines. Or, maybe there is something else at work. Some superweapon in development, or some overwhelming force. Do you really think our situation will be better in a year? In two or three?"

Barron was silent for a moment, save for the sounds of his breath. "Can you think of one possibility, one potential reason behind the enemy's inaction that works in our favor?"

"No, perhaps not." Winters voice was grim. "But, it's been almost six months, Admiral. Nearly half a year since the outposts were destroyed, and as you note, there is no sign of enemy activity. It's almost as if they're daring us to do something." Clint Winters had always been known as a hard charging commander, an admiral who often threw caution to the wind and almost always chose attacking over waiting for the enemy to come to him. But this time, he looked uncertain, hesitant. "We could be doing just what they want us to do if we launch an offensive. Add luring us in to your list of motivations, pulling us away from Striker's fortifications. Have you considered that?"

Barron nodded. "I have. And you very well may be correct. But what else can we do? A move to the front, a push into the Occupied Zone will also give us a chance to get some intel, some kind of real idea what the Highborn are up to. They attacked the outposts, which means they haven't pulled back entirely and gone home. So, why haven't they invaded yet? We're getting stronger, but they almost certainly are, too. We need to know, both what they're doing and how well our squadrons can do in a dogfight. That's not even considering the question of how long we can leave more than a hundred billion people to the mercy of the enemy. I know they're Hegemony citizens, but they're human beings. How would we react if half the Confederation was occupied?"

Barron was becoming agitated, and he paused, trying to center himself before he continued.

We've got to be cautious, ready for any kind of trap. But I am beginning to think the advantages of doing *something* outweigh the dangers. Besides, I ask again...how long can we sit here and wait? Before morale starts to crack? Before our people get distracted, their senses dulled by inactivity? Before the Senate indeed puts the choice of withdrawal or treason to us? We have to do something eventually if the enemy does not…and this seems like the best choice." It was clear from his tone, Barron was only half convinced of his own words.

Perhaps half was all that was within reach.

"You may be right, Tyler…I know that. I've got no answers, no arguments to put against your points. But I've got a feeling…" Winters didn't finish. He didn't have to.

Barron turned his head abruptly. "Admiral Griffin, put together two plans, one for a moderate-sized task force to take a picked group of your squadrons past the outpost line…and a second one, for a full fleet incursion into the Occupied Zone."

"Yes, Admiral." Barron couldn't tell if Griffin was anxious for the chance to take all of her wings forward for a major attack, or scared to death of it.

Or both.

"We will meet again in three days, and we will review both plans…and we will decide how to proceed."

Winters looked like he was going to say something, but finally, he just nodded.

"Very well, Admiral…if you will excuse me, I will get started at once." She looked at Barron, taking his nod as her leave to go.

Winters remained silent until Griffin was gone. Then he said, softly, "You're thinking about taking the biggest risk of your career, Ty. A massive gamble…and the survival of the entire Rim could rest on whether you guess right, whether we catch the enemy napping…or we walk right into a trap."

* * *

Van Striker was in the room, and Jake Stockton, and a dozen others, all men and women Tyler Barron respected, and all dead in battle over the bloody past two decades. They weren't *really* in the room, of course, just apparitions, creations of Barron's mind as he sat alone in the near-darkness of the office. He'd told himself he was leaving half a dozen times, that he was going to go back to his quarters, to see Andi and Cassie. But he knew what Andi was going to say, and also that he couldn't refuse her. He would have to let her go—he'd already as much as consented, and he'd kept the burning desire to recant those words inside him. He had already come to the conclusion that he had to agree to her plan, but somehow it seemed as though if he could simply avoid her, the subject would never come up. It was abject foolishness of the worst kind, but it was a seductive thought nevertheless.

"It is difficult, isn't it? Making command decisions like this?" Van Striker, the namesake of the very station Barron occupied, spoke calmly, reassuringly. And, of course, all inside Barron's tortured mind. Striker had been his mentor, as much as any officer had been, and perhaps the one person he ached to ask what to do. But Striker was gone, and Barron's recreation of the officer was more a sign he was on the verge of succumbing to stress than any real insight into what the dead admiral would have said or recommended.

Barron had done all he could, analyzed the options in a hundred different ways. He could stay where he was, unaware of the enemy's activities, of what was behind their seeming inactivity. Or he could strike.

Tactically, staying put was the clear winner. As long as the enemy came straight on. Striker was the strongest base ever constructed, and the three thousand fighters it carried would be a massive supplement to the fleet's wings. The system was dotted with defensive installations besides the main fort, laser buoys, missile platforms, minefields. Barron still believed the Highborn could defeat his forces if they were determined enough, but they would pay a fearful price.

Strategically, the situation was far less clear. Waiting six more months or a year for the enemy to attack didn't seem like that large a concern in a tactical sense. But the fleet and fortifications were crewed by men and women, and human beings had their breaking points. The longer they waited, staring every day at the scanners, waiting for each morning to be the one they'd been fearing, the more brittle they would become. It was a slow process. Fear grew, crept into every action, every thought. Sleep became first fitful, and then rare, and exhausted and terrified men and women stared into their screens, the dread they'd long fought off taking hold.

It wasn't Barron's decision to make, of course, not solely. But then it was, in a practical sense. Chronos couldn't reject a proposal to attempt the liberation of occupied Hegemony space, whatever doubts he might harbor as a fleet commander. His own Council was no less detached from reality than the Confederation Senate—an indictment, perhaps, of the rationale behind the Hegemony's genetic ranking system—and the pressure to push forward, to free half the Hegemony from enemy rule, would be irresistible.

And Vian Tulus was a Palatian warrior, which was all one needed to know to predict his response. He understood the need for caution, the necessity to build strength, to prepare. But inside him dwelt the spirit of a warrior, crying ever to him to advance. To a Palatian, knowing an enemy's location was the greater part of battle preparation.

No, Barron couldn't escape the decision in front of him, couldn't shift the burden to his comrades. Whatever show of debate and discussion might surround an ultimate decision, he knew his would be the voice that mattered. And the thought crushed him like a black hole's gravity.

There was a scale in his head, balanced with the pros and cons of moving forward, of launching an attack into Occupied Space and of remaining at Striker, waiting. It was almost even, a seemingly impossible decision. Save for one fact.

A   massive   move   forward   would   create   a distraction…and that would greatly increase Andi's chances of slipping into Occupied Space undetected. He felt an immediate backlash, a sense of disgust at himself for allowing his personal fears and needs slip into his command analysis.

But if she gets through…she just might find something that helps defeat the enemy…

That was true, of course, and he believed it to a great extent.

It was also immensely self-serving.

He wrestled with the thoughts, images of Andi floating before his eyes, alongside his grandfather. He was a creature of duty, born to it, trapped by it…and he owed it to all those who followed him, who'd died under his orders, to make cold, impersonal decisions. But he was a man as well, with all the weaknesses endemic to his species. He loved Andi, and the thought of losing her was more than he could handle.

His head was down on his desk, his mind lost so deeply in thought, he didn't even hear the door open, nor the footsteps across the polished metal floor. He felt something…something vague and reassuring, and he slowly came out of his near-trance.

"Andi?" She was standing next to his chair, her hand gently rubbing his neck.

"You never came back to our quarters…I figured you were stuck here. I expected to find you in heated debate with Clint or Chronos or somebody…but it looks like your argument had been with yourself." Her voice was soft, comforting, as was her touch. "So, who's winning?"

"I was just trying to decide something…what to do next." He looked up at her. She was beautiful, her hair long and full, her eyes bright blue gems in the dim flickering light. "I know you have to go, Andi…I know I can't stop you."

His mind tightened, and he could feel himself fending

off the assaults of self-loathing deep inside. "And I think I have an idea. A way to distract the enemy, to get you across into Occupied Space unnoticed."

Chapter Eleven

UWS Incassable
Vesailles System
Union Year 231 (327 AC)

"There is definitely activity at the transit point, Admiral. Energy levels have risen again, and we're starting to pick up objects emerging."

Denisov stared at the main display as the tactical officer made his report. He wasn't ready to launch the final assault on Villieneuve's remaining positions, and he wouldn't be for another six weeks, perhaps eight. He'd been impatient, anxious to push forward and end the war. Four years of fighting his own people, killing them, had damaged some part of him. He was committed, and no force he could imagine would deter him from finally killing Gaston Villieneuve, but he was exhausted as well.

"*Celadona* and *Regina* are to launch spreads of probes immediately. I want those feeds tied in directly to the flagship."

"Yes, Admiral."

Denisov had no idea what his scanners were detecting. The point led directly into Villieneuve's final pocket of resistance, but he couldn't imagine his hated enemy was attacking. He'd chased Villieneuve's loyalists across half the

Union, compelled several forces supporting him to surrender, and he'd penned his enemy into a small cluster of systems, pressed up against the sparsely populated Periphery. There was no way Villieneuve had the power to launch an offensive, and no potential ally in the Periphery strong enough to make a difference.

"*Celadona* and *Regina* acknowledge, Admiral."

The two cruisers were the farthest forward ships in Denisov's fleet. At least the half of his force he had so far assembled in the system. The rest of his ships were scattered across the Union, most of them returning from repair and maintenance operations.

His mind raced, trying to imagine anything he had forgotten, any way Villieneuve could have mustered enough force to launch an attack. No, there was no way. Unless the former First Citizen had given up. Perhaps Villieneuve had chosen a suicide attack as his final maneuver. Denisov couldn't imagine his adversary believed there was any way he would be allowed to survive defeat. Denisov hoped to spare as many spacers as possible from the defeated fleets, but Villieneuve himself had to die.

But Gaston Villieneuve would never surrender...and in its way, a pointless suicide attack would be just that.

"Probes launched, Admiral. We should have data streams in six minutes, thirty seconds." A pause. "Ship's scanners report another increase in energy levels. There is definitely something there, sir, but the scanners are having a hard time getting a fix." The officer turned and looked over at Denisov. "I know this doesn't make any sense, but it's almost as though whatever is out there is flickering in and out of...reality."

Denisov stared at the display. The officer's words didn't really make any sense, and yet they described exactly what he was seeing. Had Villieneuve developed some kind of new technology? Something that interfered with scanning beams?

He felt his insides tense. Denisov wasn't the sort to allow confidence to overrule caution, but he'd analyzed the situation a hundred different ways, and he'd come to the same conclusion every time. Villieneuve was finished.

But if he has something we don't know about...

Denisov sat, shaking his head as he watched the display. Villieneuve was no fool, and he had to know he couldn't win a straight up battle, even with only half of Denisov's fleet in place.

Not unless he thinks he has some kind of edge, something I'm not aware of...

"Bring the fleet to full alert, Commander. And I want all ships to go to full power on their scanners. I want every scrap of data on...whatever that is coming through."

"Yes, Admiral...at once." The officer's voice made it clear Denisov wasn't the only one who was worried.

What the hell are you doing, Villieneuve?

He almost gave the withdrawal order, commanded his ships to pull back. That would buy time, allow him to regroup with some of his returning forces. It would also allow his people to analyze the strange scanner readings in greater detail.

No, you're letting your imagination run wild. Villieneuve is trapped, and eighty percent of his forces have been destroyed or have surrendered. He's finished...whether you invade in two months, or you fight the last battle here.

"All ships...charge weapons, prepare to advance."

* * *

Gaston Villieneuve sat in his chair, strapped in and trying to look as calm as possible. He had always been focused, deliberate, unshakable. He'd used those traits to reach what had once served as the heights of power in the Union, and then not only survived the disaster that claimed his colleagues, but turned rebellion and defeat to his advantage, gaining even more absolute power in the end.

But he had lost his cold view, gotten careless enough to allow traitors to plot in the dark shadows, and while he'd steadfastly maintained that his forces would prevail, he'd long since lost true hope. He'd even begun to imagine an escape route, someplace he could go unrecognized, to remain out of the reach of his enemies.

Then, Percelax arrived. The Highborn had been preceded by a single cryptic message, an offer of alliance, and of immediate help against his enemies. He hadn't believed it at first, not really. Gaston Villieneuve had a lot of people who were afraid of him, but not too many allies. And none with the power to intervene and salvage his crumbling position.

Still, he'd responded, and that had led to a meeting with the Highborn representative…and a real hope of surviving, even of defeating his detested adversaries and returning in triumph to Montmirail.

There will be a reckoning that day…

He'd been cautious at first. His efforts to pursue an 'enemy of my enemy' strategy with the Hegemony had backfired badly, and in many ways, he could trace the start of his decline to that moment. But desperation left few choices, and as he sat there, he was watching the fruits of his diplomacy. His Highborn allies had only sent a limited number of moderately-sized ships, but they were vastly more powerful than anything he—or Denisov—had. And his own fleet had been hastily upgraded, at least as far as their technology levels allowed.

Now it was time. Time to crush the rebel fleet. Time to regain his power, and destroy his enemies with a finality that would almost erase them from history itself.

Sandrien was positioned back from the main fleet. Villieneuve was hopeful his new allies would help him carry the day, but he wasn't about to put himself within reach of his enemies. Denisov would come after him with a ruthless abandon if he was able to detect and close with his ship. Better to let the Highborn and their technology deal with the rebellious admiral and his traitorous spacers.

He stared at the large screen in front of him, watching as sixteen Highborn ships, none larger than a cruiser, moved forward, racing toward the enemy's port flank. Denisov had one hundred seventy ships, and Villieneuve less than sixty. He felt his nerves tingling, wondering if the Highborn were being too reckless.

That concern escalated as the display showed a large part of the opposing fleet, over sixty hulls, moving to intercept the advancing Highborn. No doubt Denisov was snapping out orders to his scanner crews, preparing to launch more probes, wondering in near panic what he was facing. But he hadn't backed down, and he was making use of his numbers with great tactical skill. Villieneuve felt his own fear rising, and some of the confidence he'd recovered when his new allies had arrived dissipated.

Then the Highborn ships opened fire.

Their guns came to life far outside firing range. At least what had been firing range, in the Union Civil War, and in every conflict Villieneuve had ever seen.

The weapons were different, still energy and light based, at least he assumed they were, but clearly not lasers, nor particle accelerators like the Confed primaries. They were electric blue, speckled strangely with moving bits of blackness, seeming almost like a glimpse into some dark and deadly abyss. And when they struck their targets, they inflicted fearsome damage.

Villieneuve watched as a destroyer took a direct hit...and vanished almost instantly. A pair of enemy beams struck a heavy cruiser, and seconds later, the vessel lay there, a dead and ruined hulk.

A flood of emotions took him, awe at the power of the Highborn weapons...and fear as well. He wanted their help, he needed it, but he felt as though he was playing with

something volatile and dangerous. It didn't take his level of
advanced paranoia to imagine such fearsome power turned
on his own forces. He told himself the Highborn needed
him, that he was a blade they could shove into the
Confederation's back…and that was true. But he knew he
had to do whatever it took to make sure the Highborn still
needed the alliance.

At least until he found a way to steal their
technology…and put the Union on a true course to
dominating the Rim.

"First Citizen…the rebel fleet appears to be
repositioning." A pause. "No, they're retreating!" The
surprise in the officer's voice confirmed the caution his
spacers had carried into the fight. They had expected to
lose, and no doubt many had planned to surrender when
things appeared hopeless.

That won't happen now…

"All ships forward, 105 on the reactors…we need to get
into range before Denisov can escape." Villieneuve felt a
new kind of panic, a fear that his enemies were so stunned
by the Highborn ships and their weapons, they were
breaking off and running before they could be fully engaged.
Villieneuve was stunned by the power of his new allies—he
was still watching as the sixteen vessels tore into the flank of
the rebels, gunning down ships even as they tried to flee.
But he was loathe to allow his enemies to escape with their
fleet anything like intact. He had regained the advantage, he
was sure of that now that he'd seen the Highborn in action,
but time was a slippery tactical element. Denisov would call
out for help from his Confederation friends, for one thing.

It was unlikely the Confeds could spare enough strength
to make a difference, but he didn't want them to have any
warning of what was coming either. His deal with the
Highborn called for the Union to attack the Confederation
as soon as Villieneuve was securely back in power, and he
intended to live up to that promise to the letter. The

Confederation border had been stripped of its defenses, save for a few fortified stations. It was open, like a bare breast inviting the knife to strike.

"The rebel forces are definitely decelerating, attempting to withdraw. The Highborn ships are following, maintaining their range and continuing to fire."

Villieneuve looked straight at the display, feeling his hands clench tightly. His ships were moving forward with all the thrust they could manage, and the rebels had to offset their inbound velocity before they could begin to move away. Still, it was a close call on whether his people would get into firing range.

He figured maybe two chances in three his ships would get some shots in, perhaps a bit better than that after the Highborn upgrades to their weapon systems. Even if they didn't, it was becoming clear Denisov's fleet was going to suffer severe losses from the attack of the Highborn alone.

Denisov's quick thinking and decision making was going to save at least part of his fleet. That was a disappointment. The war wouldn't end then and there.

But the battle would put Villieneuve's forces on the road to victory. He would follow Denisov, haunt his every move, chase his fleeing ships all the way back to Montmirail.

And then they would fight the final battle...and Gaston Villieneuve would pay many debts that day.

Chapter Twelve

Highborn Flagship S'Argevon
Imperial System GH9-4307, Planet A1112 (Calpharon)
Year of the Firstborn 389 (327 AC)

"The Hegemony and the Rim dwellers have shown considerable initiative, and we should not disregard their capabilities. They are, of course, no match for us, and indeed, their likely tendency to create false equivalencies between our order and theirs may well facilitate the fastest and least costly path to our final victory. It is far easier for us, as the superior intellects, to model and predict their plans and reactions, than it is for them to discern our own. It is on this basis that I have developed our operational plan, and I do not believe the factual data have changed sufficiently to suggest any changes are now in order. We can predict with considerable expectation of accuracy, the actions of the humans...but not the precise timing. There are simply too many variables to develop more than a range for their expected response, which I submit extends from imminently, to perhaps six to eight of their months from now."

Stockton sat along the wall, next to the other high-ranking Thralls. He seethed with burning hatred, but only in that small part of his mind still left to him. As far as he could see, the rest listened intently, sitting upright and showing the Highborn seated at the table all the respect due to superiors. To gods.

He wondered if he was the only one with disguised fury, if those raised on Highborn controlled worlds were adapted to being controlled.

To being slaves.

The whole thing sickened him, or at least it would have if he'd been able control his stomach enough. It was disturbing enough to see his fellow humans behave in such a manner—and as much as he resented and detested them, the Thralls were human beings, just like him—but to see, to *feel*, himself taking part in the whole hideous affair, was more than he could endure.

He wasn't being fair to the other Thralls, he knew that. They wore the Collar, just like he did, and he heard and saw how they behaved…but not if there was some spark of who they truly were, or who they had been, somewhere deep, trapped even as he was, watching helplessly.

"Your analysis is flawless, Tesserax, save for one factor that bears closer examination. Reports from the capital suggest the situation on the primary front has experienced some degree of decay. Your success in building the Colony, in turning the effort to bring the humans to heel, into a self-supporting enterprise has been of great assistance in that regard. Nevertheless, there is some urgency to completing the integration of the humans, and the rest of their industry, into the fold…just in case the news from the primary front continues to worsen."

"Your words are wise ones, Phazarax, and I would consider them sufficient alone to alter our strategy…if our estimates of the time required to provoke enemy action were longer. If the humans do as we expect—and I assign to that projection a probability of greater than ninety percent—their action, and our response to it, will greatly reduce the total time required to fully absorb the entire Rim.

Indeed, if the humans respond with a force at the higher end of the range of probabilities, we may indeed have a chance to end the conflict in one climactic battle. If I am wrong, we can proceed with our offensive at any time, but let us remember that such a course will likely be costly and time-consuming, and the enemy will have repeated options to withdraw, to offer multiple layers of defense. Even with our superiority in technology and intellect, such an operation could take many years. If we are able to trap the humans in the space we occupy, and destroy the bulk of their forces in one swift stroke, there is a strong likelihood we will break their will...and bring them into the fold without further bloodshed and loss. In that case, we will not only gain control of the human industry and resources in a short time frame, we will release much of the armament we have constructed here for deployment on the primary front."

Stockton listened, both the part of him controlled by the Collar, and the small bit trapped in the depths of his consciousness. He'd heard mention before of the 'primary front' before. At first, he'd assumed the Highborn were planning to strike the Rim along some other, unknown approach, but he'd come to realize his captors were, in fact, fighting someone else. Were there other humans, perhaps survivors from the empire, somewhere coreward, on the other side of Highborn space? Or had the Highborn encountered hostile aliens of some kind?

Or were they battling some self-created nightmare, even as Stockton's old comrades, and the other descendants of the empire, were doing in fighting the Highborn themselves?

"Your words are convincing, Tesserax. I propose we continue with the current plan for three more months, a quarter of an imperial year...and if the humans have not responded as we have predicted, or at least shown signs such a course is imminent, we reconvene on the issue, not necessarily to change our strategy, but at least to reevaluate it based on current data."

Tesserax nodded solemnly. "Agreed, Phazarax. My model suggests an eighty-one percent probability the humans will respond as projected within the specified time period. Are we of one mind?"

The other Highborn at the table voiced their agreement. The decision was unanimous.

"Very well, with that decided, perhaps you can update us, Phazarax, on your progress as head of the church in the Colony. Specifically, what can we expect in terms of Collar implementation and increased production levels in the three months ahead, while we wait for the humans to fall into our trap?"

Phazarax turned and looked down the table at his colleagues. "I have much to report, Commander Tesserax, and all of it quite positive. The vast genetic databases of the Hegemony, and the societal dedication ingrained in its citizens to accepting their place and obeying those placed above them, have been considerable aids to our efforts. We have been able to locate the superior genetic specimens and focus on encollaring them first. Those brought under our control, especially those the humans called 'Masters,' have proven quite useful in helping to control the rest of the populations. The lower order humans of the Hegemony appear to be highly disposed to obeying the Masters, regardless of the circumstances. The use of encollared Masters to directly supervise the as yet uncollared segments of the working classes has allowed us to exceed production targets, while reducing the number of terminations required by over seventy percent."

"That is good news indeed, Phazarax. The humans do breed quickly, and they will do so at an even greater rate when we enlighten them further with regard to their purpose and their obligations to us. Nevertheless, in consideration of events on the primary front, preserving current population levels, where possible, seems a wise strategy."

"I concur. I have endeavored to keep executions to a minimum, and in total, fewer than two billion have been liquidated on occupied worlds. That is well below pre-invasion estimates."

"That is very low indeed, and we have seen little disruption or civil disturbance despite your…light touch."

Phazarax nodded, and then he began to share details, production figures, reports on church construction…and one thing that hit Stockton like a hammer.

"…and total Collar implementation rates throughout the tier one occupied portions of the Hegemony exceed twenty percent…"

Twenty percent of Hegemony citizens wore the Collar already? The same device that enslaved him, that forced him to obey…that had turned him into a traitor against his own people? Stockton didn't know exactly how many Hegemony planets the Highborn had occupied, but what he'd just heard suggested that Collars had been implanted in tens of billions of human beings. Stockton had known for a long while the Highborn wanted to subjugate humanity, but he only realized in that instant they wanted to turn all humans, hundreds of billions of sentient beings, into drones, mind-controlled slaves, utterly devoid of free will, following the commands of their gods for all eternity, unaware even of the living nightmare they endured.

Save only for a trapped spark of themselves, a miserable and helpless remnant imprisoned for all time.

* * *

"You will have your wings ready at all times, Thrall-Commander." Tesserax looked down at Stockton. He towered over the human under any circumstances, but with the Thrall on his knees, the height difference was enormous.

"You have done well, Thrall-Commander, very well, and you will be rewarded. You will rise high in the ranks of Thralls, and you will be a hero to the masses of humans who serve us. You may even find yourself holding a place in the Church. But first, there is more to do. It is likely your former comrades will push forward shortly. They have been given the opportunity to make a grave mistake, and ample encouragement to entice them in that direction. I assign roughly an eighty percent probably that they will cross the border and engage us. We cannot be sure if this will be a full-scale assault, or simply a large reconnaissance, but in either event, we will lure whatever force advances on us deeper into our trap, and we will destroy it utterly. And you shall have your place with our forces, at the head of your vast wings."

"Yes, Highborn. I shall do all possible to serve." *No, please...no...*

"Excellent, Thrall-Commander. The sooner we are able to end this pointless resistance, the more lives we can save among your former people. Then, all humanity will be united, and they shall prosper...and serve."

"Losses are of no account, Highborn. Only victory matters. Only service to the Highborn." There was a robotic tinge to Stockton's tone. He could hear it—or, more accurately, sense it, somehow—but he couldn't change what he was saying, nor even stop the words from forcing their way out.

"Nevertheless, I would see the conflict concluded with less bloodshed if possible. Your former comrades are misguided, but they can be saved from their foolishness. When they are subdued, they will learn to occupy their rightful place in the order of things."

"Yes, Highborn."

"You may rise, Thrall-Commander. I wish to discuss tactics with you, and address some concerns. Specifically, the size of the force you will command in the coming battle.

It is larger, I believe, and by a considerable margin, than any you have led before. You command more force than any Thrall has ever led. I had some reservations about entrusting so many fighters to your command, but I can hardly place any of the Highborn into one of the vulnerable small craft…and even if I could, I don't believe superior intelligence would adequately replace your considerable experience in this branch of operations. I have pondered this for some time, and you have proven the value of experience with your training efforts. It is rare that one of the Highborn offers such effusive praise to a mere human, but you have earned these accolades. And you will soon have the chance to earn more."

Stockton felt repulsed at Tesserax's words, and even more so at the thought he was supposed to feel grateful. He was even more repelled that part of him *did* feel that way. He struggled yet again to regain control of his body, to lunge forward, to attack the monster standing in front of him. But to no avail.

Worst of all was the satisfaction he felt, the pride at the Highborn's words. The part of Stockton under the Collar's control was reacting to the praise…and enjoying it.

He felt as though he would retch, but even that outlet was denied to him. All he could do was struggle pointlessly to find some way, *any* way, to kill himself to end his misery. His slavery.

And to prevent the catastrophe that was coming for his comrades and friends, the disaster he knew he would help invoke.

But there was no way. He was helpless, trapped and condemned only to watch, as he fought against everything he believed in, everything he cared about.

Chapter Thirteen

CFS Dauntless
Beta Telvara System
Year 327 AC (After the Cataclysm)

"I don't know any other way to say this, so here it is. I know you're the most capable person for this job, and I know how difficult it will be…and dangerous. But you are right…there is no choice. Our survival may very well depend on your mission and your skills. Just promise me one thing…please be careful. Come back to me. I can't lose you." Tyler Barron had fought the bloodiest battles in Confederation history, been wounded, saw friends and comrades die, but nothing had been as difficult as letting Andi go, wishing her luck as she prepared to board *Pegasus* and head straight into space controlled by the deadliest enemy Barron had ever fought. It was killing him inside, and the only thing that allowed him to hold it all together was the idea that he couldn't contribute to the doubts and guilt Andi no doubt already felt at leaving. She was doing what she was because she believed it was the best way to protect Cassie, and everyone else as well, but he knew from his own experiences that wouldn't be enough to keep the self-recriminations at bay. She would second guess herself, wonder if she'd been too cautious, if she should have set out sooner. He'd been there many times, and he would spare her those feelings to the extent it was possible. It took all his discipline to keep himself from trying to hold her back, and the last thing he was going to do was cloud her thoughts further, and in so doing, increase the already great danger that lay ahead for her.

"There is no other way, Tyler my love, and so I will say the same to you. You've fought battles before, more than most could easily recall, but I have a bad feeling about this war…and I know you're going into Occupied Space, at least in part, to open the way for *Pegasus* to slip through. I can't argue against that while still making the case for the importance of my own mission. But be careful…please. Be ready to pull back if the enemy is too strong. There will always be another day, a chance to hold the line at Striker, or somewhere else…unless you let it end here." She paused, and he could sense the slightest bit of moisture in her eyes. "I can't lose you, either. I came from nothing, and now I have you and Cassie. That's why I will make it back here, whatever it takes. And if I get back and you're…not here…I'm going to…"

Barron nodded, and then he looked at her, struggling to hold her gaze. He fought like mad against the thoughts pouring into his head that it might be the last time, that it would be…but they forced their way in anyway. He leaned forward and took her into his arms.

"I will be back, Tyler…and I will bring the secret of how the empire defeated the Highborn. You just make sure you and this fleet are waiting for me when I do."

"I will." Barron didn't like lying to her, or even misleading her, but he, too, had a bad feeling about what lay ahead for the fleet. He knew why he was moving his forces forward, and Andi's mission was only one of the reasons. He still had no answers for the list of problems that accrued to hanging back at Striker waiting for the enemy to come, which was still his choice in a purely tactical sense. Near the top of that list stood a communique he had received form Holsten just before the fleet departed. It had been the first message sent on the new comm line extending back to the Confederation. The chain of transit point relay stations reduced communication time from Megara to Striker from two months to less than ten days.

And the inaugural message had been a warning from Holsten about Senate rumblings and unrest in the Iron Belt.

Barron held Andi for a few seconds longer, and he could feel that she was gripping him just as tightly. But he knew he had to let her go. The fleet was moving forward, and the conditions in the system were ideal for *Pegasus* to slip away. The star was active, and magnetic pulses and the locations of dust clouds and sub-planetary detritus would offer some cover, as *Pegasus* slipped out through the system's third point, one leading through more Occupied Space, but also toward the periphery of what had been the Hegemony's coreward edge.

"You have to go now." The words scourged Barron's throat as he spoke them, but he couldn't let his selfish desire to keep Andi there longer jeopardize her safety or her mission.

She took a half step back, and then she leaned in and kissed him. "Remember, I'll be back…so make sure you're here, too." She looked at him for a few seconds, running her hand lightly over his cheek. Then she turned, and an instant later she was gone.

Barron stood where he was, transfixed, fighting to organize—and fend off—a torrent of conflicting feelings. He didn't move for a long while, not until an officer stepped into the room and gave him the report he'd known was coming, but for which he was surprisingly unprepared.

Pegasus had launched. Andi was gone.

* * *

"He'll be alright, Andi…just like we will be." Vig Merrick sat a meter and a half from Andi, in his usual place on *Pegasus*'s tiny bridge. Her first officer, and one of her closest friends, a younger brother to her in every way that mattered, was trying to cheer her up. But she knew he was full of shit. Vig Merrick was no dewy-eyed optimist, and he knew just how deadly dangerous a mission they were on. He was just as aware of the hazards the fleet faced, and the danger that followed Tyler Barron and his spacers. The move into the Beta Telvara system had driven away a small Highborn force, and the forces of the Pact had retaken a single system without a shot being fired, but that was hardly a decisive victory in the war. Of course, the real achievement in Beta Telvara had been getting *Pegasus* launched, and through the point into the adjacent Rho Lexicor system, apparently undetected.

The fleet faced worse ahead, with the same near certainty that she and her people did. But time and distance were doing their job on her. The sadness was still there, and the fear, but Andi Lafarge was once again the stone cold Badlands prospector, armor in place. She opened the gates in her mind, allowed the rage at the enemy, the fury she felt at being forced from her family, to fuel her, to power her as she went forth.

As she set out to find a way to repel the Highborn.

Or to destroy them.

"I'm okay, Vig. You know me. You've seen me in action before."

"I have, Andi…but never when you had so much to lose."

She looked at Vig, and for an instant her shield of pure rage failed her, and she was vulnerable. "I never had so much to protect either, Vig…to save."

Merrick nodded. "That's true." He sighed softly. "We've

been in some tight spots before, but this is the toughest mission we've ever undertaken. I remember when the Badlands seemed like the edge of the universe. But the Hegemony is beyond the Badlands, and we're going to the other side of the Hegemony. Are you sure about that data? I see how you came to the conclusions you did, but there are some assumptions in there…and we still don't know exactly where we're going, just a series of clues we hope will make sense when we get close."

"I won't lie to you, Vig…" Though she almost *had* blurted out what he wanted to hear instead of the truth. "…there is guesswork in all of this…a lot more than I admitted to Tyler." She was silent for a moment. "But there's no choice. The fleet isn't going to win this war, Vig. The enemy is too advanced. They're too powerful." She took another breath. "They're more intelligent than us, too. We're so repulsed at the whole idea, at them seeing themselves as gods, we don't want to accept reality. They're better versions of humanity, stronger, smarter, perhaps even immortal."

"You're the last person I'd expect to admit that, Andi."

"What…you mean to tell the truth? They *are* better than we are. They were created by people to be the future, and they represent the pinnacle of imperial technology. That doesn't mean I think they're preferable, or more moral…and it damned sure doesn't mean I'm ever going to surrender, to bow down to the bastards. But it's damned foolish to ignore the obvious because the truth is uncomfortable. We're fighting an enemy that has every advantage…and the only one we have is knowledge that they were once beaten. I don't care if we have to fly into the heart of a sun, we're going to find out how that happened…because if we don't, if we go back empty-handed, we're just going to watch everyone we care about die."

Vig didn't respond. He just nodded silently, and then he

turned back to his workstation.

Andi knew she'd unloaded, that she'd dumped all her dark thoughts and realizations on him. She'd always believed in knowing the truth, however blunt. However dark and ominous. But she'd found that most people preferred lies, fantasies, delusions…even when they were facing deadly danger.

Andi Lafarge knew she was leading her people into the gravest hazard, but she also knew Tyler, his officers, the entire fleet, and then the Confederation, would fall to the enemy if she didn't find a way to defeat them. There was no place for self-delusion in that reality, no time for allowing herself to believe what she wanted to believe.

She was heading out on what would be the most important mission of her life. And she could not fail.

No matter what it took, what sacrifice it demanded of her.

* * *

"Extended line, now!" Reg Griffin tightened her grip on her fighter's controls, even as she gave the command for her wings to spread out, to wrap around the flanks of the enemy formation. There were two hundred Highborn fighters moving toward her force, and watching them approach she confirmed her worst concerns, both about the technology of the enemy fighters, and the training of their pilots. She still couldn't explain that last part, but it didn't matter anymore. All that mattered was learning how to defeat the enemy.

She had an answer in this fight, one she doubted she would enjoy when it came to a final, decisive fight. She had five hundred ships to the enemy's two hundred, and hers were piloted by long-service veterans with dogfighting experience, backed up by the picked best of the new trainees. Confidence bolstered her against fear, and she relished the respite it offered, even as she knew the advantage was temporary, that the enemy in the war overall could field *at least* as large a force as she could.

She listened as the acknowledgements came in, each of her five wing commanders sounding off in perfect order. Seconds later, she could see the ships on her scanner beginning to move, as half the fighters added lateral velocity to their forward vectors. She'd watched some of the video from the battles at the outposts...seen how the enemy forces had outflanked and destroyed the fighters sent against them. The images from Outpost Seven stuck most vividly in her mind. Susan Contrall had been a friend of hers, an old friend.

A friend who had died in one of the first encounters with the enemy fighter formations.

Griffin had been training the squadrons for half a year since then, driving them mercilessly, berating her pilots brutally for every error they made, every lapse in judgment. She'd yielded some of the love they had given her in the months after she'd leapt into the breach Stockton's death had left, and that hurt her, cut deeply. There were nicknames now, insulting ones—and a few even she had to admit were funny—whispered in the dark corners of pilots' country on dozens of battleships. That was one of leadership's burdens, she had told herself, and after a while, she'd learned to ignore it all.

Nothing was more important than getting her people through the great ordeal that lay before them. If the survivors cursed her until the day they died, she would accept that price if those deaths came when they were old and in their beds.

As long as there *were* survivors.

Her eyes moved rapidly, back and forth, checking the enemy movements, and those of her own forces. She had the edge, and she was almost sure her people could prevail, that they could win the fleet's first engagement with the enemy fighters. That seemed strange, unexpected. The enemy had at least ten thousand of the small craft, and enough launch platforms to carry them all at once.

Why would they leave a force like this here, too large for a scouting effort…and too small to face a major incursion.

She looked again, checking the status of her formation. Her two wings had stretched out to each flank, and her force now had twice the length of the Highborn line. The enemy fighters were almost within missile range. She thought for a moment, questioned whether she should authorize all her squadrons to launch. Ship to ship missiles were still in very short supply, and she had no idea how deep the enemy's stores were. She considered for an instant trying to hold some portion back, but then she saw the enemy line open up, two hundred fighters launching almost as one.

"All squadrons…prepare to launch missiles. Pick your targets…and I want those locks doublechecked." The decision had been sudden. Logistics *would* be a massive problem, especially if her people were forced to fight larger battles. But this was the first time her main forces were meeting Highborn squadrons, save only for the disasters at the outposts. They *needed* to win, and win decisively. She had to stop the fear that was eroding morale, sapping the will and the strength of her pilots, most of whom were still far more comfortable engaging in bombing runs than dogfights.

She reached out and flipped a series of switches, arming her two missiles. She tapped at her controls, selecting targets…and establishing fire locks. She glanced at the status screen. All her squadrons reported ready.

She took a deep breath, holding it for a few seconds. She'd fought at Calpharon, and the pilots who'd died at the outposts were hers no less than those in formation all around her. But she knew, in every way that mattered for the future of the Rim, for the very survival of the

Confederation and all its people...the real fight was about to begin. It would start with her next command.

"All ships...launch!"

Chapter Fourteen

225,000,000 Kilometers from CFS Dauntless
Omicron Alvera System
Year 327 AC (After the Cataclysm)

Reg's left hand clasped into a defiant fist. One of her missiles had scored a hit, and she'd watched a Highborn fighter blink out of existence. Her right hand tightened as well, though it was still griping her ship's controls, jerking back and forth in a wild series of evasive maneuvers. The enemy had launched missiles as well, and half of them were still out there, coming on strong. She'd lost a dozen ships so far to the barrage, and even as she watched, another three blinked off the display in rapid succession. But her people had inflicted vastly greater harm on the enemy. Forty-eight of the Highborn fighters, almost a quarter of the total, were gone entirely, or floating dead in space. And almost four hundred of her wings' thousand missiles were still inbound, bearing down on the enemy formation like death's scythe.

She had endured a seemingly endless barrage of grim news for the past six months, and she'd succumbed to the fear growing all around about the enemy fighters, their skills...and their vast numbers. Her people had just engaged, and they'd had by far the better of the engagement, at least so far, but she knew she'd caught a small force. Her wings had two and a half times the numbers of their enemies. She told herself that, cautioned against arrogance, against unfounded optimism. But she was a fighter pilot at her core, and the sight of a shattered enemy formation lit a fire inside her.

"Full thrust forward. They didn't leave any survivors at the outposts, and by God, we're going to repay them for that!" The words just spit forth, almost unbidden. She tensed for a moment, wondered if she had gone too far, exceeded her authority. Confederation forces didn't go out seeking to annihilate defeated forces, certainly not ones that tried to surrender.

At least not officially. War often bred brutality, even among those who decried it. If the enemy yielded, if they gave up...could she really order her people to gun them down?

Could she stop them?

Would she even try?

She wondered if Highborn forces even surrendered. They seemed the sort to fight to the death, especially since there were none of the actual Highborn themselves in those fighters, only enslaved humans, serving those they worshipped as gods. The whole idea repelled her, and it only drove her fury. Somewhere, deep inside, she pitied the humans so enslaved. But in the forefront of her thoughts, in the parts of her brain driving her forth, she only hated and despised them.

And she wanted them dead. All of them.

What kind of human being would serve those monsters...

Her jaw was clenched, her teeth grinding against each other in her mouth. The one-sided fight continued, and thirty more enemy fighters were destroyed as the rest of her missile barrage went in. The loss ratios were outstanding, and they would look great in the after action conference. But she still had no idea what would happen when she met the enemy on even terms. So far there had only been the attack on the outposts, where Highborn surprise attacks had given them the overwhelming advantage, and the current fight, where her people had the superior numbers.

That was going to be a very relevant concern if the Pact invasion continued. She knew the enemy's numbers, that they had more fighters overall than she did...at least since they had no need to hold some back for use as bombers. She tried not to let one victory, not yet even fully won, affect her cold judgment of what her people faced. But there had been so much fear, such a grim perspective, she was starved for anything she could interpret as a good sign.

And cutting down Highborn fighters—ones she wanted to believe had been in the attacks on the outposts—fit that bill. Her missiles had done their job, and now it was time to finish it before the enemy could turn about and make a run for it.

"All squadrons, charge your lasers and increase thrust to full. It's time to get in there and finish this."

* * *

"Admiral Griffin reports the enemy force has been virtually wiped out. Her people are hunting down the last survivors now."

Carlisle's words had a hard edge to them, and Barron realized his aide was excited that Reg Griffin's squadrons had not just defeated the enemy, but utterly destroyed them. Barron was pleased as well, but also a little concerned, not just because of the viciousness he heard in Carlisle's report, but also because he felt the same way. He wasn't sure if it was the arrogance of the Highborn, or the fact that he felt he had more to lose—or that Andi was out there, risking her life again—but there was a fiery rage inside him, one that challenged his ability to approach the war with cold analysis and deliberative tactics. Perhaps he'd just seen too much war, but he could feel himself succumbing to raw hatred. He could allow that, perhaps, when it came to the Highborn themselves, but he was beginning to come to the uncomfortable realization that most of those his people were killing were human beings just like themselves, men and women brainwashed by the Highborn, even enslaved with the mysterious device they called the 'Collar.'

He told himself rage and lust for vengeance would color his tactics, deprive him of much of his skill. But then he disregarded that internal warning. Logic didn't matter. Andi's departure, the scattered dust clouds where the outposts had been, the thousands dead at Calpharon...they made rationality irrelevant. Barron hated this enemy as he had no other.

"Very well, Commander. The fleet will remain at full alert." Barron still felt strange when Atara wasn't sitting at the fleet tactical station. He'd almost left her back at Striker, but in the end, he hadn't been able to do it. He was still worried about her, concerned she wasn't yet the officer she had been before she'd been wounded so horrifically. There was something else, though, something he was loathe to acknowledge. He wondered if he could trust her as he had for so many years. He didn't doubt her loyalty, not for an instant...but he wondered if she was still capable of being the granite pillar he'd relied on for so long. She was one of the toughest people he'd ever met, and he'd come to see her as invincible, relentless in every way.

But everyone had their breaking point.

Barron wondered what was happening across the system. He'd sent an advance guard forward, half a dozen battleships with escorts...and Reg Griffin to directly command the fighter wings. The scanners had detected a moderate-sized enemy force waiting there, mostly the new carriers. He'd wanted to hit them with enough force to assure victory, without pushing the bulk of the fleet too deep into the system, at least until he was sure there were no other Highborn forces hidden and waiting to ambush him.

It was caution that made sense, but it also left him almost five light hours from the forward strike force...and he realized everything he was seeing had already happened hours before.

He considered giving the fleet the order to advance, but he hesitated. He was still waiting for many of the probes to report their findings, as well as a much more comprehensive update from the advance force. Coldly put, he'd sent those ships, and Reg Griffin along with them, to flush out any traps. He didn't like to think of any portion of his fleet as expendable...but in the context of the war as a whole and the force he led, there was no way else to put it.

All except Reg. He had Timmons and Federov back with the colors, which made Griffin less singularly irreplaceable, but the loss of Stockton had left him fully aware of just how vital his key commanders were. He'd never have let Reg go so far forward...but he hadn't really had a choice. The Highborn fighters were a deadly new threat, and Reg Griffin was in the forefront of fighting them. She needed to see them up close, experience them. He knew if he'd been in her position, he would have insisted on leading the squadrons directly, and he hadn't been able to force himself to deny her that chance. Not when her ability to face the Highborn wings was one of the largest variables in whether the Pact had any chance to prevail.

To survive.

Barron wasn't in direct command of the fleet, of course, at least not officially. In a practical sense, however, the burden had fallen most heavily on him. Vian Tulus would do as he commanded, he was almost sure of that, and Chronos had become somewhat more passive, ready to follow Barron's lead without argument. That had felt strange at first, but Barron had come to realize the Confederation had become something like the lead power in the Pact. The Hegemony had been larger, and more technologically advanced—and the Confederation had originally come to that power's aid—but half of it now lay in enemy hands. The loss of the Hegemonic capital, along with vast numbers of warships and huge swaths of industry, had struck a blow more damaging than just the battle results implied. The assured confidence of the Masters, so long the Hegemony's defining principle, had been eroded by a growing sense of defeatism.

The Confederation, on the other hand, had lost none of its systems. The war hadn't even come close to its borders, at least not yet. The fear of the Highborn had galvanized its entire society, and the Rim's mercantile and industrial marvel had become energized as it had never been before. Ships rolled out of the shipyards, and weapons and ordnance poured forth from the factories in quantities scarcely imaginable.

The great effort had begun to show signs of strain, of course, in both the Senate, and among the sweating, exhausted populations of the industrial worlds. That was one reason Barron had decided to push forward, to test the enemy, see just how powerful they truly were. The Confederation couldn't maintain the pace it had for the past four years, the withering rates of construction and production...but at that moment, it was, in every quantifiable way, the beating heart of the Pact.

"The fleet will hold on station until Admiral Griffin follows up her initial report and deploys her fighters to scouting duty. Send her my congratulations, and instruct her to land and refuel her squadrons, and then to begin a comprehensive survey of the system."

"Yes, Admiral."

"And, Tilson, she is to keep a contingent of her relaunched fighters on station and ready...just in case."

"Yes, Admiral Barron."

She will know that already...and your message will arrive far too late, even if she doesn't...

But it helped Barron to issue the order, to feel as though

he was *doing something*.

Something other than waiting.

*   *   *

"Scouting groups are beginning to report in, Admiral. No sign yet of any further enemy forces in the system."

Reg Griffin sat in her small office, just aside from the cacophony that was *Vanguard*'s alpha fighter bay. The space was a borrowed one, and her permanent office was a larger, but mostly similar, space on *Dauntless*. She commanded the entire fighter corps—and her place was on the flagship. Usually.

She'd had to be with the first force to engage the enemy, however. At least the first since the destruction of the outposts. Because her people needed her there, because *she* needed to be there. For more reasons than she could easily count. She'd been prepared to fight Admiral Barron tooth and nail to get permission, but he'd agreed right away, if not without some hints of hesitation.

She understood Barron's concerns, his clear worry for her, but she also appreciated his confidence in her. She couldn't even imagine the stress crushing down on the Confederation's senior admiral, nor how the loss of Jake Stockton had affected him. He'd shown her nothing but support, but if the legendary Raptor had been lost in the struggle, how could Barron not worry about any officer in his command, and especially one charged to lead the squadrons in Stockton's place.

She was still struggling herself to accept her role as that replacement. The old saying about big shoes to fill didn't even come close. Somewhat to her surprise, Dirk Timmons and Olya Federov had deferred to her in that capacity without any signs of resentment, and she'd found that more than anything had helped build her confidence a bit. But she still felt out of place.

"All scouting teams are to continue on their assigned course, and..." She stopped suddenly. There was something on her scanner. Activity at the transit point.

The transit point coming from deeper in the heart of the Occupied Zone.

"Scanner command...are you picking this up?"

"Yes, Admiral." The same voice as a moment before, but considerably more strained. "No confirmed transits yet."

She stared at her screen for a moment, deep in thought. She hated the idea of terminating her scouting operations, pulling those ships back to the main force...especially if she was watching something like a meteor or comet fragment coming through.

But if there were more enemy forces on the way...

"Issue a recall order to the scouting groups. All squadrons are to return to primary positions." She was going to feel like a fool if nothing but a chunk of rock and ice came rolling through the point, but she wasn't going to get caught flatfooted, not with her small force almost six light hours from the main fleet.

She sat quietly for a few seconds, perhaps half a minute. Then her scanner relieved her of her concern, at least that she would look foolish.

There were Highborn ships coming through. Carriers, one after the other. She hesitated, counting softly under her breath. When she got to ten, she leapt up to her feet.

"Get my fighter ready...I'm launching immediately." He turned and stared at the aide seated about two meters from where she stood. "And confirm all search groups have all received the recall order. We need them back, now. We're not done with the fight here, not yet."

From what she could see still coming through the point, not by a longshot.

Chapter Fifteen

Forward Base Striker
Vasa Denaris System
Year 327 AC (After the Cataclysm)

"*Colossus*, you are cleared to dock at port station Beta-3. Take position two hundred meters from the station, and we'll extend the umbilicals." The voice from Striker flight control was a bit tinny over the bridge speakers. Sonya Eaton made a mental note to mention it to her engineering team. It wasn't mission critical, of course, but it grated on her craving for order.

"Bring us in as directed, Commander." She turned and looked at the display, trying to hide her astonishment at the immensity of the orbital station. Her last recollections of Striker were almost four years old, and they were of a rough cylinder, no more than a hundred meters long…instead of the ten kilometer behemoth floating before her eyes.

"Yes, Commodore Eaton." The officer at the nav station turned and began to execute her command.

Eaton sat in the center of *Colossus*'s gargantuan control center, feeling strangely at ease. She'd commanded the massive vessel for more than four years, but that tenure had been split into a short time during the Battle of Calpharon, and more than three years back in Confederation space

130

under repair. *Colossus* had fought off the entire flank of the Highborn fleet, suffering massive damage in the process. Eaton had been stunned after that epic struggle, as she still was, that the vessel had survived at all. It had taken an almost unimaginable pounding, more punishment than she'd ever seen anything manmade endure. But the skeleton of the imperial behemoth proved to be made of tough stuff, and it had not only brought her back from the battle, along with almost ninety percent of her crew still alive, it had made it back to the Confederations Iron Belt for repairs. That had been a good thing, because she was far from sure that any fleet of tugs could have gotten the hulking ship back in less than half a century.

The losses she'd suffered had been devastating to her, as they always were, but she'd been prepared for a far worse number, and she couldn't help but feel relief at ten percent casualties, and less than five percent killed. But while *Colossus* had survived and saved many of her people, the ship itself had been badly damaged. Much of the fleet had been battered, of course, but the battleships and cruisers had been quickly repaired and returned to service. *Colossus* had languished for more than three years, as attempt after attempt to conduct repairs slowed to a crawl. The ship was too big for any spacedock in the Confederation, and the destroyed imperial systems proved difficult to replace. Restoring *Colossus* to fleet service had been as much an R&D project as a repair operation. It had required the construction of special facilities, and a series of repair operations that had been at least half guesswork.

Sara Eaton had been there the entire time, nursing her ship through, pressuring the work crews…and in one case, sending her Marines to 'encourage' one particularly troublesome Iron Belt magnate to throw his full support behind the effort. The stunned expression on his face when the Marines had dragged him into her office had been one of the highlights of her life, and she would never forget it.

Eaton had lost too many friends and comrades, not to mention her only sister, in battle to manage much tolerance for corrupt and conniving shipyard owners.

Eaton had worried she would miss the renewal of hostilities, and while she'd been terribly shaken by the brutality of the fighting at Calpharon, that only made it more essential to her that she be at the front when the fleet faced what had been perceived as an inevitable invasion. Only the expected attack hadn't come. Even as the months passed in various shipyards, the news from the front had remained quiet. There should have been relief in that but, somehow, it only increased Eaton's tension. She didn't know why the enemy had taken so long, but she was sure it wasn't good, and she'd pushed ever harder to complete the work and get her ship back to the fleet. She'd been halfway to the new Striker base, when she got the word along the com chain.

Admiral Barron had led most of the fleet forward. The Pact wasn't waiting for the enemy to attack anymore…they were taking the initiative. And she was just a few weeks too late to join the advance.

Her first response had been disbelief. It made no tactical sense to her, none at all, and she couldn't believe Barron had issued those orders. The entire purpose of Striker, the reason for building such a monstrous fortress had been to back up the fleet, supplement its combat power when the next great battle came about. But then she'd put herself in the admiral's place, imagined the troubles she'd had just getting *Colossus* repaired…and then increased them a hundredfold. Barron had to deal with the Senate, and the entrenched bureaucracy throughout the Confederation, not to mention the Iron Belt industrial barons and a hundred other obstacles, and all that in addition to managing a bunch of allies, the other members of the Pact. The Hegemony leadership *had* to be anxious to liberate their occupied worlds. Eaton remembered well enough from years before, sitting two jumps from Megara, bristling for the chance to return and liberate the capital. The Hegemony Masters and Kriegeri were likely no different.

And the Palatians were always spoiling for a fight.

Eaton looked at the main display, and she couldn't help but feel surprise at what she saw. Or, more accurately, what she didn't see. The Pact's Grand Fleet, as it had come to be called, was over two thousand ships strong, by far the vastest force ever assembled on the Rim, or in the Hegemony...at least since imperial times. Four years of construction, of massing every available vessel, of repairing every ship that had survived Calpharon, had produced a force far stronger than the one defeated at the Hegemony capital. Eaton shared the caution, and even outright pessimism, of her comrades—she'd seen the Highborn fleet in action, after all—but the thought of such a massive force, formed up and ready to fight around the immense base built to serve as Pact headquarters had cultivated some level of hope.

Now, she looked out and saw fewer than three hundred vessels, a skeleton force by comparison. That hadn't been a surprise, of course—she'd received word of Barron's decision en route—and yet it still felt like one. Clint Winters was in command, of the rump fleet, and of Striker. She'd been advised of that as well, and she'd wondered just what kind of a knockdown drag out fight between the Confederation's top two admirals it had taken to get the Sledgehammer to stay behind when more than eighty percent of the fleet set out.

Now Colossus is here, too. That's more power around Striker...but Admiral Barron is out there, and he will need this ship...

Her ship increased the combat power of Winters's forces, of course, by a considerable margin. But she wasn't sure that mattered. If the enemy attacked Striker that would mean they'd already defeated Admiral Barron and the main fleet. And if that happened, the war was as good as over.

She flipped her own comm controls, activating the priority line. "Striker Base, Commodore Eaton here, commanding *Colossus*. Please advise Admiral Winters we have arrived."

"Admiral Winters knows, Sonya…"

Eaton recognized the voice immediately, and she decided she was utterly unsurprised that Winters had been in the control center awaiting her communique.

"It might take a while to get *Colossus* settled in and the umbilicals in place. Not even Striker has a dock big enough for that monster. Why don't you shuttle over in the meanwhile, and I'll bring you up to speed."

"Yes, Admiral. On my way." She cut the comm, an action that perhaps exhibited less than the requisite pomp and procedure for communications with the navy's second in command, but Eaton knew Winters had even less use for such nonsense than she did. Of course, no one hated that sort of thing more than Tyler Barron. The fleet had become somewhat less officious in recent years, and it certainly hadn't done anything to reduce combat effectiveness.

She leapt up from her seat, turning toward the nav station. "Proceed with the docking instructions, Commander. And advise gamma bay I'll need my shuttle ready as soon as possible."

"Yes, Commodore."

She nodded, and then she turned and walked across the cavernous room, and disappeared into one of the lift cars. After four years of endless repairs and titanic struggles with bureaucracy, she was back.

And she was damned sure ready for a rematch with the Highborn. She just had to convince Winters to let her move forward to catch up with Barron's forces.

* * *

"Number One, no one here doubts your intellect, nor your leadership abilities, but there are those suited to command in a crisis, and those who are not."

Akella stared across the table at Number Two. She'd once considered Thantor somewhat of a friend, and she'd mated with him as well, following the imperative their lofty genetic rankings demanded, but she had no doubt at all anymore that Thantor was her rival.

No, he is my enemy…

Akella used such labels cautiously. That was partly her own temperate nature, and partly her realization of just what an enemy was, a visualization made stark by the immense losses from the fighting at Calpharon. Thantor wanted her Seat, she was certain of that, and since her genetic rating was higher, the only way he could get it was to drive her to resign, or to have her expelled from the Council in disgrace. It had taken her a long time to realize just what drove Thantor, and she'd struggled with understanding it, mostly because she herself had no interest in political power. Her fondest wish was to be left alone, to retire to her study and her laboratory, and conduct research for the rest of her life. She served on the Council because it was her duty, and she took that obligation seriously. But she sometimes felt she was at a disadvantage in a contest against someone whose motivations she couldn't quite comprehend.

Now that the Hegemony was fighting for its life, she was prepared to put old rivalries aside, to join with her colleagues and do whatever was necessary to win the war. But it was becoming starkly clear that Thantor was not of that mind. He was scared, certainly, badly shaken by the loss of Calpharon and so much of Hegemony space. But he'd barely relented in his political offensive, and he ceaselessly blamed Akella for the recent reverses.

"Number Two, you have made your position clear. Equally clear is the fact that you lack sufficient support on this Council to upend our leadership structure for your own political gain. I ask you now, as the head of this body, the leader of the Hegemony, and one who shares a son with you...set aside your ambitions while we struggle to save our society, and indeed, perhaps all humanity." She'd hesitated to accuse him outright of conspiring to take her place, but then it all came out. She wasn't sure if it was strategy, or simply fatigue, but she just didn't care anymore. She wasn't a diplomat by nature any more than a politician, and it wasn't like the Council, the twelve loftiest genetic specimens in the Hegemony, didn't know exactly what had been going on.

Or how close she had come to defeat. She had four loyal votes, and Thantor did as well. The others had varied in their support, but it required a two-thirds majority to expel her, and that meant her rival needed all four of the centrists. He'd come close before the Highborn attacked Calpharon, but as so often happened, crisis and danger rallied the Council around the established power...and Thantor had temporarily ceased his efforts.

But not for long.

"Number One, I object to your characterizations, which are both farcical and baseless. You cannot..."

"Enough!" Akella slammed her hand down on the table as she shouted, surprising no one so much as herself. She wasn't the sort to lose her temper, but she was brittle, tense...and scared for Chronos and the fleet. The need to hide some of that, at least with respect to Chronos, only added to her tension. She could express her concern for the Hegemony's armed forces, of course, and for its top military officer as a colleague. But she couldn't admit to the true nature of her relationship with Chronos. Hegemony custom, and for Masters, law, forbade formalized and ongoing relationships. Sex was condoned for casual recreation, and for breeding with appropriate genetic partners. No one would question her decision to mate with Chronos, but the fact that the two were still deeply—and monogamously—

involved more than five years later was a grave violation of Hegemonic rules and morals. Especially since Akella had failed to produce any further children in that period. She hadn't dared have a second child with Chronos, though she had wished to. And she'd refused to even consider another pairing.

If Thantor found evidence of her relationship, it might very well be what he needed to finally destroy her. In many ways, she would view removal from the Council a blessing, but not when her people were fighting for their lives. Thantor was a megalomaniacal monster, and not someone who could lead the Hegemony through its current nightmare. If he bested her, attained the top position, the Hegemony was doomed. She was sure of that...and she couldn't allow it to happen, whatever it took.

How long would it be before Tyler Barron told Thantor just what he could do, in anatomically explicit terms...

And Barron was the more tolerant of the two senior Confed admirals. Thantor would be lucky if Clint Winters didn't just shoot him where he stood.

Akella realized she hadn't followed up after her outburst...and neither had anyone else present spoken. She regrouped her thoughts, and she looked out over the rest of the Council. There was surprise, certainly, but she wasn't sure if her anger had hurt her standing...or actually helped her.

"This is no time for political maneuvering, nor arguments between us. Most of the fleet has departed from here, returned with the other Pact forces to the Occupied Zone. You will all recall that I was against this course of action and argued against it. However, I was also aware of the imperatives behind it...and that a majority of this Council was in favor. So, I say to all of you now, while our forces are engaged in this dangerous operation, until we have some news of what has transpired, let us put disputes and arguments aside. Put your thoughts behind Chronos and his officers, and the thousands of Kriegeri manning the ships of the fleet. There will be time enough later for squabbling and posturing." Her words were hard, and she spoke them with strength and edge. But she managed to push the anger back, to sound in every way like the strong and confident leader…and not the raving lunatic she felt she was becoming.

It was a pleasing fiction, she thought, and she wondered how long she could maintain the masquerade.

She could see by the nods all around the table, and the applause that soon followed, that she had gained the Council's agreement. Only Thantor sat silently, and then, he too put his hands together and offered a short burst of unenthusiastic clapping.

She had maintained control, put aside politics and internal disputes. For a while.

How long that would last, she didn't know. But if things went badly with the fleet, she knew any renewed rancor on the Council just might not matter at all.

Chapter Sixteen

Free Trader Pegasus
Zeta Galvus System
Year 327 AC (After the Cataclysm)

"I can't believe we made it this far with...nothing. No pursuit, no sign at all we've been detected. Not even more than just a couple enemy sightings." Vig sat across from Andi on *Pegasus*'s bridge. The topic wasn't new. Vig had greeted each system they'd entered with something similar, almost as though he was offering some kind of thanks to the spacer's gods so common in legend.

Or trying to convince himself their mission wasn't as crazy as he knew it was.

"The stealth unit does seem to be effective against Highborn scanners...at least when they're not looking for anything." Andi had grave doubts the mysterious imperial device connected to her ship's drive would thwart a concerted Highborn effort to detect *Pegasus*. But the enemy had no reason to expect anything to be there, so with any luck, she and her people would be spared trying to evade intensive search efforts.

Andi was grateful, too, though it was hard to focus on such small successes given the magnitude of her task. She'd argued with Tyler, insisted she had to go, assured him she

could find what she was seeking…and now that she was
deep into the occupied space of the Hegemony, she faced
the stark reality that her data was pretty damned thin. It was
a map, of sorts, a guide to finding what she sought. But
there were plenty of holes in it, and it would take all the
spacer's fortune, and Badland's adventurer gut instinct she
had, to get them there.

"I don't like the sound the thing is making, though. I
think I'm going to have Lex take a look at it." She hadn't
mentioned that before, though it had been bothering her for
days. The stealth unit didn't sound *all* that different than it
normally did, but she could swear there was something
there, a vibration maybe. Something her gut told her wasn't
quite right. She'd considered having Lex Righter check it out
before, but she'd hesitated. She didn't want to make her
crew even edgier and more scared than they already were,
and as brilliant an engineer as Righter was, she knew the
device, half new and half ancient imperial technology would
be half magic to him. He would be feeling his way through,
much as she was doing navigationally. But if she went
wrong, they could always backtrack. If Lex made a mistake
and the unit failed because of it, *Pegasus* was deep in enemy
space and naked to the Highborn's scanners.

"Well, at least we're out of the way here. A few
populated planets in these systems…" Vig's voice lowered,
and a grimness crept into his tone. "…and a few it seems
weren't worth the effort to the Highborn."

Andi looked down at the deck. She knew just what her
friend was talking about. They'd passed three worlds, two in
one system and one in the next. From what she could tell,
they'd never been heavily populated, no more than eighty to
one hundred million each was her best guess. But those
numbers had fallen dramatically…to zero. The Highborn
had bombarded them from space and rendered them utterly
lifeless. A population that size was no doubt a rounding
error to beings who thought themselves gods, but Andi's

mind reeled at the vastness of the carnage and human suffering.

"Yes, with any luck, we won't see too many more enemy ships." That was a hope more than a projection, but there was some basis to it. It was counterintuitive to think of the 'coreward' side of the Hegemony being more sparsely populated than the 'rimward' end...but that was the legacy of the Cataclysm. The area of space *Pegasus* was approaching had been the heart of the old empire, and by all legend and accepted wisdom, it had been virtually obliterated in that polity's final death struggle. Civilization had survived, such as it had, in the Confederation and Hegemony, precisely because those sectors had been backwaters, far less important that the coreward zone...and more easily overlooked by the warring factions.

"You're right, Andi...I think we've come far enough that we won't see any more Highborn ships..." Vig stopped abruptly, even as *Pegasus*'s scanner started beeping.

It was a contact, a ship. Not a large one, but definitely of Highborn manufacture.

And a lesson to Andi in making pronouncements projecting past fortune into the future.

"Cut thrust." She gestured toward Vig's workstation as she snapped out the order. *Pegasus* had slipped past a few Highborn ships without cutting the engines entirely, but that was before the stealth unit started preying on her fears.

"Thrust at zero, Andi. But I don't think that's necessary. Look, they're moving along on their original..." Vig's words ended abruptly once again. The Highborn ship had begun blasting its engines, decelerating.

Andi stared at the screen, her eyes fixed, feeling almost as though they would burn through the display. The enemy ship's action wasn't definitive. There were multiple reasons it might decelerate, or change course. That realization made her feel a bit better. For perhaps ten seconds. Then her warning lights flicked on. Highborn scanning beams were moving across the space around *Pegasus*.

The good news was, the enemy didn't appear to know exactly where they were.

The bad news was stark, though. That ship had clearly picked up *something*, and now they were looking for *Pegasus*.

Andi reached out, flipping a series of switches, recalibrating her ship's passive scanners. With some luck—that word again—she might be able to detect the enemy beams, get a heads up they were discovered before the enemy even knew.

"Shut down the reactor, too, Vig. And tell Lex to stay down there, ready for…whatever we have to do. I'm going to need power immediately if we've got to make a run for it, so he needs to be ready for a crash start just in case."

"Okay, Andi…" Vig sounded a little shaky. The situation justified some fear, certainly, but she knew it was more than just the enemy. The words 'crash start' filled every spacer with a cold chill, and Andi knew very well the dangers of such a maneuver. *Pegasus* was a good ship, its systems top of the line. And Lex was the best engineer in space, this side of Anya Fritz. Andi figured there was no more than a three, maybe four percent chance he would lose it entirely…and turn *Pegasus* into a miniature sun.

Still, that four percent was a cold thing to see staring back from the abyss.

Andi's eyes were fixed, locked on the contact on her display. The enemy had picked up something they considered suspicious, she was sure of that. But now *Pegasus* was playing dead. She'd be hard to spot even if the stealth unit was malfunctioning. Andi knew the generator was still working to an extent, but she no longer doubted her guess that it wasn't operating at full effectiveness.

"Andi…how long can we just sit here and wait?" Vig's words mirrored the thoughts in her head. She was stubborn, in many way made of iron. She could sit and watch the enemy search fruitlessly for *Pegasus* for as long as necessary, if that was the correct course. Weeks, months…longer.

But this time, she didn't have longer. Tyler was heading deeper into the Occupied Zone. If she was going to find some way to help combat the enemy, she had to do it soon.

"I don't know, Vig…I just don't know." It was probably the most useless thing she'd ever said, but it was the plain truth.

She sat and stared, waiting…knowing at some point, if the enemy was still there, she would have to give up and make a run for it.

*   *   *

"Alright, Lex…now!"

Andi sucked in a deep breath, and she held it. The next few seconds would determine if *Pegasus*'s engines roared to life, beginning a mad dash to the transit point…or if her ship and all her people vanished in the fury of unleashed nuclear fusion.

She wouldn't know if that happened, of course. It would be too quick. She wasn't sure if that was strangely reassuring or even more nerve-wracking.

Lex Righter was down in engineering, and there weren't many people out there she trusted more than her longtime engineer to handle such a delicate maneuver. But Righter had been brutally honest with her, and he'd reaffirmed what she already knew. However careful he was, however skilled, there was always an element of chance to such a desperate and dangerous move.

She wondered if engineers could be given a course in mercifully lying to ship captains.

A loud roar shook the ship, and the very structural elements groaned and creaked under the stress. *Pegasus* sounded like she was tearing herself apart, but at least that meant the ship was still there. A few seconds later, a wave of force slammed into Andi's chest, pushing her back into her chair, and forcing that deep breath from her lungs.

Pegasus's engines were blasting at full, and the dampeners weren't even close to catching up. She pushed back against the pressure, trying to reach the controls, to get a status reading. She figured it was a coin toss whether at least one of her people had broken something in the sudden acceleration, but a fractured rib or snapped ulna was a small price to pay to escape destruction…or capture and slavery at the hands of the Highborn.

She managed to lean forward enough to get a good view of the screen. The pressure was subsiding a bit, or at least it felt that way as the dampeners finally activated.

The Highborn ship was maintaining its position…but she realized that was just the delay in its scanner beams reporting *Pegasus*'s energy output, and her motion, and of course, the corresponding delay in her own scanners detected the enemy's response. There was no way that ship was going to miss what she had just done. Not even a fully operation stealth unit could hide that kind of power surge.

Andi had watched and waited, hoping the Highborn would leave, and when she'd decided she couldn't delay any longer, she waited for the right moment, for the enemy's location and vector to be optimal to give *Pegasus* a head start.

Then she gave the order.

She'd planned it well, she thought…well enough to give her a chance to get her people out of the system. They were close to the coreward end of the Hegemony, and nothing but ancient dead systems likely lay before them. If she could get away from the Highborn ship, there was a strong likelihood none would be waiting ahead.

You hope…

She looked over at Vig, and they exchanged glances in silence. There was nothing to say. They both understood the situation, and she suspected his guess as to their chances wasn't far from her own six in ten.

She caught movement on the display as the Highborn

vessel began to decelerate. She had only guesses on the vessel's maximum thrust levels, or for that matter, how vital its commander would consider chasing down one small vessel in the system. Andi and her people were looking for ways to destroy the enemy, but she couldn't imagine the arrogant Highborn would consider that. They would probably figure *Pegasus* was some random Hegemony ship, a small freighter that had escaped the occupation. Worth chasing down, to a point. But not a crisis either.

She'd been careful in her planning, and *Pegasus* was blasting straight for the transit point. She knew what her ship could give her in terms of thrust, and that left as the only variable, the capability and determination of her foe.

The minutes went by, and any doubt that the enemy was coming for *Pegasus* evaporated. The vessel was accelerating rapidly now, coming about on a direct pursuit heading.

Andi stared, calculations running in her head at first, and then a moment later, on her screen, to double check her results. She upped her estimate on *Pegasus*'s chances of getting through the point. Seven in ten. That didn't sound bad...but it still twisted her guts into knots.

And it didn't take into consideration if the enemy would follow her...or if they would just assume they'd driven a fugitive off into dead and useless space to perish.

She didn't care to assign odds to that one. If they let her go, she would be grateful.

And if not, she would do whatever she had to do.

That's not a large Hegemony ship...we might even be able to beat it if we can take it by surprise...

Chapter Seventeen

205,000,000 Kilometers from CFS Dauntless
Omicron Alvera System
Year 327 AC (After the Cataclysm)

"Wing Three, get those ships forward twenty thousand meters. We've got to hit that lead formation hard. We're covering for the rest of the strike force, and that means we need to get up there, hit them, and get the hell out...before they can bring their numbers to bear on us." Reg Griffin had blasted forward at full thrust the entire way, even as she snapped out orders to her various formations. Her people had won a handy victory against an outnumbered enemy force in the system, but after they'd returned and refit, she'd sent most of them back out to begin an intensive survey of the system. They'd just gotten deeply into that complex operation when more enemy ships began to transit.

Reg had been angry with herself, upset that she'd deployed so many of her available squadrons to dispersed scouting ops. There were thousands of fighters with the fleet, of course but most of those, along with Admiral Barron and *Dauntless* and the rest of the fleet were clear on the other side of the system, two days or more away. Barron had been advancing slowly, with extreme caution, sending scouting forces into each system to explore the area around the point before the fleet followed. Then, he sent forth an advance guard, to move to the proposed exit point, and complete a detailed scan of the entire system. It was cumbersome and time-consuming, but Reg knew well how many times Tyler Barron had hidden himself in dust clouds and behind gas giants, lying in wait for an enemy, and he had no intention of allowing the enemy to ambush or surprise him the same way.

Reg had no argument with the admiral's tactics, save that they had left her forward with limited advance forces…just as a fresh enemy fleet appeared to be arriving.

She hadn't hesitated when the scan had first detected the new arrivals, ordering all her detachments to converge into a single strike force. Her pilots had just defeated an enemy force, if an outnumbered one, and morale was strong. Now, they were going to get the chance to repeat, this time against what looked very much like even odds.

Even if I can get all the scouting groups back and reformed in time…

She'd almost ordered the single wing she had with her to pull back, to trade space for time, but the line of Highborn carriers forced her hand. She had no idea if they were little more than launch platforms, or if, like the Confederation's battleships, they carried heavy guns as well as fighters. If she let them get too close, her own mother ships could be in danger. She'd seen enough of the ranges and the power of Highborn beams to exercise caution on protecting her battleships. And if her squadrons lost their landing platforms, every pilot she had, herself included, would die before *Dauntless* and the other ships could come up and retrieve them.

Assuming they even tried to come up. She had no idea if more enemy forces were on the way, of just what, exactly, she was up against. Admiral Barron wasn't going to push the fleet forward recklessly, not when the survival of every human on the Rim rested on the outcome of the war. She'd

sat in on the highest level strategy meetings—in Jake
Stockton's place, she never forgot—and she'd seen firsthand
Barron's reluctance. She had some idea of the factors that
had pushed the admiral to launch the offensive…but she
was absolutely sure he was nervous about it, almost
paranoid about what might happen.

She didn't blame him, not even when it pushed her into
exposed forward positions with a contingent of her fighters
corps. She would have done the same thing in his place, and
she liked to think, at least, that she wasn't a hypocrite.

She glanced down at her thrust readings. Her ship was
coming on hard, better than three thousand kilometers per
second. She felt an urge to cut back, to lay off the
acceleration, but she resisted. She was risking zipping right
by the enemy front line, getting caught between the
vanguard and the rest of the Highborn squadrons coming
up after. But there was no choice. She *had* to hit those
forward ships, engage them before they could close on her
still reforming squadrons behind. If those ships we engaged
before they could recover their formations…

She could see the range display dropping, the numbers
almost a blur. Her ships would be in missile range soon, no
more than two minutes.

"All ships, arm missiles. Commence targeting
operations."

She'd thought about holding the warheads back, bringing
her ships in close before they launched. But she had to grab
the attention of those fighters. She had to hold them back.

She counted down softly to herself, needlessly repeating
the information she was watching on the display. Her hand
tightened around her firing controls, even as she entered the
final targeting information and locked it into the computer.

She started straight ahead, and her finger tightened, just
as she leaned over the comm unit and said, simply,
"Launch."

* * *

Stockton could feel his hands moving, shifting the controls, bringing his fighter in on a course toward the Confederation squadrons. He was trying to jerk his arm, to send his ship blasting off into the depths of space, away from the Highborn squadrons he was leading, and also his old comrades...whom he was about to kill. But he couldn't budge, couldn't interfere at all with the Collar's control.

He'd trained thousands of Thralls, built a massive fighter corps that was, in many ways, a match for that of his Confed comrades and their allies. He despised himself for that, screamed silently at the universe for his inability to kill himself, to escape the waking nightmare he'd lived for four years.

But now, he was actually going to kill his people. His hand would direct his fighter, his fingers would fire its weapons. And any hope that the instincts, the intuition, all the parts of his mind that made him a great pilot, would remain under his control, and not that of the Collar and the version of himself it had created, were quickly dashed. He'd been putting on a flying display.

Maybe they'll peg me as the leader. He felt an instant of hope that one of his old pilots would kill him and end his misery. But it didn't last. In truth, he doubted anyone in the fleet could beat him...and he knew his enslaved mind and psyche would fight with all the skill and ferocity he possessed against any fighter that came at him.

He could see through the eyes he couldn't control, hear what his Collar-dominated self could hear. But there was nothing he could do to stop what was about to happen. He couldn't even close his eyes, look away. All he could do was stare right at the treachery he was about to commit.

"All wings...launch missiles." The words were his, echoing in his cockpit. He tried yet again to take control of his arms, his hands, pull them back from their deadly task.

But nothing he did could stop the arming sequence…or the firing of his two missiles.

He tried to imagine someone who had developed an abomination like the Collar. The perverse horror of a device that removed all control, provided the enslaved psyche access to all its skills and memories, and even its raw instincts, and yet allowed some scrap of the person one had been before to watch helplessly, defied his comprehension. Anyone who would employ such an abomination had to be destroyed. He would kill all the Highborn, wherever they were, if he could, send every one of them screaming to hell.

He tried to move again, one more effort at defiance, to overload his lasers, to do something, anything, to stop what he was doing.

To no avail.

He tried to turn away from the screen, from the trails of the two missiles he'd fired, but his Collar-controlled mind was fixed on the data, and that meant he had to watch.

The warheads streaked toward the oncoming formation, just over one hundred Lightning fighters in total, with close to four hundred more forming up behind. The force he now led was almost a perfect match, a fact he knew was by design. He'd even led forth a vanguard, whose true purpose had been to give the Confed forces time to reorganize their remaining squadrons before engaging his full strength.

He wasn't there that day to take on the whole fleet, to throw thousands of fighters at the combined forces of the Confederation, the Alliance, and the Hegemony. That, perhaps, was something to be thankful for…though he knew the Highborn's overall plan, and he recognized the grave danger it held for his old comrades.

His job was to give the forces in front of him a good fight, do his part to make it seem the Highborn's forces were spread out, that they were struggling to put up a defense against the Pact invasion. To lure Admiral Barron and the fleet in ever deeper…to where they could finally be destroyed.

He tried to tell himself he would break free of the Collar before then, that he would stop it all somehow. But he didn't really believe that, not anymore. Stockton would never give up…it wasn't in him. But he knew he would fail, despite his best efforts.

His misery about the future was augmented by horror at what he was seeing at that moment. Both of his missiles had found their targets…destroying two Confederation fighters. Stockton had hated himself for training the Thrall pilots, for his part in the battles they had fought, the Confed flyers they had killed.

But now *he* had killed Confederation pilots himself, his own hands on the controls, his own targeting bringing the missiles in on them, and blasting them to plasma.

The silent screams in his head turned to wild howls of misery and despair. He begged the universe to take him, to end his nightmare, even as his hands moved again, bringing his fighter toward the Confederation wings just ahead…and his display flashed, showings a full charge in his lasers.

* * *

"There is something wrong. I can't explain it, but the enemy pilots, their flight plans, the tightness of their formations…" Reg Griffin sat as a small table, flanked by two legends she'd practically worshipped as a young pilot. Dirk Timmons and Olya Federov carried the scars of their many battles, including a pair of prosthetic legs in Timmons's case. There was a grimness to each of the battered warriors, an exhaustion countered only by their unbreakable devotion to duty.

Timmons and Griffin had come up with the main fleet, and she'd asked them to join her as soon as they arrived. Her forces had driven off the second Highborn force, albeit at significantly higher losses than they suffered against the first. But she was more worried than ever, and she hoped Timmons and Federov could help her make sense of the situation.

"They are certainly better than I would have expected…in more ways than one. Perhaps they were able to secure sufficient data on our own tactics. The Hegemony must have been studying such things, and with half of that power's worlds in enemy hands…" Timmons let his voice slip to silence for a moment. "But the Hegemony didn't really engage in fighter versus fighter operations until the very end of the conflict, and even then, they faced pilots on our side raised on bombing operations, and poorly trained in such tactics as dogfighting. Yet, the Highborn pilots are quite skilled."

"Is there any way they could have obtained footage from Union sources? We certainly had our battles with them." Federov moved in her chair, wincing as she did. She'd recovered from the wounds that had taken her out of action near the close of the Hegemony War, at least as much as she was going to. Some things never completely healed.

"I don't see how. They no doubt know about the Union, but the only way the Highborn could actually reach Union space is around the edge of the Hegemony and the Badlands. That's a long way to go just to get data on fighter combat." Reg shook her head. "I've wondered if they could have intelligence assets in the Confederation. I don't like to think some of our people would help an enemy like that, but we all know the sad truth. Still, the same problems apply. How could they maintain communications with intelligence sources, with Striker and the whole fleet, and thousands of scanner buoys, between them and the border?" She paused, and her frown deepened. "There is one other thing…I'm sure it's my imagination, but…"

"But?" Timmons made eye contact.

"Well, those formations, the tactics…they remind me of

something. Back from the Union War." She fell silent again.

"They remind you of Raptor's tactics." Federov said it first, but Reg knew they'd all been thinking it.

"Yes. I know that's ridiculous. Maybe…if he'd faced them, led squadrons into dogfights against them. But how could they emulate Jake Stockton's methods, when they've never even seen him in combat against other fighters?" Reg was agitated, and it was showing in her voice. She was stressed about dealing with an enemy that seemed more capable than they should be, but it was more than that. She felt like she was fighting Jake Stockton's ghost, almost as though her old mentor had abandoned her, and was fighting against his old comrades.

The room was silent for a long while, and Reg knew they were all thinking of their lost leader. Almost four years had passed, but in ways it still seemed to Reg as though it had been just yesterday. She'd worked herself endlessly, drove herself to the brink of exhaustion, feeling Stockton's presence somehow always with her, pushing her harder. He'd had the confidence in her to anoint her as his successor, and she couldn't imagine a more terrible fate than failing her lost leader.

"I'm not sure it matters…" Timmons looked up from where his eyes had been focused on the table. "What matters is defeating them. They're better than we expected, better than they should be. Okay, we know that now. Would knowing how or why improve our tactical situation? You did what you had to do, Reg…what Jake would have done. And those pilots out there in the fleet's bays, they're a damned sight better than they were before, even since I got out here. Don't forget, that last fight was on even terms, and they caught you by surprise…and they still ended up turning tail and blasting out of the system. So, however much better they are than we think they should be, don't sell yourself, or your pilots short. One thing I can tell you about Raptor is…he worried as much as anyone, sat up nights trying to figure out how to fight against the odds. Not many people know that, because he didn't let anybody see it. The squadrons think of his as a legend, but he was just a man, one who did what had to be done. And you're more like him than you think, Reg. I can see why he picked you as his second out here, as his successor. This is going to be a hard war, and I won't lie to you and tell you anything else. But you have my confidence. I believe you can do what you have to do, that you can lead these wings to victory...and you can count on me fighting at your side to the end."

"I believe in you, too." Olya Federov managed a smile. "You *can* do this, Reg...as long as you let yourself believe it."

Chapter Eighteen

Highborn Flagship S'Argevon
Imperial System GH9-4307, Planet A1112 (Calpharon)
Year of the Firstborn 389 (327 AC)

"Your forces did well again in System GH6-2901. Your losses were on the high end of projections, but still within acceptable parameters. Such casualty levels are perhaps unavoidable, given our deliberate holdback of the enhanced missiles, and our continued efforts to allow the enemy enough success to draw them forward. It is a delicate balance, maintaining believability in the strength of our defenses, while also encouraging a continued advance into our recently-reclaimed space. You will have the chance to repeat your performance, perhaps twice more before the final trap springs. Your fighters will not deploy the new missiles until our ultimate assault on the enemy fleet, and until then, you must continue to engage in largely stalemated battles. I do not want the enemy to be given reason to pull back, to retreat to their own space. Is that understood?"

Stockton lunged forward, leaping up, wrapping his hands around Tesserax's neck, jamming his fingers into the Highborn's flesh and reveling at the hot, red blood pooling all around them.

At least that image flashed before him, a fantasy he

believed was real for perhaps one beautiful, fleeting second. But alas, he still remained in his mental prison, whatever essence remained of the man, Jake Stockton, trapped, unable to strike back, to refuse to do as he was commanded.

"Yes, Highborn. I understand."

Who is that? What thing is that speaking with my voice, pulling from my memories, using my body and my skills to serve the enemy?

Jake Stockton had his faults, he knew, but he had never been a traitor. Until now. He served the Confederation's enemy…and his hands were stained with the blood of his comrades. He'd fought all his life to survive in the face of war and danger. Now, his only wish was for death.

He'd been a fierce fighter his whole life, a merciless warrior who'd dispatched countless adversaries, but he realized he had never hated anyone, anything, as much as whatever it was inside *him*, driving his actions, forcing him to war against all he loved and believed in. Was it an alien presence, an outside force? Or was it something inside him, twisted perhaps, but still him?

He channeled all his rage, all his desperate need to end what was happening, and he tried to lunge toward Tesserax. But his body remained still, respectful and attentive to the Highborn's words.

"We will increase the size and power of the forces the humans encounter. We will position reserve units as well, scheduled to come to the aid of our forces when they are attacked. But in all cases, these deployments will be inadequate to prevail. The enemy must think we are weak, that we have positioned what strength we could, struggled to the best of our ability to hold them back. They must be encouraged in every possible way to become more confident, to believe that they can succeed, that they can liberate the Hegemony capital…and drive us entirely from the Colony." A pause, and Tesserax's face twisted into a sickening smile. "Then, they will fall into our hands. Then, we can destroy them, obliterate the military forces that stand against us, and bring humanity into our embrace."

Stockton listened, and his despair was complete as he realized, without doubt or question, that he *would* help the Highborn, that he would use all his knowledge and skill to deceive Tyler Barron and the other leaders of the fleet.

That he would help lure them into the trap...and then he would fight alongside the Highborn and kill his friends and comrades. His people.

Spacers' gods or fate or whatever force is out there...please, please just let me die...

* * *

Stockton stood at the front of the room, preparing to address more than one thousand assembled pilots. They were human, not too different looking from his people back on *Dauntless* and the other ships of the fleet. Except that he was training them to kill those comrades.

He still tried to resist the Collar, to regain some level of control over himself, even to simply hold back his intimate knowledge of Confederation tactics, but to no avail. The enemy device controlled him utterly, leaving little to him save misery and regret.

Tesserax stood next to him, the Highborn towering above any normal human present. He had come to speak to the pilots sitting before Stockton, and he acted as though he was doing them a great honor.

Worse, the pilots in the room also behaved that way, looking back with worshipful expressions. It was clear that they, too, felt as though a great honor had been done to them. Even as most of his own mind believed the same thing. He wondered if the others still had small sparks of themselves somewhere inside, as he did, or if, as beings raised from birth under Highborn rule, they had never truly developed a sense of themselves as thinking beings. He

asked himself how many would obey the Highborn, even
without the Collars, how many would rebel, would strike
back, as he would.

He suspected he would not like the answer to that
question.

Tesserax spoke with a booming voice, dripping with the
condescension that grated on Stockton's inner self. But he
couldn't prevent himself from listening. He couldn't even
wipe the obedient grin from his face.

"The enemy will deploy both interceptors and bombers
in any large fleet engagement. You have to date only faced
either interceptors or bombers alone. When you first
encounter a mixed force, it will be necessary to assign
priorities. The interceptors are the greatest threat to your
own fighters, but the bombers are a danger to the ships of
the fleet. We will therefore place a greater importance on
intercepting and destroying bombers. This may result in our
weaker wings deployed against interceptors suffering
increased losses, but no sacrifice is to great in the service of
the Highborn."

Stockton felt nauseous again, though he'd come to
realize that was his mind playing tricks on him, that the
feelings of sickness were phantoms, and not coming from
his actual stomach. Even vomiting in utter disgust was an
outlet denied him by the Collar.

"Remember, Thralls…losses are of secondary
importance. Our objective is to defeat the human forces in
opposition to us so that we may extend our sacred embrace
to all inhabited worlds. To that end, we will sacrifice as
many pilots as needed. The small craft are far more
replaceable than larger warships, and for all the training you
pilots have had, that also can be replicated. If you are called
upon to die for the Highborn, you may considered yourself
blessed, and go to your fate knowing you have served, and
served well."

Stockton listened, and his anger flared…at the version of

himself listening obediently, and at the Highborn, for such callous disregard for the Thrall pilots and the losses they suffered. There was something else nagging at him, a realization that the doctrine Tesserax had just outlined did not differ extraordinarily from Confederation norms. From his first days at the Academy, it had been drilled into his head. The battleships always came first. Always. If it came down to a choice between heavy warships and a group of fighters, the pilots got a memorial service. Every fighter jock knew that.

But it sounded far more sinister coming from Tesserax. Stockton wondered if that was something about the Highborn...or whether it was his mind rebelling, embracing his own hypocrisy. Did it really matter if a commander sent pilots to their deaths plagued with guilt and justifications of duty...or thinking of them as entries on a spreadsheet? Dead was dead, and victory and defeat existed regardless of motivation.

He told himself it did matter, but he still wasn't sure if that was true...or if what little was left of him simply *had* to believe it.

* * *

"We have received word from Percelax. His forces have engaged the Union rebels, and defeated them. Unfortunately, the enemy responded quickly to the presence of his vessels and their effectiveness, and they were able to withdraw with roughly two thirds of their forces fully or partially intact." Phazarax was clearly pleased with the news he was delivering, but just as evidently, there was some hesitation. Tesserax felt the same way, admittedly on less information than his comrade possessed.

The news *was* good, by any measure, and the gains that would likely accrue from the commitment of so modest a force made even a slight delay seem inconsequential.

Nevertheless, it seemed clear the Union rebels, the forces he had sent Percelax to engage and destroy, had able leadership. Given what he'd been able to glean of the Confederation's struggles with the Union, that was somewhat of a surprise.

Tesserax found the Confederation to be somewhat of an enigma, its chaotic unstructured society chronically plagued by corrupt and dishonest leaders…and yet it was an economic marvel, with production levels that challenged—and exceeded—even those of the Highborn. It had produced leaders like Tyler Barron and his comrades. Tesserax was intrigued by the Confederation commander, to the point where he'd imagined capturing Barron alive instead of killing him. The human would be extremely useful once encollared, and would serve well on the primary front.

But there was no time for such distractions, not until the humans were defeated and the Rim secured. Phazarax's report suggested progress had been made on the far perimeter of that struggle…but also that a final resolution there would take additional time. If his own plan succeeded, if the human fleets could be drawn deeper into his trap and destroyed, Percelax's efforts would simply hasten the mopping up efforts, bringing the Union under control long before the main fleets could advance so far into the Rim.

And if the current operation was less than entirely successful—a possibility Tesserax allowed for, but didn't really believe was possible—control over the Union would allow the opening of a second front, and it would slip a dagger right into the Confederation's exposed underbelly.

"Percelax is to be commended. Admittedly, it would have been better if he'd been able to position his forces to prevent the enemy escaping. But he can be forgiven. Our intelligence suggested no likelihood of encountering Union military commanders as capable and unpredictable as Admiral Barron and his team. Though a short term hindrance, such news is actually quite good in the long term. We are finally bringing the Rim under our control because it is our sacred purpose to rule over all of the humans, but also because the time has come for them to aid in the fight on the primary front. That is their battle as much as it is ours, both because they exist to serve us, and because the war there is to protect them as much as to safeguard our own worlds." Tesserax paused for a few seconds. He had found the fighting against the humans enlightening in many ways.

"There is something else we must consider when we have concluded the conquest, Phazarax. Late imperial theories about the effects of adversity and conflict in advancing the ability of human societies are heavily supported by what we are encountering here. The empire withered and died because its people were complacent, decadent. The Rimdwellers were forced to claw their way back from decline, and they have fought continuous wars against each other in the process, with commendable results in terms of the development of their capabilities and strength. When we do assume control, we must consider ways to ensure that the subject populations retain this strength. Their warriors, of course, will fight on the primary front, but the planets and the civilian populations of the Rim are currently far from those combat zones. We may need to find ways to simulate the effects of war...perhaps random instances of divine vengeance on selected worlds and the like."

"I agree completely with your analysis, Commander. No doubt, Church policy and doctrine will need to be updated based on the lessons learned here. Yet, first we must conclude the conquest. If the enemy continues to advance here, your forces will certainly entrap them. It is hard to imagine how the humans can continue the fight in any substantive way with their military forces virtually annihilated. And control over the Union, and an invasion of undefended Confederation space, will interfere with any desperate attempts to replace losses. With fortune, Percelax and the subject Union forces will be able to reach the Confederation production centers long before our forces here could. *That* will truly end human resistance."

Tesserax nodded solemnly. "Then, the Colony will be complete and secure, and we can return in overwhelming force to aid in the fighting on the primary front…and with victory there, the Highborn can truly take their place as a pantheon ruling over humanity, and all other life in the galaxy, for a million years."

Chapter Nineteen

Free Trader Pegasus
Undesignated Imperial System 2
Year 327 AC (After the Cataclysm)

The thumping was loud in her ears, almost distracting. Andi stood, stone still next to her chair, her eyes locked onto the display, even as she struggled to ignore the thunderous beating of her heart.

The screen was centered on the transit point, as were all of *Pegasus*'s scanner beams, and Andi's withering gaze seemed as though it might burn through the hyper-glass of the display itself. She was watching, waiting…looking for the first sign the Highborn ship was coming through. So she could destroy it.

It was a desperate plan, wildly risky. The Highborn vessel was small, some kind of courier ship or tiny freighter, she guessed. She wouldn't have had a chance against a real enemy warship, but she'd convinced herself *Pegasus* could handle her tiny pursuer.

At least given surprise. And a flawlessly-executed attack.

She was ready. Her whole crew was ready. The guns were charged, overloaded in fact, one more bet that Lex Righter's skill would suffice to keep the volatile fusion reaction in *Pegasus*'s power plant under control, even when Andi was ignoring just about every safety parameter.

Andi's nature was to fight instead of run…though she'd
tried like hell to run this time. She'd hoped the enemy would
write her off as some doomed Hegemony ship heading into
deep and dead space. But the Highborn seemed too
meticulous for that. The ship had relentlessly pursued,
broadcasting a hundred demands for *Pegasus* to surrender.

Andi had ignored them all.

Unless making obscene gestures at her own comm unit
counted as an answer.

She'd managed to stay ahead of the enemy, and she
figured she could probably keep that up, at least for a few
more systems. The Highborn were faster, but it still took
guesswork as to which vectors her ship would take after
transit. She'd managed to stay in front, but that margin was
declining. She might have kept it up anyway, bet everything
on her ability to somehow stay out of the enemy's
grasp…but she had to be free to explore, to search for the
way to the system she was after. And when she found it, she
had to stop there, something she couldn't do with a
Highborn ship on her tail.

She *had* to destroy it, and the only real chance she had
was to lay in wait just astride the transit point, and hope the
enemy assumed she would simply continue her flight across
the system. With luck—and assuming she managed to
handle it all perfectly—she just *might* have a chance. But she
had to hit the enemy on the first shot, and hit them hard. If
she missed, it was over.

And it was difficult to target Highborn ships. All she
could do was stay close, so close the gravity currents from
the transit point added one further, unwelcome distraction.
She was a good shot, she knew that. Now, that skill would
save her life, the lives of her crew.

Or they would all die.

"Andi…" Vig was sitting at his station, staring as
resolutely at the display as Andi was. "The energy reading is

fluctuating…it's just a miniscule, but…"

"I see it." Her tone was sharp, brittle. She was annoyed for an instant that Vig would think anything could slip past her just then. But he'd done exactly what he should have, what she would always want him to do. "I'm sorry, Vig." A few seconds later: "It won't be long now."

She slipped back into her chair, sliding the targeting display in front of her. She'd done all the calculations, created a dozen firing solutions, checked and rechecked the scanner links. She was as ready as she could be, at least before she had a real target.

An instant later, she did.

The scanner blip appeared suddenly, surrounded by a hazy aura she knew was mostly energy release from the transit point. The Highborn ship was a weak contact, as always, the strange Sigma-9 radiation emissions interfering with her scanners. *Pegasus*'s sensor suite was fully updated, with every improvement developed over the past four years, but Rim science had only come so far in improving tracking of the Highborn ships, and she knew it was going to take every bit of skill—and gut instinct—she had to score the hit she needed so badly.

Stay calm, Andi. It's just your life, and everyone's on this ship. And maybe Tyler's, Cassie's…everybody's on the Rim. Or, if not their lives, at least everything that makes those lives worth living…

Andi had always been strong under pressure, but the weight she could feel on her just then was almost unbearable. A fight was one thing, but knowing she could lose any chance in the first shot, that a miss was tantamount to certain death. All the fear, the tension, that would go into a battle was concentrated in one flash of time.

She leaned forward, pressing her face against the targeting scope. The contact was there, but it was shaking a bit. She knew that wasn't actual movement, but rather her scanners struggling to determine the vessel's precise location. The ship's instruments, its AI, ream after ream of analysis and programming…they all had the target pinned down to approximately a tenth of a cubic kilometer of space. But Andi had to hit the two hundred meter long hull directly.

That was where the instinct would come in.

Her finger tightened on the firing control as she pressed her face harder into the scope. She nudged the controls one way, then back a bit. She was breathing quickly, deeply…and then she held her last exhale.

He body was utterly still, her mind focused. There was nothing but the target, and her hand on the controls.

And the deafening sound of her own heartbeat.

She pressed her finger on the firing stud…but she stopped, just short of activating the lasers. She nudged the scope's controls one more time, the slightest adjustment, almost a whim…and then she pulled the trigger.

It was a sudden and abrupt move, a decision made more by her gut than her brain. She was used to the delaying factor distance played in space combat, but *Pegasus* was *close*, no more than two hundred kilometers from the enemy ship. She had the first answer she needed almost immediately. She had hit!

The second determination, the one that would decide the fight, and the survival prospects of her people, was still uncertain. She had connected, but had she scored the deadly critical hit she needed?

She didn't know, not for a few seconds, a period of time that stretched mercilessly into seeming eternity, each instant feeling like a passing geological age.

She was snapping out orders, even as she waited. "Evasive maneuvers, now!"

"Got it, Andi!" She could hear the tension in Vig's voice, and the hope. She was sure her friend believed she had scored the critical hit they needed. She was less certain.

Then, a second later, the AI confirmed it.

Her laser blast had ripped deeply into the Highborn

ship's hull. *Pegasus*'s weapons were less powerful than those of a true warship, but they were vastly uprated from anything a free trader would normally carry...and the absurdly close range meant the beams struck with considerable power.

She watched as the scanners reported explosions on the enemy ship, and expulsions of fluids and gasses into space. She dared to hope she *had* crippled the vessel in one shot.

Then, one of the deadly energy lances ripped by, no more than five hundred meters from *Pegasus*, the deadly electric blue speckled with black appearing on the screen. Whatever damage Andi had done—and it *was* considerable, she was sure of that at least—the enemy retained at least one weapon, and the energy to power it. The battle wasn't over yet.

Her whole body tensed, gripped with resolve, with pure determination as hard as a neutron star's core. The fight might not be over yet, but Andi Lafarge was going to win it. That wasn't hope, it wasn't confidence.

It was her absolute damned refusal to accept any other outcome.

"Switch to nav plan two, Vig." She could feel the sweat pouring down the back of her neck as she snapped out the order, all the while pushing her face harder into the scope. She'd scored one dead on hit, but it was going to take at least one more. And this time, she had to compensate for *Pegasus*'s wild evasive maneuvers when she did her targeting.

She'd done that before, of course, in more battles than she could easily count...but fighting the Highborn was somehow different than battling any past enemy. She despised the genetically-engineered monsters, and she would have killed every one of them if she could.

She would drag the last one from his final refuge, if she had the chance, and cut his throat herself. Still, despite the rage, the hatred, she wasn't immune to seeing their strengths. She would die before she would worship any of them, but she also understood their abilities, their intelligence, and their technology, were all far superior.

She saw the gauge on her screen turn green as her weapons once again reached a full charge. She had been waiting, honing her aim. She told herself to take her time, be cautious…but she didn't know how long she had.

Her fingers tightened, even as she was telling herself to take time, and *Pegasus*'s lasers blasted forth again…and scored a second hit. She wasn't sure she'd caught the enemy quite as directly amidships as she had the first time, and a second later, she confirmed that. She'd hit the Highborn vessel toward the bow, not a glancing shot by any measure, but not the solid strike dead center she'd managed the first time. Still, it was a second hit, more damage, and she held her breath, waiting to see if the enemy ship fired again.

Nothing.

She pushed back the hopes growing around her, even as her eyes darted back and forth, watching the charging gauge move up as her laser repowered. The fight wasn't over yet…and Andi Lafarge didn't celebrate until the enemy was dead, and often as not, cut up in half a dozen pieces and buried in different places. She'd seen arrogance and overconfidence destroy some of the most capable people she'd known, and she didn't play that game.

But the Highborn ship didn't attack again. At first, she wasn't sure what it was doing. Then, her stomach clenched hard, and a cold feeling took her from head to toe.

They were turning. They were running.

That would normally good, at least a reasonable result of battle. Absent killing an enemy, driving one away was usually an acceptable thing. But if she let the Highborn ship get through the point, they would send a warning. *Pegasus* had been an unidentified vessel, something that rated pursuit but not panic. But Andi had just upgraded that status, badly damaged a Highborn vessel. If the enemy could get a message through, she'd have real warships on her tail.

She couldn't allow that.

"Vig, bring us in, directly toward the contact." Her voice was almost feral, with just enough doubt to attest that she knew the gamble she was taking. If the enemy ship was truly damaged, if its weapons systems were all knocked out, she had a good chance of getting in even closer, scoring a kill shot.

But if the ship was luring her in, pretending its guns were down, she was serving up a perfect target. And, unlike her laser blasts on the enemy ship, it wasn't going to take a precise hit to obliterate *Pegasus*. Just about any decent shot from the Highborn gun would turn her beloved ship, and all inside it, into plasma.

That prospect bothered her all the more, because it was precisely what she would have done in the enemy's position. Assuming that ship had a gun that could still fire.

She pushed the thought away. She was all in now. She knew what she had to do, and worrying about it served no purpose. Her eyes moved back to the power display, waiting for the lasers to reach full charge. *Pegasus* was bearing down on the enemy ship, on a course so direct and straight, the enemy couldn't possibly miss if they had anything to shoot.

But still, there was nothing. Only the range dropping from point blank...to beyond anything she'd seen before. The scanner showed less than forty kilometers between *Pegasus* and its quarry, a distance so short, it almost defied meaning...but the enemy was accelerating back toward the point, on the verge of transiting.

Come on, come on...

She was watching the power gauge, as though she could somehow will it to move faster. The Highborn ship—and *Pegasus*—were *close* to the point. A few seconds more, and they'd get caught in the grav currents. That was going to make targeting far even more difficult, if not impossible.

She looked again, and she swore to herself the thing wasn't moving. The small bar of light seemed stuck. Was the reactor malfunctioning? Had a transmission line been damaged? Or was it just her mind, her fear and tension boiling over?

Then the canner turned green. The guns were ready.

She adjusted the targeting slightly. *Pegasus* was so close, she felt like she could hardly miss.

There's the arrogance, the overconfidence...no, no shortcuts. Do this right...

She chided herself, and she doublechecked her numbers...and just as she saw a massive gravity wave moving toward the enemy ship, she fired.

Pegasus's lasers lanced out, striking the Highborn ship. A direct hit, even better than her first shot. And at less than forty kilometers her small vessel's lasers struck with fearsome power.

The scanner report was almost instantaneous. She pulled back from the scope, shouting out to Vig as she looked up at the main display. "Get us out of this gravity well...now!" *Pegasus* was seconds from transiting, and Andi had no idea what effects her ship would suffer moving through the point so close behind the Highborn vessel.

A Highborn vessel that was coming apart, one that was about to...

She felt the g forces as Vig engaged maximum thrust, pulling *Pegasus* away from the point...just as the Highborn ship erupted in the blinding fury of matter-antimatter annihilation, and the whole billowing, surging nightmare slipped into the point's dense black center and vanished entirely.

Chapter Twenty

Troyus City
Megara, Olyus III
Year 327 AC (After the Cataclysm)

"I need you to go back to Montmirail, Alex...right now. I know First Citizen Ciara wanted you offworld while she...cleaned up...but now I'm far from sure she will even get that chance." Holsten turned and gestured toward a man in a Union uniform. He was standing silently, and there was a bulge under the shoulder of his jacket that, on close inspection, was clearly a dressing on some kind of wound. "This is Commander Sentivere, Alexander. He has come directly from Admiral Denisov's fleet." Holsten was silent for a moment. "The admiral sent him to request aid. Military aid."

Kerevsky stared back, the look of surprise on his face unmistakably genuine. "Military aid? But Gaston Villieneuve is cornered, down to the last of his support and resources. I don't understand."

"Apparently, the situation had changed somewhat." Holsten turned toward the Union officer. "Commander, perhaps you can share with Admiral Kerevsky what you told me."

"Of course, Mr. Holsten. Gaston Villieneuve's forces were trapped, blockaded on all sides, save for a narrow link to the Periphery. Admiral Denisov was assembling the fleet for the final push...when Villieneuve's forces launched their own attack. It was a surprise. We did not believe he had the resources or capability to launch such an operation."

"But surely, even if he managed to scrape up the ships and supplies to launch an attack, his forces were greatly outnumbered." Kerevsky looked at Holsten, and then back to the Union officer. "Did Admiral Denisov engage?"

"Indeed, we did offer battle. But Villieneuve's forces have been somehow...upgraded. Their weapons are more powerful than they were, indeed, considerably stronger than ours. And worse, he had a contingent of vessels that were more capable still. Their range greatly exceeded anything of ours, and their weapons were extremely powerful. Admiral Denisov recognized that those ships could simply blast us to scrap while staying out of our own firing range, so he ordered the fleet to withdraw. He managed to save almost two-thirds of his forces, but the rest were destroyed, or damaged badly enough to be out of action. We have very little data on the inexplicable new ships, but we fear they may be..."

"Highborn ships." Holsten interrupted, his voice stone cold, grim, without a hint of doubt. "They are Highborn ships. I don't know how they got there. They must have come all the way around the edge of the Hegemony and the Badlands, and then through the Periphery to link up with Villieneuve."

"But that means..."

"It means Denisov—and Ciara—are finished. We've had a series of advancements after six years war with the Hegemony, and then the transfer of their technology...but the Union is where they were ten years ago...and that was twenty years behind where we were then. At least they had numbers on us back in the day, but the economic collapse and all the unrest that followed, has reduced their power even farther. They're a shadow of what they once were. They might be able to threaten us while our forces are so heavily deployed in the Hegemony—in fact, the very likely *could* pose a major threat—but they have no chance of defeating Highborn forces." Holsten turned toward Kerevsky. "Which means, if Villieneuve is backed by the Highborn, the war against him is as good as over. Unless we intervene." A pause, followed by a deep sigh. "And I have no idea where to find the ships. We've barely got a picket line on the border, and nothing that can stand up to the Highborn. And everything else is out on the main front."

Holsten's mind was racing. He'd already sent *Excalibur* forward. The Confederation's first superbattleship was bound for the front. He might be able to call it back using the new comm lines...but Tyler Barron was already expecting the vessel and its contingent.

"The next three superbattleships will be ready in a little over six months, at least assuming no unexpected problems." That was an assumption Holsten was never prepared to make. "We're going to have to hope that Denisov can somehow hold out that long." He knew he was way ahead of himself. Diverting the superbattleships, and the other vessels scheduled to enter service in the coming months, would require Senatorial approval—and Tyler Barron's as well. The situation on the main Highborn front was still grave, and Barron was likely to need every hull he could get.

But if Villieneuve regains control of the Union, with Highborn support...

Holsten didn't know what to do. If he weakened Barron to divert reserves to aid Denisov, or even to garrison the Union frontier, it might be the difference between success and failure. If the war was lost in the main theater, it didn't make much difference what happened anywhere else. But if he didn't strengthen the defenses against a Union advance, they could slice right into the heart of the Confederation…to the Iron Belt industrial worlds. To Megara itself.

"Go, Alexander. Get ready. You leave tonight. I will arrange your transit." Holsten's mind raced, trying to think of how he could assemble some military force to send with Kerevsky. But even if he could find the ships—a huge enough question—he didn't have the authority. He might overreach a little, play around with force distributions, but the Confederation wasn't allied with Ciara's Union government. They hadn't even fully recognized her as head of state. Sending so much as a gunboat to aid her against other Union factions would require the last thing he wanted to deal with.

It would require Senate approval.

* * *

Cliff Wellington eased back in his command chair, surprised for about the fiftieth time by the smoothness of *Excalibur*'s engines. He was a veteran of the Union War, and he'd served the earliest days of his career in warships without the seemingly magical effect of the dampeners. Thrust levels had been limited in those days not by available power, but by how much punishment the human bodies of the crew could take. Vessels had used special couches, and even tanks of various kinds, but none of it had worked particularly well, and especially not in combat, when crews couldn't be drugged and immobile.

Modern warships had thrust capacities five or ten times what those vessels of two decades before had managed, and *Excalibur* was another leap forward. The Confederation's first antimatter-powered vessel was also the fastest in the fleet, despite also being the largest. In every sense, *Excalibur* was a superweapon, second only in power and mass to the salvaged imperial wonder of *Colossus*.

Excalibur had only one real weakness, and that was one, if the last reports he'd received were correct, would soon be solved. The new pride of the Confederation navy relied on Hegemony sources for its antimatter fuel. The Hegemony were allies, of course, at least in the fight against the Highborn, but Wellington had lost too many friends—and been wounded twice himself—in the prior war against that power to feel good about such a dependency.

If production commences as expected, we might have a shipment of our own antimatter less than a month after we reach the front.

That couldn't come soon enough for Wellington. He knew he had much more to worry about than fuel deliveries from the Hegemony—or from the Confederation's new production planet—but it was hard to take his mind off of any perceived vulnerability.

"Let's give these engines a run and see what they can do." He'd held back on pushing his ship to the limit of her abilities, partly to save that antimatter fuel that so concerned him, and also because the two dozen other ships accompanying *Excalibur* were conventionally fusion powered, and had no hope of keeping up with the battleship at full thrust.

But he also needed to put the vessel through its paces. He had no doubt *Excalibur* would quickly find its place in the front of the battle lines, and before that happened, he wanted to know just what the miraculous new ship—and its handpicked crew—could do.

Tyler Barron had entrusted him with the powerful new vessel, and its escorts. He had elevated Wellington to the senior captain in the entire fleet, and save for Commodore Eaton on *Colossus*, the highest-ranked ship commander. Wellington had always been intensely loyal to Barron, and ready to follow the admiral into hell itself, if that's where he led. But now, he felt even greater pressure to live up to Barron's expectations, to make sure *Excalibur*, its crew—and its captain—were one hundred percent ready when they reached the front.

That was a duty he would see fulfilled, however hard it was on his ship, and on the sweating, overworked men and women in its crew.

*   *   *

Anya Fritz drew a breath, slowly, methodically, feeling the cool air move through her nose and down into her lungs. She wasn't much for stress relieving techniques—tension had, as often or not, been a source of energy driving her—but she had never dreaded an order more than the one she was about to give.

Nor had she ever been as impatient for one. It was a contradiction, something she knew made no sense. But then, perhaps there was some kind of twisted rationality to it...at least when it came to something as awesomely powerful, and unbelievably dangerous, as antimatter.

Fritz had been working for almost four years, heading a project that had involved nothing less than harnessing the entire energy output of a planet. The world for the Confederation's first antimatter refinery had been carefully chosen, one with enough volcanic and seismic activity to harness, without so much that it jeopardized the massive facilities constructed on its surface. The planet's extensive plains were covered with solar panels, their effectiveness enhanced by the thinness of the atmosphere, and the space above was ringed with satellites capturing even more of the power output from the system's sun. The world's tides, waterways, even the heat from its molten core had all been tapped, every captured watt feeding the insatiable appetites of the antimatter production units.

Now, with the flip of a switch, she would activate the solar collection facilities, the geothermal power generators, the two hundred fusion power plants operating off the planet's tritium-rich oceans…and when she did, if her work had been done correctly—and her repeated rounds of testing had suggested it had been—antimatter would begin to flow into the specially-designed collection tanks, stored there in immense magnetic bottles until it could be loaded onto specially-designed freighters, and moved to the battlefront, to fuel the Confederation's advanced new ships and weapons.

"Admiral Fritz…all final checks are clear. All systems green. All stations report ready and awaiting your command."

Fritz took another breath, deciding a few seconds later that stress relief was a fantasy. No zen, balance, mind-centering crap was going to calm her down, not when she was about to open the floodgates to a torrent of antimatter. If all went well, it would take less than one thousandth of a second for the facility to produce more of the precious substance than every other source had in a century of Confederation history.

That was more power than the human mind could easily grasp…and every bit of it earmarked for man's foremost pursuit. War.

She felt something like regret at that thought. Fritz wasn't a dewy-eyed pacifist, not by any measure. Her life had *been* battle, repairing and maintaining warships so they could stay in combat. So they could survive long enough…to kill. Still, she couldn't help but wonder what peacetime marvels such a quantity of antimatter could power, what great achievements it could fuel. Even for one of her grim determination, the fighting had become too much. The Confederation's history, that of the entire post-Cataclysm Rim, had been filled with conflict and strife. But the last twenty years had seen almost nonstop war. Strangely, the past three years had been the quietest she could recall, though that calm existed under the shadow of looming invasion, and the dark and dismal threat of utter defeat.

"Admiral? Should we…"

Fritz turned toward the officer, and her glare silenced him mid-sentence. Her people didn't exactly love her, as Barron's spacers did him, but she knew she had their respect. And they were scared to death of her. Given a choice of one option, that's the one she would have picked. It was the most useful.

"Activate the refinery. Let's start producing some antimatter."

*   *   *

"Antimatter production has begun. The Quasar facility is operating at ten percent of expected capacity, but Admiral Fritz will shortly begin increasing that." Holsten paused, looking out at the gathered Senate. He preferred to deal with politicians in small groups, or better yet, one on one. He detested addressing the entire Senate, but he hadn't seen a way out of it this time. "Admiral Fritz has also requested a transfer to the front lines as soon as the operation has ramped up to full production." Holsten knew there would be arguments, that many would want to keep the Confederation's foremost engineer right where she was, watching antimatter production with a withering intensity that would make a hawk seem blind. But Fritz had been very clear when she'd accepted the task to oversee the construction of Quasar, and a return to combat status had been paramount among her conditions.

"I can also advise you all that *Excalibur* has been dispatched to the front lines, along with roughly two dozen other new vessels. She should reach Base Striker in about six weeks."

"That is all well and good, Mr. Holsten, but I think this body would like to hear all of your intelligence on the situation in the Union. And I do mean *all* of it." Cyn Avaria spoke out of turn, a departure from the Senate's normal procedure. That wasn't a particular surprise...she'd never given the slightest indication she thought the rules she imposed on others applied to her. She was one of the most powerful Senators, and the head of the Reds, one of the two dominant power blocs.

She was also an absolute pain in the ass, at least as far as Holsten could see. He'd imagined some of his black ops people throwing her in the back of a transport a hundred times, but kidnapping or assassinating a sitting Senator was a bit too far, even for Gary Holsten.

At least so far it was...

"Senator Avaria, I was going to get to that in due time." A lie, at least partially. He hadn't *really* thought he'd get out of the briefing without discussing the uncertain and crumbling situation in the Union, but if the Senators had given him the chance to do just that, he'd have taken it. He'd secured Emmit Flandry's promise not to bring it up, at least. But word had spread, and fear was growing.

"I think now is a good time, Mr. Holsten."

God I hate her...

"Of course, Senator. "The truth is, there is much rumor and fearmongering, and little hard data. Until recently, all intelligence suggested both that Sandrine Ciara's forces were on the verge of defeating Villieneuve's loyalists and that she intended to honor her overtures and establish a lasting peace between our nations. I have no reason, at least none based in hard fact, to assume that has changed in any material way." Another lie. He didn't have what he'd like to have in terms of data, but the information he did possess had been keeping him up nights. Still, there was no reason to unleash panic and chaos in the Senate. At least not until he could turn it to his own needs.

"Please, Mr. Holsten...do not treat us as fools. You serve at the behest of this body, and you can be removed and replaced if you find yourself unable to meet your obligations."

Holsten mostly ignored the threat. He'd always kept enough information on the important Senators to secure his position...and somewhere along the line he'd stopped being amazed that none of them ever seemed to lack dark secrets he could discover. But he had an even better guarantee of his place as head of Confederation Intelligence. Tyler Barron. When Barron had first risen to prominence, Holsten had been somewhat of a guide and a protector. But those roles had been reversed. Holsten could have burned every one of his red files, and not worried for an instant about his position as the head of Confederation Intelligence. Not while Tyler Barron still supported him. The Senate knew Barron had contempt for their political games and corruption—and most of them despised the admiral—but more importantly, they also knew he was the one man who could likely rally the entire fleet behind him...and depose them all.

Barron actually doing something like that seemed almost inconceivable to Holsten, but he also knew how the Senators' minds worked. He doubted most of them could imagine someone not caring about political power...and that made Barron a tool he could use to keep them in line. A very powerful tool.

Not to mention Barron was unquestionably the Confederation's best hope of staving off the Highborn. The distance from the main front somewhat diluted the fear the Senators felt. But only somewhat. They'd all seen plenty of images and data, and they were scared enough.

"I could come in here, Senator, and spew out baseless rumors and wild guesses, like those you have undoubtedly heard. But my job is to gather intelligence...reliable data on the situation in the Union. Until I have some basis in fact to report otherwise, I maintain that the likeliest scenario remains a victory by First Citizen Ciara's forces." He knew none of them would believe him—hell, he wouldn't have believed himself—but it was the best he could do. If the Senate decided to divert forces from the main front, the consequences could be catastrophic.

And if Gaston Villieneuve does have Highborn support, the effects of not doing so will be, too…

He didn't want to think about that.

He didn't feel good about minimizing the urgency of the Union front, especially since he was as worried about it as anyone on the Senate floor. But it came down to simple strategy. An existing threat took precedence over a potential one.

And he wasn't going to leave Tyler Barron hanging. If the Union became a threat, worse, one with Highborn support, he'd figure something out.

Somehow.

Chapter Twenty-One

Free Trader Pegasus
Undesignated Imperial System 12
Year 327 AC (After the Cataclysm)

"There's a lot of debris in this system, Andi. A *lot*. I don't think I've ever seen anything quite like it."

Andi was looking at the main display, thinking exactly what Vig had just said. There were dead hulks floating all around, the remains of various kinds of ships and other constructs. Hundreds of them.

The system was a mystery to her, but according to her best analysis—and a few hopefully lucky guesses—she had reached her destination.

The capital of the old empire.

She looked out at the system, no fewer than three planets dead within the habitable zone, and two more just outside that looked as though they'd been terraformed to tolerable levels. A half dozen gas giants farther out, surrounded by halos of manmade debris, shattered wreckage Andi guessed they were the remains of once great constructions for harvesting tritium and helium-3 from the planetary atmospheres.

She'd seen the great Core worlds of the Confederation, with their billions of inhabitants. But even Megara seemed

like a backwater compared to the planet straight ahead. She
tried to imagine the billions who had once lived there, the
almost unimaginable population of the whole, massively
developed system, but those thoughts were derailed,
subsumed by the realization that all those people, those vast
almost ungraspable multitudes, were all dead. There were no
descendants, no ongoing civilization, no living legacy of
their lives, only the silent death of an unimaginably large
graveyard.

The Rim had suffered badly enough in the Cataclysm
and its aftermath, and she'd seen the dead, decaying worlds
of the Badlands often enough, and up close to boot. She'd
had somber thoughts there, of course, images of those who
had once lived and worked in the places she'd visited, of
men and women, probably not terribly unlike herself, or
those she knew. But she'd never seen anything like the black
and oppressive emptiness of the system through which her
ship now plied its way. *Pegasus* hadn't landed yet, and space
was empty and open everywhere, but the sense
of...haunting...was irresistible.

She felt cold, surrounded by an eerie darkness, as though
the very space howled with the screams of those long gone.
Everywhere she looked seemed to be filled with ghostly
faces, and ancient cries of terror and death. She'd always
know the empire had been vast, its population enormous,
just as she'd realized billions had died in the horror of the
Cataclysm. But now she began to understand just how
grossly she had underestimated the human cost of
mankind's great nightmare. The empire had stretched from
where her people sat in their ship, all the way back to the
Far Rim and the Periphery...and likely much farther
coreward. Billions hadn't died in the empire's fall, she
realized. Trillions had. Numbers like that were imaginable in
a theoretical way, thinking cells in the body or atoms in a
chunk of metal...but the thought of deaths in such
numbers, each victim a man or woman, with a life,

memories, loved ones, was almost impossible to grasp. It shook even Andi's hardened psyche.

She marveled at the incalculable wealth she saw, the raw value of imperial technology arrayed before her eyes…and for the first time, she didn't care. She had all she could ever need, and the things she wanted in life now were beyond price. She'd forego a million ancient computer chips and the king's ransom they would bring in the markets of the Confederation…for one fleeting second with Cassie in her arms, one touch of her hand on Tyler's cheek, the merest feeling of his warmth.

She hadn't come for wealth, nor for artifacts to increase the historical record, save only on one subject. The Highborn. And what she needed wouldn't lay in the shattered holds of ancient shipwrecks, nor in the gutted, shards of old orbital stations. No, her trail led to the capital itself, to the center of the vast, nearly planetwide metropolis that had served as the empire's center and the seat of its imperial government. To the great vaults beneath the ancient city's central zone, which she could only hope had remained proof against the ravages of war and the decay of time.

"The imperial capital would have been a massively developed system, Vig…and it looks like this one fits that bill. The records specified the fourth planet as the capital. There were references to two moons as well…and the fourth is the only habitable planet here with two satellites." She paused. "I think we have found what we're looking for." She was far from *sure* of that, but so far the system had passed muster in every way.

Andi was exhausted, scared…worn to a nub. She'd long been used to the haunted nature of the Badlands, to the feelings of isolation that wore so heavily on prospectors and their crews…and drove no small number to early retirement, and sometimes madness. But this was something else entirely, and she felt as though she had left the domain of the living, and moved on into some dark dimension of the dead.

She'd been driving herself to the brink and beyond…ever since the battle with the Highborn vessel. *Pegasus* had won that fight, and she'd come through it with only minor damage. And the enemy had been destroyed before they could transit and send a distress call.

At least she hoped they hadn't been able to get off some kind of message. But even if she *had* prevented her adversary from sending out a warning, she had no idea how the Highborn would react to a missing ship. Would they send vessels to search? *Pegasus* had won the fight because she'd had surprise…and because Andi and her people had gotten damned lucky. A missed shot, a more suspicious enemy commander, almost anything could have turned victory into defeat. Andi allowed herself the satisfaction of the win—that was almost an instinctive reaction—but she didn't fool herself. If any more Highborn came looking for the destroyed ship, her chances of winning another fight were something between zero…and some tiny fraction above zero.

She'd raced across the systems since then, working day and night with Sy and Ellia, analyzing the scanner data, matching it with their various sources, making snap decisions on where to go next. If she had indeed found the capital of the old empire, perhaps the luck that had seen her through the battle was still with her.

But even if it was, Andi knew fortune was a fickle mistress. There was no guarantee past favors would be repeated…and as dangerous as the journey was, Andi had a feeling it was about to get worse.

"Bring us into orbit around planet four, Vig. Our data mentions a great city, but I doubt we're going to find anything but ruins, if that. We'll pull in everything we can from the scans, maybe even send down a few probes. We should be able to get enough data to suggest that a vast city is—was—down there." She took a deep breath. "And then we'll land." The words echoed in her ears, and it took all she had to control her nerves, to remain calm—no, that wasn't quite accurate—to *appear* calm to her people.

She heard a sound behind her, and she spun around, her hand reaching to her belt, to where her pistol usually lay. But she relaxed almost immediately. There were no enemies on her ship, and even the ghosts she could feel lurking around the system were unlikely to go stomping around the decks of her ship.

"My people have rather more data on these core imperial provinces than yours, I suspect, if simply because our systems lie so much closer to these central areas of the empire than yours on the Rim." Ellia's head had poked through the hole in the deck. She finished climbing up the ladder onto the bridge, and she turned and looked over at Andi. "I do not know if I will be able to confirm that this if this is indeed Pintarus lying before us, but it does match all of the specifications we have of the empire's capital world." A pause. "Added to the fact that it also fits with your own data offers a compelling argument that we have reached our destination." The Hegemony Master had been an invaluable addition to Andi's efforts to track the empire's efforts against the Highborn. She'd had some resentment toward Ellia and her people at first, lingering feelings from the bitter days when the Confederation had battled against the Hegemony. But those had quickly faded, and in addition to Ellia's clear intelligence and extensive knowledge, Andi found herself just liking the Master.

"Take the third station…the scanners are just starting to feed in some real data." Andi gestured toward the often-unoccupied number three seat on *Pegasus*'s bridge. Her ship, its control room, its cabins, the various tubes and accessways that led into the depths of its structure and mechanicals, were utterly familiar to her, every control, every keyboard, every twist and turn. She'd never known any place in her life as well as she did her ship.

But *Pegasus* wasn't her home anymore. For years, since her days as a child fighting to survive the Gut, Andi had felt adrift, unanchored. *Pegasus* had been the closest thing she'd ever had to a home, and she'd developed a strong emotional attachment to her ship. That was still there, but it was different now. She had a home, a *real* home, at least she would if her family made it through the war. As much as *Pegasus* had served her well, brought her back from one dangerous mission after another, she was ready to let the vessel slip into her past. If the Confederation and its allies somehow defeated the Highborn, if they achieved the miracle of peace, Andi was ready to take one last walk through the corridors, and put the ship into permanent storage. *Pegasus* deserved a rest, and Andi had a family, a life to lead. Assuming either of them got the chance…

"This all checks out so far, Andi. We know very little about Pintarus, but what we do have matches this system perfectly. The number and distribution of planets is correct, as are the general sizes of the planet's two moons. There are the correct number of transit tubes. I could calculate the odds of encountering a system with so many similarities by pure coincidence, but I don't believe we need the actual number to realize it is infinitesimally small." A pause. "With the caveat that not all of our data on the system is certain, and much is based on conjecture and extrapolation, I would say it is very likely we have, indeed, found Pintarus."

Andi listened to Ellia's words, and she found herself nodding gently. She agreed with her comrade's logic and analysis, and she'd come to trust Ellia's conclusions. She was satisfied that she had found what she'd sought, at least the planetary system, if not yet the secret of how the empire defeated the Highborn.

She'd heard of the lost imperial capital, of course, wondered as she'd plowed through the Badlands what wonders might remain at the empire's core. Now, though, she didn't really care. Saving all she held dear depended on finding how the empire had overcome the Highborn, and for that reason, she would search the ruins for as long as it took. But the wonder, the curiosity, even the greed at what priceless marvels might be buried under the sands of the planet before her...none of it was there, as it had been so many times before. She wanted to finish what she had come for, and get back as quickly as she could, to all that truly mattered to her.

"I imagine you're right, Ellia. I've never been particularly comfortable dismissing the possibility of coincidence, but in this case, perhaps one system in a thousand would have a comparable layout." Even as the words escaped her lips, she realized the odds were far greater than that. Not one system in ten thousand, even a hundred thousand would so closely match the parameters of their search. She knew, with growing certainty in her gut, and something close to that in her head, that the planet *Pegasus* was approaching was indeed the legendary world of Pintarus.

"Let's up the thrust, Vig. We came all this way...if this is what we were looking for, let's not waste any time." *A voice inside her head whispered softly...w*e might be out of time already. Tyler might...

She slammed her mind shut to those thoughts. They could serve nothing, and only hinder her. And the one thing she could do, for Tyler, for everyone she cared about, was to focus on the job in front of her. The empire had driven the Highborn out, there wasn't any doubt remaining about that.

That meant there *was* a way, some weakness, some weapon or tactic to threaten or harm them. Whatever that was, Andi was going to find it, and she was going to bring it back. She would see the Highborn monsters destroyed, or at least driven away...and she would finally attain peace, and the life she longed for with aching need.

Or she would die in the cold depths of dead space, striving for that goal until she drew her last breath.

Chapter Twenty-Two

CFS Dauntless
Cobol Ventaris System
Year 327 AC (After the Cataclysm)

Barron looked up from his desk, distracted from his work by the familiar sound that told him someone was outside his door. It was an annoying tone something between a bell and a buzz. Some engineer on the construction team when *Dauntless*—still the new *Dauntless* to him—had been built, had chosen it as the default, and in ten years, he had never bothered to change it.

Ten years…has it really been that long? He'd spent more time on the second *Dauntless* than he had on the original, though first loves of that sort never completely died. His old ship had seen a heroic demise, saving the fleet, and possibly the Confederation, in the process. He consoled himself with the idea that there weren't may ends for a warship better than that, especially since the crew had escaped the final end. Obsolescence and a trip to the scrapyard were the likely fates of warships that survived their wars, an end Barron considered ignominious, if inevitable.

He reached toward the controls, to see who was at the door, but before he did, the AI answered his question.

"Admiral Travis is requesting admittance."

Barron was startled. Atara Travis had once been his most frequent visitor, and perhaps the single officer he'd trusted most, both in terms of her loyalty, and her no nonsense willingness to give her raw opinion on any question. Barron had studied the writings of the great heroes of the Confederation's past, most notably the reams of notes his grandfather had left behind. He'd learned much, but nothing so intently as the danger of arrogance, the destructive potential of unrestrained ego. War heroes were showered with honors, and used shamelessly by politicians, and he understood how easily such things created pompous fools surrounded by sycophants. He'd promised himself long before, that he would always seek officers with the guts and directness to give him things straight, and Atara had been the queen of that group.

But since she'd been wounded—so badly hurt she'd hadn't been expected to survive—some bit of the spark she'd had inside her had gone out. She'd been quiet, reserved, largely keeping to herself. Barron had respected her desire for privacy wherever possible, but he had ached at losing so much of one he'd considered almost a sister.

"Admiral...I'm sorry to disturb you..."

"Atara, it is always a pleasure to see you." He looked down at the work in front of him. "And I could use a break from all this." He gestured toward one of the chairs facing his desk. "Please, sit. You know this room as well as I do, I daresay." Not only had Atara spent endless hours in Barron's office, but her own was just across the small corridor, slightly smaller, but otherwise almost identical. She hadn't spent much time there since her return to duty, but Barron had steadfastly refused to authorize its use for any other purpose.

"Tyler...I want to...apologize..."

"Apologize? What could you possibly have cause to apologize for?" He looked at her intently, and he could see she was troubled.

"For being the next damned thing to useless these past few years. For letting it all get to me…in ways I never thought it could. And for letting my own disappointment in myself worsen the problem and make myself my biggest obstacle." She paused, and Barron could see a first. Atara Travis, so long a block of granite, so proud and strong he'd often leaned on her when he felt weak, fighting back tears. "For not being there for you. I let you down, Tyler…and I can't tell you how sorry I am."

Barron felt as though he'd been punched in the gut. There was truth in Atara's words, perhaps, but he'd never considered it in such terms. She had served long and dutifully, and she'd suffered immensely from her wounds. It was true she hadn't been like her old self, but Barron had never thought of that as a failure on her part.

But I should have known that's how she would see it…

"Atara…there is nobody in this fleet I trust more than you. That was true before, and it's true now. You needed time, and I tried to give that to you. We came so close to losing you."

"You didn't lose me. I know it might have seemed that way, but I'm still here. I'm back." Barron could tell from the shakiness of her voice she wasn't *entirely* back. But he could feel her fighting, pushing against the doubts and fears, trying to find the route to the officer she had been. That had been missing since she'd been wounded, and he was thrilled to see it again.

And he wasn't about to do anything to stand in her way. Because she deserved to be herself again…and because he needed her back.

"You still have the last word around here on rosters and assignments, Atara. Give yourself as much of a load as you want…but don't push yourself too hard. Give yourself time."

"I've had time. Too much time. I need to push myself…hard." She looked at him, and in her eyes, through the uncertainty and the glistening moisture, he saw something. A hint of that old spark.

"If you want to drive yourself into the ground, it's your call. You're the one person in this fleet I never feel I have to check up on. Keep the fleet running. I trust you implicitly." He still had some doubts, but he knew what Atara needed from him. His confidence. The same unlimited, unquestioned trust she'd always gotten from him. And if he had to suppress a few lingering doubts to give her that, or at least a partial illusion of it, then so be it.

"Thank you, Tyler." He could hear the strength returning to her voice. It was tentative, but it was real. He'd told himself Atara would find her way back, but as he stood there seeing it happen, he realized how close he'd come to giving up hope.

"So, is that all you wanted? To ask for more work?" He smiled at her, something very close to a laugh.

She returned the grin, but only for a few seconds. Then her serious grimace returned, and she took a deep breath. "No, there was one more thing I wanted to discuss with you. I understand why we're advancing, why you didn't have a choice. The Senate, the Hegemony Council...all the other reasons. But I thought we should discuss some tactics, some ideas and contingency plans."

She looked right across the table, her eyes dry now, her gaze as powerful as it had ever been. "We are walking right into a trap, after all, Tyler. It's probably worth figuring out how the hell we're going to get out of it when it closes on us."

* * *

"The humans are doing exactly as we had hoped, Tesserax. Soon, we will be able to spring our trap...and perhaps conclude this conflict before it continues any longer or costs more resources. Ellerax will be pleased. The report I have seen suggests that the additional resources of the Rim and its environs will be most welcome on the primary front."

"I agree completely, Phazarax, save perhaps for assigning the label of hope to our expectations. It is not terribly difficult to analyze the inferior human brain, nor to predict their thoughts and actions. Their political leaders, in particular, exert an influence that is quite easy to pattern, even to extend into outright prediction. Their military leaders are cautious, that is clear from the slow pace of their advance and the intensity of their system scanning operations. However, they had no choice but to commence their advance, as we determined would be the case, and we need little more from them to ensure their destruction. Their caution and their alertness will avail them little."

"Indeed. I did not intend to understate the sophistication nor the accuracy of our predictive routines. The humans *are* predictable, at least usually. I have found them to be capable, however—on occasion at least—of doing most unexpected things. I have worked closely with them as I have labored to establish the Church hierarchy through the occupied systems. There have been instances, acts of rebellion, efforts that were, in many cases, seemingly illogical, and almost always suicidal. I would also submit that these events have taken place on Hegemony worlds. As you know, our review parameters suggest a greater degree of unpredictability in specimens from the wilder cultures prevalent on the Rim proper."

Tesserax scowled, but the frown dissipated quickly. "I will take your concerns into consideration, Phazarax. Clearly, there is little to be gained from overconfidence." Tesserax turned and looked over at the large horizontal display in the center of the room. There was a star map depicted, thirty systems all around the last reported position of the human fleet. "Nevertheless, I remain optimistic." He lunged out with his hand, pointing to a system. "Here is where we will strike first, Phazarax, with enough force to halt the human advance, and to send them fleeing back toward the border. We will pursue, but allow them to stay ahead of us, even as additional forces attack from lateral transit connections. The constant fighting will reduce their strength, fatigue their crews, erode morale. We will maintain constant pressure, but we will allow them to reach here…" He moved his hand, his finger pointing to another symbol on the map. "Imperial System GK4-3979, the one the humans call Beta Telvara. The first system they entered when they crossed into the areas we control. They will be worn by the time they get there, battered. Their ships will be damaged, their fighter squadrons depleted." Tesserax's voice took on a sinister tone, almost feral. "And it is where our blocking forces will deploy…and we will trap the humans between them and the pursuing fleets."

Phazarax nodded. "It is a brilliant plan, Tesserax, and I have no doubt it will result in total victory over the human forces."

The Highborn commander stared back, a dram malevolence in his gaze. "It will be more than victory, Phazarax…it will be annihilation."

* * *

Stockton sat at a small desk, reviewing rosters and organizational charts. He could have been sitting in his quarters on *Dauntless*, or in his office—his old office, overlooking the battleship's alpha flight deck. But this time he was somewhere else, somewhere foreign, even alien. But it was more than location eating away at what little remained of his soul. He was working for the enemy, diligently rearranging the wing formations, shifting units based on their performance, all to hone the Highborn's assault forces, increase their effectiveness.

So they could kill more of his friends, his comrades.

Stockton had given up trying to break free of the Collar,

at least in terms of hope and expectation. But he still pushed constantly against the device's influence, still struggling to regain control with no expectation of success. It was just about all he had left. Resistance. Even utter futility was better than nothing. Better than abject surrender.

He'd wondered if the Collar had been designed to leave some part of him unchanged but imprisoned. Just enough of who he'd been to ensure endless torment? He wanted to believe that, if only because it fueled his hatred of his enemy, which was the only other thing that remained to him. But he didn't think the Highborn had been deliberately cruel in the device's design. He didn't think they cared enough about humans, at least not as individuals. They needed humanity, to feed their egos, their sense of themselves as superior beings, as gods. But they considered each individual human specimen to be of little value.

Most at least. It was abundantly clear, from the efforts they made to capture him and the time Tesserax spent with him, they valued his abilities. At least until they'd learned how to replicate them.

The torture of watching himself reduced to slavery, a torment worse than any physical abuse he'd endured, was likely unintentional, perhaps even unknown to the Highborn, nothing more than an unanticipated side effect of the device.

It still fueled his rage, though. The thought that his enemies couldn't be bothered to understand the full effects of their diabolical creation was almost as bad as his earlier suspicion that simple cruelty had been a play. He doubted the Highborn had even thought about it, or spared a moment to consider the effects the Collar had on those who wore it, on who they were. Who they had been.

Worse perhaps, as he raged, as fury seemed to fill him, his eyes were still scanning the reports, and his hands still moved across the keyboard, updating the wings, rearranging pilots based on their performance in the recent battles. The kernel that was still Jake Stockton cried out to the heavens in unimaginable pain…but his body and most of his mind, his memories and skills, labored silently in the service of the enemy he despised.

People had imagined hell for millennia, and a thousand versions existed of it in literature, in belief systems. But Jake Stockton couldn't imagine any of those visualizations could equal the terrifying nightmare that had trapped him. Even his wishes for death seemed only to generate biting laughter from the universe.

Chapter Twenty-Three

Reconstructed Hall of the People
Liberte City
Planet Montmirail, Ghassara IV
Union Year 231 (327 AC)

"Your ship is at the spaceport, ready to launch at any time, First Citizen." The aide looked tense, fearful. Ciara wasn't entirely clear if that was genuine concern for her from a loyal minion, or just a worry that she wouldn't be among those she took with her when the end came at Montmirail.

She looked up from her desk. Her eyes were red and bleary, her normally impeccable clothing rumpled and undone. She was struggling to maintain her focus, but she felt punch drunk, distracted. She'd been on the verge of victory. Perhaps she had jumped to that conclusion, become too confident. But her understanding had been based on Admiral Denisov's reports, and on multiple streams of intel data. Gaston Villieneuve had been beaten. She was sure of it. One last offensive, one final strike, and the Union's old dictator would be gone, the road open for her to build a new society...and to consolidate her own power.

That last attack never happened. Instead, Villieneuve, supposedly down to his last resources, launched a devastating assault of his own, badly mauling Denisov's fleet, and sending the rest of her admiral's forces fleeing back to Montmirail. Ciara had been furious when she'd first heard, and she'd even suspected Denisov of treachery.

Until she saw the scanner footage. And replayed it in her nightmares ever since.

"Very well, Simone. See that full discretion is exercised. There is no point spreading panic when we are still not sure what will transpire."

"Yes, First Citizen." The aide bowed her head and then turned and left the room.

Ciara was on the fence. Part of her wanted to go immediately, to escape from Montmirail before it was too late. Denisov was preparing the fleet for action, for a defense of the capital, but even as she tried to imagine the forces loyal to her, utterly victorious until so recently, she saw those hideous images, the enemy ships.

Highborn. They are Highborn. They can't be anything else.

Ciara didn't know all that much about the mysterious enemy that had so challenged the resources of both the Confederation and the Hegemony. But she had enough intel to be scared shitless.

What hope she had fought to maintain began to slip away. She'd fought so long and hard, come so close. Kerevsky could likely obtain sanctuary for her in the Confederation, as long as she escaped from Montmirail and reached the border. And, of course, assuming the sometimes foolishly brave admiral, was smart enough to break off from a losing battle soon enough to escape himself. Her fear wanted her to go—and maybe her good sense, too—but the instant she stepped onto her ship, her struggle was over. Her hopes for lasting power, so irresistible a drug, would be dashed. She would be a refugees in the Confederation, most likely housed in moderate comfort...and watched by Confed Intelligence until the day she died.

If she stayed, if Denisov somehow prevailed and found

some way to repel the enemy…fleeing early would cost her everything.

She looked at the screen on her desk, at the fleet's deployments. *Can you do it Andrei? I know you're good—you'd have lost the whole fleet by now if you weren't—but the enemy is so advanced, so powerful…*

Maybe. She was no expert in naval tactics, but she realized there *was* one way. Killing Gaston Villieneuve.

The Highborn had arranged some kind of Alliance with Villieneuve, that seemed apparent. But what would happen if Villieneuve died in the battle? Perhaps the Highborn would withdraw.

Or switch their support to the other side…

Ciara had fully intended to honor her promises to Kerevsky, to forge a peace treaty and even friendship with the Confederation. But the Confeds were at war with the Highborn. She'd thought about that in fleeting terms before, but now she realized something with cold certainty. The Confederation was very likely going to lose that war. Ciara had made promises, but if there was any way to kill Villieneuve, and to take his place as the ally of the Highborn, perhaps she could salvage things after all.

Denisov wouldn't like it…but surely, he'd realize there was no other war. And if he didn't, well, Ciara had come to genuinely like her admiral, but if the officer's sense of integrity threatened her only way out…well, anyone was expendable in that situation.

We have to reach Villieneuve's ship and kill the bastard, or none of his matters.

And Andrei Denisov will sacrifice himself, if necessary, to do that. He hates Villieneuve as much as I do…

She reached down to the comm. "Get me a secured line to Admiral Denisov at once."

*   *   *

"You have all served well, with courage and distinction. Whatever happens, you will always have my gratitude, and my profound respect." Denisov stood in the center of *Incassable*'s flag bridge, addressing his command staff. They had been with him, as a group at least, for more than four years, and they had served him well. Many of the individual officers had served under his command far longer, and no small number had been with him in the Confederation. He wished them all peaceful and enriching lives, but he knew they would likely have neither.

He'd raced to repair what damage he could in his ships, and he'd placed Montmirail's defenses at their highest readiness. But inside he felt only despair. He couldn't explain what he'd seen, except to assume that somehow, Gaston Villieneuve had managed to ally with the mysterious Highborn. He had no real evidence that the ships he'd faced were those of the enemy the Confederation was fighting so far out beyond the Badlands...but he couldn't imagine what other force could have displayed such might, such unfathomable technology.

He'd been caught by surprise, and the only positive note had been that he'd listened to his instincts, and fled the battle almost at once. He'd still lost almost a third of his ships, but he had preserved a force in being, and brought it back to defend the capital.

For all that will accomplish...

Denisov was an experienced commander, one who'd seen his share of battles, and his tally of victories as well. But he knew he couldn't defeat the force that was almost certainly coming. He knew that Barron had employed his fighter wings against the Highborn to considerable effect, and his first thought had been to emulate the Confederation tactics. But his own squadrons were depleted and inferior in every way. He'd struggled to put as many hulls into service as possible to feed the fight against Villieneuve, but restoring the Union's battered and demoralized fighter groups had been a lesser priority. He had squadrons, and no small number of his pilots were veterans of the fighting against the Hegemony, but all told, he would get no more than four hundred of them into space, and Union attack ships were decades behind the Confed Lightning IIIs, and even worse with bomber kits installed.

Denisov was proud of his spacers, and he considered himself a patriot. But he felt shame as well, sadness that the mighty Union had fallen so far, that with twice the systems of the Confederation, it had never been able to match its rival's technology or economic might. Now, his people were very likely going to die. They were going to die because they lacked the numbers, the tech, the weapons to face this new enemy.

They were going to die, because destruction in combat was a far preferable option to falling alive into Gaston Villieneuve's hands.

He'd considered running, pulling his fleet out and dashing for the border. It was the sensible option, and the only one that offered even a chance of survival. But he just couldn't abandon the Union capital to Villieneuve's renewed tyranny, not without at least trying to mount a defense. If he fled, his spacers would once again be outlaws in their homeland. They would leave behind friends, families, loved ones.

Denisov knew what it felt like to be an exile. He'd made friends in the Confederation, served proudly alongside Tyler Barron and his spacers. But he'd hid the aching loneliness he had felt, the longing for a home he'd never expected to see again. Could he do that to his people? Would they follow him once again to such a fate?

"Admiral…First Citizen Ciara is on your line."

Denisov's head swung around, an almost involuntary reaction. He'd already reported on the situation and his plans, and he hadn't expected to hear from Ciara again until after the battle. If there was an after.

"Put her through, Lieutenant." He slid his headphones forward, over his ears. Whatever Ciara had to say, he doubted it was anything he—or she—wanted the entire bridge crew to hear.

"First Citizen…"

"Admiral, listen to me carefully. I know the enemy—and they *must* be the Highborn—are too powerful, that your fleet is likely facing defeat. But if you can identify Villieneuve's flagship…and destroy it…" Her words faded out for a few seconds.

Denisov's first reaction was disapproval. The idea of targeting a specific enemy leader didn't sit well with his sense of honor. But then his hatred flared hot. Gaston Villieneuve was on the verge of regaining absolute power…and if there was any way to stop that…

He didn't imagine killing his hated foe would save his fleet, or prevent the Highborn and the rest of Villieneuve's fleet from destroying his own. But ridding the universe of Gaston Villieneuve was an accomplishment, perhaps even one worth dying for.

"I understand, First Citizen." He didn't say any more. He didn't have to. If it was possible, if he got any chance—regardless of whether the battle was won or lost—he would kill Villieneuve.

* * *

"Bring your ships forward, Gaston. My forces will destroy the rebel fleet, but it is up to your ships to engage and destroy the Montmirail defenses. I believe that will serve our purposes better than my own forces blasting them to atoms at long range. We want your people to see you as a liberator and a hero, not an invader." The Highborn didn't say anymore, but the words, 'and a coward' seemed to hang in the air.

Villieneuve listened to Percelax's words on the comm.

The Highborn was making sense, of course...but Villieneuve had been completely prepared to allow his new allies to crush all of his enemies. Denisov's fleet was the largest danger, certainly, and the Highborn ships would almost certainly crush any defense the rebellious admiral tried to mount. But the fortresses around the capital were far from insignificant, and his ships would have a serious fight on their hands. He had no doubt Ciara had seen to sweeping out any of his loyalists who'd remained. Treachery seemed unlikely, but perhaps fear could accomplish something similar. Perhaps he could secure the surrender of at least some of the fortresses. But then he shook his head.

They know too well not to expect mercy when I reclaim power...

His reputation had long been useful, the fear that billowed out before him everywhere he went had won many victories for him, without even firing a shot. But it didn't exactly encourage his enemies to surrender...

"Of course, Commander Percelax. My people will be in position and ready to assault the fortresses, as soon as you have destroyed Denisov's fleet.

Villieneuve hated Andrei Denisov. He'd imagined the admiral's death, always in excruciating detail, a thousand times, and he'd promised no shortage of horrors he'd inflict in the exceedingly unlikely event the officer fell into his hands still alive. But what he didn't let anyone else see, what he tried to hide, even from himself, was that he was terrified of the admiral. Denisov was a gifted tactician, a strategist far beyond the mediocre talents the Union's system tended to produce. Before the Highborn had come, Villieneuve had endured months of waiting...waiting for the final attack, for Denisov to come and destroy what remained of his fleet, and to hunt him down. Those thoughts had grown into something like a stark, almost uncontrollable terror. He would face the fortresses, if only to maintain his standing in the eyes of his new allies. But he would wait, and allow the Highborn to rid him of Denisov first. Once the admiral was gone, morale would collapse throughout his fleet, and likely on the fortresses as well. Perhaps he *could* manage to secure their surrenders with promises of amnesty. It would be foolish for any of them to accept his assurances, of course, but it was an error others had made before...and the terrifying might of the Highborn, combined with Denisov's death, just might push at least some of the station commanders to yield.

If they didn't, he would have to destroy them. He would take losses, but he was reasonably confident his fleet was strong enough, and something close to sure the Highborn wouldn't let the attack fail even if his Union ships weren't up to the task.

He would keep his flagship back, close enough to appear to be in the fight, but not in any real danger. Then, he would return to Montmirail, to where he belonged. The planet sat in the center of his display, the Union's capital, a world he hadn't seen in more than five years. He was back, close enough to stare at sensor images, at least.

In a few hours, perhaps a day or two, he would again set foot on its surface, reclaim the reins of power that had been stripped from him.

And he would wash away his enemies, anyone even suspected of being untrustworthy.

He would wash them away in rivers of blood...

Chapter Twenty-Four

Free Trader Pegasus
Planet Number Four (Pintarus)
Undesignated Imperial System 12
Year 327 AC (After the Cataclysm)

Pegasus rocked hard, the ship shaking wildly as it skipped along the upper reaches of Pintarus's atmosphere. Andi wasn't completely certain that she had indeed found the legendary imperial capital, but after analyzing the scanner readings a hundred different ways, she finally allowed her instincts to make the decision. And her gut told her, the blackened, ravaged planet below indeed held the sorrowful remnant of the once-vast metropolis that had been the center of an empire ruling over trillions of human beings for a hundred centuries.

In other circumstances, she would be eager, her mind racing at the chances to learn more of the empire, to discover new secrets of its awesome technology, to uncover fresh details of its horrendous fall. But all she wanted as she sat and endured the rough ride down was to find what she was looking for, and to get the hell out, to return home. Andi had once craved profit, and she still felt a hunger for knowledge…but none of it could match the ache she felt to get back to her family.

Dark thoughts crept all around, worries about Tyler and the fleet, images of Cassie enslaved, or left crying and alone amid the fires of invasion and conquest, tugging at the body of her governess. Andi had seen too much darkness, too much misery, to overlook such possibilities.

Especially when they were as likely as they were just then.

Andi understood fear very well. She had always tried to hide it, to portray an image of the unshakable adventurer. But she'd damned sure felt stark terror, more times than she could count. The final moments of her epic battle with Ricard Lille, times spent crawling through haunted ruins, battling old imperial security systems, watching enemy spaceships moving on *Pegasus*, waiting to see if incoming fire connected, or if her people lived for another few moments. She knew just what it felt like, and the thought of her daughter experiencing anything like what she had almost broke her, even as she sat quietly on *Pegasus*'s bridge.

"I'm updating the landing sequence, Andi, seeing if I can't give us a smoother ride in. It's not like we're coming in against some kind of defensive array."

Andi look over at Vig, but she didn't say anything. *You hope we're not coming at any active defensive system…*

She didn't think there was a huge danger of any operational planetary defense networks down on Pintarus's surface. The old orbital forts, more than a hundred of them, a vast array, had all been reduced to useless scrap, and it didn't seem likely ground installations had fared any better. Not based on what the scanners had revealed of the utter obliteration that lay below her descending ship.

It would be a different story once her people were on the ground. She'd run into functional—or partly functional—security bots and the like on more than one occasion, and she was about to set foot on the capital of the empire. She couldn't imagine the kind of security that had existed…or what might remain still prowling around in the ruins. It wouldn't take much of a remnant of that awesome ancient power to kill her and every one of her people.

The ship shook hard again, throwing her forward into her harness. *That's going to leave a bruise...*

She winced at the pain. It was no big deal, certainly nothing that was going to take first—or tenth or a hundredth—place on her list of injuries. But that didn't mean it didn't hurt.

I must be getting old...

She could see from the display, *Pegasus* was less than three kilometers from the surface. Andi was *Pegasus's* primary pilot, of course, but Vig had handled most of the landings. She'd almost brought the ship down herself, but her longtime comrade deserved better than to get pushed aside just when *Pegasus* was about make her most celebrated landing.

"See if you can stabilize her at around a kilometer and a half, Vig. That should be close enough for intensive scans. We've got to find what we're looking for. We haven't got the time or the manpower to search the whole planet on the ground."

"Got it, Andi. About thirty seconds, then we can do a few tight orbits."

They weren't exactly going to be orbits, not so close to the ground, but Andi detested people who pointlessly corrected things like that. She knew just what Vig had meant.

She'd have preferred orbiting. It would certainly have been a more comfortable ride. But she had to get lower, closer to the ground. She was looking for signs of certain structures, trying to pinpoint precise details she'd gleaned from a dozen different sources. She could scan mountain ranges and large land masses from orbit, but to pick out the wreckage of a building, or a central pavilion—especially when all she might find was a shattered portion—she had to be *close*.

She flipped a switch, and then she spoke softly into her headset. "Prepare to begin sensor scan and analysis."

"All systems are ready, Captain." *Pegasus*'s AI had known its share of different voices. Changing them had been somewhat of an affectation for Andi, and somewhere along the line, it had become an outright habit. The current incarnation was female.

She had spent considerable time programming the AI as *Pegasus* approached the planet. The details she was seeking could take months to find by eye, years even. But the computer could go through vast scanner input data in seconds…and now it knew what Andi was seeking.

Her stomach lurched a bit as *Pegasus*'s descent slowed and then stopped abruptly. The ship was hovering about fifteen hundred meters above what looked like the dried bed of what had once been an ocean. Andi turned and looked over at Vig, even as *Pegasus* pitched hard up and then back down. "These are some serious wind currents." She didn't expect a response. There was nothing to say. She'd been on some hostile worlds before, but Pintarus had been the imperial capital. She imagined it had been a pleasant and temperate planet.

And it was, almost certainly…at least before the Cataclysm…

She wondered what nightmares had claimed the planet, what gruesome destruction men had unleashed on each other there. The seas were dried and pocked beds, the few signs of city development little more than twisted ruins, melted into slag and rehardened. But most of the developed areas were simply gone, utterly vaporized or buried deep under the surface that had now been mostly reclaimed by the encroaching forests and jungles.

"How are we going to find what we're looking for, Vig? If it's even here, it's probably buried somewhere. It will be a miracle." She could feel herself beginning to despair, the true magnitude of the job she'd come to do weighing on her with oppressive force.

"We'll find it, Andi. You did your work, the way you always do it. We've got enough landmarks to search for...at least some of them will still be recognizable enough to spot."

Andi looked over at Vig, staring intently for a moment. She'd been waiting for the uncertainty in his voice, for the inevitable signs he was bullshitting her. But he was solid as a rock. She sat for a moment, gathering her strength, rebuilding her confidence. She'd come all the way beyond the Hegemony, to the very center of the old empire.

I'll be damned if that is going to be for nothing...

"Okay, Vig...let's get moving. The AI's got the data...we're probably best letting it direct the scanning sweeps."

She turned and looked up at the display. She knew the computer would find what she was looking for, if it was found at all. But that didn't mean she wasn't going be searching herself, trying like hell to beat the machine.

* * *

Andi had tried, but she hadn't beaten the AI. A planet is a large place, almost unimaginably vast to one searching for individual buildings and geographic features. Her eyes were sore, burning, and she didn't even try to guess how many square kilometers she'd scanned with them. But the alert had come from the AI, not from her. She still wasn't sure yet that they were in the right place. The matches were far from perfect. But the broken and battered wreckage of ancient buildings, what little was left of them, looked like it could be the section of the capital city she sought.

The AI had done immensely complex calculations, factoring in the position of the nearby ocean—what was left of it—mountains, the remains of what appeared to be bits of an old transport line, and it had assigned an Eighty-one percent probability that it had brought *Pegasus* down within a kilometer of what Andi sought.

Actually, an annoyingly precise 81.074%, which Andi was sure was some kind of bullshit the machine generated to make itself seem more important. The AI had also added the somewhat annoying caveat that its analysis relied on the accuracy of the data Andi had provided. Somehow, it pissed her off, having her own AI give her a disclaimer.

Even the machines are well versed in CYA…

She pushed those reactions away…and focused on what she thought of the odds, assuming they meant anything. Eighty-one percent was pretty good by most standards, but when the survival of so many people, of everyone she loved, hung in the balance, that nineteen percent seemed like a dark void, pulling her in.

Even if they were close to what they had come for, that didn't mean they would be able to find it, that what they sought would be there, or that it even existed anymore. Imperial data storage media were usually durable, and what she had come for *could* have endured over the centuries.

But it could have been vaporized more than three hundred years before, too.

She stood on the sandy soil, next to a section turned to glass by the heat of *Pegasus*'s engines. If the AI was right, she was standing near the center of what had once been the capital of the empire, less than a kilometer from the imperial palace itself.

Though it appeared little, if anything, remained of that vast structure. *No doubt, it was a primary target for someone…*

If she'd interpreted her research correctly, if her translations had been accurate, if the records she'd examined had been reliable…she was standing almost exactly at the sight of the old imperial intelligence headquarters.

The building was gone, along with all the nearby structures. There were crumbled chunks of debris, some masonry and some jagged shards of metal. Andi had seen imperial steel before, but she still marveled at the brightness of the completely untarnished material. She leaned down and picked up a piece, wiping it on her sleeve. A sheen of dirt came away, and the steel gleamed as though it had just come out of the foundry.

"It's a pretty amazing vista, Vig...but we've seen sites like this before."

"Nothing like this, Andi." A pause, as Vig looked around, a stare of amazement on his face. "The scanners suggested there were underground gaps and caverns just below us. From the looks of things around here, the city was bombarded with some kind of kinetic weapons, mass drivers or something similar. It's possible the impacts fractured the geological structure below, that some sections of the city, most of it even, sank down before they were obliterated. Three centuries is more than enough time for the dirt to cover it over, especially with this wind."

Andi looked off to the east, the direction from which most of the air currents flowed. She closed her eyes against the gritty dust in the breeze, and she reached up and pulled the goggles on her head down. She looked out again, squinting, as though anything she saw would be meaningful. "This planet is a wreck, Vig. They destroyed it. Not only the city...but the oceans, the weather, even the mountains look half collapsed. They turned their capital, a world that was home to countless billions, into an utter ruin."

"Are we so different, Andi? How close have we come to destroying what little we've managed to rebuild? The empire stood for ten thousand years. Can you honestly say you believe our own civilization will?"

Andi didn't answer. Vig knew her response to that question. There was no need to say it.

"If there are caves below, we've got to find a way down. If the buildings are truly buried, under meters—or kilometers—of dirt and rock, we'll never find it." *Pegasus* wasn't large enough to carry full-blown excavation equipment, and even if it had been, she hadn't thought about it. She wondered for a moment about lifting off, using the ship's lasers to bore into the ground...but that could just as easily cause a massive cave in, or destroy any artifacts that still existed.

"We've got some idea where to start, Andi. The AI produced a map of underground gaps and caves. It may not be entirely accurate, but *Pegasus*'s scans are pretty powerful." Vig paused, looking at Andi's unconvinced expression. "Look, Andi...if the buildings are collapsed, if it's all a big pile of debris, or it's buried outright, maybe we don't have much chance. Perhaps we might as well head back and do what we can at Striker. But it the bombardment caused a whole section to sink down, if it's open down there...if there's a way in, we might be able to find the old intelligence headquarters. Their data storage vaults would be highly secure. They could very well have survived the bombardments that destroyed the city."

"Maybe so, Vig...maybe so. Anyway, we came this far. We're not going back empty handed. Andi could feel her determination building, her strength returning. The chances of her people making it past the enemy and finding the imperial capital had also seemed miniscule. Yet, now she stood on ground the old emperors had walked upon, where the throngs had once gathered. She wasn't going to fail now.

She simply refused to accept that she might not find what she had come for...and she dared the universe to challenge her on that.

* * *

"Two weeks, Vig. Two weeks and nothing but dead ends." Andi pulled a small rag from her belt and wiped the sweat from her face. Her people had been searching almost without rest, crawling through every bit of surface wreckage, and exploring every crevice or opening in the ground. She couldn't say they'd found nothing. They'd uncovered enough artifacts to rival any fortune the Confederation had ever known, enough even to crash the markets for imperial technology. They'd also more or less confirmed they were in the right place, or near it. The planet was indeed Pintarus, or at least half a dozen broken chunks of massive structures had borne that name, carved into surviving masonry or etched into almost indestructible imperial steel.

Andi was also sure they were in the correct place on that fabled planet. A hundred bits and pieces of detritus had proven that, almost beyond any doubt. But the ancient headquarters of the imperial intelligence services, the location that held the files Andi had seen referenced, the records of the fight to defeat the Highborn, were still nowhere to be found.

"It's been two weeks, but I wouldn't say we've found nothing. We know we're in the right place…and if we can't find what we're looking for, we'll go back and then return with a larger expedition, one with the proper equipment…" The volume of Vig's words lowered, and Andi knew he had realized the problem. *Pegasus*, with surprise, with a stealth unit, with a lot of luck, and the fortune to win a battle against a Highborn ship, had barely made it. Now the enemy was no doubt more watchful, driven by the loss of one of their vessels to increase their security, even in the backwater sectors of the coreward Hegemony. *Pegasus* would be lucky to get back…the chance of leading some kind of major expedition all the way to Pintarus seemed unfathomably remote.

No, if they didn't find what they had come for, and soon, they never would. At least not before the Highborn destroyed the fleet…and embarked on their subjugation of the Rim.

"Andi…over here."

Andi turned. She recognized Ellia's voice immediately, and she could tell from the excitement in the tone, the

Hegemony's foremost expert on imperial history and lore believed she had found something.

"What is it?" Andi jogged toward the sound, even as she shouted back her question.

She turned a corner, around a small pile of dirt and rocks, intermixed with debris. Ellia stood there, with a pile of broken masonry she'd pushed aside...revealing an opening about twenty centimeters in diameter. Andi raced over, grabbing the small lantern her comrade handed her. She held it next to the gap, and she pressed her face forward. There was a large opening inside, a tunnel stretching beyond the reach of the lamp...and heading down into the ground.

Andi turned and exchanged glances with Ellia. It wasn't the first thing of the sort they'd found, but it was the largest. And it was almost exactly where Andi had expected the old intelligence headquarters to be.

"Vig! Lex! All of you. Over here now...and bring all the excavation gear we've got." Andi was excited, even as she instinctively tried to restrain it. She certainly wasn't an optimist my nature, nothing of the sort...but for some reason, she believed they had just found the way to what they were seeking.

She reached up, pulling at the edges of the hole Ellia had opened, tearing away chunks of dirt and broken pieces of debris with her bare hands, even as she heard the others coming up behind her.

* * *

Andi stepped down the path, scolding herself for moving too quickly, for exercising none of the caution one of her experience should be expected to exhibit. And then she ignored her own warnings yet again.

Her foot rolled off a loose rock, and she almost lost her balance, but she recovered, and continued on as wildly and recklessly as before. The tunnel—and it wasn't really a tunnel, at least not in the sense that it was a deliberate path someone had created—continued down from the surface. One side seemed to be mostly the wreckage of a massive building of some kind, and the other was predominantly loose rock and dirt...looking far less stable than the cautious, deliberate part of her mind liked.

But that part of her was utterly subordinate at the moment. She realized that for all her insistence on taking the dangerous journey, her determination to find what she had come for, she hadn't really believed there was a chance.

Until now.

There was something ahead, an opening of some kind...and even more astonishingly, some kind of light source. It wasn't bright, nor did it provide much illumination in the twisting tunnel, but it meant there was some kind of power source still functioning.

That could be good...and it could be very bad. Andi had fought her share of imperial security systems before, but she shuddered to think of the protections that had surrounded the central core of the capital, and even more, the headquarters of the empire's intelligence service.

But nothing could restrain her. Every impulse to show caution, every fear of what might lay ahead, was countered by the face of her daughter, of all people in the vast and tumultuous region of the galaxy still inhabited by humankind, the one person for whom she had come the most.

She followed the path another five or six meters, and then she put her foot down...and the rocky ground underneath crumbled. She fell forward, her body flooding with adrenalin as her foot slipped into nothingness, and her body began to follow. The dim light gave her a view into the distance horizontally, but as she slipped into the abyss in front of her, there was only darkness.

She had been too reckless, and now she was going to die.

Then she felt something on her, her jacket tightening, pulling back. She was transfixed, staring down into the black depths, consumed with fear for an instant that seemed to last a lifetime…and then she realized someone was pulling her back.

She turned her head, even as she fell backwards, on top of the man behind her.

Vig.

He'd been coming along just after her…and she realized immediately, she owed her life to his quick instincts. Her wild urge to race down, to see what they had found, subsided for just a moment. She was trembling, and even as she struggled to control it, she felt her stomach convulse, and she leaned over, emptying its contents. She coughed and gasped in some air, and then she turned her head again and looked at her shipmate and friend. "Thank you, Vig." It seemed inadequate, but it was all she had.

"My pleasure, Andi. You've pulled me out of worse before." He had slid out from under her, and he was pulling himself to his feet. "I'd wager I owe you more than a few from back in the day." He reached down, extending his hand to her.

Andi tended to react poorly to proffered help, almost defiant in her independence. But Vig's aid had just saved her life, and she grabbed his hand and accepted it again, this time to bring her aching body to its feet, and to steady herself. She stood still for a moment, silent, taking a series of breaths, trying to calm down. Then she turned and stepped forward, paying far closer heed to the ground in front of her. The chasm that had almost claimed her stretched along the left side of the tunnel. The narrow passage itself widened just ahead, into a broad flat space, overlooking an immense open area, a vast cavern, formed when a section of the capital had slipped down into planet's shattered crust.

She stepped out onto the small ledge and she stopped

and stare, utterly stunned by what lay before her.

The great chamber extended beyond sight in front of her, and before her eyes stood the greatest marvel she had ever seen. Immense pillars, some laying at various angles, others almost straight, and atop them, statues, huge stone and metal statues, depictions of men and women, standing tall and proud, adorned with strange and elaborate regalia.

And beyond, disappearing into the dimly-lit distance, were buildings, or what remained of them, vast and imposing, speaking, she knew somehow without any real evidence, of imperial pride and might. Some seemed reasonably intact, others had fallen in on themselves, ravaged by their downfall beneath the surface.

Andi looked out, over the stunning panorama. She was unable to speak, to pull her eyes away, even to think of anything, save one startling realization. All she could do was marvel at what she saw, and repeat the same thought again and again.

We found it.

Chapter Twenty-Five

CFS Dauntless
Alantra Vega System
Year 327 AC (After the Cataclysm)

Tyler Barron sat in the center of *Dauntless*'s bridge, trying to keep his face from twisting into a dark grimace. He had never been happy with his decision to advance into Occupied Space, and he'd been fighting doubts since the moment the fleet set out from Striker. The reasons he'd agreed, even overruling Clint Winters's objections, were still valid. From the Confederation Senate to the Hegemony Council, the political leaders had been growing impatient. The Masters wanted to reclaim their lost systems, and the Senate wanted the war to proceed, so it could end...they could get back to their normal pursuits of sleazy deals and building political power.

It wasn't just the politicians, though. There were reports of unrest from the Iron Belt worlds, and signs the pressure was building throughout the Confederation. Worse, perhaps, Barron couldn't imagine the nations of the Pact could match the production levels of the Highborn, or at least exceed them by enough of a margin to make up for the technological difference between the two sides. He'd considered it a hundred different ways, and he couldn't come up with one scenario where his people weren't losing ground by waiting. He'd have preferred the enemy come to him for the final showdown, but they hadn't obliged him in that regard, and as much as he'd valued the period of relative peace and happiness with his family, the bill for that had finally come due.

But nothing had him more on edge than the fact that events so far had only supported the wisdom of his decision to move forward. The enemy appeared to be overextended, struggling to defend the vast expanse of space they had seized. The fleet hadn't passed through any major Hegemony systems yet, at least none that were densely populated with highly developed industry, but they were getting close. And every effort the Highborn made to stop them had failed.

He should be happy about that, he realized, but it only weighed heavier on him. It was counterintuitive, he knew, but he was sure of it. *Something* was wrong…the more he thought about it, the more certain he became. But he couldn't call off the offensive on an unsupported hunch, and even less so because enemy resistance had been weaker than expected. He'd believed the situation with the Senate and Council had left him no choice before he'd left with the fleet. If he returned, back to his starting point, deterred by a series of encounters the politicians would characterize as victories, the shit would truly hit the fan. There might even be calls for his resignation…and he honestly didn't know what he would do if it came down to that. He had no respect for the Senate, or at least not for the Senators themselves. But the idea of seizing power himself was repellant to him, and all the more so because he believed he could pull it off. Tyler Barron didn't want to be a dictator. He didn't want to be a politician. No thought horrified him more. He simply wanted to serve a republic, just one run by honest representatives, and not villainous slime. One that would instill pride in him as he led his spacers forward in its defense.

You might as well ask for three wishes…

"Admiral, we're getting readings from the lateral transit point."

Barron was startled by the report, and he turned and looked over at his aide's station. He even felt the tension, the dark mood weighing on him, fade a bit as the familiar sound of Atara Travis's voice worked its way through his distraction. She'd continued to serve in her role as his senior aide over the last few years, of course, if on a much reduced duty roster. But there was something different, something in her tone that he hadn't heard in four years.

Atara was back. The *real* Atara.

He felt relief, not only because he cared about his friend, but because he knew he would need her. She'd been a vital part of every battle he'd won, and if he and his people were going to find the road to victory in the current conflict, Atara would be a vital part of the team.

"Full scan. Starboard pickets are to launch a spread of probes." Barron paused for a few seconds, and then he looked down at the fleet display, checking which battleship was closest to the transit point. "*Triumphant* is to launch a patrol to investigate the point."

"Yes, Admiral."

Barron figured most people would think he was overreacting. The readings were low powered, and that likely meant something mundane was coming through, a small asteroid or some similar chunk of celestial debris. Even if there were ships coming through, the readings didn't indicate more than a few moderate sized vessels. Nothing that threatened the fleet. At least so far. But Barron was already on edge, and he'd been reminding himself constantly since the fleet had left Striker not to be careless, to take everything seriously.

There was no indication in Atara's voice that she

disagreed with anything he'd said. That was another reason he was glad to have her back...*really* back. She was even more paranoid than he was. Barron was old enough a veteran to not really care what anyone else thought of his decisions, but he was human, too. It always felt good to have someone else confirm that you weren't crazy.

Or that both of you were crazy. He wasn't sure which.

"All orders sent and acknowledged, Admiral."

"Very well." Barron leaned back in his chair, sinking deep into thought. The fleet had encountered a number of enemy armadas, but none large enough to seriously threaten the forces he commanded. He'd expected—feared—that the enemy had been outproducing even the shipyards of the Iron Belt. The enemy had added half the Hegemony—and the more industrialized half—to whatever it had started with. But he hadn't seen any indications of those force levels, not so far. Barron couldn't escape the thought that there should be more enemy forces out there. Why had they come at him with such small fleets? Were they testing him, trying to evaluate any advances the Pact forces had made? Or were they trying to see how their fighters performed? If that was their intent, Barron acknowledged with considerable regret that they had much with which to be pleased. He still couldn't explain how the Highborn had so quickly brought their wings up to such a high degree of proficiency.

But where are the rest of their forces? What are they planning?

"Admiral, Captain Jeffries reports contacts from the forward transit point. Enemy ships coming through. He confirms forty vessels transited, and more coming."

Barron turned to respond, but before he could, Atara spun around and met his gaze. "Energy levels have spiked from preliminary levels at the lateral point as well. *Triumphant* reports enemy ships coming through there as well. No estimates yet on numbers or classes."

Barron took a deep breath. Was the enemy finally striking? Were they making a stand?

He didn't know, but he damned sure wasn't taking any chances. "Fleet order...all squadrons are to prepare for launch. All ships to red alert. All formations are to stand ready to receive redeployment orders." He was ready to respond, to send his fleet against the enemy. But he couldn't make any real decisions, not yet. Not until he had more data. He needed to know the sizes and compositions of the forces coming through the two points.

"Yes, Admiral."

He needed to make a choice, and the one his gut was urging ran against every bit of tactical instinct he had. Should he divide his fleet, advance against both enemy forces? Or pull back, order the advance guard to retire toward the main force, even at the cost of taking heavy losses?

"Atara, I need every bit of data we've got on the incoming forces, the instant we get it."

"Yes, Admiral. We should have updated information in one to two minutes."

The firmness of her voice felt both familiar and unfamiliar. He hadn't heard it in quite some time, and he'd missed it. He didn't know what his fleet was moving into, another skirmish, or a decisive battle. Or the overwhelming enemy assault he'd feared since he'd left Striker. But he knew one thing with reassuring comfort.

Atara Travis *was* back...and she had a fire burning inside her. He knew her well enough to realize she was battling her demons, that she had something to prove, if only to herself. He was still edgy, paranoid, grim about the fleet's prospects. But for an instant, the sound of his friend's voice almost filled him with sympathy for the enemy.

* * *

"Wing Seven command, watch it. They're extending their line, trying again to outflank our formation. You're what we've got out there, so you've got to stay on them." Reg Griffin's voice was raw, coarse. Her people had come a long way in learning fighter versus fighter tactics, but they were far from proficient. She was losing patience with them, not because they hadn't worked hard or done their best...but because they were all going to die if they couldn't outfly the enemy. The Highborn were hitting the fleet again, this time from two points. The coordinated attacks indicated a high level of planning and a lot of skill at timing. It all added up to trouble in Reg's mind, both in front of her at that moment, and even worse, in her expectations of what lay ahead.

It certainly suggested the Highborn were getting more serious about stopping the Pact fleet. And that had her insides tight. She'd lost enough people in the recent battles, but she believed deep down that they had only seen the tip of the iceberg, that a truly massive fight was coming. The Pact fleet was the largest formation to exist since the empire's fall, and whatever small forces had come at her people so far, she didn't doubt the enemy would eventually deploy its own massive armada. The battle she could feel out there was going to be truly immense...and it was going to be bloody. And as much progress as they had made, her people weren't ready for it. Not yet.

She stared at the screen watching the enemy outflanking efforts...and wondering for what had to be the thousandth time how the Highborn had become so adept at fighter tactics. The moves were perfectly timed, and more than once, they'd been so abrupt, and so perfectly positioned, they'd caught her by surprise. It had been all she could do to keep up, to shift her units in response. She'd managed to hold her own, barely, but she couldn't ignore the fact that she'd clearly yielded the initiative. Whatever Highborn, or perhaps one of their minions—Thralls, she remembered they were called—was commanding the force in front of her, he knew what he was doing. Far better than any of the enemy should after so short a time deploying fighters.

She looked down at her port display, at the running casualty figures. There was a certain amount of guesswork involved, but for the most part, the AI kept pretty accurate track of the loss totals. Her people still had the edge there, though not by the margin she would have liked. The enemy had lost just over a hundred ships so far, to her seventy-four. That was better than the reverse, of course, but despite the fact that she was currently facing fewer than six hundred enemy ships, she knew very well that the Highborn possessed, less recent casualties, of course, an absolute minimum of ten thousand. That was roughly equal to the Pact's entire strength, including bomber squadrons and forces left at Striker. The current fleet had just over eight thousand, and barely five hundred of those were in her advance force. The lead units had done most of the fighting so far, but both her scanners and her comm alerts had confirmed that there were enemy forces attacking from the system's second transit point as well. She had no idea of the size of the attacking formation there, nor the state of the fighting. That data would trickle in, though she would have to listen and follow it on delayed comm reports. *Dauntless* and the rest of the primary battleline were almost a light hour behind, and that meant they were nearly two days from the forward forces. The enemy might be coming into the system from two directions, but the battles fought would be separate affairs.

Her eyes moved over the display, checking on the positions and statuses of her various units…and then they stopped, fixed to a single dot on the screen.

It was an enemy fighter, a single one, not looking as though it was part of any unit. And its movement filled her with an icy cold. For an instant, she thought she was watching Jake Stockton, as though somehow his ghost had come to fly across the battlefield. She closed her eyes for a moment, but when she looked again, the contact was still there, flying with a skill she could hardly comprehend. She pulled up the AI's stored results and confirmed that the ship she was watching had taken down four of hers so far in the battle.

Whoever was flying that ship was an accomplished ace. That was clear. What she couldn't prove, but suddenly believed without doubt, was that she was staring at a large part of the explanation for the proficiency of the enemy forces. Did they find a prodigy of some kind? Some human with a natural affinity for fighter ops? That explained some of it, but still not all. Not even Jake Stockton himself had been that good in his first battles. Experience was the missing link. No one could be *that* capable without a lot of combats under his belt. And yet, it was clear the Highborn hadn't utilized small craft before the current war.

Whatever…you know what you have to do…

She angled her ship's thrust, altering her vector toward the enemy contact. Whoever was flying that ship, he was clearly superior to the others. Eliminating him would hurt the enemy's combat strength, seriously if that pilot had something to do with their training and organization.

Reg felt something strange. Fear, yes. The pilot she was targeting was *good*, and she knew a victory against him was far from assured. But something else, too. A hesitation. Was it some kind of respect toward another pilot, one of clearly great skill? That seemed unlikely. She despised the Highborn, and perhaps even more the pathetic humans who served them. But there was something about that ship, that pilot.

It didn't matter. There was no time for such foolishness. She'd found one of the enemy's leaders, she was sure of that. And he was too good for any of her people to handle, perhaps for most of them. Timmons and Federov might have a chance, but they were back with the main fleet. That made this target, pilot zero, she dubbed him in her mind, her responsibility.

She pushed her thrust up to full, moving straight toward her target…and then she saw the enemy formation begin to decelerate. The Highborn force was breaking off, and her target altered his own thrust vector. She pulled the throttle harder, as if pressure on the control unit would somehow draw more power from the engines. Her ship continued forward, accelerating, but not with enough power. She wasn't going to catch the enemy before he withdrew, not this time.

She stared, watching the Highborn squadrons break off, and her people followed, taking a heavy toll on their fleeing enemies. And she watched that single ship, that pilot, moving back toward the Highborn carriers. No, she wasn't going to catch him, not then and there. But she'd marked him, branded his ship and his flying style in her brain. She punched at the keys on her control panel, saving the contact, instructing her AI to scan for the specified flying style in any future battles.

Next time…next time I will get you…

* * *

Barron looked across *Dauntless*'s bridge, toward Atara. The unspoken communication the two had often shared in battle and other difficult situations was back. Though, this time it was telling him they were both uncertain, that neither of them had any idea what was happening.

The lateral attack had been spirited and aggressive, but no match for the main body of his fleet. The enemy forces had withdrawn and transited out of the system after suffering heavy casualties. The forward forces under Garrison Jeffries had also repelled the enemy assault from the forward point. For a few hours, the system seemed free of Highborn forces, something that Jeffries scouts had virtually confirmed through systematic search patrols.

Barron had almost been ready to relax, or at least what passed for relaxing since the fleet had crossed into Occupied Space, and then the communique arrived. Jeffries forces had encountered a fresh enemy force coming through the point. Thirty vessels had transited when the message was sent, and two fresh updates had brought that total over one hundred, with more still coming.

The data was still incomplete regarding enemy ship classes present, and there was no report yet of fighter activity. But Barron knew the data he was reading was half an hour old. The main fleet had been moving forward, but it was still going to take a day to reach Jeffries's ships, and that only if he ordered his newest and fastest ships to accelerate at full.

Just the kind of thing an enemy would do to split up our forces, fight us in piecemeal bits…

Barron knew it could be a trap. He knew that because it was precisely the kind of thing he might try in the enemy's place. He could get up there in a day, with maybe a third of his combat power, but the rest would trickle in over the following thirty-six hours.

And if the enemy comes through the flank transit point again while the fleet is stretched out like that…

The tactical decision seemed a simple one. Keep the fleet in formation, and advance at the speed of the slowest ships. Except that such a course almost guaranteed the destruction of Jeffries's entire force. There was no way his small flotilla could hold out for that long. Garrison Jeffries was a skilled and veteran officer, and the advance guard had some of his best spacers, but numbers had a way of asserting themselves at a certain point.

And Reg Griffin was up there.

Barron detested deciding who lived or died based on their perceived worth, as though a rookie had less right to live than a seasoned veteran. But war was a cruel mistress, and it rarely left him the luxury of choices based on ethical considerations. He might have been able to abandon Jeffries and his people…but not Griffin. She had done something he'd have believed impossible, or at least she'd come close to doing it. She'd stepped into Stockton's shoes, and brought his demoralized and despondent wings back. If he lost her—if the wings watched another beloved commander killed—the effects would be devastating.

Spreading the fleet out over a light hour or more of space was dangerous. It practically begged the enemy to spring a trap on him…the trap he'd been expecting since he'd left Striker.

But not doing it would cost him perhaps the one person who could hold the squadrons together, to get from them the maximum effort and sacrifice he knew he'd need. Reg had become a phenomenon, and Barron wasn't even sure Timmons or Federov could take her place. The pilots who had idolized those two legends from past days were mostly gone, dead or retired. Reg Griffin had become the living heart of the fighter corps, the current, and young, fighter corps…and if she was lost, or worse, if he abandoned her, the consequences could be horrific.

"Atara…" He knew what he had to order, but still he held back for a few seconds. "All ships are to proceed at best possible speed. Send a flash communique to Captain Jeffries. Tell him we are coming to his aid, and he is to pull back and buy as much time as possible."

"Yes, Admiral." Atara's tone spoke volumes to Barron. It was clear she didn't like it, but she didn't disagree either. No doubt she'd come to all the same conclusions he had. If the enemy came through the lateral point in force while the fleet was strung out…

Barron shook his head and looked down at the deck. He felt as though he was making a grave error.

But he didn't have a choice.

Chapter Twenty-Six

Ruins of Pintarus City (Former Imperial Capital)
Planet Number Four (Pintarus)
Undesignated Imperial System 12
Year 327 AC (After the Cataclysm)

Andi looked up at the statue, unable to control the amazement she felt. The empire had fallen more than three centuries before, but the monument in front of her, and the others scattered around, were far older. She'd spent most of her time searching for the records she'd come to find, but the statues exerted a strange pull on her, capturing her attention every time she passed them.

This one was particularly compelling. It was the largest of all those she could see, and a quick spectral analysis suggested it was the oldest as well, at more than ten thousand years. That placed it firmly in the earliest days of the empire, a period from which almost no records had survived.

The statue was special in another way as well. The monuments her people had found mostly had plaques on them, but they'd been worn and damaged, unreadable. But this one bore a name. Altharic I.

There was also a date, and while some of that was damaged, she could make out a number...36.

If that is imperial reckoning, this could be the first emperor…

She stepped back, her eyes moving up and down the great monument, almost feeling an ancient and ghostly presence. Andi wasn't the sentimental sort, but the thought of what she was seeing—at least what she suspected it might be—someone who had lived so many millennia before, who had founded the very empire in whose wake and ruins she and her people lived, was overwhelming. For a moment, she felt the urge to explore, to research, to gather every bit of the vast store of precious historical information that lay all around her.

Then she remembered why she had come. She remembered war and death…and the desperate attempt to save those she cared for.

She turned slowly away, feeling a strange bit of melancholy before the discipline slammed back into place. She was just about to turn and walk over to where her people were searching when she heard a voice, calling to her.

No, screaming.

She turned, pulling the pistol she wore at her side out as she raced down the steep and jagged path toward the main search area. She was unclear for a moment whose voice she'd heard, but after her mind crunched on it for a few seconds, she realized. It was Sy.

Sy Merrick was her computer expert, and one of her oldest friends. Andi's mind filled with images of Sy, lying dead and bloody on the ground, but then she heard another yell. Whatever had happened, her friend was still alive.

At least at the moment.

She whipped around a corner, and she stumbled to a halt as she saw a flash up ahead. It was a beam, a laser, invisible for most of the distance it covered, but bright and easily detectable where her crew's excavation efforts had stirred up a large cloud of dust.

The visible part of the laser allowed her to look back, to

see where the shooter was situated. She turned, staring over the debris and rubble covering what had clearly once been a great open square…and she saw it.

An imperial bot. She was sure of it. She'd encountered them before, and if the one partially visible from behind a mound of broken masonry was of a different type than she'd seen, there were more than enough similarities to eliminate any lingering doubts.

The memories of her encounters with imperial security bots still woke her up some nights, covered in sweat and struggling to hold back her screams.

But those were all badly damaged, barely operational. That thing looks like it's in almost perfect shape…

She crouched down behind cover and fired half a dozen shots at the bot. She didn't think her pistol was going to damage it…but it might draw its attention from Sy, and whoever else it had targeted.

She wasn't sure if she'd succeeded…until a few seconds later, when a section of collapsed wall in front of her blew apart, covering her with a painful shower of stone shards and debris.

She could feel blood trickling down her face, and another two or three small wounds on her arms and midsection from the effects of the blast, but she was still there, and more or less intact. And she had what she'd wanted. The security unit was focused on her now.

Somehow, it didn't seem as great an idea as it had initially.

She crawled along the ground, staying low, taking advantage of what cover she could find. She cursed herself for not bringing more armament with her. She'd gone out the first few days armed to the teeth, but when no security systems had responded to the search efforts, she'd let herself slack off.

That's always when you get in trouble…

She was scared, and a little unsure what to do. There

were heavier weapons in the small base camp her people had set up near the primary search area, but she was far from certain she could make it there. She'd have to cover some open ground, and she had a pretty good idea just how accurate imperial bots could be with their fire.

She wriggled her way forward, peering around the edge of a pile of debris. She wondered if the bot was still tracking her, of if it had lost contact.

That question was answered when she saw more sparkling light in the dust clouds, and the bot's laser tore into the wall behind her, bringing down a cascade of crumbling stone. She lunged to the side, just as a large pile of masonry hit the ground where she'd been standing. She was covered in a blanket of dust, but otherwise unharmed.

She reached down to the small comm unit clipped to her jacket. *At least you didn't go out completely unprepared…*

"Vig…can you hear me?"

"Yes, Andi…I've got you. It looks like you've got the thing's attention. Hang tight and stay low. The Marines are moving into position, and I just made it back to the camp."

A second later, Andi heard the sounds of fire, the heavy rattle of the Marines' assault rifles. She'd almost forgotten Tyler had made her take half a dozen of them, every one a veteran handpicked by Bryan Rogan himself. She wasn't used to having quite that much firepower at her disposal, and despite her still-vulnerable position, she couldn't help but laugh when she saw the burst of fire that erupted all around the bot. Masonry shattered, and dirt and chunks of stone flew all around. The bot itself was mostly under cover, but what little was exposed took at least half a dozen hits before it sank back down.

Andi knew imperial war machines well enough to know it wasn't destroyed, not yet. Even the battered and barely functional units she'd encountered in the Badlands had been tough to put down. If the one facing her people now was fully operational, she expected it would put up one hell of a fight, even against her Marines.

She lunged forward. Destroyed or not, the bot's retreat had given her an opening, one that wouldn't last. She stumbled forward, running so hard she barely managed to stay on her feet. She dove forward, just as part of the bot appeared around the edge of a wall of debris and opened fire again. She rolled forward, landing hard against a twisted pile of metal and wincing at the pain. She could feel more blood on her arm, and she looked down and saw that she'd taken a gash out of herself. It hurt—a lot—but Andi had always been good at compartmentalizing pain. She had bigger things to worry about just then…like survival.

She heard something moving toward her, boots on the gravel, and she looked up.

"Here, Andi…" It was Vig, reaching out, handing her a heavy rifle and an ammo belt.

"Thanks, Vig." She grabbed it, and next, she took a small pouch he held out. *Grenades*, she realized.

She looked back around him, toward the rough line Rogan's Marines had formed. They were firing on full auto, hosing down the entire area around the bot.

All save one.

At first, Andi thought the Marine had dropped down on his belly to grab cover. But then she saw the blood everywhere, and the huge hole in his armor…and beneath that, his back. She'd lost people before, men and women who'd been with her longer than the Marines had. But it still hurt…and she suspected the dying was not over. Not yet.

"Is everybody else okay, Vig?"

"Sy and Ellia are in the building off to the side. I think they're okay, but I'm not sure they can make it back, not until we take that thing out. The others are fine, except…" Vig turned his head, glancing over at the dead Marine.

"That thing's got us pinned down. We're going to have to come at it from more than one angle."

"Andi…"

"There's no choice, Vig. Let me get the thing's attention again…and have the Marines ready. It won't take long to damage the bot, not with those guns they've got. Assuming I can get them a decent shot."

"But if that thing comes out after you, it will bring all its weapons to bear. Andi, you know the ones we've faced were half-wrecked already. If that thing focuses on you with all it's got…"

"Just be ready…and make sure the Marines are on the ball." Not really necessary, she knew. General Rogan had selected the very best of the Corps. They didn't need to be told what to do. They knew.

She turned and slipped back the way she had come, diving to the ground as she emerged from the battered half wall that had provided her cover. She pushed herself down hard, as though she could force her way into the dirt itself…and she waited.

Waited to see if the bot blew her to bloody chunks. Or if the Marines struck fast and hard enough.

She could hear their fire coming from the side, and also the bot's weapons opening up. Walls exploded behind her, and more debris fell all around. But then, the fire from the bot ceased. She stayed low, listening to the Marine rifles blasting away, but not daring to raise her head. Then, finally, she looked up, slowly, cautiously.

The bot was on the ground, just in front of the debris it had used as cover. It was still moving, and still firing too, though its targeted system seemed damaged. The laser appeared to be knocked out, and the projectile rounds were ripping forward in a wild pattern, still potentially dangerous, but far less deadly than controlled fire would have been. She put her hand in front of her eyes when a pair of grenades landed near the thing and exploded with a flash. When she looked again, the bot was *still* moving…but its weapons all appeared to be knocked out.

She scuttled back behind the wall, and she pulled herself

up to a prone position. She looked back at the Marines...just as a flash ripped across from another direction, and the Marine closest to her fell back, screaming in pain.

She'd seen it, too clearly. *Another* laser, visible only where it passed through dust and smoke, had struck his arm, pulling it right off. No, not ripping it away so much as disintegrating it entirely. She figured there was a chance the Marine was still alive, even that he would survive, at least if he got some treatment soon enough. But there was another problem. That shot had come from a different direction, a different bot. And when Andi took a chance and popped her head up to look, she saw that it wasn't one, but three of the units, all situated off the far right, beyond the camp.

That was more firepower than her people could handle, even with the Marines. She had no doubt about that, none at all.

Pegasus...

Maybe...just maybe *Pegasus*'s weapons could take out the bots. But her ship was up on the surface. And even if any of her people could get there, if *Pegasus* opened fire on the ground, it could very well collapse the entire cavern, burying everyone—and the precious information she'd come to retrieve—below millions of tons of rock and metal.

And if they didn't try, they were all going to die.

"Vig...can you get back to the ship?" She leaned her head down, even though she knew the comm would pick up what she was saying anyway.

"Maybe...I know what you're thinking, Andi, but if I..."

"Shut up, and just listen to me. It's our best chance...our only chance. I'll use my rifle's sights to send you targeting data from here. If you run if through the AI, we just might be able to keep the targeting precise, keep the damage to the area around those bots."

"That's a wild guess, Andi, and you know it. Even with dead on targeting, this whole place could collapse."

"And if you waste time arguing with me, those bots will kill us all. Go! Do as I say!"

There was a very short silence. Then, Vig's voice, grim but definitive. "Okay, Andi…I'll see if I can make it up there. I'll signal you when I'm ready."

Andi just nodded, and she wriggled forward, right against the nearly shattered wall. It would take Vig at least ten minutes to get back to the ship and get the guns powered up. And she had to hack her gun sights, connect them to her comm so she could spot for him. That was a delicate enough job on a table in *Pegasus*'s lower level. Lying on her side, in pain from half a dozen cuts and gashes, trying to avoid enemy fire, it seemed damn near impossible.

But impossible wasn't an option. Andi Lafarge didn't give up.

Chapter Twenty-Seven

UWS Incassable
4,000,000 Kilometers from Montmirail
Ghassara System
Union Year 231 (327 AC)

"Division Two is to reposition at full thrust. I want those ships to come around the rear of the fleet, and take position in front of the Montmirail fortresses." Andrei Denisov sat on his flagship's bridge, directing his fleet with all the skill and resolve he could muster.

Which mostly meant constant repositioning efforts, trying to keep as many of his hulls away from the small force he was now certain were Highborn ships. He knew that wasn't a solution, nor a path to victory. The cold reality was, there was no way to save Montmirail, to hold off the enemy fleet as long as those Highborn forces were still in action. Delaying the inevitable end accomplished nothing...save for one possibility.

What he *could* do, just maybe, and assuming he could survive long enough, was kill Gaston Villieneuve. He'd identified the flagship of the former First Citizen's fleet, and he'd done all he could to push his beleaguered and savaged forces forward...a desperate charge to reach *Sentinelle*, and blast it to atoms. That wouldn't save his own life, nor those of his spacers, but it would be victory of sorts. Whatever nightmare loomed in the Union's future, whatever domination by the shadowy and mysterious Highborn, it could only be worse with Villieneuve in the picture.

"Admiral, the unidentified vessels are increasing their acceleration rates and pursuing Division Two."

Even as the officer made his report, Denisov turned and looked at the display. The Highborn were coming on at nearly twice the maximum acceleration rate of even the newest and most advanced of his ships. His mind had always been quick with calculations, a blessing that quickly turned into a curse as he realized none of the ships in his second division were going to escape to reach the fortresses. Not one.

I should order them to turn about, to close on the enemy. At least that might delay the Highborn…for a short while.

The idea of sending loyal spacers to certain death came hard to him. There was always great risk in battle, but sending spacers and ships against those Highborn vessels was just murder. As purely and simply as if he put a gun to each of their heads and pulled the trigger.

They're dead already…

The thought was only the truth, but part of him rebelled against it. The ships could still fight, they could still fly. That gave them a chance…*some* chance, at least.

He could feel his head shaking, rejecting what he tried to tell himself. He'd never been good at ignoring facts in favor of what he wanted to believe, and he'd always been amazed at how adept most people were at the exercise.

"Belay that last order, Commander. Division Two is to reverse thrust and close on the enemy at flank speed."

There was a short silence, then the officer responded, the hesitation clear in his voice. "Yes…Admiral."

Denisov listened as the comm officer relayed his command. He wondered what thoughts were going through Commodore Simonetti's mind, and those of his officers and spacers. They knew, almost certainly, he was sending them to their deaths. Would they obey? Would they mutiny? Would they turn and try to flee?

You already sent them to their deaths. You insisted on making a stand here, on trying to defend Montmirail, even though you knew you had no chance. They're all going to die for nothing...unless you kill Villieneuve...

"All ships in central division, remove all safeties. We need maximum forward thrust now, whatever the risk. All fire is to be focused on *Sentinelle*." His main division, perhaps forty percent of his hulls, were the only ships with any hope of reaching Villieneuve's flagship. Division Two was being sacrificed to buy the time his center needed to go after the enemy leader. The rest of his fleet served no purpose but to stay in position and die. He felt the urge to give them the order to flee, to allow any vessels close enough to the transit point a chance to escape. But could be maintain control over the remaining ships, the forces formed up around *Incassable*? It was enough to ask men and women to die...but would they do so while their friends and comrades were fleeing, leaving them behind?

He held back. He couldn't take the risk. There was no tactical reason to withdraw the rest of his ships.

Tactical reasons, my ass, his thoughts roared inside his head. *Those men and women aren't supplies, they are human beings. And they fought hard. They deserve some chance to survive...*

He looked at the display, at Villieneuve's flagship. That was his destination. There could be no thought of escape for himself, no question of any other course of action...not until that demon was destroyed.

But he *had* to let the rest of his people go. He couldn't destroy a monster by becoming one. Some of his people would have a chance to get out of the system. If they could make it back to the Confederation border, maybe some of them could survive, even to fight again. He couldn't deny them that chance, however slim.

"First Division with *Incassable*. We're maintaining course and thrust, moving on *Sentinelle*. Division Two, hold position, keep those unidentified ships off our backs as long as you can." A pause, one last hesitation before the human being inside him blurted out, "The rest of the fleet is to break off…and make a run for the transit point."

"Yes, Admiral." The officer was scared, that was clear. But there was strength in his tone, more than there had been earlier. *He will die well. I hope we can all die well.*

Above all, he hoped he could do what he knew he had to do. It was his sole purpose then, the reason he existed.

Time for you to die, Villieneuve…

* * *

"Yes, Andrei…come on. Come forward…and kill me." Gaston Villieneuve stared at *Incassable*, and the thirty or so ships formed up behind it, hurtling toward his flagship. Admiral Denisov was clearly determined to do just that, and it was becoming clearer and clearer that his desperate charge just might make it. *Sentinelle* was in trouble, perhaps grave trouble. Villieneuve figured Denisov had better than even odds to destroy the battleship.

He roared with laughter.

Yes, *Sentinelle* would likely fall, Denisov's ships tearing it apart, even as they themselves were surrounded and brought to their own ends. Indeed, Denisov was sacrificing himself to take Villieneuve with him. It was a noble effort, a display of astonishing courage.

And foolishness.

Villieneuve turned, looking at a row of monitors before his eyes moved back to the small screen in front of his chair. Yes, Denisov would likely destroy *Sentinelle* before he met his own end. There was only one problem with his plan.

Gaston Villieneuve wasn't on the flagship.

Denisov had every reason to believe he was, of course.

The orders sent out from the flagship's comm had been in Villieneuve's own voice. That had been a simple matter of recording much of what was broadcast, and beaming the rest on tight laser comm to the battleship from the small cutter positioned far back from the action, where Villieneuve sat and watched as his forces, and those of the Highborn, obliterated the enemies that had come so close to destroying him.

Villieneuve smiled as he watched the finale of his long ordeal unfolding before him. He'd held immense power for decades, first as a member of the Presidium, and then, in the aftermath of that body's destruction, as the Union's sole and absolute ruler. And he'd come close to losing it all.

Now I will have it back…and I will keep it this time. He would enjoy watching Denisov die. It was something he'd long imagined, and in darker moments, had almost despaired of seeing. Now it was before him, the final moments of the traitorous admiral's life.

Time to die, Andrei…I only wish I could give you my special attentions, stare into your eyes as you discovered the true depths of agony…

* * *

So close…you were so close…

Sandrine Ciara leaned back in the cushioned acceleration couch and closed her eyes. She'd waited…almost too long, hoping against hope that Denisov would find some way to prevail. But when the admiral had given the order for part of his fleet to flee, and set out himself on a desperate suicide effort to destroy Villieneuve, she'd realized all was lost. Denisov just *might* manage to kill their mutual enemy, but something inside her refused to believe it. Villieneuve was a hideous monster, but he was a genius as well, and she couldn't see him meeting his end this way.

And she couldn't afford to wait around to see.

She felt the pressure as the shuttle blasted off, moving toward her orbiting ship...toward escape. She was almost certain she would be given sanctuary in the Confederation, but she didn't know what she'd do next. Certainly a life as a glorified prisoner seemed unattractive compared to being First Citizen of the Union.

But far preferable to what would await her if she fell into Villieneuve's hands.

"First Citizen, if you are not fully strapped in, please do so now."

The title mocked her now, the position she'd struggled so hard to attain, the one now being stripped from her, as if in slow motion.

"I'm strapped in." Her tone was brusque, sharp. *You have to watch that. You need to keep the few people you've got left close to you.*

She knew her loyalists were already departing her in droves, and what few remained would soon be lost as she abandoned them. She had the resources to escape, but many of her followers did not. They remained on Montmirail, awaiting Gaston Villieneuve's retribution.

She imagined they'd all be frantically trying to erase any records pointing to their cooperation with her. She almost laughed. Hope could drive people to believe almost anything, and fear even more. But her profession had taught her that such things, electronic trails and the like, were almost impossible to completely eliminate.

And Gaston Villieneuve was a master at uncovering such things. Few, if any, of those who'd rallied to her would escape discovery...and torment.

Thousands would die horribly, tens of thousands. She had no doubt Villieneuve would sweep through the capital like Death's scythe, and she knew the man well enough to realize he wouldn't lose any sleep over the innocents caught in his broad based purges.

"First Citizen...we're going to be undertaking some

evasive maneuvers. I just wanted to warn you."

Her stomach went cold. Evasive maneuvers? What were they evading? Worst of all, perhaps, the pilot was clearly scared.

"What is happening?"

"The ship is under attack. We're going to have to get through some fighter groups to dock."

She knew, in one crushing instant...she'd waited too long.

"We're going to get past enemy fighters? In a shuttle?"

"There is no choice, First Citizen. Unless you want to return to the surface."

She considered that for a moment, but even before she could discount it, the option was ripped from her. The ship shook, hard. The pilots were clearly trying to escape from some pursuer. For a few seconds, she let herself hope they had gotten clear.

Then the ship rocked again, and flipped over, plummeting from the sky toward the ocean below.

*   *   *

"We have to abandon ship, Admiral. You have to come with us now."

Denisov heard the words, but it took a few seconds for his mind to make sense of them. He had done what he'd come to do. He had destroyed *Sentinelle*. He had killed Gaston Villieneuve. *That* was his victory, and all he would have. Now, the choice was a simple one. A quick death, or a chance to survive as a prisoner of the Highborn. Or the most fleeting of chances to escape, to crawl back toward the Confederation border with a few ragged survivors.

Villieneuve's death had made the idea of capture slightly less unthinkable, but Andrei Denisov did not wish to live as prisoner of the Highborn either. Neither did he have the will to survive the thousands of his loyal spacers he'd condemned to death. He wished the survivors among his people fortune in their attempts to flee. But he would die with his flagship.

"Go, Pavel. You have served well. Escape if you can, or make your peace with the Highborn. Take my best wishes with you, for that is all I have left to give, and all of mine that will leave this ship." He turned and looked up at the aide, and he nodded gently.

"Admiral…you *must* come with us. You can't stay here. We may not be able to escape the system, but we're going to try."

Denisov nodded again. "Your spirit is magnificent, Pavel. You are one of our very best. But my road is nearly finished. It ends here."

"*Incassable*…is anyone there?"

The voice coming through the comm was strangely familiar. For an instant, Denisov thought he was hearing things. *No, it's impossible. Villieneuve is dead.*

"Right now, you're telling yourself I'm dead, that you killed me with *Sentinelle*. For all your tactical brilliance, you are a damned fool, Admiral. Did you really think I would let you get to me, expose myself to your foolish and suicidal ideas of honor? No, my old friend…I am here, alive and well and ready to take back all you tried to steal from me."

No…no, it can't be…

"This is some kind of trick. It's impossible…" But he knew it was true. Despair flooded over him, like dark billowing clouds of an oncoming storm. He had been ready to face death, knowing at least he had rid the universe of Gaston Villieneuve. Now he would perish in utter failure, defeated, humiliated by the man he hated worst in the universe. He silently beseeched death, bade it come faster and take him from his pain.

"I have ordered the ships around *Incassable* to cease fire, Admiral. You will not die in the ruins of your flagship. If you would escape the fate that awaits you in captivity, you will have to kill yourself. If *Incassable* is to be destroyed, it will be at your hands, not mine. One final disgrace for an officer finally brought low by his treachery, and his foolishness. You have failed, Andrei Denisov, more utterly and completely than any who has come before you." The grim satisfaction in the voice grated on Denisov, tore from him everything save misery and darkness.

No…no…no…

It was all Denisov could think. He'd lost, in every way that mattered. His life was in ruins, his dreams utterly destroyed. The only relief would be death, and that as soon as he could get see that his people on *Incassable* got their chances—however remote—to escape.

His aide slammed his hand down on the comm unit, cutting off Villieneuve's line. "Admiral, we…"

"Pavel, I am entrusting you to take care of my people here on *Incassable*. Go to the shuttles, take your chances to get away. I only wish you had better hope for success than I expect you do. You have been a reliable and honorable officer, and…"

"Come with us, Admiral. You can't stay here." There was desperation in the aide's voice.

"I cannot come with you, Pavel, my friend…but nor will I stay here, at least not in any form that will do Gaston Villieneuve any good."

"No…please. Come with us."

"Go, Pavel…every second lessens your chance of escape." He turned toward the officers remaining on the bridge. "All of you. Go with Pavel. Try to escape. But don't let yourselves fall into Villieneuve's hands."

The aide looked around the bridge, and then back at Denisov. "I am sorry, Admiral…please forgive me…"

Denisov was confused, unsure what Pavel meant. Then, he saw the shadow of the officer's fist approaching him…and everything went black.

* * *

"They always say Union manufacture is inferior to that in the Confederation. I've long bristled at that, thought it terribly unfair. I am gratified to see that our safety mechanisms are so effective. When I received the report that your shuttle had been shot down, I despaired for your safety. But here you are, alive, and if not exactly well, better than one might expect after surviving such a crash."

Ciara looked up, bleary eyed, confused. Her memories were starting to come back. Her escape attempt, the battle…

Her stomach clenched suddenly, as realization returned in full. She had lost, her effort to take and maintain control over the government utterly defeated. Even her desperate attempt to escape had failed. And Gaston Villieneuve stood above her, staring down with feigned sympathy that couldn't hide the malevolence in his eyes.

No…not this…

She was afraid of death, terrified. Still, she would have taken her life, whatever monumental instant of focused control and determination it would have taken. Anything except falling alive into the hands of her deadly enemy. Thoughts passed through her mind, what he was likely to do with her, all the more terrifying in its way for the fact that she had condemned so many others to similar fates. Some part of her understood the balance of it all, realized she deserved no sympathy…certainly not from the dead faces of her own victims, staring back from the abyss. But mostly, she just felt, pure, unrestrained terror. She tried to respond, to shout, to plea pointlessly for mercy, but her throat was a parched and silent desert.

She tried to lunge from the bed, to make some mad, pointless dash for escape. But her arms and legs wouldn't move. She was restrained, unable to do more than angle her head slightly.

"We have had to restrain you, of course. After all you have been through, we couldn't risk your harming yourself, could we? I also thought perhaps it would be wise to drug you, to paralyze your vocal cords. We wouldn't want you saying anything...unfortunate, would we? Not in your current situation." Villieneuve stood just next to the bed, and behind him she could see soldiers...and something else. The figure appeared to be human, but it was large...very large. Two and half meters tall, at least, and with an immense build. There was something else about him, a strange sense of presence, of one who looked and seemed of a higher order.

One of the Highborn...

She had assumed the Confederation's enemy had been Villieneuve's newfound ally, but she hadn't been sure, not until just then. She had planned for every eventuality, at least she thought she had. The mysterious Highborn reaching across a vast route around the Hegemony, the Badlands, and the Periphery, to reach Villieneuve and aid him in his struggle, had never occurred to her.

Villieneuve reached down, gently stroking her cheek. "Rest now, Sandrine...and when you are well, when you have a bit more energy, we will...talk." He smiled, a sickly sight that made her already roiled stomach a shriveled wreck. "Yes, Sandrine...we have so much to talk about..."

Chapter Twenty-Eight

Forward Base Striker
Vasa Denaris System
Year 327 AC (After the Cataclysm)

"Admiral...we're receiving a message from *Excalibur*."

Clint Winters turned and looked over at the aide. "On my line, Commander."

Winters had been spending a lot of time in Striker's main control center, for no other reason, perhaps, than it made him feel less useless. He understood why Barron had left him behind, entrusted him to gather the newly constructed units and prepare Striker and its remaining fleet for whatever might happen.

Whatever? You know exactly what he was thinking. If the fleet is defeated, even destroyed, he wants you ready to hold the line here...and you will try, fight as you always have.

But could he win? Was there a reasonable chance of turning back an enemy assault without the forces Barron had taken into Occupied Space? Winters would have answered that question with a firm and resolute, 'no,' when Barron had first left, but since then *Colossus* had returned from its lengthy period under repair, and *Excalibur* had just transited into the system with two dozen escorts. The return of the ancient imperial warship, and the Confederation's first scratch-built vessel powered by antimatter seemed like massive additions to his strength. They were far from the only ones.

Confederation production had exceeded even his wildest hopes, making the nation the clear and unquestioned heart of the Pact. But the remaining Hegemony systems had continued to produce as well, and the Arbeiter working in the shipyards and factories, and the newly-trained Kriegeri manning those vessels, acquitted themselves quite well, too. Even the Palatians, with a far smaller industrial base and a vastly greater distance from the front, had expanded their forces considerably. No more than a week before, Vian Tulus's fleet had added three new battleships along with a vast train of ordnance and supplies.

Even Striker's defenses had grown. The base itself had finally been completed after nearly four years of immense effort…but the network of minefields, laser buoys, and fortresses surrounding it continued to grow. Winters found himself in command of a force of considerable strength, even with the main fleet gone.

Anything with *Colossus* and *Excalibur*—and the biggest fortress ever built—was a serious force. Part of him regretted that the two massive ships hadn't arrived in time to accompany Barron, and part was glad he had them. If Tyler Barron was defeated, if the admiral didn't return, Winters would mourn one of the few true friends he'd had in his life. But he would also be tasked with the last responsibility that friend had given him…finding a way to stop the Highborn. *Colossus* and *Excalibur* would be of great help in that goal.

"Admiral Winters…I request permission to dock *Excalibur* with Fortress Striker." Cliff Wellington's voice was crisp, alert. He sounded almost eager to be up near the front with his new command.

That won't last…

Blood had a way of washing enthusiasm into the gutter.

"Permission granted, Captain. Welcome to Striker." Winters looked down at his screen for a moment, and then he said, "Docking station eleven will be good." A pause. "That's a big tub you've got there though, Cliff, so ease her in."

"Yes, Admiral."

"And come up and see me as soon as you're settled. I'll bring you up to date, and we'll work your ships into the OB."

"I'll be there in an hour, Admiral…faster if I can make the docking approach on my first try."

Winters cut the line. He sat quietly for a moment, then he turned toward his aide. "Contact Commodore Eaton, Commander. Advise her I would like to see her in my office as soon as possible. And send Captain Wellington as soon as he arrives." Barron had taken Vian Tulus and Chronos with him, but much of the cream of the Confederation high command was now at Striker. Winters had strict orders not to send any additional forces forward, but that didn't mean he couldn't prepare his defenses…and maybe work out a contingency plan or two.

Just in case circumstances compelled him to…massage…those orders…

* * *

"We cannot advance, Captain. I have specific orders to remain at Striker, and do everything possible to keep the fortress fully prepared to defend against any attack that might come." Clint Winters sat at the end of the table, acting in effect as the overall commander, even though his position as such was far from clear. The documents that formed the Pact had been deliberately vague on the chain of command, not because ambiguity was in any way desirable, but because the distances between the respective capitals and governmental bodies necessitated an agreement that would quickly gain the acceptance of all parties. Arguing over whose officers would outrank whose could have taken years, and by the time the politicians finished their debates, the Highborn would have been having lunch amid the ruins of Megara.

Such confusion would have been highly problematical already, save for one thing. Everyone had been willing to accept Tyler Barron as the informal leader of the Pact's military. Vian Tulus was Barron's blood brother, and Chronos and Barron had forged something of a friendship, despite having been bitter enemies for six years.

But Winters wasn't Barron, and the fact that he'd been designated as commander by that very officer didn't guarantee everyone would agree. Ilius was in command of the Hegemony forces that remained at Striker, and Tulus's legate was a commander named Vestilius. By all accounts, the officer was a skilled and courageous warrior...but he was old Palatian through and through, and by that Winters meant in every way that made him a pain in the ass.

"We have a very considerable fleet here now, with the recent arrivals. What if Admiral Barron encounters enemy forces he cannot handle?"

Winters shook his head and raised his hand up toward Wellington. The officer was a skilled veteran, but he had limited experience serving at the upper levels of command. "Captain, as I said, Admiral Barron was quite clear. So, unless you are prepared to recommend mutiny, I suggest we move on to the next topic at hand." Winters knew his remark had been a bit of hyperbole. He wasn't ready to ignore what Barron had asked of him, not yet. But he knew there might come a time when he was ready to plunge in after his friend, and if that day came, he doubted he could think of it as mutiny.

So much is in the eye of the beholder...

Wellington didn't look satisfied, but he didn't say anything else either.

"However…" Winters leaned back in his chair and looked out at the others. "Admiral Barron did not leave any orders against our conducting preparatory drills…just in case something should change, and we are charged with advancing to his aid. To that end, I have a few fleet orders I wish to implement, and I would like to issue them jointly from the three of us." There were a number of officers present, but Winters was looking right at Ilius and Vestilius, the commanders of the two largest fleet contingents after the Confederation's. Winters tended to be a bit of a rampaging bull when issuing orders, but he had enough statesman in him to recognize that his position as effective commander of the fleet largely depended on the continued support of the Hegemony and Palatian leaders.

"What would you have us do, Admiral Winters?" Winters knew Vestilius was simply asking a question, but somehow, the arrogance of the Palatian grated on him. In truth, Tulus's legate had done nothing so far save support his plans and follow his…suggestions. But Winters still found the warrior abrasive.

Perhaps two wildcats stuffed in a bag together can never truly get along…

"First, I would transfer fighters and crew from the fortress to any battleships with less than full complements, even those housing regulation wings that can accommodate additional squadrons. I would maintain homogenous wing structures on ships where possible, simply due to differences in ordnance and equipment, but based on my preliminary analysis, we may have to intermix squadrons on some vessels. This will require close examination of supply manifests, to ensure that all vessels are stocked with the required items. I don't want to see any avoidable snafus, flight crews standing in front of stacks of ordnance that won't fit in the fighters they're refitting and the like. With everyone's agreement, I would like to appoint Captain Jahn to see to the shuffling of forces and supplies." Winters looked down the table at the logistics officer who'd been instrumental in organizing the massive flow of ordnance and supplies from the Confederation to the war zone. He wasn't an Academy graduate, like most of the top Confed officers, but his competence was beyond question. Jahn had come to the service as a volunteer, the scion of an Iron Belt industrial dynasty who'd come forth to answer the call, and who had contributed more than any other single man or woman to the efficiency of the supply lines supporting Striker and the fleet. He didn't have any tactical experience, but his organizational ability was beyond question.

"That certainly seems to make sense, Admiral. After all, if we are attacked here, the transferred squadrons can just as easily launch from the battleships as the fortress's bays." Ilius had been silent, grim and noncommittal as usual. He had been almost a model of physical perfection, like so many of the Hegemony Masters, but years of war and terrible wounds had scarred his face, and left him with a permanent limp, as well as a hunch forward when he stood or walked. "And I can think of no one more capable of managing such an operation than Captain Jahn."

Winters looked around the table, seeing no signs of disagreement. Jahn didn't say a word, but he nodded slightly when the admiral's eyes passed over him.

"Second, I would have all ships maintained in a state of readiness, prepared to embark on four hours' notice." He knew that would be the more controversial suggestion.

There was a small rustling around the table. Having warships ready to depart in such a short time would require something close to maintaining a constant alert status. It meant a lot of work, but perhaps of greater concern, it would also wear down the crews after a while.

But again, there were no objections. Only Vestilius voiced any opinion at all, and his was typically Palatian. "I am under so such orders as you, Admiral, to remain here while the fleet takes the war to our enemy. My ships will be

ready to depart at any time, on far less than four hours'
notice." It was an empty boast, of course, one that spoke
more of Palatian pride and honor than engineering reality.
The warrior ethic of a culture didn't speed up the process of
powering up reactors and preparing ships for the rigors of
interstellar travel.

But all things considered, if Clint Winters had to face an
enemy like the Highborn, he was just as glad to have some
Palatians with him.

"Your eagerness does you credit, Commander Vestilius,
but I urge you to remain with the rest of the fleet here
until…the situation changes. Tyler Barron knows what he is
doing, and I believe Imperator Tulus supports him
completely. So, perhaps you have no formal orders, but if
Vian Tulus was here now, I daresay he would endorse
Admiral Barron's orders wholeheartedly."

Winters considered Tyler Barron one of his few true
friends, his best friend, in fact. But he wasn't sure he could
ever quite forgive his commander for leaving him behind,
and especially for saddling him with the diplomatic duties
that came along with his quasi-command position. He hated
it, despised every torturous second…but the expression on
the Palatian commander's face, and the simple, if somewhat
sour looking nod that stood as his answer, proved again that
as much as he detested such duties, he could handle them
when he had to.

The Palatians were the weakest of the three major
powers in the Pact, and by a considerable margin, despite
what he didn't doubt were their own heartfelt beliefs that
their courage and warrior spirit more than made up for any
deficit in hulls and technology. Nevertheless, their
contributions were far from irrelevant, and if the Pact
somehow managed to prevail, to hold off the Highborn, it
was very likely the margin of victory would be far less than
the strength of Palatian arms.

Winters didn't really believe they were going to prevail,

though, even as part of him dug in every more deeply, determined to somehow do just that very thing. But if victory was somehow attainable, he didn't doubt that would come down to the fact that years before, a future Palatian Imperator took a liking to a Confederation officer named Tyler Barron.

One more achievement.

Winters knew Tyler had always struggled to live under the shadow of his grandfather's glory…but he'd come to believe his friend's efforts had overtaken those of his illustrious ancestor. As far as Winters was concerned, Tyler Barron was the greatest hero in Confederation history, bar none.

The Palatians might have joined the Pact anyway, of course, despite their history of eschewing allies and relationships, but he couldn't imagine they would have been as controllable, as effectively integrated into the overall force structure, as they had been under Vian Tulus, Barron's friend and blood brother. That could very well be the difference between victory and defeat all by itself.

Ilius broke the long silence, and pulled Winters from his thoughts. "Admiral, if I may ask a salient question…it is all well and good to prepare to set off after the main fleet, but what, exactly, would constitute sufficient reason to…massage, as you put it…Admiral Barron's orders that we remain here?" Ilius looked right at Winters. "Under what circumstances would we move forward?"

Chapter Twenty-Nine

Beneath Ruins of Pintarus City (Former Imperial Capital)
Planet Number Four (Pintarus)
Undesignated Imperial System 12
Year 327 AC (After the Cataclysm)

The shockwave threw Andi against the rock wall behind her, and then to the ground with a disconcerting—and painful— thud. Pain radiated out from half a dozen places, but two decades of combat instincts told her she hadn't been seriously hurt.

She just felt like it.

She wanted more than anything to stay still for a while, to rest and do her best not to move at all, but there was no time. She knew what had happened. Vig had reached *Pegasus*, and he had fired the ship's topside laser turret. While the weapon was a light one compared to the armament of a true warship, it was still designed for combat in space at ranges measured in thousands of kilometers. At a distance of a hundred meters, not even the attenuating effect of a planetary atmosphere would substantially reduce the weapon's hitting power. Andi could hear sections of the massive cavern coming down, cascades of rock and debris crumbling off in the distance, and she knew there was a good chance the whole place would collapse, that she and the others would be buried along with the old empire's ashes.

But the only alternative had been dying under the onslaught of the three most fully-functional imperial bots she'd ever encountered. Two of her Marines were dead already, and two more were wounded, along with several members of her crew. Vig had gotten back to *Pegasus* and somehow managed to fire the laser in less than ten minutes, faster than she'd dared hope…and it had still been almost too late.

You hope 'almost.'

She pulled herself up into a prone position, pausing for a second on her hands and knees as she tried to clear her head. She'd sent Vig dead on targeting data, she was sure of that. But even under the best of circumstances, blasting the ground, hoping to score precision hits on targets as small as bots, thirty meters below the surface, was far from a sure thing. And the more shots it took to take down the targets, the more chance the whole cavern roof would come down, killing or trapping them all…and dooming any chance to aid the effort to defeat the Highborn.

She crawled forward, to the old piece of wall—now nothing more than a pile of crumbled debris—that had served as cover before she'd been thrown back by the blast. She peered over the top, her eyes darting frantically around, trying to pinpoint movement or a flash of reflected light, anything that might give her an idea of the status of the imperial security units. There was nothing for an instant…and then she saw motion. She ducked down, just in time, as a stream of fire ripped over her head, hundreds of small projectiles further obliterating the wall behind her.

At least one bot was still active.

She turned and looked laterally, down to the Marines' position. They were firing again, three of them at least. One of the wounded was still up, fighting. The other was lying behind his comrades, ominously still. Andi knew they had to get him to the ship if he was going to have any chance, but there was no way to carry him out of the cavern, not while any of the bots were still active.

"Vig…nice shot, but we've still got incoming fire. I think you might have gotten at least one, but you're going to have to take another shot." A lie, or at least an embellishment. She had no idea if he'd actually taken down any of the bots, but a little encouragement wasn't going to hurt. She looked up at the ceiling of the cavern, her eyes moving back and forth to the bits of rock and dust dropping down to the ground below. Another shot would be dangerous…

The gunfire over her head resumed, showering her with masonry and metal fragments from the tortured remains of the building behind her.

Not taking another shot meant almost certain death.

She dove forward, crawling around the edge of the half wall in front of her. She pulled her rifle around, and peered through the AI-assisted sight. She caught a glint, light reflecting off something.

One of the bots…

She took a deep breath, and then she said, "Okay Vig…spotting data coming now…" She flipped the small switch on her sight, activating the transmission function, sending the targeting data to *Pegasus*.

She held the rifle a bit longer, long enough to be sure Vig had gotten a good transmission, then she rolled back around behind the cover, hyperventilating as she lay there on her back, trying hard not to calculate the chances one of the bots might have gotten a fix on her while she'd been partially exposed.

Or the chance she was about to become buried under millions of tons of rock and debris…

The fire from the bot increased in intensity, and she realized there had to be at least two of them still in operation. The sounds were all coming from the same basic location…the spot she had just transmitted to *Pegasus*.

"Now Vig…fire!" She shouted, almost impulsively, not wanting to risk allowing caution or fear to stop her. She gasped hard and held her breath, waiting as the seconds passed, one, two…

Then the sounds of debris crashing down again, the almost deafening cracking sounds as the rock above split along multiple fault lines…and began to crash all around.

She looked up, terrified for an instant, shaken by a visualization of the top of the cavern above coming down on her. Andi had faced death numerous times, been tortured by Sector Nine, despaired of escape or victory in more instances than she could easily count. No one would call her soft. But the idea of being buried alive ranked up there with the worst things she'd experienced, and she found herself paralyzed for a moment, lying still, waiting to see if she would live to the next instant.

The sounds of the collapse got louder, and she coughed and choked on the dust billowing throughout the great underground cavern. But the roof held, at least where she lay.

She pulled herself up, struggling to regain control of herself. She crawled to the edge of the pile of rubble she'd been using as cover and peered out, cautious of the enemy. The fire had ceased, but that was no guarantee the bots had been destroyed.

She looked over toward where the imperial security units had been, and she was shocked at what she saw. Mountains of debris, meters high, everywhere around the bots' positions. Unless the units had moved at the last instant, even Andi's normal caution and pessimism failed to stop her immediate conclusion.

The shot had taken them out.

She could hear the Marines moving already, checking on their dead and wounded. And there were shafts of light streaming in from a great new hole in the cavern's roof now, replacing the previous dim artificial light that had gone dark with the last attack. Whatever else Vig's last shot had hit, it appeared that whatever power source had remained had been knocked out.

"Andi!" Her ears were still ringing from the sound of the cave in, but she recognized Ross Tarnan's voice. Ross had been one of her people back in the days when she'd been a Badlands prospector, through good times and bad, including a few when she'd barely managed to hang onto *Pegasus*, much less gather a fortune. He was loyal, and an old friend. And she could tell instantly, something was wrong.

"Ross...what is it?" She pulled herself to her feet and she moved toward the sound of his voice.

And then she stopped in her tracks, her eyes fixed on the large building across the square. The imperial intelligence headquarters.

The building where Ellia and Sy and their people were combing through records, searching for what they had come to find. The building that stood now, half collapsed under an avalanche of rock and dirt from what had been the cavern ceiling above.

Andi came close to panic, though her mind later warred with itself to determine what had hit her first...fear for her friends, or that whatever secret to defeating the Highborn might have been there had been destroyed. She knew the answer she wanted to that question, the one she knew she should have. But she wasn't sure, and she felt a wave of self-loathing in response to her uncertainty.

"...about to try to go in again. I commed Vig, and he's on the way down with some gear."

She realized Ross had been speaking while she'd been immersed in her thoughts. His words came back to her slowly, though she was running eight or ten seconds behind.

Ellia and Sy were in the building. And Ross had been trying to get them out.

"Show me...how far could you get?"

"Not far, Andi. This way." He waved as she approached, and he turned and jogged back toward the building, or what was left of it.

She ran up behind him, and then she lunged around, climbing up a pile of debris in front of what had been the left side of the building. She stumbled, cursing herself for letting panic and guilt keep her from looking where she was going. "Have you tried to raise them on the comm?" She knew the answer, but she asked anyway.

"Yes, nothing...but this building has some kind of strange material in it. Even before the collapse, we could only communicate if they were close to an exit."

It made sense, of course. She couldn't imagine the old imperial intelligence service had been particularly fond of anyone trying to listen in on...well, anything.

But it was decidedly inconvenient at the moment.

"Andi..."

She spun around. Vig's voice was unmistakable. He was a little out of breath, but otherwise he sounded fine.

"Vig...that was a...good shot. You saved us all." He had saved them all. She was certain they wouldn't have held out much longer against the bots. But she also suspected he blamed himself for the damage to the building...and those members of the crew who lay inside.

"Maybe not all..." He didn't go any farther. *Pegasus* had its own culture, and while dewy-eyed optimism had no place in it, never giving up or writing off any of their own was also a core tenet.

"Come on...let's go." She extended her arm, pointing. "Over this way. I think we can get into the section that's still standing." She looked up at the building, and the exposed structural elements. Half of it was still standing, but she wasn't sure how long it would stay that way.

She scrambled up, climbing over a twisted knot of steel girders, and toward what looked like an interior wall, now exposed by the building's partial collapse. "Here...bring that drill up here, Vig."

He climbed up right after her, and he pulled the heavy portable drill off his back. "This thing is pretty powerful, Andi." He looked up at the side of the building, an interior cross section that stood next to the debris that had been the other half of the massive structure. "This place doesn't look too sturdy."

Andi moved forward and grabbed the drill, pulling it, and Vig on the other end, toward the wall. "Give me that thing, Vig...this is my responsibility, and if this place going to come down on anyone, it's going to be me. You can pilot *Pegasus*, get the others home. Go."

Vig still held the other side of the drill, and he stared right back at Andi. "I don't refuse your orders very often, Andi, but this is one of them. Besides the fact that it would take a platoon of Marines to drag me from your side here, that's my sister in there. So, are we going to waste time arguing, or are we going to do this together?"

Andi opened her mouth to argue, but she'd known Vig a long time, and she could tell from his eyes and his tone he wasn't going to give in. There were small chunks of masonry skittering down the edge of the building as well, as if her awareness of its instability needed some kind of reminder.

"Okay, Vig, let's get this thing going." Andi pulled at the front, and shoved it up, positioning the bit on what looked like the side of a door of some kind. She pulled back and nodded, and Vig flipped the switch. The drill cut into the masonry like a knife through butter, but then it almost stopped, amid a hideous, squeaking sound.

Imperial steel. Dammit...

"We're going to have to find another spot, Vig." Andi wasn't surprised that the intelligence headquarters had steel reinforced walls. She would just have to find a way around, some route in that didn't require cutting through the incredibly durable metal. She wasn't sure if she had anything on *Pegasus* that could even burn through imperial steel—that depended as much on the thickness of the material as anything else—but she was absolutely certain anything that could do it, was almost certain to bring the rest of the building down.

She looked up, trying to decide if the stream of crumbling bits seemed heavier to her. She didn't like the answer she came up with, so she ignored it.

"Over there, Vig. Let's try over there."

She was running out of time. She knew that…but she couldn't give up. Not on her friends. Not ever.

Chapter Thirty

CFS Dauntless
Alantra Vega System
Year 327 AC (After the Cataclysm)

"We're picking up more energy readings, Admiral. It looks like additional enemy forces are about to transit in." Atara sat at her station, rigid, unshakable, as she had been for so many years before she'd come so close to death. Barron felt more certain than ever that his right hand was back, and none too soon. The knots in his stomach suggested he was going to need her help as he never had before.

"Full alert, all ships." He turned, reaching down and flipping the controls on his comm. "Stara...I need a status report on wing readiness." His voice was soft, calm, nothing like it had been moments before as he'd issued various commands on the bridge. It had become almost a subconscious act for Barron to treat Stara Sinclair gently, even as he relied on her to do her job. Jake Stockton's death had hit him hard, and it had almost destroyed morale in the squadrons. But Stara and Stockton had been lovers for years, and Barron could only guess at the pain she'd felt at his loss.

Whatever grief she'd endured, though, it had done little to reduce her efficiency. On the contrary, her apparent need to work around the clock had turned her almost into a machine, one apparently devoid of emotion, and barely dependent on sleep and food. On one level—one shameful level—Barron was almost grateful. Her total dedication to her duties had been crucial in helping Reg Griffin reforge the squadrons into the weapon he needed. He did his best to deflect the guilt, telling himself her cold devotion to duty was something that *she* needed. That might have been true, but it didn't change the fact that Barron had to have those wings as ready as they could possibly be...and he would have done almost anything to ensure they stayed that way.

"Admiral Griffin's wings are being refit now, sir. They should be ready to launch in roughly thirty minutes. The rest of the fleet squadrons are on full alert and ready to launch on your command. I can scramble them in less than five minutes."

Barron nodded, a pointless gesture since he wasn't on a video connection with Sinclair. "Very well, Stara. Good work." He wondered if praise even mattered to her anymore. She was the closest thing he'd ever seen to the hollowed out husk of a human being, turned almost into an unstoppable robot. Whether that was her way of escaping from the pain, or a driving need for vengeance—or both— Barron didn't know. He knew a thing or two about grief, himself, but it had been four years. He wondered if Stara should have gotten over it by then, returned to something of her old self.

Would you get over losing Andi? Ever?

The thought had been an instinctive one, and it allowed fears and emotions he'd kept bottled up to escape for a few seconds, worries about Andi, about what was happening to her...out there. He indulged them for a few seconds, and then he managed to slam the door shut again. He didn't have the luxury of such things. To many lives depended on him being at his best.

"Get the pilots in their ships, Stara. I'll be issuing the

launch command shortly." Barron wasn't about the send thousands of fighters out, not until he actually *saw* what came through the point. But his gut rarely lied to him, and it was telling him he was going to need all he had…and soon. The enemy resistance had been light so far, far lighter than expected, and many of his officers had dared to hope the Highborn production capacity was far lower than had been feared. Barron himself did not subscribe at all to that theory, though he knew he would find no satisfaction in being proven right.

"Yes, Admiral. We'll be ready."

Barron held his hand over the comm, feeling like he should say something else to her, as he often did when the two spoke. But he knew Stara was holding her emotions in check, even as he was, and he respected her efforts. He tapped the comm, shutting down the line without another word, and then he looked up, just as a line of Highborn ships began pouring through the transit point.

Large Highborn ships, a new class almost as big as the heavy battleships his fleet had fought four years before at Calpharon. And the battlewagons were each followed by a trio of smaller, now-familiar vessels.

Carriers…

He took a deep breath. He'd wondered where the enemy had been, why they hadn't put up a stronger fight. Now he knew.

They'd been waiting, holding back, likely trying to draw him farther from his supply lines and from any possible reinforcements. That wouldn't matter if his people managed to win the fight…but it was going to be one hell of a long and dangerous retreat if they lost.

And the fact that he felt like a damned fool who had fallen right into a trap wasn't making it easier to focus on the battle at hand.

"All available squadrons…launch when ready." He directed the command to Atara, but first his hand wavered over the comm unit. He might have given the order to Stara directly, but he found it difficult to speak with her, depressing on multiple levels. He wasn't proud he felt that way, but he couldn't deny it either, and he took the chance to avoid another exchange so soon after the first.

"Yes, Admiral…issuing fleet launch order now." He could hear as Atara relayed the command, to Stara, and to every flight deck in the fleet.

He stared at the screen, watching as more and more ships poured through. His squadrons would be launched and formed up within ten minutes. Then it would be time to advance behind them, and to close with the Hegemony forces. Barron was worried, fighting off a feeling that his fleet faced grave danger. But he couldn't withdraw without even engaging the enemy, trying to sustain the offensive…and the faster his people advanced, the more chance they had of catching the Highborn while they were still transiting.

He found himself looking around the bridge, his eyes moving from one veteran officer to another. His people were among the best he'd served with, a match for any group he'd led before. He didn't know what lay ahead, what they were about to face. But he was sure of one thing.

Whatever the Highborn sent through that transit point was going to get one hell of a fight.

* * *

Reg Griffin felt the g forces slamming into her as her fighter barreled down the launch tube. The miniature dampeners on the new Lightnings were highly effective, but they couldn't handle the massive acceleration imparted by *Dauntless*'s launch catapults. Her eyes were closed, but she opened them just as her ship slipped out of the tube and into the deep blackness of space. Thousands of fighters were launching, all around the fleet, beginning to move into the formations she'd prescribed. She was about to face her greatest test, a massive struggle against the largest Highborn fleet yet encountered in the current advance. She had no real idea what the new large enemy ship class was, or what weapons it mounted, but with the mass of those vessels, they were almost certainly battleships of some kind. She had no idea if they carried fighters, as the Rim capital ships did, or if the Highborn restricted their squadrons to the smaller purpose-built carriers. She didn't know which would be worse, either. The last thing she wanted was to face even more enemy squadrons…but the thought of the weaponry those ships could carry if they were dedicated battlewagons terrified her.

"Alright, wing commanders…you all know what to do. Form up your squadrons, and get ready to go in. We're going to hit those bastards before they can get more ships through the point or launch more fighters. So, full thrust, all the way in, and then we fight it out until it's over." She'd trained her people again and again for just the scenario unfolding in front of her. Now, she would see how well she had done…if she had given them the tools to survive the crucible they were about to enter, or if she had failed them, and was about to lead them as sheep to the slaughter.

She could see the enemy fighters launching from their own platforms. She would have the edge, for a while at least, as enemy vessels continued to transit into the system. It was hard to estimate just how many Highborn fighters the ships in position carried, but she had some idea of the capacity of the small carriers. If the battleships didn't have any squadrons of their own—and she hadn't seen any launching from the big ships yet—she would have at least a two to one advantage in the initial stages of the battle.

That advantage hadn't resulted from any tactical brilliance of hers, only from the inherent advantages of the defender against a transit point assault, benefits bestowed largely by the limited lateral size of the points. But whatever the cause of her edge, she intended to take full advantage of it. She had all of her available fighters in space, or still launching. Two thousand bombers sat in the fleet's launch bays, waiting for the orders to follow. She'd almost brought them out right away...the fleet could certainly use the help against the forward Highborn vessels. But the line ships would have their own numerical edge at first, and Reg didn't want to worry about protecting bombers, not yet. Her interceptor wings were pure predators just then, with one mission, and one mission only.

To destroy the Highborn squadrons.

She could see the enemy ships falling into their formations, once again with a precision that unnerved her and defied explanation. She'd seen the first Hegemony fighters going into action during the previous war, looking more like a confused mob than any kind of polished military unit. But Highborn squadrons had flown almost like veteran formations from the start.

The Highborn had enjoyed the same respite the Pact had, of course, several years to hone their skills before plunging into battle. But it wasn't so much time a new fighter corps needed as experience, and leaders with the battle hours to teach the new pilots. That was something the Highborn simply couldn't have...and yet their wings were almost a match for hers.

Almost. She was still willing to give her people the edge, though she wasn't sure if that was entirely objective analysis, or something colored by loyalty. It didn't matter just then. All that was left was for every pilot to fight hard...and to prevail, somehow. If the Highborn kept feeding ships through the point, she was looking at the largest fighter battle in known history.

She was ready, as much as she could be. And she was damned sure not ready, too.

Not to mention scared out of her wits.

None of that mattered, either. There was only one

important fact. It was time to go in.

Her hand moved the throttle, feeding power to her engines, and she felt as though a wall slammed into her as she blasted toward the Highborn formations at maximum thrust.

* * *

"All ships…forward at full thrust. To battle!" Vian Tulus sat in the center of *Fulgur*'s bridge. He'd transferred his flag to the Alliance's newest ship, as much as anything, a nod to the efforts the industry back home had poured into feeding new vessels and weapons to the front. Palatian production couldn't match the astonishing efficiency of Confederation industry, nor could his new flagship stand up to a vessel like *Dauntless*, much less the rumored new superbattleship class led by a vessel called *Excalibur*. Tulus had never seen the first of the new Confederation behemoths, but Tyler Barron had shown him the specs, and he didn't doubt all he had heard—and more—was true.

None of that mattered, of course, not to Palatians. He would have led his people forward in lifeboats armed with plasma torches if that had been the only way into the fight, the only way to stand beside his blood brother in the glory of battle.

Vian Tulus was a Palatian to his core, and he felt the call of battle…but he was also an analytical man, far more so than most who'd previously occupied his position. He owed some of that to Tyler Barron, no doubt, but he fancied at least part of it had come from his own sources. That bit of his brain, and the thoughts if produced, were extremely valuable to him…most of the time. They were a hindrance just then, however, when there was nothing to analyze, no option before him save to fight to the end. Any distractions that wore away at his simple Palatian warrior's code were counterproductive at that moment. He knew just how dangerous the enemy was, and how remote the chances of victory for the fleet truly were. A Palatian wasn't supposed to have such thoughts, nor imagine that courage and the skill of warriors could be overcome by tonnage and ordnance.

And yet there was a darkness woven deep in his race's creed.

The Palatians had been enslaved for a century, before they had rallied and driven away the offworlders. The war that had freed his planet had begun with simple slaves carrying farm implements, even sticks and stones. Tulus was well aware of the legends, and the actual history, that had helped to form the warrior's code, but as he watched the Highborn ships streaming through the transit point, he understood the realities of technology and numbers, too. The Highborn were far more advanced than the Confeds and the Hegemony, and even farther ahead of the Alliance. The enemy's science nearly matched that of the old empire, and their weapons and defensive systems were still only partially understood.

Tulus fixed his eyes on the display, and he struggled to center himself, to drive away all thoughts save those of battle. If his association with Tyler Barron had caused him to lose something of a Palatian's simple and relentless drive to fight whatever the odds, he knew he had gained much more, and that the warrior he had become was a far more formidable adversary than the one he had been.

I thank you, my brother, for all you have given me. I am here, at your side, as we go into the fight, together, as one…

* * *

Stockton looked at the screen, the part of him that was still the man he'd been deep in hopeless misery. He had killed Confederation pilots already, gunned down warriors who'd served him, who'd idolized him. He hadn't been able to control himself, but such testaments and protestations stood in his mind as frail and shadowy excuses. The men and women he'd attacked were still dead...and he was about to kill even more, and lead the Highborn squadrons into a battle that would likely see thousands of his old comrades massacred before it ended.

He tried, yet again, to gain control of himself, of any part of him, just for a few seconds, to overload his reactor, or pop open his canopy, anything at all that might kill him and end his pain. But he failed, just as he had a thousand times over the past four years. He was imprisoned as securely as ever, helpless, even as he heard his own voice snapping out commands to the Highborn wings.

The attack was a powerful one, not strong enough, perhaps, to entirely defeat Tyler Barron's fleet, but strong enough, almost certainly, to deter the admiral, to send him heading back the way he had come.

Which was just what Tesserax wanted him to do.

Stockton desperately wanted to warn Barron. Even a few scant seconds on the comm would give his old friend a chance to adapt, to at least know what he was facing. To know he was already deep into a trap. But it was impossible. Stockton had to sit and watch the Highborn attack unfold. No, worse, he had to help it succeed.

His eyes moved over the small screen in front of him, checking his formations...and the incoming Confederation forces. There were Palatian and Hegemony squadrons out there, too, but Stockton knew the heart of the wave of ships coming in consisted of his old wings. There were a lot of new pilots out there, the number of squadrons alone told him that. He wished them all well, even as he knew he would do everything possible to defeat them, to destroy them.

Perhaps one of them will kill me, and end this nightmare. He tried to believe that, but he knew how unlikely it was. That was ego, perhaps, but it was also stone cold analysis. He was the best pilot the Confederation had—at least when they'd still had him—and the odds of anyone in the force heading his way taking him down seemed remote. There were good pilots out there, certainly, and a few top aces, too…and it was always possible a group could swarm him, bring him down. But he'd been flying for more than twenty years, and he could count the opponents who'd truly challenged him on one hand.

And not one of them had ever truly beaten him.

His eyes focused on a small dot on the screen. It was a pilot, at the leading edge of the approaching assault. The flying style, the skill…it was excellent. The pilot was clearly a master.

And familiar as well.

He'd fought a skilled pilot before, a battle that had ended inconclusively. He could feel his mind, the part controlled by the Collar, focusing on the target, identifying the threat, hands moving, adjusting his vectors. He was going after that pilot.

He cringed, screamed silently in the lost part of himself that was still his. He railed against the conclusion forming in his mind, denied it even as he became more and more convinced it was true. Stockton knew he was good, but even he didn't think he could pick out a specific pilot by watching his flying.

Or *her* flying.

But as he continued to watch—and as he involuntarily began to close on the contact—he became more and more convinced.

That was Reg Griffin out there, his protégé, the pilot he'd left behind as his successor. She was leading the wings, standing in his shoes.

And he was going to kill her.

Chapter Thirty-One

Beneath Ruins of Pintarus City (Former Imperial Capital)
Planet Number Four (Pintarus)
Undesignated Imperial System 12
Year 327 AC (After the Cataclysm)

"Sy? Is that you?" Andi had heard a voice, but it was distant, soft, behind too much rubble for her to be sure.

"Andi?" Still faint, but the speaker was clearly shouting. "Yes…it's Sy. We're back here. Everybody is okay, but we can't get out."

Andi felt a rush of relief that almost took her off her feet. For a few miserable, fateful moments, she'd been sure her friends were dead. "Stay put, Sy…we're coming to you." She almost turned up the power level on the drill, but she stopped herself. Sy and the others were still alive, but they wouldn't be for long if her impulsiveness brought the building down.

"Stay put, Sy…we're on our way." She turned and exchanged a quick glance with Vig, who looked just as relieved as she was.

And as edgy, looking up at the building as she had been doing every few seconds…and likely trying to ignore the bits and pieces of masonry and twisted metal dropping down as the drill bored its way deeper.

"Keep that thing steady, Vig. I think we're cutting through a stable section here." *You* hope *it's a stable section…*

"I've got it, Andi. I think we're almost through. With any luck, we won't have to do anymore cutting after this." Vig did a good job of making pure conjecture sound like reasoned analysis. It was an endearing quality, at least in moments like the current one.

Andi nodded. She wasn't sure there was any factual reason for such optimism, but she decided to go with it. The thrill of discovering that her friends were still alive had buoyed her spirits, driven back her usually dark view of things.

She watched as Vig continued to drill. The seconds, then minutes, began to wear down her optimism…as did the continued cascade of rubble sliding down the jagged wall above her. The idea of defeating the imperial bots and finding her friends alive, only for them all to end up buried under the rubble of the very building they'd come so far to find, fit in with her view of the universe with disconcerting ease.

"I think we're through, Andi."

Vig's words were a lifeline to her, and once again the darkness and pessimism were driven back. She leaned forward, looking toward the end of the drill. There was an opening, no more than a quarter of a meter so far, but it was clear there *was* an open area beyond.

"Alright, Vig…let's keep it easy…" It took all she had not urge her friend once again to drill faster.

The opening widened slowly, until it was nearly a meter in circumference. Vig pulled the drill back, and he started to say something about remaining cautious, but Andi was already crawling through.

She dragged her leg across a jagged section of the opening, wincing as she heard the chunk of metal rip open the front of her pants…and felt it dig into the flesh below.

She pulled back, rolling over slowly as she tumbled through the opening and onto the hard, debris-strewn floor beyond.

Her hands moved to her leg. She could feel the blood, warm and wet, but when she looked down, the injury was less serious than she'd feared. The cut was at least ten centimeters long, but it wasn't deep at all. Her reactions had saved her from worse, and she resolved on a simple medical expedient. To simply ignore the wound.

Barely a scratch...

That wasn't true, of course, and she knew she *should* stop and at least bandage it up. But her friends were somewhere in the ruins of the building, and just maybe they had the secrets she had come so far to find. There would be time for such luxuries as first aid. Later.

She pulled herself up to her feet, gritting her teeth as she struggled to ignore the pain in her leg...and in a dozen other places. She could hear Vig coming through behind her, but her eyes were focused ahead, into the darkness of the building's interior. She was about to curse herself for not bringing a light with her when illumination appeared almost in response to her frustration. She glanced back and saw Vig holding a lantern, angling it forward, throwing as much light into the building's interior as possible.

At least one of us was prepared...

She climbed over a pile of debris, moving deeper in. She could hear Vig right behind her, bringing the light forward as she pressed on.

"Sy? Ellia?" Andi called out, her voice somewhat hushed. She didn't really think a shout was going to bring the building down—at least not unless it was going to collapse anyway—but she held it back nevertheless.

"Andi?" Sy's voice.

"Sy? I can hear you...we're on the way." She pushed forward, reaching out, grabbing hold of a vertical girder as she climbed over another pile of rubble.

"We're over here, Andi."

The voice was close. Andi could feel her excitement growing…even as a small cascade of debris fell almost directly in front of her. She looked up, and for an instant she thought the building was going to come down. But it held.

"Sy…"

"Here, Andi…"

Andi stumbled forward, toward an opening in the wall ahead. Her eyes caught something. She wasn't sure at first, but then she realized.

Light.

She headed to the opening, and even as she did, the light moved…and Sy came stumbling through the doorway.

"Sy!" Andi's excitement almost took her, but she restrained herself. She walked forward, cautiously, throwing her arms around her friend, even as she saw Ellia step through next, and the rest of the team after her. "I'm so glad we found you." She tightened her arms, hugging her old companion for a few more seconds.

Then Sy stepped back, and the smile slipped from her face. "Andi…"

Andi could tell something was wrong. Her eyes darted around frantically, but nobody seemed to be missing or seriously injured. "What is it, Sy?"

"We *had* it, Andi. I know how the empire defeated the Highborn." Her voice was dark, somber. Clearly, there was more to the story than just that.

"You found it?"

"We found out *how*, Andi, at least partly. It was a biological weapon, a genetic one." Sy paused, looking at Andi as her eyes welled up with tears. "We had it, Andi…the formula, the complete data on how it worked, how to produce it…everything."

Andi felt her stomach clench.

"It was in a database I had just managed to access…I was almost in, ready to copy it all…"

Andi could hear her friend's words even before she spoke them. She just stood there and closed her eyes as Sy continued.

"It was destroyed, Andi...in the collapse. The whole thing...obliterated. There's no way we can get to the wreckage, and even if we could...imperial tech is difficult enough. I could never extract anything from something so damaged."

There was silence, broken for perhaps half a minute only by the sounds of pebble-sized debris falling from the ceiling. Then, Sy spoke again.

"We *had* it, Andi. We had it in our grasp...and we lost it."

* * *

The despair had been immediate...and all consuming. But it hadn't lasted, at least not at full force. What seemed like utter defeat had been quickly replaced by thin strands of hope. What had been an end to Andi's quest proved to be just another step.

"There were two remote bases, located out where the Highborn couldn't find them. That is where the weapon was actually developed before it was brought here and used by the imperials. The Badlands, Andi...the bases were in the Badlands...or at least in the space your people have come to call the Badlands. One was a planet called Aquellus..." Ellia was speaking, the Hegemony master clearly struggling to sound optimistic.

Andi felt her heart sink, the fragile spark of hope that had flared in her extinguished. She had been to Aquellus. She'd almost died on the ocean planet, and she'd lost several of her friends there.

She'd also seen the base on that world utterly obliterated when the Sector Nine operatives she'd been facing had released the antimatter stored there.

Aquellus had been where she'd found the folio that had begun her efforts to understand the Highborn, the start of the trail that had led her all the way to Pintarus.

I was there. The answer was there, right in front of me...and I left without it...

She felt the withering blast of self-recrimination, even as she knew it wasn't fair. She'd had no idea then that the Highborn even existed. She hadn't even known Tyler Barron yet, and the idea that she'd be struggling to aid the fleet that had always hunted her kind would have seemed preposterous.

Still, she'd been so close...

"Aquellus was destroyed, Ellia. At least the base on the planet was. Antimatter explosion. Nothing is left. I know...I was there."

The Hegemony master returned her gaze, a look of surprise yielding almost at once to one of sympathy as she saw the pain in Andi's eyes.

"That is...unfortunate, Andi. But the records we found indicate there were *two* different institutions, no doubt a redundancy to insure against discovery by the Highborn. The other planet is in the Badlands as well, though on the far side from Aquellus, close to the outer edge. A planet called Bellastre."

Andi looked back at Ellia. The name was almost familiar, as though she'd heard it somewhere or seen it on some map. *That could be wishful thinking, too.* "Do you have a location?"

Ellia looked down. "No, Andi. No precise locational data on either, just some vague references. I was able to conclude they are both in the Badlands, and that Bellastre is on the outer perimeter. But no specific positional coordinates, no route to get there." A pause. "Still, I *have* to believe we can find it. We *do* have some system data that should be sufficient to confirm it if we're able to locate it...much as we did here."

"We came all this way to get directions...back in the

other direction from where we started?"

Ellia didn't answer right away. Andi understood. They very well might have found what they'd come for already…if they hadn't blasted the place to dust. Andi was angry with herself, while at the same time realizing she hadn't had a choice. If she hadn't let Vig use the ship's lasers, they'd all be dead by then. Whatever overwhelming frustration they all felt, at least they were still alive. Still in the fight.

But those shots destroyed what we came to get…we came here for nothing…

Another half-truth, she knew. The information Ellia and Sy had secured was extremely valuable. First, it confirmed what she had hoped. The empire *had* developed a method for driving the Highborn out. Andi had imagined more of a physical weapon system, but the more she thought about it, the more she realized a biological approach was probably better. Especially if what Ellia had just told her a few moments before was true—and the only record of that was now the Master's memory. The Highborn had fled only months after the weapon's initial implementation, and the artificial virus did not harm normal humans. The idea of using the Highborn's engineered genetics, turning the genes that fueled their feelings of superiority against them, appealed to Andi's vengeful side.

And that was a large and potent part of who she was…at least with those who asked for her wrath. The Highborn had taken her from Tyler, from her child. She would try to destroy them because they were a deadly threat…but she would also do it because she *wanted* to.

"Okay, let's get back to the ship now…before the rest of this place comes down. What we want is far from here, on the other side of Striker." She turned around. "Vig, get back up to the surface, and get the ship ready. We're lifting off as soon as we can get everyone back onboard."

"Yes, Andi…we can be ready in twenty minutes, maybe

fifteen if Lex and I hurry."

"Then hurry." Vig nodded, and then he turned around, moving back toward the surface.

Andi glanced around, looking over the ruins of the cavern, and the patchy light now streaming through the gaping hole in the roof. Two of the Marines were carrying out the last body. Andi had never been one to place any real value on the physical remains of the dead, no matter how close they were to her. But she respected the Marines, and she knew they valued bringing their lost comrades back from their battles.

And there was no question they had saved the rest of her people. Her crew would never have held out long enough for Vig to get back to the ship, not without the Marines. She'd almost argued with Tyler about taking them along, and now she just closed her eyes for a few seconds and breathed a sigh of relief. She hadn't succeeded in her mission, at least not completely.

But she hadn't failed either.

At least not completely.

"Let's go, Ellia, Sy…it's time to get the hell out of here."

Chapter Thirty-Two

Reconstructed Hall of the People
Liberte City
Planet Montmirail, Ghassara IV
Union Year 231 (327 AC)

"I must thank you, Sandrine. Your efforts to rebuild the Hall of the People were rewarded with great success...even if the rest of your insurrection ended rather less triumphantly. My office—the one you styled your own for a period of time—is quite magnificent. Though, I have had to remove the garish furnishings. You proved somewhat more capable than I'd expected as a rebel, but I'm afraid your tastes in interior design still leave much to be desired."

Ciara could see Villieneuve's face staring down at her, even as she endured his gloating. Something like that would have been infuriating, if she hadn't been utterly consumed by the certainty that far worse awaited her.

She'd spent two weeks in the hospital, and her wounds had been mostly mended. She was still sore, and she suspected she wasn't really fully healed. But that didn't matter. Not while she lay strapped down to the cold metal platform, unable to move.

Unable to do anything expect listen to her feared and hated enemy taunt her...before he gave the order for her true nightmare to begin.

"Now, Sandrine, as much as I enjoy our little chats, I'm afraid we have some serious business to discuss. My people have rounded up a considerable number of your accomplices, but it has been some years since I have been on Montmirail, and I'm afraid my knowledge of goings on in the capital is not what it once was. You can help me with that. You can help by providing a list of *everyone* who participated in or cooperated with your fraudulent government. Everyone, in fact, who aided you in any way. I want them all, even the cooks who prepared your meals. I am quite resolved to sweep Montmirail clean of all traitors." He paused, and when he continued, a malevolence slipped into his voice. "You *know* you will help me, Sandrine, one way or another. You are quite aware how effective our methods can be. My recollection is that you were not terribly hesitant to employ them in your own operations back in the day. So, why not just tell me what I want to know? You will do so in any event, but if you cooperate, perhaps things can go less harshly for you."

Ciara looked back at Villieneuve. Restrained as she was, it was all she *could* do.

"You may speak, Sandrine. I have ordered the cessation of the drugging protocol that paralyzed your vocal cords."

"You will...torture...me anyway..." Villieneuve had told her the truth. She *could* speak, though every word was an ordeal. They came out as virtual whispers, and the idea of yelling or screaming seemed as unlikely as getting up and walking out.

"You are probably right, Sandrine." He smiled, a sickly, terrifying grin that froze her insides. "You caused be terrible harm. You stabbed me in the back after I favored you, advanced you. Do you believe you have a right to expect anything else? You, one who tortured your own victims, who saw their mangled bodies thrown into the disposal units like old garbage?" He paused, but not long enough for her to respond. "You have earned what awaits you, Sandrine...but still, I might be inclined to lessen the severity a degree, to grant you a quicker death. *If* I am convinced you have provided me all the names I seek."

She didn't believe him, not really. But any hope of lessening the torment that lay ahead for her exerted a powerful pull, enough even to compel her to betray all those who had supported her, who had served her faithfully. She hadn't often allowed ethics and morals to guide her actions, but the thought of exposing her allies, those few who might have escaped detection, sickened her. Still, she knew she'd do anything to escape the horrors looming over her, even for the slightest chance of lessening her torment.

"Release me. Allow me to leave...and I will tell you what you want to know."

Villieneuve laughed caustically. "Sector Nine *does* teach operatives to negotiate, that is clear...still, Sandrine, I think your starting position is a little extreme. You know that is not going to happen. Even if I was willing to overlook all your transgressions against me, if I released you, you would only continue to conspire against me. It is in your blood, and I understand it, as few could. Do you really expect me to believe you will go to the Confederation if I release you, settle somewhere—assuming they will have you—and grow vegetables, or squeeze out a couple babies?" He laughed again. "No, Sandrine, you are a creature like me, and for that affinity, I am willing to offer you this chance just one more time. Give me everyone—*everyone*—who participated or assisted, or even sympathized with, your traitorous rebellion, and I will grant you a reasonably quick death." He stared at her, and her already cold blood almost froze. "Refuse this last chance, and I will still get everything I need. Your resistance will only delay my efforts a bit, and there won't be much of you left to execute when I'm done."

She stared back, stuck between stark terror and her near certainty that she couldn't trust a thing Villieneuve told her.

She was wavering, trying to maintain what remained of her courage, but she could feel it slipping away.

Then: "Gaston, if you have a moment." It was the tall man. His voice was deep, almost defying disobedience in anything he uttered.

Villieneuve turned immediately and walked out of the room. She could feel *his* fear…and with what remained to her of clarity and control, she relished it.

* * *

Andrei Denisov sat silently in the center of the cruiser's bridge, staring at the screen in the front, and at the battleship it displayed. He had been furious at his aide when he'd first awakened. Not for striking him, though assaulting a superior officer *was* a capital offense in the Union service, but for compelling him to live. Pavel Milovia had not only gotten him out of the Ghassara system, under the nose of Villieneuve's fleet, and those of his Highborn allies, but he had also managed to reassemble close to three dozen ships from the fleet. The survivors had been mostly cruisers and escorts, fast ships that had managed to flee the beleaguered capital system in time, but now two battleships had joined them. It wasn't enough force to mount any kind of serious fight against Villieneuve or his allies, but it was too much for Denisov to ignore in favor of wallowing in self-pity. The cold misery was still there, but he could feel the call to duty pulling him slowly from it, and back to where he belonged.

And from where he wanted more than anything to flee.

"Admiral, *Casaleon* and *Muralan* are in position on the flanks as ordered. The fleet is ready."

Ready…ready for what? For me to lead it? To call these battered hulls a fleet, as though that would make it so? What can they—we—do? There is only one choice. Flee again to the Confederation…and watch and see what kind of nightmare becomes of our home…

"All ships are to engage engines at 20g thrust. Course

directly for Alsatiana transit point." Denisov had led his fleet to almost total destruction, and in every way he was still capable of *feeling* anything, he found it grotesque that he was still in command of the survivors. But his attempts to step aside, to stand down, even to surrender himself to his spacers, to accept their judgment of him and whatever punishment they decreed, had been rebuffed by the almost unanimous support of all who remained of the crews of his once powerful fleet. Acclamations came at him from all directions. From the bridge of the cruiser *Declanne* first, where he'd placed his flag, leading first six refugee ships, the seed of a force that now numbered thirty-four hulls. From the comm unit, in rapid succession, as every ship that joined the growing flotilla affirmed him as the choice of its officers and crew to lead them all. Even from the dead and dying in the sickbays, men and women who'd been broken and burned carrying out his commands. Spacers lying burned in agony, leaning upward and saluting him with their dying strength. It was too much to endure.

He'd tried to refuse, but it quickly became apparent that fate wasn't done with him yet. He was still the admiral, at least as far as the spacers were concerned, and that meant the walls of his prison were unbreakable. The death he'd intended, the end that could only relieve him of his misery, was out of reach, at least until the fates of war so decreed that he die. Duty bound him more tightly to a losing cause than any chains could have.

"Admiral, Captain Droute wishes to know if you want to transfer the flag to *Casaleon*."

Denisov turned his head, but he didn't answer immediately. He'd never even thought about moving to the larger of the heavy ships. Regulation stipulated that a fleet commander fly his flag from an available battleship, and the largest one available unless age and other factors provided clear cause to choose another vessel.

What the hell does regulation matter now anyway?

The navy he had served was gone, dead. He'd considered his fleet fighting years earlier alongside the Confeds to be the rightful Union navy, even if it served in exile. But the pathetic cluster of ships he had left made that point of view seem ridiculous. He and his people were fugitives, nothing more...and they would be lucky to escape across the border into the Confederation.

He took a deep breath. "Negative, Lieutenant. I'm going to stay here. Please offer my thanks to Captain Droute for his loyalty, but I think getting the fleet to a place of relative safety is my first and only concern right now."

"Yes, Admiral."

Denisov closed his eyes for a moment, and he tried to tell himself his cause was still alive, that as long as he had ships under arms, his people weren't truly defeated. Such efforts had worked for him in the past, but now they failed utterly. All but ten of his ships had heavy damage, and his supply situation was critical. If his people were engaged before they could cross the frontier, they were finished. And even if they escaped, they were a tattered remnant, incapable of action on their own, even of fueling and arming their own ships.

That looked a lot like defeat to him, no matter how many wild mental gymnastics he attempted.

* * *

"I appreciate your anger, and your thirst for revenge. Indeed, nothing is so grating as the arrogance of an inferior." Percelax towered above Villieneuve, astonished that the Union dictator seemed to miss the true meaning of his words. He'd shown something approaching respect to Villieneuve, and to label such efforts as tiresome was a remarkable understatement. It took considerable control not to order the Union leader to his knees, to beg favor from one who was as a god to him. But expediency was his primary concern, at least at that moment.

"Nevertheless, Gaston, from what I know of this subject, and of her past dealings, I believe she can be useful to us alive…and well."

Villieneuve was shaking his head, even as Percelax finished, something that infuriated the Highborn and further tested his patience. Still, he held his anger. There would be a time, but it was not quite yet.

"Percelax, I am deeply grateful for your aid in defeating my enemies. Your forces were greatly helpful."

Our forces were critical. I would say so! You would have lost without us. Indeed, you were on the verge of utter defeat when we contacted you.

Still, the Highborn said nothing.

"However, your people do not understand mine, I fear. It is essential that Sandrine Ciara receive the treatment that is due her. She has information I need, and while I can likely expose most of those involved in her treason without her, she is the surest and quickest way to uncover them all. Besides, it is essential to make an example of her. Even if I was willing to grant her clemency as an individual—which I most certainly am not—I could never take such a step. Anything except the harshest of punishments would only encourage others to try as she did. Your people may have different motivations, but the Union population is controlled by fear, by stark terror of the consequences of disobedience or rebellion."

You do not know anger, you lowborn mongrel. One day, I will show you how the gods feel rage…and you will quake in abject terror…

"You know little of the resources at my disposal, Gaston, nor the technology behind them. Your methods of torture are primitive tools for interrogation, unpredictable and often slow to achieve complete success. I can assure you, we can obtain a list of names for you, a quite complete one, at least as far as Sandrine Ciara's knowledge extends, and we can do so almost immediately, and without injuring her."

"There is no concern about injury, Percelax. We are quite skilled at keeping subjects alive until their interrogations are complete. And when hers is done, she must die anyway."

"No." The word was firm, the voice loud and commanding. "I told you Sandrine Ciara would be useful to us...and shortly, I will show you how. For now, you must accept my word on the matter. Surely, you are indebted to us for all we have done for you. Do as I...request..." It took considerable effort not to say 'command.' "...and you will have our thanks, and our continued support."

Villieneuve was silent, and for a moment, Percelax thought the Union dictator might find the courage and resolve to resist. That would force his hand, and complicate his mission. Tesserax had been clear. If at all possible, he was to control the Union through diplomacy and not force. At least until it was time to execute Plan Alpha.

A moment later, Villieneuve nodded, the Highborn knew the human had given in.

"I will do as you ask, Percelax...for now. But I cannot guarantee anything permanent."

The impertinence of the human was almost unbearable...but Percelax knew he wouldn't have to take it for long. Soon, Villieneuve, and all the humans on the Rim, would learn their places.

They would learn them, or they would die.

Chapter Thirty-Three

CFS Dauntless
Alantra Vega System
Year 327 AC (After the Cataclysm)

"All primaries, open fire!" Tyler Barron hadn't had to give the command, of course. The fleet had been under orders to fire the instant the enemy came into range. But it made him feel better, gave him the illusion of having more control over the situation than he did.

Such were the tricks that helped him find his way through impossible situations.

"All primaries engaged, Admiral." Atara's voice was reassuring as well. Not what she said, just the fact of having her there, of *really* having her there. He was deep in enemy space, feeling very much as though he'd led all his people to their doom, and if he faced the kind of battle he suspected he did, there was nothing he wanted, *needed*, more than having Atara Travis at his side.

He could hear the distant whining of *Dauntless*'s main guns firing. He still found himself expecting the lights to blink out for a second, but the newer ship's power generation dwarfed that of his long lost old *Dauntless*. The second ship packed a heavier punch, too, with a quad turret instead of the old double gun.

The particle accelerator's beams lanced out, and he watched as they scored a hit on one of the lead Highborn units. Doctrine called for targeting battleships first, but Barron had ordered the fleet's gunners to focus on the smaller carriers. That was a massive gamble, especially with the firepower of the heavy units, but if he could blast the enemy launch platforms, just maybe his wings could gain tactical superiority in the system. Then he could get his bombers into the mix, perhaps even convert some of the interceptors back into attack ships to hit the Highborn battle line.

It made sense, or it didn't. Barron wasn't sure. So much depended on variables, not the least of which was when the hell the stream of incoming Highborn ships would cease. He still had numbers, but that advantage was slipping away steadily, and he had no intel at all to tell him what the enemy had to throw at him. They could match his fleet in hulls, which would be a huge advantage for them with their superior technology. Or they could have ten times as many ships as he did. The only bright spot in that scenario was that the end would come quickly.

The war against the Highborn had turned tactical orthodoxy on its head. From the doctrines developed to deal with the enemy's longer ranged and more powerful weapons, to the difficulty of targeting their mysterious hulls through clouds of Sigma-9 radiation, to the terrifying and unexpected realization that they had not only developed their own fighters, but deployed them en masse, Barron and his colleagues had bounced from one tactic to another, always reacting, trying to catch up with the situation.

Ideally, he'd have held his line ships back while the bomber squadrons hit the enemy battleships. That had become a more costly tactic with the deadly Highborn point defense missiles…and a downright impossible one now that space was filled with thousands of enemy interceptors. He'd had to convert most of his wings back to the anti-fighter ops they would have conducted a decade before, against a different enemy, and that left him without the bludgeon the bomber squadrons had been. Which, in turn, made it essential to push his own heavy units forward, to run through a deadly stretch of space nearly eighty thousand kilometers long, where his weapons were out of range, but the enemy's deadly blue-black beams were not.

That particular nightmare had been moderately less dark than it might have been, this time at least. The enemy fleet was still transiting, and the fact that his own ships had been fairly close to the point provided a chance to hit part of the Highborn force before reinforcements could deploy.

Less dark didn't mean without cost, however. He'd lost four battleships outright, and a large number of his forward ships had sustained various levels of damage. The battle was just beginning, and the death toll already numbered in the thousands. He wouldn't let himself imagine what the final totals would be.

Dauntless shook, and for an instant, he thought the flagship had taken a hit. But a quick glance at his small screen confirmed that it had merely been an aggressive evasive maneuver. His ship had been lucky so far, and for all the skill and dedication of her crew, Barron knew luck was just what it had been. The randomized evasive routines had been designed before the battle, and they were largely executed by the ship's AI. There was some human interaction, a touch of intuition thrown into the mix with the devilishly complex mathematics, but mostly, the difference between a vessel slipping through unscathed and one getting blasted to rubble was little more than mathematics, and how well those complex calculations did in guessing the angles of incoming fire.

In other words, how well the computers, mixed with a touch of a veteran navigator's gut, guessed.

Barron was looking up at the display as *Dauntless*'s main guns fired again, and two of the four weapons scored hits.

That was a far better targeting rate than he could have rationally expected, but he still felt disappointment at the two misses. It wasn't rational, but amid Barron's cold skepticism, and his realistic analysis of combat situations, on some level he believed his people could do anything.

A murmur of stifled shouts rippled around the bridge as a pair of Highborn carriers vanished in rapid succession. No fewer than six beams from the Pact battleline had struck each in rapid succession. It was by no means first blood...Barron's own fleet had been battered badly enough closing into range, but it was manna for his scared and sweating spacers.

The butcher's bill was still far from even, and Barron knew his people could never destroy as many enemy ships as they lost. But getting up on the scoreboard caused a surge in morale all around the bridge, and no doubt the entire fleet.

And even in it's grim and troubled admiral.

*   *   *

It's you again...

Reg Griffin's teeth were grinding together, her sweat-soaked hand clasped tightly on the throttle. She was staring at her screen with focused intensity, and a level of determination she could barely understand.

She'd never wanted to kill anyone so badly in her life.

She had no verification, but she was sure anyway. The ship facing hers was being flown by the Highborn pilot she'd sparred with before, the one who'd battled her fiercely, until their drawn contest was interrupted by other events in the battle.

I'm going to get you this time...

Her eyes were narrow and fixed, her breathing shallow and erratic as her focus tightened on her adversary. She knew she had to direct the strike force, that she didn't have the luxury to pursue personal vendettas...but there was *something* about that pilot. She had no real information, nothing on which to base any analysis. Still, somehow she was sure she was looking at part of the reason the Highborn squadrons were so effective. A prodigy, maybe, or some product of genetic manipulation...something. She *had* to kill that pilot, not just because she wanted to, but because she was certain he was immensely important to the enemy wings.

She brought her ship around, altering her vector to a direct course toward her enemy. She could feel the thrust bearing down on her, but all the discomfort only fed her bloodthirsty predator's instinct. She could feel the sweat pooling up around her hairline and at the top of her neck, a few errant beads slipping downward across her face. She ignored them, just as she did everything else. She had thousands of pilots behind her, under her command, but this was her responsibility. If she sent anyone else at the enemy fighter, she might as well blast them to atoms herself. She had her command responsibilities, too, but her wing commanders, and Timmons and Federov, could handle those, at least for a while.

While she did what she had to do.

Destroying that fighter, killing the man or woman she was becoming sure was the overall Highborn fighter commander, was *her* job, and she continued on, feeling the relentlessness driving her as though it was a physical force. Her cockpit seemed uncomfortably hot, but a quick glance confirmed what she already knew. Her life support systems were working perfectly.

She breathed deeply, trying to center herself, to focus on her enemy. The kilometers were flashing by, bringing her closer to the deadly fight she knew lay ahead. She was about halfway to firing range when her target's abrupt thrust modifications made one thing startlingly clear.

The Highborn pilot was changing his own vector. *He*

was coming after *her*, even as she was bearing down on him.

She felt a shiver down her body with that realization, and the confidence she had felt when she'd first set out after her prey partly melted away. She remembered the last fight, the incredible skill of that pilot. She was going to go in, try to beat him, but she suddenly wasn't sure she could prevail.

She wasn't sure who was the predator...and who was the prey.

* * *

Stockton tried to move his hand, to upset the delicate maneuvering that was bringing him toward the Confederation fighter. He'd given up on trying to gain control over his motor functions, at least mentally. But the reflex died hard, and every time the Collar-controlled part of him did something of particular concern, he found himself struggling pointlessly, and utterly without effect.

He wasn't sure Reg Griffin was in that ship, of course, but he'd have bet on it. Even if it wasn't her, it was one of the fleet's best pilots, which meant it was someone he knew well, a man or woman who'd worked directly with him, who'd probably toasted with him in the officer's club.

Now, he was going to kill whoever it was.

His hand was tight on the fighter's controls, his eyes narrow with the grim determination that had taken him to the very top of the fighter corps, made him such a deadly and stone cold killer.

He prayed silently, begged any force in the universe to allow that pilot to win the fight about to begin, to take him down. To end his personal hell. There was a chance, perhaps, especially if that *was* Reg Griffin. If anyone in the fleet could take him out, it was probably her. But the confidence that had led him to so many victories, and the ego that lay at the core of every great pilot, asserted themselves. He believed he would win, as he had in all of his great dogfights…and he understood with sickening realization that he was resolute, determined to blast that ship, and its pilot, into oblivion.

He tracked the approaching ship on his scanner, and then he launched his first missile. It was a decoy, a shot intended to herd his prey rather than to score a deadly hit, and he watched as it worked perfectly, as the opposing ship moved away from the incoming missile, along the exact vector he'd expected.

He could feel his deepest thoughts, his instincts, his gut reactions, all serving the Collar-controlled version of himself. It repulsed him, but there was nothing he could do but watch. He saw the Confed fighter moving across his screen, and he felt his hand tightening, launching the second missile.

The warhead ripped across space, coming in just ahead of its target, dead on for the fighter's projected course. His target altered its thrust vector and plunged into a wild evasive routine, even as it sent its two missiles his way. Those shots were desperation plays, he knew, intended to keep him busy and prevent him from closing while the Confed pilot tried to elude his skillfully-placed missile. In that regard, they were successful. Stockton knew better than to ignore approaching warheads, especially ones as well-targeted as the two heading toward his ship, and he launched into his own evasive routine, even as his eyes remained fixed, watching with eager anticipation—and utter horror—as his missile fired its own thrusters in an attempt to stay fixed on the target.

To kill Reg Griffin.

He watched the weapon closing on the Confederation fighter, even as his hands moved wildly back and forth, trying to shake the two warheads his adversary had sent his way. He'd pretty much lost one, but the second was hanging on tightly, drawing more and more of his focus as he struggled to escape its deadly approach.

He wondered if the Collar allowed the controlled side of him to feel the stark terror of battle. He was free of that, for once. He would welcome death's embrace. His only fear was that he would prevail, that his chance at oblivion would slip away.

The ship lurched hard to port, and then back to starboard, and then it went into a deep dive into the Z plane. The missile was still in hot pursuit, but Stockton knew Confederation ordnance like he knew his own name. The weapon was seconds from depleting its fuel, and when its thrust capacity was exhausted, even the slightest of vector changes would push his ship aside from the weapon chasing after it.

He watched, feeling the old excitement, and in the part of his mind that still belonged to him, despair, as the missile ceased thrust and maneuver, and went ripping by, missing his fighter by at least eight hundred meters. It had been a deadly chase, and a close call, but it was over. He had escaped his opponent's missiles.

He looked back at the main display, and he could see that his adversary had done the same, escaping his own missile by an even slimmer margin. The Highborn missiles carried more fuel than their Confed counterparts, but his weapon, too, had run out of power, and moved harmlessly past its target.

He took a deep breath, even as his hands moved over the controls, bringing his ship back on a course toward the Confed fighter, and the laser duel that would decide their contest.

* * *

We've got to break off...

Barron continued to watch the battle unfold. Morale among his staff remained high. By every account, the fight was going well. He'd caught the enemy coming through the point, and he'd hit them in stages, achieving tactical superiority at every phase. He'd even managed to keep the loss ratios slightly in his favor, which was an achievement against Highborn arms.

But he was more certain than ever that he'd led his people into a trap. It was the way the enemy continued to come through the point. Fleet transits were slow operations, by any measure, but the Highborn were coming through even more slowly than the physical constraints of the point could explain. It was almost as if they *wanted* him to believe he was winning.

He turned and looked at the long range displays, his eyes searching for any signs of enemy activity through the lateral transit point, now over a day's travel behind the main fleet. He'd left pickets, of course, but any warnings they sent would also take over an hour to reach his flagship. The enemy could be coming through that point again, taking position behind his fleet...and, without any proof at all, that's what he believed was happening.

If he listened to his gut, ordered a retreat, and there were no enemy ships back there, he would look like a damned fool. Especially if the Highborn forces still coming through the forward point slowed and then stopped. Giving up a chance at a victory in Occupied Space, a chance to *really* drive back the Highborn, would damage his standing, and his grasp on the top command. The Senate might use the whole thing against him, and while he was pretty sure he had Akella's unshakable support, if the Hegemony Council believed he had thrown away a chance to retake their systems and their capital, he doubted even Number One's steadfast support could prevent the other Masters from demanding he be replaced.

If he ordered the withdrawal, on nothing more than his instincts, he risked being crucified by his political enemies, his career and his power destroyed. And if he ignored his gut, and it was right as it had been so many times before, his fleet could be utterly destroyed, and the war lost in one fateful, horrific battle.

He sat silently for an indeterminate time. He was aware of the seconds passing, and the minutes, but he had no idea how long it had been when he finally turned toward Atara's station.

"Atara..." He knew she would instantly hear the vulnerability he was trying so hard to hide.

She spun around, and her eyes met his. She nodded, so slightly it was barely perceptible, but he knew at once. She understood. And that made it easier for him to issue the order.

"Retrieve all squadrons. The fleet will conduct a fighting withdrawal as soon as the wings have landed."

He could hear the hushed reaction around the bridge, and he was sure most of his people disapproved. But he had to do what he thought was best, even if that meant standing alone.

In the end, he didn't give a shit about political games. If the Masters and the Senate wanted to fire him, so be it. He would welcome the escape, at least he would have if he hadn't realized so clearly that his future, and his family's, and that of everyone on the Rim, depended on winning the war.

His eyes caught Atara's again, and he knew he wasn't by himself. Even if the two of them were the only ones in the fleet who understood his motivations, it made an enormous difference that it wasn't just him.

"Yes, Admiral. Issuing fighter retrieval now." Her tone was loud, firm, unshakable. He could feel her lending her authority to his, daring anyone in earshot to question the orders he had just given.

Barron the man was empty, broken over worry about Andi. But Tyler Barron, the Confederation's great admiral was still determined, still at his post...and deeply grateful to have his compatriot, his friend, back at his side.

For all his grit and determination, for all the battles he'd fought and desperate situations he had endured, he wasn't sure he could have pushed through this one alone.

But he wasn't alone…and that was one thing he *could* be sure about.

* * *

Reg was soaked in sweat, struggling with all the resolve she could muster to control the shivering that threatened to take her. The battle had been fierce, desperate. She and her adversary had both come close to victory. But every time she'd thought she had the enemy, he'd managed to pull some maneuver she hadn't expected. She was working her way to a realization that was difficult enough for any pilot to accept, and certainly for one of her stature.

Her opponent was better than she was.

Not immensely so, nor so much as to make her victory impossible. But if she'd been betting on the outcome, she'd have slid her chips from the spot in front of her, to that before her enemy. She couldn't explain how a Highborn pilot had gotten so good so quickly, nor why his tactics seemed uncannily familiar, as though she was watching Jake Stockton's ghost, manifest on the battlefield.

She fired suddenly, an action provoked almost entirely by raw instinct, and one that came close to hitting her target. Her laser pulses ripped by her enemy, coming within two hundred meters of the Highborn fighter. That was close.

But close isn't going to win this fight…

She angled her ship hard, trying to keep her own evasive maneuvers fresh, unpredictable. She dodged a shot from her opponent, and she was coming around to fire again when her comm buzzed.

"All wings, break off at once and return to base. Repeat, all wings, break off and return to base. This is a fleet withdrawal order."

Reg couldn't believe what she was hearing. She shook her head, tried to tell herself she was hallucinating. It didn't make sense. Her personal battle had been close and deadly, but the overall battle was going well. It didn't make any sense to pull back. Then the message replayed.

She was in shock. She'd been in a desperate fight to the death, but the wings had achieved near dominance across the line. It was numbers more than anything making the difference, and while that had sapped some of her satisfaction, success was success. There would be more Highborn fighters in the battle soon enough, but it was beginning to look like her interceptors had opened the way for a bombing attack. She'd been about to issue the launch order for the attack squadrons.

And now they're calling us back?

Confusion surrounded her like a dark gray cloud. She felt the urge to disobey, to order her squadrons to press their advantage. But she didn't have it in her to mutiny against Tyler Barron…and she suspected he knew something she didn't. She'd been anticipating some kind of trap since the fleet had crossed into Occupied Space, much as she knew the admiral had. Could it have finally sprung, even if she couldn't yet see it?

A laser blast ripped by her ship, so close she could see it outside her cockpit as it lanced through a small cloud of dust.

That was close…

She stared back at her screen, adjusting her scanners and her thrust. She was far from sure she even *could* break off, not without exposing herself to her deadly enemy. That was nothing but a truthful analysis of her situation, but it was also self-serving to her almost irresistible desire to destroy her enemy. If she fought, if she managed to defeat the pilot she was facing, her escape would be far easier.

Then, her adversary tested her discipline. He came in almost directly toward her, blasting his engines at full and firing wildly. The laser pulses tore by her, four, six, eight shots, all coming closer than half a kilometer from her ship.

She evaded them all, barely. And then the enemy ship whipped past, blasting its engines to decelerate and return to the fight.

She had her chance. Her chance to obey Barron's order.

Her chance to flee, to escape.

To run from the enemy she had sworn to defeat.

She hesitated for a few seconds, her hand pulled in different directions as her mind warred with itself. She bristled at the idea of fleeing from the fight, but in the end, discipline and loyalty won out. Her opportunity wouldn't last. *It's now or never…*

Her hand slipped to the starboard, and she blasted her engines at full…away from her opponent, and back toward *Dauntless.*

Another day…we will meet again…

Chapter Thirty-Four

Free Trader Pegasus
Beta Telvara System
Year 327 AC (After the Cataclysm)

"I think I've got a better line on the system, Andi. There's still a lot of conjecture, but I've managed to cross reference some mentions in the files we managed to secure, and I feel pretty good we've got it narrowed down to a manageable sector. Two dozen systems, maybe…and I'd wager we can eliminate half of them once we get back to Striker's databases. We could probably nail it down exactly, if that outer area of the Badlands was better known."

Andi looked across the table at Sy, offering an almost involuntary nod in response to her friend's words. She was still trying to rekindle her morale, to fight off the somber feelings trying to pull her down. She'd been sorely disappointed when her people had come away from the old imperial capital empty-handed.

Though you were far from empty-handed…

Andi wasn't a person anyone would call overly optimistic, but she'd let herself hope she would find what the Pact needed on Pintarus. The cost she'd paid, in leaving her daughter behind, in tearfully saying goodbye to Tyler as he went off yet again to fight some hopeless battle, in the

Marines who'd died down in the cavern, was still an open wound. And now, she knew, she would go back to Striker, hold her daughter in her arms for a passing instant, and leave again almost immediately. It would be harder this time than it had been, and she doubted she would even get to see Tyler. The fleet was off somewhere, deep in Occupied Space, no doubt fighting one terrible battle after another. She would have just enough time to look around their quiet and brutally empty quarters, kiss her daughter, and then she would be off again, seeking the way to defeat the Highborn.

To save Cassie…and if she was fast enough, maybe Tyler and thousands of his spacers as well.

"Keep working on it, Sy. You've done a great job so far. You and Ellia saved the mission by getting that data out. I'm sorry we lost so much of it, but at least we still have a trail, even if it's a pretty cold one."

Andi found it odd that she could speak the words to bolster her friend's morale, yet they were cold and empty to her own ears.

"You could use some sleep, Andi…" Sy looked concerned.

Andi stared back, wondering about the last time she'd seen Sy back in *her own* quarters and on the merits of well-meaning hypocrisy.

"Not now, Sy. This is the border system, the one where we set off from the fleet. There should be some pickets here, at least. We might be able to get an update on the status of the operation." A pause, as her thoughts drifted yet again to Tyler, to memories of their precious time together. "Once we transit out of here, it's a straight shot to Striker. I'll get some sleep then."

"Andi…"

The tone of Vig's voice on the comm told her something was wrong.

"Vig? What is it?" She was already on her feet, ready to head toward the small ladder that led up to the bridge.

"I was scanning for the fleet comm ships, Andi. But there was nothing. Either they withdrew…" Andi knew there was no way the comm ships Tyler had left behind would have abandoned their posts. "…or they were destroyed. I cut off the active scans immediately, but now we're picking up some kind of activity right around our exit point."

Andi felt her insides freeze. Tyler had been worried he was walking into a trap. He hadn't told her that directly, of course, but he had never truly adapted to how perceptive she was. It was hard to lie to Andi Lafarge, even in the most well-intentioned of ways.

She had been worried he was heading into a trap, too.

And if those are Highborn ships out there, that pretty much eliminates any doubt…

She turned and raced across the main section of *Pegasus*'s lower deck, leaping up and grabbing one of the ladder's rungs, as she had a thousand times. She scrambled up into the small vestibule just outside the bridge, and she burst through the open doorway.

"Status?"

Vig was already out of her chair, moving to his own station as she slid into hers. "Nothing new. I think they must have picked up some sign of our active scans, but I've got those shut down now, and the stealth unit is fully operational."

Andi stared down at the small screen in front of her workstation. The passive scans provided far less information than the active ones, but it was enough to see that there were at least a dozen ships in front of the transit point…and that none of them had Pact beacons transmitting.

That didn't make it a certainty the vessels were Highborn, but Andi didn't have any real doubts. She tried to push aside the implications an enemy presence in the system had on the status of Tyler's fleet. She had to focus on getting *Pegasus* through whatever was up there, and back to

Striker. She didn't have the secret to defeating the Highborn, but she and her people on *Pegasus* were the only ones who knew where to look for it. Nothing was more important than that, not even chasing after Tyler with warnings that there were enemy ships along his lines of communications.

He'll know that well enough when he stops getting status reports…and Tyler will have scouts out ahead of the fleet, even if he is heading back toward Striker. Still, the urge to rush to his aid—even though there was little real help she could give him—was almost irresistible.

She reached down and tapped her comm unit. "Lex…I need you in engineering, now. I want your eyes on that stealth unit until we're out of the system." She figured she had about a 50/50 chance of eluding the enemy…as long as the unit remained operational. She'd have given herself better odds, but the fact that the Highborn were searching for her already was less than helpful.

"I'm on it, Andi."

She nodded and shut the line. Then, she turned toward Vig. "We're going to have to build up some velocity out here, Vig. And, we'll need a dead on line toward the point." She didn't like the idea of blasting her engines at all, but she knew she didn't have time to waste. She might not be able to help Tyler directly, but Clint Winters needed to know the enemy had forces behind the fleet. She knew he had firm orders to stay at Striker…but maybe he would ignore those, at least enough to send a force to clear away a few Highborn ships and reestablish communications with Tyler and the fleet.

"Calculate a straight line from here to the point, and then go to thirty percent on the engines." She debated with herself what was better, higher engine output or a longer period of acceleration. It came up more or less a coin toss, and her gut told her to cap the thrust level.

"On it, Andi. Just doublechecking the calculations now."

Andi looked at the main display, but her eyes weren't seeing anything. She was considering all she knew, speculating, analyzing…wondering just what the hell the enemy was up to. Had they simply sent a small force to cut the fleet's communications? Or was something more dangerous happening?

She didn't know…but she intended to figure it out.

"Alright, Vig…as soon as you're sure of the numbers, nudge up the thrust. Let's go to thirty in three increments."

And let's hope to hell those ships don't manage to pick us up…

* * *

What the hell…

Andi sat at her station on the bridge, the place she'd remained for three days, eating what little she had consumed right there, drinking barely enough water to fend off dehydration, and actually moving only for brief moments when necessity called.

She'd watched the Highborn ships with stinging, bleary eyes, and she'd grown increasingly edgy. But now, she felt as though she'd been punched in the gut with an iron fist.

The scanner readings weren't clear or conclusive…but they were too many to ignore. The dozen ships she'd spotted from the other end of the system were still more or less where they had been. But there were new contacts as well, hints of things that might be more ships…in places that seemed conspicuously like the kind of spots a task force would choose if it was trying to hide.

"I don't like the looks of this, Andi…" Vig was staring at the same data she was, and clearly coming to the same conclusion. It was a realization she fought against, one that shook her resolve.

There wasn't a small flotilla of Highborn ships positioned in the system to block Tyler's communications. There was a full blown task force waiting to ambush his fleet, and block its way back home.

Implications raced wildly in her mind, and understanding gelled into conclusions she hated. If the enemy had a force waiting to intercept Tyler's retreat, they had an expectation of forcing that very withdrawal.

I have to warn him, get to him...

But she couldn't.

If she even tried to reverse course, blast the engines hard enough to turn her ship from its current vector back toward the point leading in the direction of Barron's fleet, *Pegasus* would be detected. Not certainly, perhaps, but she guessed the chances were somewhere north of ninety percent. And if they were spotted, they were dead. The chances there were functionally one hundred percent.

She couldn't help Tyler that way. If he was driven back, if the enemy had sprung the trap they'd all feared, it had likely already begun. Tyler knew about it, and she couldn't do anything useful to aid the fleet. Still, she wanted to see Tyler, to be with him in whatever struggle lay ahead.

But more than that, she wanted to do something to save him. And she'd realized immediately the only way she could do that. She had to get back to Striker, to Clint Winters. She didn't know how much force remained at the great base, how many new ships had arrived after she'd left, but it was the only place she could reach that might possess enough force to make a difference. If she could get there, and get back in time, those ships just might make the difference.

Assuming she could convince Winters to disobey Tyler's orders.

"We've got to get to Striker *now*, Vig." Every fiber of her being longed to unleash the full power of *Pegasus*'s engines, to blast at maximum acceleration right for the transit point. But the thrusters were shut down, as they would remain. She'd been focused on escaping, but now it was even more vital that her ship get past the Highborn waiting just ahead of her.

"Shut down the reactor, Vig. We can manage life support and passive scans on the batteries until we transit." Every instinct inside her called for decisive action, but her intellect remained in control. The best chance of helping Tyler—of saving him and his entire fleet—was to continue on her present course, and to trust in the spacer's gods that *Pegasus* would slip by unnoticed.

"On it, Andi." Vig leaned forward and moved his hands over the controls, just as Andi tapped her comm unit again.

"Lex, we're shutting down the reactor. Close down the vents…we'll have to hold any radiation in the chamber until after we transit." One more problem. She couldn't risk leaving any kind of trail for the enemy to spot…but by the time *Pegasus* transited, the reactor core was going to be damned hot with radiation.

That was a problem she'd deal with if they got through.

When we get through…

She sat, silent, not a sound on the bridge save the vents pouring out clean air…at a rate far below normal. Andi hadn't noticed any difference yet, but the power saving protocols were likely to make things quite stuffy on *Pegasus* by the time the ship reached the transit point.

Andi looked over at Vig's station, just as her friend picked up his head and gazed her way. Neither of them spoke, but they communicated nevertheless. They were about twenty minutes from transiting, and every second of that time could be the one when a Highborn ship picked them up. The enemy ships weren't battleships, but they didn't have to be, not to take on *Pegasus*. Andi loved her ship, and she knew it was far more powerful than it looked, but against even a Highborn cruiser, it might as well be an unshielded lifeboat. Just about any hit, even the most glancing of blows, would vaporize *Pegasus*, and kill everyone onboard…and destroy the information that still might lead to a way to defeat the enemy.

The only way to defend against an enemy attack would

be to evade, to avoid getting hit, something impossible with *Pegasus*'s reactor shut down. Even if it had been an option, it would take the ship off course, away from the transit that was its only true escape.

Andi had bet everything on stealth, on sneaking past the Highborn. Now, there was nothing to do except ride that out, and count the minutes, the seconds.

And hope.

Chapter Thirty-Five

CFS Dauntless
Velitara System
Year 327 AC (After the Cataclysm)

Dauntless shook hard, as the Highborn beam clipped the ship's port side. It was a glancing blow, in the terms commonly applied to personal combat, a flesh wound. But no hit from the deadly Highborn weapons was insignificant, and his screen filled almost immediately with a fairly extensive damage report.

He felt an instinct to grab the comm, to call down to Fritzie and get the real story. But Fritz wasn't on *Dauntless*, she was back in the Confederation heading up Project Quasar. Barron couldn't argue that wasn't a more important use of her almost immeasurable talents, but he still wished he had her back in engineering, keeping his flagship in the fight with her uncanny ability.

The fleet had been in almost constant combat for days now. Barron had been granted the meager satisfaction that his instincts, his concerns of a trap, had once again been correct. It was cold comfort.

The fleet had faced Highborn ships sitting astride its line of retreat in multiple locations, and it had taken a sustained and bloody fight to push through and escape from the system. When his ships emerged on the other side of the point, he knew the enemy would be in hot pursuit...and his first scanner reports had quickly told him things were far worse than that.

A Highborn task force was deployed just in-system from the point, and his people endured another battle to break free, and continue their increasingly desperate retreat, looking behind them every passing moment, to see if their pursuers were coming through yet.

The same story repeated itself in the following system, and once again, he was about to order his ships to red alert, and to scramble Reg Griffin's increasingly ragged and exhausted squadrons. Barron had slammed the gate down on his emotions, struggled to face the situation with machinelike precision. But it was a long way back to the border, and with each enemy attack, he lost a little bit of his remaining hope that his people would escape.

You led them here, dammit, you can lead them away!

Determination had taken Barron far in his career, but he knew it wasn't magic. And he wasn't sure anything short of a sorcerer's conjurings could save his fleet.

"The Highborn task force looks smaller than the one in the previous system, by at least twenty percent in hulls."

Atara's unsolicited report had been intended as much for the other officers on the bridge as for him, though he suspected she was doing what she could to prop him up as well. Barron didn't doubt his fleet could defeat the forces currently in front of them, but he didn't have much time, not with the force he knew was on his tail. And rushed battles sacrificed tactical elegance, buying victory with buckets of blood instead. He would break through the force in front of his fleet, but he would lose more ships and spacers in the process. Worse, he was almost certain the same situation would await him on the other side of the next transit.

He'd done some rough calculations, basic guesstimates

on how much of the fleet might make it back to the border. His totals varied widely, but all of them were south of half, and some lower than that. And he hadn't dared to imagine larger enemy forces waiting in the systems ahead.

"All units…battlestations. Prepare to engage the enemy." He paused, hesitant to issue the rest of his order. "All squadrons are to scramble at once…interceptors and bombers will launch simultaneously." He sighed softly, hoping he'd kept it low enough to hide from his comrades. Griffin's pilots were exhausted, and most of them were already strung out on stims. He'd really hoped he could give them a rest, at least a day without combat, but it didn't look like that was in the cards.

"Yes, Admiral. All ships, red alert. All wings scramble."

Barron looked at the display, and the pressure of a lifetime at war suddenly pushed down on him from all sides. How many had died under his command? Tens of thousands certainly. *No, hundreds of thousands…millions if you count the Marines…*

He'd never even considered a career outside the navy. As his grandfather's only direct descendant, he'd never really had a choice. He'd been eager in his early days, and then discipline had taken him the rest of the way. But how much blood could one man wallow in before it destroyed him?

"All ships, increase to full thrust. Let's get through the dead zone to our own firing range as quickly as we can."

He stared straight ahead. Yes, one day war would probably destroy him.

But that day had not yet come.

* * *

Vian Tulus felt the adrenalin surge that always accompanied combat. He'd chafed at Barron's withdrawal orders in Alantra Vega, and his Palatian spirit had cried out against the ignominy of retreat. To his view, attack was always preferable to defense, and taking the war to the enemy was the surest road to victory.

Tulus's views on such things had changed somewhat in the years since he'd taken Tyler Barron as his blood brother. He fancied, with some solid reasoning, that the two had benefitted each other, that their bond had made each of them stronger. But in his lucid moments, he realized he had learned more from Barron than his blood brother had from him.

Alantra Vega was just another proof of that. Barron had been right to retreat, his nose had indeed sniffed out the trap the Highborn had laid for the Pact fleet. Tulus knew without doubt that he, on his own initiative, would have plunged forward…and that he would have led the fleet even deeper into the enemy's snare. He had become far more deliberative and thoughtful of his actions in the dozen or more years he'd known Barron, but the Palatian inside had never died.

That spirit surged now, in its glory fighting the enemy, even though the battles now were struggles to escape, to open the way for further retreat. To try to get at least some of the fleet back to the border, and to Striker. It was early to call the entire offensive a disaster, but it didn't take tactical wizardry to see that was where it was in grave danger of going.

All that remained was to determine how great a catastrophe it became.

"Sir, we are about to enter firing range. All batteries report full charges and readiness."

Tulus looked over at the officer. The young warrior's voice had been slightly tentative, but he knew that had nothing to do with any fear of battle. His people had encountered more difficulty dealing with his reforms than they had fighting an enemy with vastly superior technology. Tulus had done away with generations of tradition, sweeping away the old forms of address, and mandating that he be called simply, 'sir' in combat situations.

Tulus had learned as much from the Confederation Senate and from nations like the Union as he had from Barron, the perils of arrogance and the narcissistic pursuit of political power and recognition. An Alliance Imperator was a hero warrior, who earned his position in battle and not in dark and shadowy back room deals. Still, Palatia had not always managed to maintain the purity of such things, and some of his predecessors had succumbed to the pomp and privilege of the office. He suspected he had as well, at least at times, but he'd also made an effort to return to his roots, and to those of the Imperator's chair, to remain the simple and honorable warrior, the man who kept his oaths and stood in the line of battle whatever the odds.

This was such a fight, and his warriors looked to him. His allies needed him as well…the fleet could not hope to escape without the very best every contingent, every warrior, had to give. It was a difficult situation, one he suspected was wracking Tyler Barron with pain and regret that he'd led his people there, that he hadn't pulled them back sooner.

But to Vian Tulus, it was the vision he'd nursed since childhood, the unbreakable warrior standing tall against the overwhelming enemy. The shame of retreat was almost gone, washed away by battle after battle, by the blood of warriors, heroically shed.

In that moment, Vian Tulus embraced his Palatian soul, the primal scream of the warrior.

"All ships…it is time. Open fire."

* * *

Chronos watched his staff at their stations, snapping out commands into the comm units, coordinating the actions of his fleet. His part of the fleet.

The Hegemony Master, Number Eight of the Council, one of the most genetically perfect humans known, had allowed his position to slip from the unchallenged Pact military command many believed he should hold. He hadn't submitted to Tyler Barron's authority in any formal way, but in every practical sense that mattered, he had done just that.

He'd felt some resentment at first, but far less than he might have anticipated. He'd long fought against Barron and his Confederation comrades, and he'd come to respect them, first as enemies, and later as allies, if not as outright friends. There was more to it than that, however. He hadn't yielded his authority to the Confederation—though that body had clearly taken the lead as the most productive and powerful member of the Pact. His willingness to follow the guidance, if not the straight out orders, of another, was limited to Barron himself. It went against all his beliefs and a lifetime of cultural indoctrination to so accept an outsider, one who hadn't even submitted to genetic testing.

Though, do you doubt Tyler Barron's test would reveal him to be of Master status, very highly rated Master status?

He had no doubt at all, nor did he have reservations about Barron's tactical abilities. Pressed to name one man or woman as the most capable military leader in human-occupied space, he would offer his enemy turned ally without hesitation.

There was no place for ego, not in a fight against an enemy like the Highborn. Chronos had long doubted the shadowy threat, even questioned the existence of those his people had long called, 'The Others,' but the old legends had proven not only to be true, but the real threat was vastly greater than any had imagined. It was difficult for a leader of the Hegemony, so long assured of its supremacy over humanity, to acknowledge that half his nation, and its capital, were in enemy hands, and that any hope of reclaiming the occupied systems, or even of surviving, depended on the aid of allies.

He looked up at the display, watching the formations moving slowly across. There was nothing slow about those ships in real terms, he knew. Much of the fleet was moving at a velocity of one or two percent of lightspeed, putting thousands of kilometers behind them with each passing second.

He felt the urge to issue some kind of orders, but he knew there was nothing more he could do. The fleet was vast, and its battle plan was well founded. The operation was more of a fighting withdrawal than a real battle, and there was nothing else it could be, no other options the fleet could embrace.

That didn't mean ships weren't being destroyed…and men and women killed. The fleet's losses had been severe, if somewhat lighter than he might have feared, and there was still a long way to go before they reached the shaky border that separated Highborn-Occupied Space from that still controlled by the Hegemony.

Assuming they just don't follow us all the way back to Striker…

Chronos had always had a deliberative approach to things, but as he sat on his flagship, watching his fleet fight their way out of a trap, the reality that his nation, half of it anyway, was gone, pressed in on him from all sides. The offensive had been intended to liberate those worlds, to return to Calpharon and reclaim the capital. Now, his best hope was for the Pact fleet to escape at least somewhat intact…and prepare to endure an inevitable renewal of the Highborn invasion. He looked into the depths of his mind, into his visualization of the future, and he couldn't see a path to the liberation he sought. All he saw was a desperate—and perhaps hopeless—defense, and more defeat.

Will you ever see Calpharon again?

He cut off the thought abruptly. He didn't think he'd like the answer.

Chapter Thirty-Six

Forward Base Striker
Vasa Denaris System
Year 327 AC (After the Cataclysm)

"You have to do something, Clint!" Andi stood on one side of the table looking across at her friend, the Confederation navy's second in command…and perhaps Tyler Barron's only hope of returning to Striker alive.

The two were standing next to the conference table. They'd been in the room for almost ten minutes, but neither had made a move to sit down. The thought hadn't even occurred to Andi. She was too tense, too wired, to sit.

She was also upset, her concern for Tyler only growing since *Pegasus*'s narrow escape from Beta Telvara. She still didn't know if the Highborn ships had spotted Pegasus, or if her ship had slipped through undetected, but she'd spent half the trip across the next system twisted forward on her seat, a nervous wreck, watching for hours to see if the enemy ships followed *Pegasus* through the point.

Waiting to see if all of her people were going to die.

There had been no pursuit, however, at least none she'd detected, and now she was back on Striker. But the stress was still there, the flames fanned by the final scanner data *Pegasus* had gleaned before transiting, the readings that showed just what Tyler and his fleet would face if—*when*, she told herself—they made it back to Beta Telvara.

"Andi…Tyler gave me orders, clear orders. He made me promise him I would follow them, no matter what. I gave him my word." Winters was clearly on edge as well. Andi didn't think the Sledgehammer would be overly concerned about disregarding orders…but breaking a promise to his closest friend was another thing entirely.

"You've got the fleet deployed like its waiting for your order to advance." Andi could see surprise in Winters's expression. People tended to underestimate just how much tactical knowledge she'd gained in her years in and around the fleet.

"I shouldn't be surprised that you saw that, Andi. But it doesn't change the fact that I promised Tyler. We had this very conversation. What if something went wrong? What if he needed help? His answer was always the same. He wanted me here, getting ready to defend Striker if things went bad."

"You're one of Tyler's closest friends, Clint, and I know what your word means to you. But Tyler couldn't foresee every possibility. If we were talking about going after him deep into Occupied Space, I would understand doing as you promised. But this is the system just across the border. It's not even far from Striker…and the enemy force is right beyond the point. We *can't* stay here and let the fleet be trapped and destroyed. We can't let him die, with no chance to escape…" Andi realized her face was wet. She'd lost her usual control, and the tears she'd fought so hard to hold back poured out.

"Andi…" Winters walked around the table and extended his arms, hugging Andi. But she pushed him away.

"I'm fine," she said, fooling neither herself nor Winters with the lie.

"Andi…" Winters just repeated her name, and then he paused. The room was silent, save for Andi's soft sniffles.

Finally, the admiral took a deep breath and said, "You're right, Andi. Tyler might break me down to spacer third class for it, but I can't leave him out there." Another pause. "I won't." The two words came out like a hammer striking an anvil.

Andi felt a rush of excitement. She hadn't really doubted she could convince Winters, but she hadn't known Tyler had extracted a personal promise from his friend either. She felt a flash of anger. Tyler Barron had never been hesitant to put his own life at risk to save his comrades…but he'd gone to such lengths to prevent his comrades from risking themselves to save him. The frustration bubbled up, countered by guilt for being angry at him, while he was still out there, in terrible danger.

She didn't want to lose him. She *couldn't* lose him…

"When can the fleet set out?" Andi pulled herself back to the topic on hand, using Winters's decision to steady herself, to quiet her tortured mind.

"Four hours."

The response was unexpected. Despite her still-active captain's rank, Andi was far from an expert in fleet operations. But everything she did know suggested any time frame less than days seemed unrealistic.

"Four hours? Is that even possible?"

"Well, I promised Tyler I'd stay here, Andi…but I didn't say anything about not running fleet readiness drills. The fleet just might be at yellow alert…" He looked at her and smiled. "Let's go, Andi. Let's go pull that husband of yours out of the mess he got himself into."

*   *   *

"We are ready, Admiral Winters…fully prepared for an effort that is well overdue. Let us go forth to the aid of the invasion fleet. Let us secure a safe return for Admiral Barron and the Imperator." Vestilius's voice was haughty, dripping with arrogance. He hadn't called Winters a coward for waiting so long, not exactly at least, but the Confederation admiral's dislike for the senior Palatian commander at Striker grew a bit, seemingly every time the two spoke.

"We were obeying orders, Commander Vestilius, and it is with great hesitation that I now override those commands. New data and intelligence have only now justified such action." Winters was annoyed with himself immediately for taking the Palatian's bait. He had neither the time nor the desire to trade barbs with a puffed up Alliance officer who saw himself as some fearless, legendary warrior.

Any warrior without fear is just a damned fool…

"Nevertheless, Admiral…the Alliance forces are prepared to set out at any time. Indeed, I urge you to hurry the other contingents, so we are not forced to wait."

Winters gritted his teeth, fighting back against the fresh wave of anger. He would have despised Vestilius utterly, save for one important fact. For all the Palatian's bluster and foolishness, he was indeed the closest thing to fearless Winters had seen, and one hell of a tactician as well.

And the fleet needed such men.

"We will depart in thirty minutes, Commander. See that your people are ready." The last part came out with a bit more edge to it than he liked, more of a barb than an order. But then, he was only human, and no one could grate on someone quite like an old line Palatian.

He turned and looked over toward Andi. "You should bring your people aboard *Excalibur*, Andi. *Pegasus* is one hell of a ship, but she has no place in a fight with the Highborn."

Andi looked around her, still trying to process the size of the superbattleship's bridge. She'd been on *Dauntless* more times than she could count, and even the current and second ship of that name, for all its size and power, was dwarfed by the Confederation's newest war machine.

Winters's words made sense, certainly in a purely tactical sense. Andi had no idea how things would progress when the relief force reached Beta Telvara, and she doubted *Pegasus* could be of much help in any scenario she could conceive. Still, her ship had served her well, and she just couldn't see leaving her behind, not now.

"I appreciate the offer, Clint, and you're probably right. But I think I'll bring her anyway. She got us through and back here—barely—and I don't think it would be right to leave her behind."

"Andi…Tyler is my friend, and so are you. When we get there…well, you know *Pegasus* isn't large enough to fight Highborn ships. Promise me you'll stay back, out of range."

Andi smiled without answering. She just leaned forward and kissed Winters on the cheek. "Thank you, Clint. For everything." She straightened up and turned toward the bank of lifts, walking across the bridge and slipping into one of the cars.

Winters just watched, his mind pulled between his obligations to two of his closest friends. *I will try to keep her safe, Tyler…though she doesn't make that easy.*

And, I will do whatever I have to do to break through those enemy forces in Beta Telvara, Andi…to bring Tyler home.

* * *

Ilius watched as the transit point grew larger on the display, at least the dull gray projection that represented the bizarre perversion of spacetime that allowed interstellar travel. The Hegemony commander was tired, not in the sense of normal fatigue, but just bone deep exhausted, physically and emotionally. He'd been terribly wounded in the war against the Highborn, seen his capital taken and half his nation occupied by the enemy. He'd watched the Hegemony, once a power that embraced its destiny with unquestioned confidence, reduced almost to a junior partner of the

Confederation, a power that had been its enemy six years
earlier. Things were more complicated than that, of course.
For one thing, Ilius now believed his people should never
have been enemies with the Confeds. The Rimdwellers
didn't follow the genetic ranking system of the Hegemony,
that much was true, but they were worthy nevertheless.
They had come to the Hegemony's aid, and they had fought
alongside his people, bled with them. He still found it
difficult to sort out all his emotions, but he knew one thing
without a doubt.

He was one hundred percent behind Admiral
Winters…request…that the Hegemony forces at Striker
move out with him to go to the aid of the main fleet. That
unquestioned support came from multiple places, the
realization that the fleet's defeat probably meant the end of
any hopes of winning the war, the desire to rescue his
comrades and his old friend, Chronos…and the growing
belief that, as difficult as it was for a Hegemony Master to
accept, any hope to defeat the enemy lay in Tyler Barron's
tactical brilliance.

Ilius felt something else, too, something that seemed
strange for a man about to head off into battle against a
force of unknown size and power. Relief.

He had tried to fill in for Chronos, to provide Akella
with the aid and support he could muster in her struggles
with Thantor and his allies on the Council. He knew his
friend's interest in Number One went far beyond the
political, or even the fact that the two shared a daughter.
Ilius had been appropriately shocked when Chronos had
confided in him about his feelings for Akella, and admitted
the two had been lovers for years. Such a relationship would
be frowned upon in any segment of Hegemony society, but
for a Master, it was criminal. Akella had already drawn
criticism on herself for having only two children…if her
enemies found out about her long and illegal
relationship…they would destroy her.

Ilius had remained silent about that, in part because he wouldn't betray his friend's confidence, but also because he believed if Akella lost control of the Council, if Thantor gained power, the Hegemony was truly and completely doomed.

He turned back and looked at the fleet display, at the clusters of various icons moving slowly toward the transit tube. Winters was taking every ship from Fortress Striker, from *Colossus* and the new Confederation behemoth, *Excalibur*, to the smallest escorts, even a pair of repurposed freighters he'd managed to turn into ersatz light carriers. Ilius had been worried enough about what would happen if the invasion fleet, along with Chronos and Barron was lost. If the rescue force met disaster as well, there would be nothing left at all. Just one massive fortress, mounting immense weaponry, but fixed in space without any support.

Ilius had always considered all possibilities, including how to handle failure and defeat. But he couldn't think of that just then, for one simple reason.

Failure wasn't an option.

Chapter Thirty-Seven

Highborn Flagship S'Argevon
Imperial System GH6-4521 (Omicron Alvera System)
Year of the Firstborn 389 (327 AC)

"You have done well, Jake Stockton. You have served with admirable skill and dedication, led our new fighter corps with distinction. And you will not find me ungrateful. But now, we approach the final battle, the struggle to crush the human resistance. Your former compatriots are trapped, fleeing from this fleet...into the maw of another. The end will come soon."

Stockton listened to Tesserax, with blind hatred, and also with gushing devotion. He was a man torn in two, one side forsaking all he had once believed in to serve a vicious group of creatures produced in a lab who thought themselves gods. The other side was forced to watch the nightmare unfold, unable to strike back, even to stop himself from using all his skills and knowledge to help defeat his old comrades.

"I have reviewed the reports from your recent battles. The performance of our squadrons is commendable, despite the somewhat heavy losses we have incurred. But we have identified several areas of concern, however, specifically certain human pilots we have targeted for elimination. You have engaged one of these yourself, twice I believe, at least if our analysis is correct. The third time must be the last. You have failed to destroy this enemy. You must see that this does not happen again."

Stockton could feel his acknowledgement, and his shame at failing to destroy the pilot he'd twice engaged. *Reg Griffin...it has to be her...*

He raged impotently against the regret he felt for not killing his friend, and the shameful way his mind practically screamed out, begging forgiveness from the Highborn.

"I will not fail again, Highborn." He felt his head bowing, his body dropping to his knees, despite his greatest effort to remain standing, defiant.

"I know you will not." Tesserax paused, allowing Stockton to remain prone for close to a minute. "Rise," he said finally, and Stockton obeyed, all the while the hatred seething hot in the imprisoned corner of his mind.

"May I ask, what are the plans for the final assault?"

"You may indeed ask, Jake Stockton, and I will tell you, if only because you will play a major role in its execution. We have pursued the humans, but we have held back, remaining close enough to keep the pressure on them, but apparently failing to catch them and stop their escape. That was the plan from conception. Your former comrades will draw some confidence from the fact that they have come so far with losses that, while heavy, have been less than they might have expected. The proximity to the border, and thoughts of a final straight course back to their large fortress will stoke that fire. They will be on their guard, of course, but distracted as well by the prospect of escape."

Stockton listened to the Highborn's words, and he became sicker and sicker with each passing moment.

"They will no doubt accelerate at or near their full thrust potential in an effort to reach the jump point and move across the border...which, of course, is little more than an arbitrary line on a map. Then, when they believe they are almost there, our blocking forces will emerge from their hidden positions, and form up in front of the jump point, just as this fleet enters the system behind them. They will be trapped, cut off from escape, sandwiched between our two forces." Tesserax smiled, a grimace Stockton believed was the most horrific thing he'd ever seen.

"Then, they will be destroyed, Jake Stockton, utterly obliterated…and the way will be open for our combined fleets to advance toward their Striker base, and crush any remaining resistance."

Stockton was frantic inside, but his head simply nodded, and he said, "Magnificent, Highborn. Your plan is a masterpiece, one surely to result in utter and complete victory."

Stockton hated himself for saying the words, but even in the imprisoned part of his mind, he had to acknowledge, the plan *was* brilliant. He tried to tell himself Tyler Barron would find a way to counter it, to avoid destruction…that the fleet would somehow manage to escape. But he couldn't make himself believe it.

"You will be there, of course. You will have another chance to destroy that enemy pilot, to make up for your failure. I trust you will not disappoint me again."

"No, Highborn. I will do as you command. I will find and destroy that pilot…and then I will lead our wings forward, to the total destruction of the human forces."

* * *

Stockton climbed out of his fighter, dropping down to the flight deck. Highborn launch bays weren't as well designed as those on Confederation ships. That was understandable enough. The Highborn technology was superior, but much of what went into the design of bays was gained through years of experience. It took a bit longer to launch the squadrons than it did, on the Confederation ships, at least.

The Highborn don't have Stara either…

He'd tried not to think of his lost love. He was in hell, beyond redemption, beyond solace. She was gone to him, and he would never see her again. But she lingered stubbornly in his thoughts, bringing him a bitter mix of pain and fear.

Pain at the loss…and fear for her, for what would happen to her if the Highborn prevailed. He was lost, resigned to darkness until death took him, but there was still hope for Stara.

She would fight to the end. He had no doubt of that. And she would be invaluable to Tyler Barron. Speed of launch operations was one advantage that still rested with his old comrades, though the Highborn had the edge in most other areas.

Stockton was fully aware of what his Collar-controlled psyche saw. He'd become used to noting what he could of things around him, without any control over where he went, or even which direction he looked. But he didn't need to see anything to know what was going on just then. He hadn't encountered Reg on the just-completed sortie, or whoever it was he'd faced twice. That was no surprise. His orders had been precise, and they'd restricted him from pushing the combat too aggressively. Tesserax didn't want to provoke the final battle on this side of the transit point. The final climactic fight would take place in Beta Telvara.

That was where he would kill Reg Griffin.

That was where the Highborn forces would bracket and destroy Tyler Barron's fleet.

Stockton felt as though he was screaming, a dark and piteous howl that existed only in the recesses of his mind. He was trapped as he had been for four years, and now, he would watch his comrades die. He would help crush them.

And when he saw *Dauntless* destroyed, he would know that Stara, too, was gone. Stockton had suffered in his life, fought back against wounds and loss and pain…but he had never fallen to such a dark and desolate place as that he now occupied. Even his prayers for death had gone unanswered. He was trapped in a nightmare that never ended, from which there was no awakening.

He walked over toward a group of technicians, and he snapped out a series of commands. Or, he listened to himself issuing the orders. He'd known what he was going to say, of course, even before he had. His lack of any control over his actions didn't prevent him from hearing—feeling?—the thoughts in his Collar-controlled brain.

Even as he'd felt himself speak the orders to the flight crew, he was aware of the cold and grim determination, the relentlessness with which he would pursue Reg Griffin when the battle was joined again. He'd always had a dark side—every great warrior did—and now that part of him served the enemy, as all his skills and experiences did.

Everything he was, everything he had become in more than two decades at war would be used to kill his friend, the comrade he'd left behind to take his place. Then he would lead the Highborn wings against the rest of his old squadrons, and open the way for the Highborn line to destroy the fleet. To kill Tyler Barron.

To kill Stara.

The misery rolled over him from every side, burying him in hopelessness, even as his eyes caught the countdown clock on the wall, the numbers showing less than one hour until the Highborn fleet began to transit after Barron's forces.

Before his journey to treachery and utter, black despair was completed.

He couldn't scream, couldn't cry, couldn't utter the slightest complaint.

He couldn't even stop himself from feeling the anxious, creeping anticipation that filled the Collar-controlled part of him. He wasn't only going to help kill everyone who'd ever meant anything to him.

He *wanted* to do it, bristled at even the slight delay that lay ahead.

He had become a monster, and he hated himself with greater intensity than he'd ever despised any enemy…and he could feel his sanity slipping away, what little remained of Jake Stockton slipping away, as fine dust caught in the wind and scattered to oblivion.

Chapter Thirty-Eight

CFS Dauntless
Beta Telvara System
Year 327 AC (After the Cataclysm)

"Readings confirmed, Tyler. There is an enemy force in position astride our course to the exit transit point. A large force."

Barron turned toward Atara's station. The news was clearly bad, and her tone only made it worse. But he *really* knew things were dire when his friend addressed him informally on the bridge. Atara was like a sister to him, and apart from Andi, he was closer to her than anyone else. Despite that, she'd always shown considerable discipline in according him the respect she felt the commander was due in front of others.

"One more fight before we get home. We'll handle it." Barron spoke loudly, his words almost reflexive, and intended more for the officers on the bridge than for Atara. His longtime aide knew as well as he did the fleet had more problems than just the ships waiting ahead. They weren't going to outrun the Highborn forces pursuing them. The fleet had barely escaped from the last system, and Barron knew his people had, at most, hours before their enemies followed suit. Then, they would be fleeing desperately from one enemy force...right toward another. His mind raced, every tactical option he could think of quickly considered and rejected. There was no way, nothing he could do. His people were going to be attacked from two sides, sandwiched between Highborn forces, surrounded, and perhaps even englobed. The enemy had planned it all perfectly.

The fleet was going to be destroyed.

Barron knew such things were rarely as total and complete as they seemed, and terms like 'destroyed' were rarely as fixed as their meanings suggested. Some of his ships would almost certainly escape, scattered remnants, perhaps, damaged and militarily ineffective. He could almost see it in his mind, a line of straggling ships, limping back toward Striker, the dazed survivors onboard staring blankly at their screens and wondering if the enemy would follow and finish them. Whatever happened, the fleet as a unit, the great combat force he had led on a failed quest to liberate the occupied systems of the Hegemony, would be functionally obliterated.

The only real question was, how badly could his people hurt the enemy before they were crushed? He had no real idea of total Highborn strength, or what other reserves, if any, they possessed. If he savaged their forces, even as his own fleet died, could he weaken them enough to buy his survivors, and his comrades at Striker, and back on the Rim, time?

Would it even matter? Was there any way to prevail in the war if his own force was defeated? Could even Confederation industrial might keep up with the immense power of the Highborn? The ships he was about to lose represented billions of manhours of labor, and trillions of credits...not to mention the very special, and highly-trained men and women aboard them. It would take years to replace them all, if it was even possible.

And the Highborn weren't going to give the Rim years.

He took a deep breath, trying to remain calm in the face of what seemed to be certain doom. He'd faced death before, and as much as he wanted to live, he'd always been aware of the risks of his profession, prepared on some level for the sacrifice he'd always known he might be called upon to make. But it was harder now. He wouldn't just die a warrior who'd finally failed to outrun fate. Thousands of spacers would meet their ends, too…and he would leave Andi behind, and his daughter as well.

Will she remember me? Barron wondered how much Cassie would recall when she was grown, whether he would be more than the vaguest of memories in some recess of her mind. Whether she would have more of her father than a few old pictures and a scattered, incoherent recollection or two?

Then, his thoughts turned truly dark. When the fleet was gone, so too was the last *real* hope to defeat the Highborn. The cold truth was, Cassie wasn't going to grow up, or if she did, she would do so as a slave, condemned to worship a twisted race of genetically-engineered monsters for the rest of her life.

I am so sorry, my sweet girl. I have failed you so completely…

Barron felt as though he was coming apart. He loved Andi and Cassie, with all the intensity he possessed. But as much as they'd added to his life, they weakened him now, stripped him of the cold view of the heroic warrior. He could face his own death, grim in his resolve to the end, but not a failure that condemned those he loved to misery and despair.

And in that, unexpectedly, a new strength began to form.

He felt his teeth grinding, and he realized his hands were clenched tightly into fists. His people might be trapped, they might not seem to have a chance…but no fate was absolute, and they could still fight. Until every ship was destroyed, every veteran spacer killed, it wasn't over.

He had an idea, one born of intellect, experience, tactical

brilliance...but most of all pure stubbornness. Barron couldn't allow the Highborn to destroy or enslave his family. He *wouldn't*.

"Fleet order...all ships are to decelerate at full thrust. We're moving back toward our entrance point."

Even Atara looked stunned as she listened to his command. "You want to reverse course, Admiral?" It was perhaps the first time he'd ever heard his comrade checking to confirm an order in front of the bridge crew.

"That's *exactly* what we're going to do. The enemy will be coming through that point any time now, Atara...and we're going to meet them as they transit. And we're going to give them one hell of a reception. It we can get back quickly enough, we'll have the edge as they transit. Then we'll come about and deal with those ships on the other side of the system." It was crazy, unintuitive. If it worked, the histories would call it genius. Barron had been leading his people on a desperate retreat for weeks...and now he was going to turn about, back the way they had come. It made sense, in its own way. It was the only option that allowed him to face the two enemy forces separately, at least for a time. Even at Highborn thrust levels, those ships at the far point would take almost a day to reach his position. If the fleet continued on its current course into the system, the two enemy forces would converge, and they would hit his fleet more or less simultaneously.

If he had to take on overwhelming forces, he'd rather fight them one at a time. Even if it meant moving farther from home to do it. He might even find a way to slip around the enemy blocking force once he drew them from the transit point. He was too much a realist and a veteran to believe his people could truly prevail, but maybe a few more of his ships would make their way back, escape from the trap springing on them.

And almost certainly, he would spill more Highborn blood, destroy ships that Clint Winters and the warriors at

Striker wouldn't have to face.

A moment later: "All units confirm, Admiral. Revised maneuver plan is being implemented." He could tell from Atara's tone she had finally comprehended his reasoning, even that she agreed with the decision. That didn't mean she believed they would prevail, but when the choice was between bad decisions, Atara had always been in favor of the option that allowed her to come closest to wrapping her hands around the enemy's throat.

Barron tapped his comm unit. "Stara, it's Tyler Barron. I need the wings ready to launch as soon as possible. We're not moving toward the force at the far side of the system, we're coming about, and we're going to hit those bastards the instant they come through after us. I'll want Admiral Griffin and her people deployed before the Highborn ships transit in."

"Yes, Admiral...understood. It was clear from the venom in her words that Stara Sinclair was also onboard with the plan. Barron knew grief and a need for vengeance had warred in her mind for four years. He couldn't do anything about the pain of loss, but if killing Highborn could offer her any therapy, she was about to get a massive dose.

No amount of killing could compensate Stara for Jake Stockton's loss, or Barron for the realization that he would likely never see his daughter again...but that wasn't going to stop either of from trying to drown their misery in enemy blood.

* * *

"Forward, all ships. All batteries, prepare to fire on my command." Vian Tulus sat, appearing calm, even as his insides were twisted into knots. He felt the urgency of the moment, the call to fight with a ferocity unlike anything that had been seen before. There was tension as well, the knowledge that the Rim could very well fall to the enemy if his people, if the entire fleet, fell short on the destruction meted out in the coming hours.

And, as much as he tried to deny it to himself, he was scared as well. He knew the odds, the vanishing chances he had of surviving the battle that was about to begin.

If I must die, let the battle be one worthy of a song…

It was a noble thought, in the best traditions of Palatian Imperators.

Assuming anyone is left to write the song…

"All units report prepared for action, sir. The fleet is ready."

Tulus just nodded, and then he turned toward the display. The Highborn forces were coming through, but Barron's abrupt decision to reverse course had caught them by surprise. They were transiting in a long column…and Reg Griffin and the fighter wings were already closing hard, with two thousand bombers formed up right behind her interceptors. The bombers would begin their attack runs soon, braving the dangerous swarms of enemy point defense missiles, and deadly lances of their defensive beams.

But this time, the enemy will have something to worry about besides the fighters and bombers…

Just maybe, the battleline's advance and engagement would create enough distraction to give the attack ships some cover, and more of the small craft would make it through.

Tulus's flagship shook hard, a significant hit from the feel of it, and a reminder of the cost his people were likely to pay to aid the bombing wings. He'd never heard of battleships being used as diversions for small craft. It was almost always the reverse. But the Highborn line was still forming up, and that limited the damage they could inflict on his ships. It was a priceless opportunity to close before the Highborn could bring their full strength to bear. And if those two thousand bombers could get in with their formations reasonably intact, they could gut the Highborn vanguard.

If they did well enough, Tulus would see that they, too, got a song. Assuming he lived long enough.

"We've lost a pair of starboard batteries, sir, but the engines and reactors are undamaged, and the rest of the offensive array is operational."

Tulus nodded, acknowledging the damage report. *Not as bad as I feared…*

A few seconds later, one more word slipped into that thought. *Yet.* Worse was coming, and very probably soon. But his people were close now, and there weren't enough Highborn ships in position yet, at least not enough to wipe his line out.

He knew he should have cleared his advance with Barron, but as much as he respected his blood brother, the Confeds tended to get a little squishy about casualties. They were brave, and they died in droves when need be, but for all he'd become an honorary Palatian, Barron had never been able to view sending men and women to their deaths quite the same way Tulus did. He would never see glory as a thing worth dying for…and as much as his blood brother had changed *him*, Vian Tulus still heard the warrior's call.

He was leading the greatest force the Alliance had every fielded, in the most desperate battle it had fought. If that wasn't a thing worth a death, he didn't know what was.

The minstrels will sing of what we do here for a thousand years…

* * *

"Let's go, people…we all knew this day would come. Either we destroy this fleet coming through the point, or they'll do the same to us. This isn't a battle, it isn't a contest…it's a raw, blood-soaked struggle to the end. Only one side makes it through, so when you've launched your torpedoes, you use your lasers. But *no one* breaks off, not until I give the

word. Understood?" It was a question she knew six
thousand pilots couldn't answer, at least not that she could
hear. But she'd led them into enough deadly battles to know
what they were saying in their cockpits, spread across
seventy thousand kilometers of open space.

"Bombers, you're in this, too. I want you tucked in right
behind the interceptors. As soon as the enemy fighters are
cleared away, you go in. No delays…just blast your way in
and let those plasmas go. And take it in *close*…so damned
close you can see the paint peeling on their hulls."

Reg could hear the acknowledgements coming in, a tidal
wave of voices on the comm. She couldn't make much of it
out, but it didn't matter. It wasn't for her. She knew her
people would obey her commands, whether they
acknowledged or not. The shouts were for them. Morale
was a strange thing, and compelling men and women to do
terrifying things was as much an art form as it was
psychology.

She brought her ship around, checking a few times to
make sure her formations were in place. The battle was
mostly in the hands of the wing and squadron commanders
now. She was focused, waiting to send the bombers in, but
beyond that, she had one other task she set above all others.

She was looking for someone, for a specific ship…and
she suspected the pilot of that fighter was looking for her.
They'd fought twice, deadly duels that had pushed each to
the limits of their abilities. She'd held her own, more or less,
but in the deepest depths of her mind, she'd come to an
unexpected and disturbing conclusion.

That pilot was better than she was.

Not enormously so, nor enough to deprive her of a
chance at victory. But the fight would be the greatest of her
life, and the deadliest. It would take all she had, every bit of
skill and strength she could muster. If she could prevail, she
would almost certainly deprive the enemy squadrons of their
leader.

And if she failed, the Pact wings would lose theirs, the officer who had led them back from the brink after Jake Stockton's death.

Reg's stomach ached. It felt as though it was shriveled into a tiny ball, and even as she took hold of herself with iron discipline, she could feel her hands quivering slightly. She was determined, ready…craving the death of her enemy.

And she was scared, more abjectly terrified than she'd ever been in all her years at war.

There were thousands of fighters behind her. The wings she led had the advantage in numbers, at least until more of the Highborn ships were able to transit and deploy. It was an opportunity, and she intended to exploit it.

Her eyes scanned her display, searching for one single ship.

Nothing.

He might not even be with these forward forces…

She considered that for a moment, but then she dismissed it. In the end, it had only taken one thought to reach her conclusion. *Would you be anywhere but with these forward wings?*

She looked again, her eyes moving from one cluster of ships to another. She didn't have any real way to ID her enemy, but she was confident she'd know when she saw him.

Then her eyes froze.

One ship, apart from any formation, flying with a grace and style the masses of fighters on both sides lacked. It was far from a certain identification, but Reg had no doubt at all. Her hand moved, almost on its own, altering her thrust angle, beginning to change her course, to head for the fight of her life, the one she'd come for.

The one that would likely be her last.

She wondered if she'd spotted her enemy before he did her, some uncertainty nagging at her…but seconds later she got her answer.

The ship was changing course, too, heading right for her.

And it had launched a pair of missiles directly toward her fighter.

Chapter Thirty-Nine

Confederation Border Outpost Twelve
Sigma Delaris System
Year 327 AC (After the Cataclysm)

"Commander, we're picking up energy output from the transit point."

Larson Jaymes was sitting at his station, in the middle of the outpost's small control center. The outposts on the Union border were small installations, devoid of weaponry, by terms of the peace treaty between the two powers that had demilitarized the border.

It was also a place the Confederation navy had, in recent years, sent its problem officers and spacers, those one step away from being bounced out of the service. The practice had been in place, informally, of course, since the start of the Hegemony War, and it had continued with the subsequent conflict against the Highborn. Jaymes owed his continued presence in uniform to those conflicts, in fact, and the insatiable demand they had created for ever more officers, ships, and spacers. If there had been any meaningful stretch of peace, Jaymes knew he'd have been expelled from the service, certainly after the third time he'd been drunk on duty.

"Which transit point? The system has three." Jaymes

wasn't drunk then. In truth, he'd cleaned up his act, and he hadn't had a drink in months. But he'd been as close to asleep as a man could be when he was still awake. The Union border had been silent for years, first in the aftermath of the last war between the two powers, and subsequently, as the Confederation's old enemy had slipped into chaos and civil war.

"*The* transit point, Commander. The one from Union space."

Jaymes looked up with a rapid jerk of his neck. He wasn't the most attentive officer at times, but his aide was telling him the one thing he'd been trained to handle, the sole reason he and his sixty-four spacers were stuck in a cold metal cylinder on the very edge of Confederation space, was happening.

Ships were coming in from Union space.

He felt a momentary panic, but then it mostly passed. He was hardly privy to the latest intelligence on conditions in the Union, but based on what he did know, it seemed impossible the enemy was invading. *A group of defectors, maybe? Or some foul up in freighter manifests?*

"We're picking up contacts now, sir."

Time seemed to slow, and Jaymes could feel his mind racing, trying to come up with a list of possible explanations. He'd have been scared of an unexpected Union invasion, if he hadn't been as well briefed as he was on the disruptions within that power. He'd heard some unsettling rumors about recent events in the civil war there, but he couldn't come up with any way, a bankrupt and exhausted Union could mount an invasion of the Confederation.

Though the border is stripped clean…it wouldn't take much to burst through the defenses…

Even Grimaldi, the massive fortress that had been the nerve center for operations in two successive wars with the Union, had been neglected, most of its fighter wings transferred to the Highborn front, its aging weapons neglected and allowed to decay.

"We're picking up ships now, sir. Union warships." A short pause. "Confirmed."

Jaymes still couldn't imagine how the Union could possibly mount an invasion, but he felt a twinge inside nevertheless. If he was wrong, if the Confederation's longtime enemy *was* coming, he knew very well who would be the first to die. Outpost Twelve didn't have any armament at all, just the sophisticated scanner array fueling the growing panic inside him.

"Transmit a challenge, Lieutenant." Jaymes was staring at the display as he spoke. His nerves were a wreck, but even as he issued the order, he could see something was wrong.

The Union ships were moving raggedly, in considerable disorder. Some clearly had greater thrust levels than others, and a closer look revealed atmosphere and radiation leaks, and signs of hastily-patched hulls. Those ships, whatever they were, had been through hell. They looked more like a battered and defeated force than any invasion fleet. Still, Jaymes knew the protocols well enough.

"Send a flash transmission back to Grimaldi, Lieutenant...and bring the outpost to full alert."

"Yes, Commander." A short pause, then: "Commander, we're receiving an incoming message. I have an Admiral Denisov on your line…"

* * *

"Andrei, I got here as quickly as I could. I'm sorry to keep you all the way out here. I would have authorized your people to move on to Grimaldi, but I wanted…to be cautious about allowing any rumors to spread." Gary Holsten extended his arm, grasping the Union admiral's hand. In truth, he'd been more concerned about the *truth* getting out than he was any rumors, or at least what he feared was the truth. It had been far easier to quarantine the outpost and its tiny crew than it would have been at Fleet Base Grimaldi.

Even if Grimaldi had been stripped to a skeleton crew.

"Thank you, Mr. Holsten. I had nowhere else to go. I'm not concerned for myself, but my spacers…"

"Of course, Andrei…you are all welcome. I will see that any who wish it are granted asylum, and any who elect to return will be allowed to do so." A pause. "And it's Gary, Andrei. We've known each other how many years now?" Holsten and Denisov had worked together for some time during the Hegemony War, but the Union admiral had been gone for more than four years, fighting in the Union Civil War. For most of that time, Holsten had been sure his ally would prevail.

Good reminder…never be sure about anything…

"There will not be many who wish to return…if any at all. I'm afraid nothing but death awaits any of them on Montmirail, and perhaps worse."

Holsten nodded, and he remained silent a few seconds before he spoke. He knew very well there were worse things than death, especially at the hands of a man like Gaston Villieneuve. "Tell me, Andrei, what happened? It seemed you were close to victory? Did Villieneuve have some hidden forces, something he slipped past us all?" *Please, let it be that…*

"Yes, in a manner of speaking…Gary. He seems to have found some kind of ally…one with technology considerably in advance of our own." Denisov pulled a small tablet from a pouch at his side, and he tapped the screen, turning it on. "Here is some scanner footage from the battle at Montmirail. One of the mysterious ships."

Holsten looked down at the screen, knowing what he would see even as he prayed it wasn't so.

"They are Highborn, are they not?" Denisov's voice was deadpan, his exhaustion and despair overwhelming his efforts to control them. It was clear he already knew the answer to his question.

Holsten's eyes focused on the ship displayed on the tablet…and his heart sank. "Yes, Andrei…that is a Highborn ship." He sighed deeply. "They must have traveled around the perimeter of the Hegemony and the Badlands, and through the Periphery." It was a long way, almost impossibly so. But Highborn ships did have considerably higher thrust capacities than anything on the Rim. The time spent in interstellar travel wasn't crossing the great gulfs between suns. The transit points reduced those journeys to seconds in duration. It was crossing the systems, from one point to the next that took time. And 40g of additional thrust could really cut time from such trips.

"How many of these ships were present?"

"Sixteen confirmed." Denisov hesitated. "I know that doesn't seem like many, but they outranged us by a huge margin. None of my ships could even close with them…and my fighter squadrons were all configured for interceptor operations. They were badly depleted as well."

Holsten nodded. "There was nothing you could have done, Andrei. We struggle at the front, with our latest and most advanced units. Your people went right from the Hegemony War into your own civil conflict. Your ships are at least twelve or fifteen years old, and most of them are considerably older. You didn't have any chance against the Highborn. Even if they'd had fewer ships, the truth is they could have stayed out of range while they blasted your fleet to scrap. You couldn't catch them, and you couldn't fire back, and without sufficient bomber strength, there was no way for you to hurt them. You did well to get any of your ships out."

"That's kind of you, Gary, but I lost more than eighty percent of my command…adding in the losses on the ships that did escape, fewer than fifteen percent of my spacers made it out. They're dead, the rest of them…and if they're not, it's only because a few ships were captured, and the crews fell into Villieneuve's hands." Denisov looked down at the deck, and he fell silent.

Holsten could almost hear what he wasn't saying, though. Any captured spacers were suffering all the more because he had survived, and extricated some of his people. There was no doubt that fact had enraged Villieneuve.

"You did the right thing, Andrei. You could have served no purpose by dying at Montmirail. Your skills are incredibly valuable, and your spacers deserve to have you in command."

"Command? Of what? Three dozen ships, most of the damaged, and every one of them an out of date relic? Is that a fleet? And even if it is, technically, it's one I can't supply. Not even with the useless, obsolete weapons that failed us so badly at Montmirail."

Holsten had always been impressed with Denisov's strength, but now he could see the admiral was close to coming apart. "Andrei...you're here now. You're with friends. We'll help you care for your wounded, repair and resupply your ships. I'm going to tell you something Tyler Barron told me a long time ago. The fight isn't over until *you* give up. I know things look dark now, but you came to our aid when we were fighting the Hegemony...and we won't stop until our enemies are defeated. All of them."

Holsten held his head firm, resisting the urge to shake it at his impetuous suggestion that Confederation forces might invade the Union and overthrow Gaston Villieneuve. He was likely to have enough trouble with the Senate. He tried to imagine convincing them to allow a battered Confed navy that somehow made it through the war with the Highborn turning about immediately and attacking the Union. The thought made his head hurt.

One realization slammed into him like a train, and he struggled to remain calm, to breath regularly and keep the panic at bay.

The Highborn hadn't made an immense trek around the

Badlands just to help Gaston Villieneuve. They had done it to take control of the Union.

No, they have *taken control of the Union…*

Holsten had long argued that the Union wasn't a threat, that its fleets were depleted, its science behind, its economy in shambles. Now he faced a Union backed by Highborn technology, its fleets supported by Highborn ships. A theoretical and manageable danger had now become a very real—and extremely dangerous—one.

If the combined Highborn and Union forces invaded, they would punch through the thinly defended border in a matter of weeks, and they would cut off the heart of the Confederation from the main front.

Worse, they could move right on the Iron Belt and the Core…while most of the navy was cut off, forty jumps away.

He had to do something. He had to find some way to strengthen the border.

But how?

Chapter Forty

32,000,000 Kilometers from CFS Dauntless
Beta Telvara System
Year 327 AC (After the Cataclysm)

Reg watched as the enemy missiles continued past her, flying off into space on unchanging vectors. They would continue on until they struck something, a planet, a sun, or perhaps they would make their way in a few hundred thousand years, into intergalactic space. Whatever their fate, they weren't her problem anymore.

She was drenched, and her body slid around inside her flight suit, becoming more and more uncomfortable with each passing minute. The shaking in her hands had gotten worse, and it had spread to her legs as well. She'd escaped her enemy's missile attack...by the slimmest of margins. But the cold truth had taken hold of her.

Ten seconds more fuel in those weapons would have doomed her.

She sucked in a deep breath, and she pushed back against the nausea. She hadn't prevailed, not yet. She hadn't even gained an edge. She'd simply survived the first exchange, as her opponent had done with hers. Both fighters had expended their missiles. Now, they would settle things once and for all, at close range with lasers.

A true dogfight.

She shook her head, as though the motion would clear her jumbled thoughts, and bring her the clarity she craved.

Her eyes were fixed on her opponent. There were other fighters around, from both sides, engaged in their own combats. She thought about calling for aid, trying to overwhelm the ship opposite hers. But none of her people could handle a pilot as skilled at the Highborn leader. Timmons or Federov, perhaps, but they were on the far side of the formation. She'd put them there deliberately…to keep them away. She knew very well she might die in the coming moments, and the strike force couldn't lose *all* its leaders. The two remaining Horsemen, Jake Stockton's old comrades, were the only ones who could step in if she died, the only pilots who could lead the wings, give them any chance at victory.

She couldn't risk that, not even to save herself.

Besides, it had become a matter of pride. She'd fought a pair of draws with her enemy, but despite the lack of a decisive end to either combat, she couldn't lie to herself. She'd gotten the worst of it both times. She wanted revenge. She wanted to prove herself…in her own mind, at least.

Her hand tightened on her controls, her finger resting over the firing stud. Her lasers were charged and ready, and the range was quickly counting down on her screen. She was almost there…but so was her adversary.

She was ready to shoot, but even as she did, as she opened fire and tried to kill her enemy, he would be doing the same. In a few seconds, it would begin…and then any instant could be her last. She might not even have any warning. Not knowing it was coming, being alive one second and possibly dead the next, was the hardest part for her to accept. She could feel the tension inside her, almost as though her body was tightening, curling up.

She sucked in one long, deep breath…and then she

clenched her fingers, and her cockpit echoed with the high-pitched whine of the lasers firing.

* * *

Olya Federov leaned forward, her hand tight on the bomber's controls, her mouth barely a few centimeters from the comm unit. "All wings, you've got your targets. We're going in now, and you all know what to do." She nudged up the power to her engines, feeling the g forces increase as her bomber accelerated. She'd given herself the largest Highborn ship as a target, one of the big battleships, the class she'd seen in the footage of the fighting at Calpharon. It was a big monster, and she suspected it could take a lot of damage. But she had two hundred bombers right behind her, and a force like that could *put out* a lot of damage.

Even if only half of them made it through.

Federov was a veteran, a legend in the fighter corps only a rung below the place Jake Stockton had occupied. But she'd never been at her best in a bomber. She'd made her bones as an interceptor pilot, as an ace dogfighter. She'd flown bombers during the Hegemony war, of course, as most pilots had, but she'd never reached the level of proficiency she'd always had facing other fighters.

But when Reg Griffin asked her to lead the bombing run, Federov understood. She was aware of the danger, of the deadly fire the bombers would face. If she could get them in fast enough, before the enemy got more ships up to the line, maybe—just maybe—they would escape with less than crushing losses. But that meant moving forward while the interceptor battle was still going on.

If any of those Highborn wings break off and get away from our interceptors…

Bombers could evade point defense attacks, but the cumbersome craft were like a flock of sheep before hungry wolves when facing interceptors. All she could do was trust in Griffin, and the dogfighting wings, who still had at least a fifty percent edge in numbers.

She stared at the screen, watching the battleships growing larger as she closed. For a moment, she thought perhaps none of the ships in front of her mounted the deadly point defense missiles…and then she saw them launching.

They were sporadic, spread out far more than they had been in the scanner data from Calpharon. But that didn't mean they weren't dangerous. They were going to take out bombers, a lot of them.

They were going to kill her people.

"Stay tight on those evasive routines…all of you. Nobody has permission to get scragged by a missile, you all understand that?" It seemed pointless to remind them all yet again, but she'd found such things to be effective. And even if it only saved one of her people, it was worthwhile.

There was one cluster of missiles on the screen in front of her ship. That seemed like light fire, and it was to an extent. But she also knew those weapons would split into multiple smaller warheads…and every one of those would still be strong enough to take her ship out if it could get within half a kilometer before it detonated.

Her finger tapped away on the small keyboard off to the side of her main controls. She activated the AI-assisted evasive routines, and she leaned over the comm. "All units…get your evasive maneuvers started now. Those warheads are going to split any time. And remember, those things don't have to actually hit you. Let one get half a kilometer from your ship, and you're finished." It came out a little harsher than she'd intended, but Federov had never been one for soothing tones.

Or for bullshit. A lot of her people were going to die, and many more if they didn't do what she told them to do. They needed to hear that, and the needed to pay attention. Loud and hard was the way she'd always given it to her subordinates. It was the way it would stick.

She tapped her throttle, even as the four or five missiles nearest her vanished from the screen, replaced by clouds of smaller dots. At least two of those were a threat to her own ship, and as she panned her eyes across the display, she found herself estimating how many of her fighters the missiles would take out.

She breathed deeply, holding it for a few seconds, and then exhaling with considerable force, even as she pushed her arm forward, and fed power to her engines.

* * *

Barron looked out, watching the battle. He was proud of his people, and he felt a closeness to each of them. He sincerely believed every one of them deserved to survive, to return home victorious, and spend the rest of their lives at peace with their families.

He also knew that wasn't going to happen.

His desperate tactic had worked, better even than he'd dared to expect. The Highborn Vanguard had been crushed, almost obliterated, though his people had paid a heavy price for that success. He'd never seen a Highborn force so battered, so close to outright annihilation. But the image on the scanner drained away his enthusiasm. His people had destroyed a lot of enemy ships…but there were far more of them moving up.

And they were *still* coming through the point.

His problems had only increased, his situation worse in many ways than it had been. His numerical superiority was gone, or at least it would be once the newest enemy arrivals were able to deploy. His fleet was going to be overwhelmed, and every tactical instinct in him was screaming to withdraw.

But that was impossible. If he turned and ran, he would fly right into the blocking force, which had been moving toward his fleet, and was already almost hallway across the

JAY ALLAN

system. If he turned and ran and engaged them, the forces his ships were currently fighting would follow, and they would slam into the rear of his fleet. If he stayed, continued the fight in place, the blocking force would complete their journey across the system and attack from the rear.

Either way, his forces would be bracketed, surrounded. If the enemy kept pouring more ships into the system, it would be even worse, even more quickly. His fleet would be completely englobed.

Breaking off, making a run for it, meant almost certain death.

But so did staying where he was.

Barron glanced over at Atara, and her return gaze confirmed that she understood the situation exactly as he did. His move against the pursuing force had been out of the box thinking, but now he had nothing. Tactics, courage, resolve…they all played a role in combat outcomes. But there was a point when mathematics took control, became the absolute arbiter of battle.

Things were close to that point, if not there already. He wondered if he'd made a mistake, if he should have allowed his people to break formation and make a mad dash for home. His experience and understanding of the tactical situation told him only a small fraction would have made it, but now he would fight the final, fateful stages of the battle far across the system, nowhere close to an escape route.

Barron had commanded in his share of desperate situations, but he had never been so mentally exhausted, so utterly without any idea of what to do next.

"Admiral…" There was something in Atara's voice. Surprise? Certainly. But something else, too. Was it hope? What could she have possibly seen to drive away the black curtain of despair?

"What is it?"

"We're picking something up, sir. I think it's…"

* * *

Reg Griffin's laughter echoed off the canopy of her fighter. It was a caustic, bitter display, an outpouring of vengeance and hatred...and a way of saluting her comrade. Olya Federov had led the bombers in, and she'd gotten through the enemy's defenses with more than three quarters of her ships still in formation. That was partly because of how stretched out the of enemy fleet was, but her evasive maneuvers had been nothing short of brilliant. He survivors plunged through the final layer of enemy point defense, losing another five percent of their number to the hyper-accurate beams, and then they planted their plasma torpedoes directly into the guts of the Highborn ships.

They were targeting the carriers, just as the forward battle line units were doing. It was a gamble, one that ran counter to normal doctrine, but the fact that the Highborn not only possessed fighters, but had them in massive numbers, had turned everything on its head. Reg had no idea how many launch platforms were with the enemy fleet, but she didn't have to have an exact count to know taking them out was a good thing.

Perhaps her people could maintain their superiority. Denying the enemy squadrons a place to land was an effective strategy. It didn't matter how good they were, or how advanced their ships were. If they couldn't refuel and rearm, they were finished.

We might be able to refit and relaunch...and keep the pressure on. Perhaps she could even fit out more of her ships as bombers.

Or Olya or whoever else might do that...if I'm not there...

Reg was excited to see her wings performing so well...but she was losing hope of leading them out herself for any second assault.

She was fighting fiercely, better she believed, than she ever had. But it wasn't enough. It was close to what she needed. But close in a one on one dogfight was just about the most useless thing imaginable. Dying because one was a half second behind an adversary or missed by twenty meters, didn't change the reality of being dead.

She still couldn't understand how a Highborn pilot had gotten so good, so quickly, but such thoughts were rapidly leaving her mind, chased out by more primal sensations, like despair and fear. She'd just dodged a pair of shots that had almost finished things, including one deadly lance of laser energy that had come less than twenty meters from her ship. She was still hyperventilating from that one, and she knew the more rattled she became, the less effective she was. Fear was beginning to do her enemy's work for him.

She tightened her hand on the controls, and she grasped in her mind for any way to control fear, to refocus her thoughts on the fight at hand. She was at a disadvantage, she couldn't deny that…but it wasn't over yet.

You can win this battle, dammit. Just stay on it, don't give up…

But such things were easier said than done, and she wrestled fiercely on the brink of despair. She was a veteran, and that strength prevailed…barely. She still wasn't convinced she could win, but she was damned sure going to keep trying.

If her opponent wanted her to stop, he would have to finish her, and if he gave her any opening at all, that was just what she was going to do it him.

*   *   *

"We're definitely picking up additional contacts, Admiral…besides the enemy blocking force. Behind them, on the far side, toward our exit transit point." Atara was trying hard not to sound confused, but Barron knew her too well to be fooled. She had no more idea what was happening than he did. The idea of more Highborn ships, beyond the two vast forces already bracketing his fleet, was horrifying enough. But the last place the Highborn would be coming from was through that point. Striker was only a few transits beyond, and even with the outposts gone, he'd placed enough pickets there to get warning to Clint Winters if any enemy forces tried to push through.

Barron remembered his words with Winters, just before the fleet set out. He'd been determined then, and he'd meant every word he'd said. But he wondered if he had been wrong, if *Colossus* and the rest of the ships at Striker, including, he suspected, the new antimatter-powered *Excalibur* would have made a difference. Had he consigned his fleet to destruction, and all his people to death?

"We're picking up beacons now, Admiral." Atara was suddenly excited, and the doubt had mostly vanished from her tone. "They're Confederation signals...and Hegemony ones. And Palatian, too!." She looked across the bridge, and their eyes connected. "They're ours, Admiral. I don't know how, but those ships are ours!"

Barron felt a rush of emotions, confusion, then clarity...and a flash of anger that quickly faded. Suddenly he understood. Clint Winters had disobeyed his orders. He had led the ships at Striker forward after the fleet. That was insane, foolish, reckless. How far would he have gone, how deep into enemy territory, if he hadn't run into Barron's people back in Bata Telvara. But his anger couldn't get any traction. The Sledgehammer had disobeyed his orders...but his comrade and second-in-command also given him—and his spacers and his fleet—a chance, at escape at least, if not at victory. And he wasn't going to throw it away.

He felt renewed vigor, and the hopelessness that had begun to take hold was suddenly gone.

Chapter Forty-One

CFS Excalibur
Beta Telvara System
Year 327 AC (After the Cataclysm)

"Get me more thrust. All ships, push reactors. We've got to catch those bastards." Clint Winters was snapping out orders, some of them containing language that would have been frowned upon in the Academy. But the Sledgehammer had a reputation for firing out commands that were both loud and dirty, and he was living up to his own legend in every way as he led the relief force forward.

He'd expected to engage the enemy almost immediately. Andi's description of the Highborn locations had been precise, and if he knew one thing about his friend, it was that he could take every word she uttered as incontrovertible fact. But, of course, Andi had come through the system over a week before, and ships could change locations at any time.

That hadn't made much sense at first. A position astride the transit point seemed the perfect place to lay in wait, the ideal spot for trapping Barron's retreating fleet.

Then, the long range scans came in, and with them, complete clarity. Barron's ships weren't somewhere deeper in Occupied Space, making their way back to Beta Telvara.

They were in that very system already, on the other side from where Winter's ships had just entered…and they were in the middle of a fierce struggle with Highborn forces that had pursued them.

Winters might have hesitated, wondering what had happened, but he knew Tyler Barron too well for that. His friend had spotted the enemy trap, and instead of racing across the system and making a run for it—just what the enemy had wanted—he'd turned about and hit his pursuers as they transited. It was bold, daring, decisive.

It was Tyler Barron.

And it was perfect. Barron had made his decision alone, a desperate attempt to find a way take on the two enemy forces individually. But now, Winters's fleet was going to engage the blocking force. There were still a lot of Highborn in the system, and even with everything the Pact could muster present, it was going to be a hard and deadly fight.

But at least there was a chance, if not of victory, of escape.

"Admiral, Commodore Eaton advises that she can increase *Colossus*'s acceleration to 90g."

Winters turned, and he nodded. "Have her increase to 90g. And, let's get *Excalibur* up to 75g, at least. Those are antimatter reactors down there, so let's see what the hell they can do."

"Yes, Admiral."

He could hear the hesitation in the officer's voice, and he understood. He was violating every tactical principle in the book. It made no sense sending his most powerful ship ahead alone, while he followed in the second strongest, leaving the rest of the fleet strung out behind.

But it made less sense to allow the Highborn blocking force to reach Barron's fleet before he could engage them. He'd come to rescue Barron's people…not to watch them outflanked and destroyed while he looked on helplessly. If he could get close enough before the Highborn made it across the system, he might force them to turn and deploy to face his attack.

That would be hard on *Excalibur* and *Colossus*, and on the Hegemony battleships that would be next in line behind them. But the rest of the fleet would be coming up next.

"Gunnery stations…prepare to open fire." The Highborn had the range advantage over every ship in the Pact fleet…save two.

The two that were advancing at the forefront of Winters's force.

Colossus's massive old imperial batteries were a match for anything the enemy had…and while *Excalibur*'s main guns were untested in combat, the specs were clear that they could fire on targets almost as far out as the Highborn ships could.

And the railguns on the Hegemony battleships just behind weren't that much shorter ranged.

"All gunnery stations report ready to fire on your command." A few seconds went by. "Admiral, scanners are picking up energy readings from *Colossus*. They've commenced firing, sir!"

Winters smiled, and he nodded, a barely perceptible move, and one acknowledging Sonya Eaton's skill and preparedness. Winters had mourned the loss of Sonya's older sister, Sara, as had the rest of the fleet. The elder Eaton had been one of the navy's most popular officers, and one of its most capable. But her sister was rapidly filling her shoes, and when Tyler Barron had given her *Colossus*, he'd put her in charge of the single most powerful war machine any of the Pact powers possessed.

And she had never given him reason to regret his choice.

Winters watched as the scanners updated *Colossus*'s shots. Damage assessments began to scroll down the display as two of the massive weapons scored hits, and a dense cloud of radiation spewed out from the forward Highborn ship.

Winters felt his hands clench, and he pumped his fist in

silent congratulations. Then his eyes saw as the distance to the lead targets ticked down, into *Excalibur*'s range.

"All batteries…open fire."

* * *

Stockton could feel the excitement and exhilaration that only came to him in battle, when he was fighting a worthy opponent. When he was on the verge of victory.

And he hated himself for it.

It was Reg Griffin out there, he was almost sure of that. He recognized her fighting style, the things he'd taught her, and those personal touches she'd brought with her. She was, in many ways, his greatest student, and she'd come close to equaling her teacher's ability.

Close…but not quite.

Combat was never a sure thing. Reg Griffin was perfectly capable of killing Stockton, but he figured he had at least four chances in five of defeating his adversary.

His friend.

He felt an urgency to finish the battle, to kill Reg, so he could attend to his wings, to the problems that had been mounting all the while he'd fought his duel with his old protege. Casualties were far beyond the most pessimistic projections, courtesy more than anything of Admiral Barron's unorthodox move to turn about on the pursuing force. He hadn't expected his wings to be outnumbered for so long, but he realized he should have. He'd fought with Tyler Barron for two decades, and he cursed himself for underestimating the Confederation admiral.

And deeper down, he felt the warmth of a smile. *Well done, Admiral…*

It was also clear the Pact bombers, and even the advance elements of their battleline, were all targeting the carriers. He was losing launch platforms faster even than fighters, and finding his people someplace to land was rapidly becoming a major concern.

The targeting priorities were as daring a move on Barron's part as his course reversal. It posed a dire threat to the Highborn wings, at least the most forward ones…but the bill would come due when the undamaged Highborn battleships were able to mass sufficient strength to start tearing apart the Pact battleships from outside their opponents' ranges.

But the fighters, and where to land them…that was *his* problem.

Land them in the center of the damned sun…I will lead them there myself…

But his thoughts of sabotaging the wings were as impotent as they had been for four years, and he knew he would do everything possible to safely land the squadrons, and lead them out again against his old comrades.

First, he would kill Reg Griffin, and in doing so, he would not only betray a friend, he would allow the best chance he'd had in four years of escaping into the arms of death slip by.

It was time. He could feel it. He understood it in his mind.

And he made one last, desperate effort—ultimately futile—to stop himself, to keep his hand from the controls. Even to delay, to make a mistake, give Reg an opening. To no avail. The Collar was as securely in control as ever.

His eyes narrowed, focused on his target. He felt the predator's thrill at an impending kill, and he despised himself as the high flooded over him. He was going to kill his old comrade, his friend.

And to his utter disgust, he was going to enjoy it.

His ship banked hard, and his hand closed around the throttle, his finger tightening on the firing stud.

*   *   *

"Admiral…request authorization to bring the bomber wings in immediately. If we can get everyone docked quickly enough, we might be able to get out in time to hit the force moving on the rear of the fleet."

Tyler Barron listened to Olya Federov on the comm, but his attention was split. He was still checking the scanner reports, trying to piece together just what kind of relief force had arrived.

Trying to decide what he should do. Should he press forward harder, do as much damage as possible to the enemy fleet *still* transiting in? Or should he pull back, make a run across the system…and just maybe, trap the enemy's would be blocking force between the two Pact fleets? There wouldn't be time to fight that out, to take full advantage of the positioning…not with so many ships coming through that would almost certainly follow him. But he was sure he and Winters could give the blocking force one hell of a beating.

"Yes, Olya…get all your people back onboard. As quickly as possible." Barron knew the evasive maneuvers of the fleet's line ships would make landing operations difficult. He also knew he had the best officer in known space to direct it all. Stara Sinclair had brought thousands of fighters back into the bays, even while their mother ships were locked in their own desperate battles. It wasn't supposed to be possible, even, at least not by the book. But Barron had seen her do it. More than once.

"Atara, the bombers are coming in. Alert all ships, and advise that Commodore Sinclair will be directing landing ops."

"Yes, Admiral."

Barron nodded, and he leaned back, wrestling with the next decision he had to make. Reg Griffin's fighters were taking great advantage of their temporary numerical advantage. But if he was going to break off, he had to get them back aboard. He was already too late, and every passing moment only worsened the problem.

But if he was going to keep up the pressure on the enemy fleet as it transited, he wanted those fighters out there. The enemy would be at a tremendous disadvantage as it continued to launch additional wings piecemeal, as their carriers arrived. Pulling the fighters back would give away a chance to hurt the enemy even more than he had already.

Leaving them out there risked being compelled to abandon them entirely when he decided to make a run for it. That was something he couldn't allow.

"Atara, get Reg Griffin on the line. We've got to pull back the entire strike force."

"Yes, Admiral." A few seconds later: "No response from Admiral Griffin, sir. I've got Dirk Timmons."

Barron tried his best not to imagine the worst about Reg. Too many people were counting on him just then to allow a moment to worry about a friend. "Warrior, this is Admiral Barron. We can't reach Admiral Griffin. I need you to take command of the interceptor wings, and prepare to break off and return to base. Olya Federov is landing the bombers right now. Stay in the fight for fifteen minutes more, and then get the hell back here, *as fast as you can!*"

*   *   *

Reg jerked her hand hard to the side, her ship's thrust angle moving sharply, and the wall of g force slamming into her from the side. She could see the vague glimmering of laser blasts ripping by just to the port side of her fighter, slight hints of the trajectory of her enemy's shots as they passed through intermittent clouds of gas and particulate.

That was close…

She was soaked in sweat, and she felt as though she was staring right into the eyes of death. But the trembling had passed. She wasn't sure if she had overcome her fear, or merely accepted the inevitability of defeat. She didn't care.

She was still fighting, struggling against her enemy with all she had, every scrap she could dig up. And if she had to die, that was the way she wanted to go.

The Highborn fighter had dueled with her for almost twenty minutes, executing one elegant maneuver after another. The attacks had been deadly dangerous, but they had also been conducted in ways that made her own counterattacks difficult, if not impossible. But now, something had changed.

The enemy ship was coming in hard, right toward her. For an instant, she wondered why her opponent had given up his choreographed dance, his tactic of wearing her down, gradually increasing his advantage in the battle. Then she realized.

All it took was a quick glance at the long-range scanner, and the blasted and crippled hulks that had been three dozen Highborn carriers. Her enemy had increased the intensity of his attacks because he'd run out of time. He needed to direct his wings, find a way to get them back to landing platforms that could accommodate them. And that meant ending the one on one duel, and doing it quickly.

Reg felt a new wave of fear, but with it she sensed opportunity as well. Her enemy was a terrible danger as his ship came tearing toward hers…but he was more vulnerable as well. The risk she faced, the growing shadow of death closing on her also offered her a chance at victory.

She stared at the screen, her mind racing, calculating alongside the targeting computer, putting all her attention and focus into lining up her shot.

Her last shot.

She, too, was sacrificing defensive effort, betting all on one last attack…a wild gamble that she could get off the killing shot before her adversary did.

She drew a deep and ragged breath, adjusting her targeting every half second or so…and then she fired.

She waited to see if she'd delivered the kill shot…or simply left herself open to her enemy.

She got a partial answer seconds later, as a laser blast ripped by so close, it looked almost as though she could have reached out and touched it…and then a second shot hit her fighter dead on, and she could feel the stricken craft disintegrating all around her, hear the wild hiss of her life support slipping away.

* * *

Stockton felt a deep, jolting pain at the base of his head, almost as though he'd been turned inside out. He shouted, a primal scream of torment as his head seemed to explode inside his skull. He could hear and feel crackling sounds all around his cockpit as arcs of high amperage electricity snapped all around. He felt half a dozen more shocks, one after the other, every one of them painful and distracting.

He'd been hit, that was immediately clear. It was evident the shot that had struck his ship hadn't quite been the kill shot his opponent—and the part of his mind that was still *him*—had so desperately wanted. His fighter was damaged, and he was injured. But he was still in the fight.

And none of it drew his focus from what he was doing. His eyes remained fixed, and his right hand was tight on the throttle. His enemy was there, in his sights. To his unabashed horror, he knew it was time.

His fingers tightened, and the lasers whined as they sent their deadly pulses of concentrated light to the Lightning craft he knew carried Reg Griffin.

Half his control panel had shorted out, but he had one screen left, and his adversary's ship was displayed dead center on that. His first shot missed, by less than three meters.

But the second slammed right into the fighter, tearing open the entire starboard side…and a few seconds later, the entire ship broke up, bits and pieces spinning off in a dozen directions.

Stockton stared at the now empty space where Reg Griffin's fighter had been, and he felt the satisfaction of the predator, the almost unrestrained rush he had always enjoyed after victory in combat.

And somewhere else, in that lone and helpless part of his brain, there was only despair, and guilt so deep and biting, he prayed to any power that might aid him to empower one of his old pilots, to send one of them to defeat him and end his suffering at last.

*   *   *

Andi was staring at *Pegasus*'s display. She'd been trying to get a read on the massive fighter battle taking place across five hundred trillion cubic kilometers of space, but her attention had been diverted to what had seemed to be one great duel between pilots. She'd guessed the pilot in the Lightning was Reg Griffin, a few seconds before the fighter's ID beacon confirmed it. She'd been leaning forward, and her body tensed rigidly, becoming more and more astonished at the abilities of the Highborn pilot Reg was fighting.

Then, suddenly, Reg's ship vanished from the screen.

Andi gasped, and she felt her insides convulse. It took all the will she could muster to hold the contents of her stomach down. She had considered Jake Stockton one of her very few true friends, and she'd mourned his death terribly. But she'd quickly gotten to know Reg, and she'd developed a strong attachment to the pilot.

The pilot she'd just watched die.

She felt a wild rage growing inside her, a fury that defied any satisfaction. She wanted Highborn blood, and if she could have, she would have consigned their entire accursed race to utter extinction. The distance to the main fleet was still too great for any but the haziest of scanner data, but

Clint Winters had managed to pinpoint *Dauntless*...and he'd sent her word that Tyler was still alive. That was an assumption, she knew. It didn't appear the flagship had suffered serious damage yet, but that didn't mean there weren't casualties aboard. But the news had been gratifying nevertheless.

For about five minutes...until she'd watched Reg Griffin die in front of her.

"Andi..."

Vig's voice cut through the gloom surrounding her. Her eyes remained fixed forward, watching Reg Griffin's killer bank away and blast hard from the scene of the epic battle. She was consumed with the desire to chase down that pilot...and frustrated at her inability to do more than watch the ship fly back toward the main battle.

"What is it, Vig?" She immediately regretted the caustic anger she'd allowed to slip into her tone.

"We're picking up a signal. It's faint, but I think it's a transponder...from a pilot's survival suit."

Andi had barely been listening, but a few seconds later, Vig's words sunk in and suddenly made sense.

"Location data on the screen," she snapped, her own hands moving over her controls, zooming the display area to a small zone around the area where Reg's ship had been destroyed. She adjusted the data, accounting for the intrinsic velocity of the destroyed ship.

A velocity that would impart to anything—anyone—who had ejected from it.

A few seconds later, a small blinking light appeared...right where Reg's ship would have been.

"Vig, set a course for that point...now!" Andi had promised Clint Winters she'd keep *Pegasus* out of the fight, away from the enemy forces. She had already partially broken that pledge by bringing her ship much farther forward than caution allowed. Now, she was going to lunge even farther, right to the very edge of the great fighter battle still raging.

She tried to tell herself it was okay, that Clint Winters hadn't *really* believed she would stay back, and in that fact lay some sort of absolution.

She didn't take breaking promises lightly, but if that was Reg Griffin floating out there, she just couldn't leave her. The pilot could be wounded, her survival gear damaged. Even if all was well, her life support would run out far before the fleet could pick her up, even under the best circumstances.

And the fleet is going to have to make a dash to escape the system, which means there won't even be *any rescue operations…*

Besides, Clint Winters was violating orders, breaking his own promise to Tyler. Andi knew she had played a role in that, of course, but she latched on to it…and tried to justify her actions, even to herself.

Andi looked back at the display, her hands flying about on her controls, trying to enhance the signal, to confirm the beacon was, in fact, from Reg Griffin's escape pod. But there was too much interference from the battle raging all around. Her gut told her it was Reg…but she had no real proof.

But Andi Lafarge had always listened to her instincts, and they hadn't killed her yet.

"Full power, Vig…if that's Reg Griffin floating around out there, we're her only chance…"

Vig just nodded, and Andi knew her old friend had left one glaring question unasked.

What chance did *Pegasus* have of moving that far forward, finding Reg and bringing her aboard, and then getting out in one piece?

Andi didn't know…but she was going to find out.

Chapter Forty-Two

CFS Dauntless
Beta Telvara System
Year 327 AC (After the Cataclysm)

"Full thrust, all units. We're going home." That was beyond oversimplification, but Barron figured they were words his people needed to hear. The arrival of reinforcements hadn't eliminated the danger of utter destruction, but it had at least given his people a chance. Just maybe, they could fight their way out.

Even as he turned back and looked at the display, he could see that much of the blocking force was decelerating, preparing to come about and engage the newly-arrived Pact forces. The Highborn ships that had planned to trap his fleet in a wedge between hostile forces were now facing that very danger themselves. And Barron was going to make the most of it while he could.

"Atara, I want all ships ready to open fire the instant we are in range of those ships. If we push the engines hard enough—and maybe a little over redline—we should be able to engage them about the same time as the bulk of Admiral Winters's forces do."

"Yes, Admiral!" He could hear the old bloodthirsty

sound in Atara's voice, and his mind flashed back to a dozen other desperate fights.

He still wasn't *sure* the newly arrived fleet was commanded by Clint Winters, not technically, at least. But he didn't have any real doubt. First of all, he didn't know anyone else with the guts to so overtly disregard his clear orders.

Second, the directness and ferocity with which the fleet was coming in, chasing down the Highborn ships at what looked like maximum thrust levels, had the mark of the Sledgehammer all over it.

Barron looked down, checking the status of landing operations. Federov's bombers were all back in the bays, but half the interceptors were still out there, waiting in landing queues or forming a rearguard to hold back the newly-arrived Highborn wings.

Blasting the battleships' engines at full thrust was going to make it hard for those last fighters to keep up, to get back before they exhausted their fuel. But it was a chance he had to take. He couldn't risk what remained of the fleet's battleline for less than a thousand fighters. He wondered about a life that had enabled him to reduce the possible abandonment of a thousand pilots to basic mathematical analysis.

What else might I have done, have been, if I had not been born a Barron...

"Atara...alert the wing commanders of the rearguard. The fleet is pulling out, and they're going to have to keep up. Fifteen minutes...they are to hold for fifteen minutes, and not a second more. Then I want them back here, I don't care if they burn their engines down to molten goo to do it!"

Because any of them who don't do it are going to die...

* * *

"You've got the ship, Vig!" Andi leapt up from her chair,

and she raced back toward the ladder leading to the lower deck. She could hear Vig's voice in the background, but she was already sliding down, and she couldn't make out what he was saying. She wanted to be at *Pegasus*'s controls, but she *needed* to be down in the airlock. Vig could handle the ship as well as she could, as much as part of her hated to admit that, but she wasn't sending any of her people out on the exceedingly dangerous operation of hauling in what she hoped—without any real proof—was Reg Griffin's survival pod.

She bounded across the lower deck, almost losing her footing as the thrusters kicked in before the dampeners could compensate. Vig wasn't just pushing *Pegasus* forward, he was moving the ship in a zigzag pattern, being cautious to evade any enemy fighters that might notice the vessel's approach and decide to take a few shots.

That was smart, the kind of veteran move that only confirmed her confidence in her friend. It also made it pretty damned difficult to get around on the ship.

The others were all strapped in, and Andi threw up her hand as she saw several of them moving their hands toward the harnesses. "Stay…there's nothing any of you can do right now." That was true, more or less. She probably could have used some help trying to haul Reg's pod into the ship, but she'd resolved to handle that herself. Apart from that, she needed Vig at the controls and Lex in engineering…and for everyone else to stay the hell out of the way.

She tore open the door next to the airlock, pulling one of the suits from the rack inside and climbing into it. She was trying to move too quickly, and she almost lost her balance, her hand reaching out and catching her before she fell. She stood still for a few seconds, one foot in the suit and one out, and then she finished. She zipped up, not an easy thing to do alone with her hands in large bulky gloves, and then she muttered a command to the small AI that ran the survival gear. "Activate life support."

The suit puffed up a bit as cool air pumped in, and Andi stood for a few more seconds until the small green light to the inside of her faceplate illuminated. The suit checked out. She was ready.

She opened the inner airlock door and stepped inside. A moment later, the door slid shut, and she could hear the sounds of the pumps evacuating the chamber. Thirty second later, the outer doors were open, and Andi Lafarge was in space, clinging to the hull of her ship.

She looked around, feeling like a fool almost immediately. She was enough of a veteran of the deeps to realize what a tiny thing a human being was in the utter vastness of space. She snapped a quick order to her AI, and a small image projected inside her helmet. Her suit was linked to *Pegasus*'s main system, and her portable display gave her the scanner reading she needed to track down what she hoped was Reg.

"Vig, about two kilometers forward. Six degrees in the Y axis, and 44 in the Z." She knew she didn't have to provide such detailed instructions. Vig had the scanner data, too, and he knew exactly what Andi was trying to do.

"Andi…first be careful. EVAs are always dangerous. And…" A pause. "Well, we don't have much time. We have to cut our evasive routines to try to get close enough to that beacon, and well…"

Andi understood, even though Vig hadn't managed to get the word 'hurry' out of his mouth. It didn't tend to align all that often with 'be careful.' But Andi wasn't going to put the rest of her people at any more risk than necessary, not them, and not the tenuous trail they had to a way to defeat the Highborn.

That meant she was going to hurry. *The hell with careful…*

She climbed out of the airlock, her magnetic boots gripping the metal of *Pegasus*'s hull. She had a lifeline, of course, but it was only twenty meters long. If Vig couldn't get close enough, and Andi got a visual on Reg…well, it wouldn't be the first time she'd ended up floating free, relying on her air jets to make it back to the ship.

She clung to *Pegasus*'s hull, her eyes fixed on the projection in her helmet. She was struck by the seeming peacefulness of space, despite the fact that she knew she was in the center of one of the largest battles ever fought. She was well aware of the almost unimaginable distances involved in space travel, but it still felt like a surprise that she couldn't see any ships…or explosions and combat.

Time passed, and she could feel the ship's deceleration, and finally something that felt very much like *Pegasus* had come to a dead halt.

That was dangerous, she knew. She was sure Vig had Ross Tarnan in the topside turret by then, but it wouldn't take a lot for a few Highborn fighters to cripple her ship, if not destroy it outright.

Two minutes…you've got two minutes to find her, and then you have to go back in and get your people out of here…

She looked all over, again, a pointless effort. If she found Reg Griffin, it would be on her scanner, not with her naked eyes.

"Andi…right off to the starboard. Fifty meters, almost directly on the ship's Y plane…"

She turned and looked, but even at such close range, she couldn't see anything. But the contact was there, on the small projected display, and she felt a burst of excitement. Her hand dropped to the tether, and she was about to unclasp the latch when *Pegasus* lurched slightly.

She wasn't sure what had happened, not at first. The thrust—if that's what it was—had been too light even to be the positioning jets. Then, she realized.

Vig is clearing the air lines. He's using them to push the ship toward Reg…

It was beyond precision flying, and Andi knew she might have to let go her belief that Vig was *almost* as good a pilot as she was.

She watched as the contact drew closer, and finally she could see it, the tiny blinking light of a Confed escape pod. She let herself drift away from the ship, her tether still in place, and she maneuvered her way toward the pod. Vig's repositioning had been almost perfect, an uncanny degree of accuracy for such a thing. She reached out, and she grabbed hold of the pod…and then she affixed it to her tether. She breathed a sigh of relief as she activated the winch…and then she felt the line pulling her—and Reg Griffin—back toward the ship, and to safety.

Or as close to safety as she could get on a tiny ship in the middle of a titanic battle.

*   *   *

"Full power to the engines. The fleet is withdrawing, and it's time to follow." Sonya Eaton sat on *Colossus*'s cavernous bridge, snapping out orders to the aides gathered around her. It was a bit primitive, in a way, for her to rely on so many human officers when so many of her orders required the advanced number crunching of the computer systems, but she was more comfortable dealing with other people than directly with an electronic interface.

The old imperial AIs that had run the vessel, and likely interacted very closely with its captain, were a part of the ship that had not been restored. The Rim powers and the Hegemony had made great strides in information technology utilizing recovered imperial artifacts, but no one had matched the great sophistication of the empire's old thinking computers.

Colossus was still fighting, its massive weapons lancing out, cutting into the closest elements of the Highborn fleet. The enemy was badly strung out, the result of Barron's aggressive move against the attack forces moving into the system, and Clint Winters's unexpected assault on the flanking force. There were still enough Highborn ships in the system to obliterate every vessel under Barron's and Winters's commands, *Colossus* included, but it would take hours, perhaps days, to reorder them sufficiently to launch an organized assault.

That fact gave the fleet its chance to escape, and *Colossus* and *Excalibur* and a small line of heavy ships were safeguarding that operation, fighting one rearguard action after another. But now, it was time to break off...and to follow the rest of the fleet through the point. There were Highborn ships close enough to follow, to prolong the fighting, but not enough to stop the withdrawal. The fleet had advanced right into an ambush...and though a series of near-miracles, it had escaped, even caught part of the enemy in a trap of sorts.

Now it was time to get out. The Pact couldn't spare *Colossus* or *Excalibur*. If any Highborn followed closely behind, the ships that had already transited would overwhelm and destroy them. With any luck, the fleet would make it all the way back to Striker without suffering further losses.

What happened then would depend on what the enemy did, whether the shaky stalemate continued...or the Highborn forces reorganized themselves and came right at the fortress, initiating the battle that could very well decide the war once and for all.

Eaton had a good enough grasp on all that to be glad it was Tyler Barron's problem, and not hers. Her job was starker, simpler. Get *Colossus* out of harm's way before it suffered any more damage...and be ready for whatever came next.

* * *

Andi felt her hands clench even as she let out a loud yell. She'd been watching three Highborn fighters close with *Pegasus* for the past few minutes and now, thanks to Ross

Tarnan in the topside turret, there were only two.

Pegasus was no warship, but her guns were heavier than those carried by a one-man fighter, and that advantage might just save Andi and all her people. The ship didn't look like a militarily significant target—though if the enemy had any way of knowing the wife of the Pact's senior admiral and the pilot who commanded all the fighter wings, were both onboard, she suspected half the enemy fleet would be chasing her down. Instead of three fighters.

Two fighters…

Still, danger was danger, and either of the remaining attack craft could seriously damage *Pegasus* if it got into range and scored a hit. Andi's spontaneous effort to save Reg Griffin had worked. The pilot was injured and unconscious, but she was going to be just fine.

Unless they all got blasted to atoms.

Andi had paused for a few seconds, torn between rushing to the bridge…or down to the bottom turret. It was a question of navigation versus fighting…and as much as she acknowledged Vig's abilities as a pilot, if *Pegasus* was going to make a mad dash to save all their lives, she'd decided *she* had to be at the controls. They had to escape those interceptors pursuing them, but they were never going to survive just fighting. The more time that elapsed, the likelier it was that more enemy fighters would engage.

"Lex…I need that power now. I don't care if the damned reactor melts, as long as it gets us the hell out of *here*." She worked the controls even as she spoke, pouring all her piloting skill into trying to shake *Pegasus*'s pursuers. She'd planned to head back through the Confederation wings, wildly transmitting the beacon that identified *Pegasus* as a friendly. But the fighters had suddenly broken off, and they'd blasted back toward the battleships at full thrust. She understood at once. Tyler had issued a withdrawal order. She'd even smiled for a few seconds. Maybe Clint Winters's intervention was actually going to work. She dared to imagine she had helped in her way to save the fleet. To save Tyler.

But the withdrawal left *Pegasus* far more exposed than she had been. Her ship was fast, assuming the already-tortured reactor and engines could take even more abuse, but if the enemy wanted her badly enough, they could catch her.

She slammed her fist down in her lap in frustration as one of Tarnan's shots went *just* wide of the closest fighter. She was frustrated her gunner had only taken down one of the enemy ships, but she knew that wasn't fair. She had enough firsthand experience to understand just how difficult it was to hit a fighter.

"You've got all the power I can coax out of her, Andi…and I can't guarantee when she's going to give up the ghost entirely."

Andi just nodded, and she jerked her head abruptly to the side, shaking off some of the sweat that had been pouring down her face. She nudged the acceleration higher…and then even higher. *Pegasus* had never let her down…and she was willing to bet the day that would change had not yet come.

It was going to be a race now, a desperate run to the transit point, following the fleet as it retreated…with all the might of the Highborn right behind her.

She would either make it, or she wouldn't, and there was nothing to be gained about thinking about it any deeper, or pondering what ifs.

She pushed the controls even farther forward, and *Pegasus* began to shake wildly as the vessel blasted out more thrust than it even had before.

Fifty-fifty.

Despite her best efforts, Andi hadn't been able to stop herself from estimating their chances.

Though she thought her numbers might be a touch optimistic…

* * *

"What exactly, Admiral Winters, was unclear about my orders for you to remain at Striker, *no matter what*?" Tyler Barron's voice was rough and raspy, but he suspected his second-in-command would sense the lack of any real anger in it almost as quickly as Atara had. *Dauntless* had transited along with the rest of the fleet, and they were all enjoying a passing moment of relative safety.

"Well, Admiral…I just figured it made more sense to mutiny than it did to allow the Pact to lose it's top admiral. Besides, your wife would have had my hide if I hadn't set out with the whole fleet."

"Andi…you saw Andi?" Barron hadn't heard a word about *Pegasus*, or any update on the status of Andi's mission.

"Yes…she came back to Striker. She was the one who told us about the ambush the Highborn were planning. She is why we're here, Tyler. She's a force of nature, that one."

"She is, indeed, my friend. So, let's say you get a pass on insubordination, just this one time." Somehow, Barron doubted it *would* be the last time. "Is Andi back at Striker?"

The silence on the line told Barron all he needed to know, and it confirmed his worst fears.

"She wouldn't stay back, Ty. I tried to get her to come with me on *Excalibur*, but…"

"She brought *Pegasus* out here?" Barron turned, his eyes moving to the display, and then to Atara. He hadn't seen Andi's ship, not in Beta Telavara and not among the retreating fleet units still trickling through the transit point. He'd almost let himself feel relief at the number of ships that had made it out, but now there was only a void, and a deep, yawning worry about where a single free trader was, a tiny ship that had no place in a battle like the one just ended.

He felt a flash of anger at Andi, at her recklessness, but it was immediately washed away by guilt and fear. "Atara…"

"No sign of *Pegasus*, Tyler…not yet." A pause. "But there

are still ships coming through."

Barron appreciated Atara's effort, but he knew the fleet couldn't wait much longer. He'd left the Highborn forces in massive disarray, and he was fairly certain he had time to get his fleet out of harm's way, to return to Striker before the enemy could conduct a true pursuit. As long as they didn't waste any time.

Could he leave…without knowing? Without waiting for Andi's ship to return?

If she returns…

He'd tried to clamp down on that last thought, but it had slipped out anyway.

He sat, silent, still, almost in a state of shock, and he watched the minutes slip by, then an hour, two. The flow of ships transiting from Beta Telavara slowed…and then it stopped. He knew there were still ships back there, crippled vessels that would never escape. He'd done everything he could to rescue those crews, and many of his ships were packed with refugees, survivors of vessels that had been left behind.

Was *Pegasus* one of those ships? Or had it been…

Every second passed in agonizing slowness, and with every one of them, Tyler Barron's spirit sank. He could feel his hope slipping away, and in the part of his mind that wore his admiral's stars, he knew he had to give the order, to pull the fleet away from the point, and set a course back to Striker.

He could feel wetness in his eyes, and he struggled to remain cool, emotionless. His people needed their admiral, not a heartbroken husband…and the billions on the Rim needed the navy to stay in the fight, to hold back the enemy that would turn them all into slaves and supplicants. It was bigger than any one man, any one woman. No matter how much he loved Andi, he was a prisoner, to his heritage and his duty.

And now he had to leave, to pull away, not even

knowing what had happened to her.

"Atara…" He managed to speak the name, but the order he had to give proved more difficult. He hesitated, took a deep breath, and said, "The fleet will head toward the exit point at full thrust."

"Yes, Adm…Tyler, the display!"

Barron's head whipped around, and he could see the energy spike from the transit point…and a single ship emerging into the system. For an instant the scanners offered nothing more than a location. But then the stats began to flow in…mass, dimensions, thruster output. They were all familiar, deeply, gratifyingly familiar.

"It's *Pegasus*!"

Barron hadn't needed Atara to tell him that, but he was grateful for the confirmation nevertheless.

He could see that Andi's ship was damaged, that its thrust was barely half its normal levels. But that, he could do something about.

"Atara…fleet order. All ships, proceed to Fortress Striker at full thrust." He turned and leaned over his comm. "Clint, you've got fleet command right now. Get our people out of here." He tried to hold back a smile, without real success. "I'll be right behind you."

Back to Atara: "Let's lock the approach beacons on *Pegasus*, Atara. It's time to get that ship docked and get the hell out of here."

Chapter Forty-Three

Forward Base Striker
Vasa Denaris System
Year 327 AC (After the Cataclysm)

"You can't go away again. No!" Cassie stared at Tyler Barron with an insistent frown on her face. Barron knew her words came only from her love for him, and for Andi, but they cut him like a knife. He wasn't going anywhere, that much he could promise her. But she was.

The invasion had failed, and if Andi's and Clint Winters's intervention had averted total disaster, there was no question of any renewed offensive. The campaign had proven beyond doubt that the Highborn forces were vaster than even the most aggressive estimates…and the enemy fighters had proven to be as effective as feared. Tyler Barron knew what he had to do. He had to get ready, prepare to meet the Highborn once again in battle, this time in defense of Fortress Striker…to hold the path back to the Rim and to the Confederation itself.

He was still unsure about tactics, deployments, just about everything he would have to have ready. But he was sure of one thing. Cassiopeia Barron would be nowhere close to the fortress when it became the center of a monumental battle. He knew very well his daughter's future rested in many ways on the outcome of the war, but he was damned sure not going to allow her to be anywhere she'd face immediate danger.

"You can't go either! Promise me!" Barron winced as his daughter turned toward Andi and unleashed a barrage with the same brutal severity her mother was wont to direct at those who stood in her way. There was no way to explain to a five year old child, even one as intelligent and incisive as Cassie, why her parents had to send her away. 'We love you, which is why we can't be with you' was a difficult argument to make to a child, no matter how intelligent she was, or how true the words were.

"We will talk about it later, Cassie. For now, let's just spend some time together." Barron had precious little time to spare, he suspected, but just then, he would settle for a few quiet hours, just the three of them. He knew he had to speak with Andi as well, discuss her intentions to leave almost immediately for the Badlands, to seek out the phantom weapon the empire had supposedly used to defeat the Highborn. Barron didn't doubt such a resource existed…but it was too tenuous a goal to justify watching Andi leave yet again.

At least she won't be going into enemy space this time.

Though if we can't hold here, everything might be enemy space…

Barron pushed it away, with all the force he could muster. He had a few weeks, days even, with his family, and he wasn't going to let anything ruin that.

War would come again soon enough, and he would be there to meet it, as he had always been.

* * *

"Andi, I don't know what to say. Thank you." Reg Griffin was propped up on a pile of pillows, staring right at the door as Andi stepped into her hospital room. The pilot had been injured, though not severely, and by all accounts, she would be out of the hospital the next day, and back on duty in less than a week.

"It was just dumb luck that we were so close. What happened, anyway?" Andi felt almost immediately as though she'd blurted out too much. She hadn't believed any Highborn pilot could match Griffin, but she didn't want to exacerbate Reg's self-recriminations.

"There is this pilot...he's good, Andi, really good. Unlike anything I've seen before." A pause, then: "No, that's not exactly true. He flies just like..." Reg hesitated again, and Andi moved over to the side of the bed, looking down and waiting silently until her friend continued.

"He flies like Jake Stockton. The way Jake...did..."

Andi didn't know what to think of what she was hearing. Her first instinct was usually to doubt almost anything she heard, but Reg Griffin wasn't the unreliable sort. Of course, the pilot had been through a lot.

"Could it be coincidence? Or, maybe they studied their own scanner records from the early battles, when Jake was still..." Andi looked down at the floor, and the two remained silent for a moment. Then she stared back at Reg. "I just wanted to stop and see you, because I'm leaving in the morning. I think we found something that will help fight the Highborn...but it's still just a trail, not an actual weapon yet."

She leaned forward and put her hand on Reg's shoulder. "Don't let this enemy pilot get into your head, Reg. Tyler's going to need you." She forced out a smile she couldn't imagine looked anything less than fake, and then she turned and walked out of the room.

She had twelve hours before *Pegasus* was heading out, one evening and night, and she was damned sure going to spend it with Tyler and Cassie.

Then she was going to leave them again...to go out there and find a way to save them both.

* * *

"We likely accomplished one thing. We've proven to the Senate the importance of continuing to support the war effort. They can't look at the reports and the scanner footage we sent down the pipe and not realize the magnitude of the danger." Barron didn't much care for the slang title that had already attached itself to the string of relay stations that vastly reduced communications time to and from Megara. But it was easier to call the thing the 'pipe' just like everyone else was doing than it was to try to fight a trend that had already taken hold. Barron was just glad to have the thing operative, and the reduction in two way communications time from six months to just a couple weeks had all kind of tactical implications.

Including a few he imagined might come back to bite him. He'd dealt with the Senate long enough to realize there were times when a solid lag in communications was a blessing.

"You accomplished much, Tyler, and you have my profound thanks. Our great test still goes on, the struggle for survival, for freedom looming as tall as ever. But the enemy suffered considerable losses as well, including many in their new fighter wings. That, at least, is a good thing.

The massive battles the Pact fleet had just fought would serve Akella even more usefully than him. The Senate would be scared to death, but they were far enough away that they might focus some of that against him, place the blame on their senior admiral. The Hegemony Council was too close to the action for that kind of nonsense. If Striker fell, the chance to hold onto the rest of the Hegemony would almost certainly be lost. The once-mighty Masters would be reduced to refugees, likely housed on Megara in considerable comfort but with a status lying somewhere between guests and well-tended prisoners. Even Thantor had backed off on his attacks on Akella, and her position as

Number One seemed secure, at least for the time being.

Chronos had reaffirmed his allegiance, and his willingness to allow Barron to retain the top command, as had Vian Tulus. The Palatian Imperator had been wounded in the last of the fighting, and Barron imagined his blood brother would consider the resulting twenty centimeter scar something fit for a song.

The situation was no better than it had been before he'd led the fleet forward, but aside from the realization of just how many ships the Highborn possessed, it wasn't any worse either, as least as far as he could see. He'd suffered losses, but the enemy had as well. Indeed, he'd reviewed the scanner recap of *Excalibur*'s first battle, and he'd been awed by the superbattleship's power. He would have three more of them in a matter of months, and they would be most welcome. With any luck, the enemy would give him those months…though he figured he might well have used up his current allotment of fortune. Plainly put, he was concerned that maybe his luck had run out.

He got confirmation of that just a moment later.

"Admiral Barron…" An aide stood in the open doorway, looking at Barron and the assembled leaders nervously.

"Yes, what is it?" Barron was a little annoyed. He'd left strict orders not to be disturbed.

"Sir, we've received a priority communique on the pipe. It's for you, Admiral, from Mr. Holsten at Confederation Intelligence. It's about the Union border, sir…and Admiral Denisov."

Chapter Forty-Four

Highborn Flagship S'Argevon
Imperial System GH3-2307 (Beta Telvara System)
Year of the Firstborn 389 (327 AC)

"You did, in fact, eliminate the human fighter commander, or at least a review of all available scanner footage suggests that you did. That is a success, certainly, however our wings took losses far in excess of both expectations and the casualties the enemy suffered. I understand this was not entirely your fault and, in consideration of the difficulties encountered in transiting the fleet, and the resulting force mismatches, your squadrons performed well by several measures. For these reasons, I will neither punish you, nor remove you from your command responsibilities. We will soon begin our invasion, and your wings will be at the forefront of the attack. You will have a chance to redeem yourself, to claim a share of the glory of victory."

Stockton listened to Tesserax's words, and most of his mind responded with sniveling gratitude. He felt his body drop to a prostrate position before the creature who called himself a god, and he looked on from the part of his brain that still belonged to him with disgust and exhaustion.

He'd seen hundreds of his comrades killed...and he himself had destroyed Reg Griffin's ship, stripped his old wings of the leader he'd left behind in his place. The sole scrap of solace he'd managed to gather to himself over the past four years had been the knowledge that he'd left his pilots in good hands. Now, he'd taken even that from them.

But guilt and misery were finite, and Stockton was already at rock bottom. He felt distracted, almost unable to think about anything. Even watching himself, his body and his brain, supplicating before the hated Highborn had mostly lost its effect on him. He'd craved death for four years, and for all that time it had been denied to him. He wondered if things could be any worse, if he could reach depths his soul had not yet plumbed.

"Go now, Jake Stockton. You are a mere human, despite your undoubted skills. You must rest. We will have need of your services again, soon. I would have you ready, prepared to face the challenges ahead."

Tesserax gestured with an arrogance that infuriated the inner Stockton. But, as always, he was powerless even to respond. The portion of his mind that was an abject slave— the greater portion by far—understood the dismissal. Stockton could feel his head bow deeper before he rose and left the room, returning to the small cubicle that had served as his quarters for four years.

The door slid open, and he stepped inside, sitting in the room's single chair. He sat with his hands on his desk, a sparse affair like everything else in the room, barely large enough for the workstation that occupied most of it. His mind was reviewing the battle against Reg Griffin, and also planning new ways to direct the wings, to take advantage of the fact that his old comrades had lost their leader. Again.

Their morale would be weak, shaky. Perhaps he could use that to his advantage.

Stockton endured the thoughts, and he despised himself again for his weakness. He'd struggled a thousand times to try to break the Collar's hold, to reclaim some control over himself, his body, his mind. Reg Griffin had come close to taking him out, and for a brief few seconds, as electrical discharges flew around his cockpit, he'd almost believed she had succeeded. But in the end, his only injuries had been a few light burns, and a headache that had lasted for three days.

You're just as useless as you've been for four years, he railed against himself, throwing all he could into a pointless effort to move his hand, to slam his fist on the table.

He didn't manage that, but he was staring down at the desk…and he saw his index finger move. It was slow, a motion of no more than two centimeters. But somehow, he knew *he* had done that. Not the Collar-controlled part of his brain, but *him*.

He focused, trying to push all distraction away, and he tried again. He could feel the effort, almost unbearable, but then he saw it again.

His finger moved, tracing a short line down the surface of the desk.

*   *   *

"We might have achieved more if we hadn't underestimated Tyler Barron and his comrades." Phazarax had been careful to characterize the failure as a joint one, and not Tesserax's error. He was the head of the Church in the Colony, and that was a position that afforded him considerable latitude, and quite a large amount of immunity from the actions and resentments of others, even the viceroy of the Colony himself. Still, he didn't want to provoke his comrade. Such rivalries offered little gain and only potential loss. Their duties differed considerably, but they were both tasked with bringing the humans to heel, and integrating them into the domains of the Highborn. Success would benefit them both, as failure would accrue to them jointly.

"No mere human can outthink one of us, Phazarax. Tyler Barron's maneuver was simply crowned with luck, a random decision that aligned with other variables to produce a temporary advantage. A ninety percent chance of success is still a ten percent probability of failure. Yet the fact that said ten percent avails in one instance does not suggest change is desirable in a subsequent ninety percent chance. The humans escaped, with rather less damage than would have been optimal, and they inflicted greater losses on us than expected. That changes nothing. They did, indeed, suffer considerable casualties themselves, and a continuation of hostilities soon after the close of the recent battle will only accelerate the decline of their morale."

"You may be right, Tesserax. Indeed, you are almost certainly correct. I must caution you, however. The Church has encountered greater resistance than expected from the subject populations of the former Hegemony, especially the segment known as Kriegeri. Executions and implementation of torture are running four hundred thirty and six hundred ten percent respectively above projections. In short, the humans are far more resistant than we had expected...and there is little doubt the wild societies of the Rim will be even more so than the Hegemonic populations, inured as they are to a highly structured society."

"They are still only humans, Phazarax. Perhaps they have more courage and animalistic stubbornness than we had anticipated. It is possible that many are willing to die rather than to change. But that does not give them the technology or the intellect to stand against us in battle. We will complete the conquest, and when we do, your Church may kill and punish as many as it takes to impose widespread acceptance. I have no doubt pacification operations may indeed take longer than we had hoped. But we have been able to operate the industry and produce considerable output, even with populations not fully broken. I reject the notion that the base and primitive traits of the humans will meaningfully extend the duration of the conquest."

"And what if such resistance translates to more tenacity and courage in battle? What if their astonishing production can be sustained for a longer period? What then?

"Such concerns are of no consequence. A greater victory in the recent campaign would have been welcome, but it was hardly necessary. The enemy suffered considerable losses, and while ours were heavier than projected, there is little doubt we possess all the strength required to conclude matters. It is time to activate the next step of our plan, to finish this with one great blow. It is time to implement Attack Plan Alpha."

* * *

"You have wanted this for a very long time, Gaston, have you not?" Percelax sat on the raised platform, leaning back in his chair as the Union's restored dictator walked across the floor.

"Indeed I have, Lord Percelax. The Confederation has been a thorn in my side for all of my life. Now, I am on the verge of gaining vengeance for all the injuries I have suffered at their hands."

"You shall have your revenge, Gaston, and much more." Percelax found it somewhat difficult to converse with the human as though the two of them were equals. Villieneuve should have been on his knees, offering thanks for favor, and begging for a continuation of such grace.

These humans on the Rim will have to learn how to worship us. That is likely to be a hard lesson for many.

Percelax looked down at the arrogant human in front of him, pulled from the edge of destruction only by his intervention and now restored to his petty notions of power. Villieneuve exhibited some empty signs of gratitude, but Percelax knew the human's true goals were to extract the aid he needed, at the least possible cost. Villieneuve thought to use Percelax and the Highborn, but it was he who would be the tool, the blunt and disposable instrument.

You will come to understand and respect your gods, human...sooner than you can imagine.

Villieneuve was quite intelligent, at least by the standards of the Rimdwellers, though he seemed a particularly sociopathic example of his kind. But to Percelax, he was less than nothing beyond whatever utility he offered. Villieneuve no doubt believed he was taking advantage of his new allies, betting on taking control of the Confederation with the arms and technology the Highborn provided...and making himself too powerful for them to overcome. Villieneuve planned to betray him, Percelax didn't even consider that a variable.

He did, however, find it laughable hubris on the part of a mere human, one who had been too weak to defeat his enemies himself.

"I have much to do, Percelax, so if you will excuse..."

"Gaston, there is one more thing while you are here." Percelax gestured, the merest flick of his finger as it rested on the armrest of his chair. The response was immediate, as ten Thralls, soldiers in full combat gear, jogged into the room, dropping to their knees the instant they reached a long red line on the floor. "Hail Percelax, we obey and beseech you for your favor."

Villieneuve glanced quickly to each side, seemingly caught between confusion, and approval at the obsequious conduct of Percelax's minions. And perhaps a bit of fear about what was happening.

Well grounded fear...

"These Thralls will escort you to one last appointment before you leave, Gaston."

"I am quite pressed for time, Lord Percelax." Villieneuve seemed edgier, nervous. "Perhaps later."

"I'm afraid I must insist." He gestured again, and the Thralls closed in around Villieneuve. "This will not take long, Gaston. Not long at all. Though it will, I am afraid, be quite painful. It is necessary, however." A short pause.

"Have I ever told you about the Collar, Gaston?"

Blood on the Stars will Continue with
Attack Plan Alpha
Book 16

Appendix

CFS Excalibur-Class Superbattleship

Excalibur is the first Confederation ship class to fully employ a combination of its own newest technology with that of the Hegemony, provided per the terms of the Pact Treaty. It was designed at a rapid pace in response to the dire situation on the front, and the *Excalibur* itself, the first, and to date only, vessel of the class to launch, was constructed at the Kirovsky Shipyards, orbiting the Iron Belt planet Belgravia.

Excalibur is more than twice the size of *Repulse*-class battleships such as *Dauntless*, and the vessel carries a massive arsenal of weaponry and defensive system, much of them representing major leaps forward in Confederation technology.

Offensive Array

1 – Spinal mount antimatter-powered hyper-velocity railgun, launching 120kg projectiles.

4 – Quad 10gw "primary beam" particle accelerator mounts (16 guns in total).

40 – Omega fourth generation 2 gigawatt laser cannons.

20 – Ground bombardment pulse cannons.

10 – Plasma mine launchers (1,000 mines held in magazine).

Defensive Array

60 – 200 megawatt point defense lasers in double turret mounts.

20 – Blast gun anti-fighter pellet launchers (developed from railgun technology).

4 – Deflector screen projection systems (designed to warp and distort incoming energy weapons fire.

Small Craft Contingents

180 – Lightning III ("Black Lightning") assault fighter-bombers (12 squadrons, 2 assault wings).
30 – Attack Wave ("Ironfist") heavy bombers (crew of 6).
20 – Heavy assault shuttles (capacity 20 Marines).
20 – Standard Fleet shuttles.
2 – Admiralty-3A class fleet command cutters.

Power Generation

Dual "Confed-1.0" antimatter reactor system.
12 – 15 gigawatt fusion reactors (backup power).

Complement

Primary ship crew – 1,620
Fighter-bomber pilot and flight crews – 960
Marine contingent – 840
Admiral's command staff – 40

Total – 3460

The Pact

The Pact is the document forming an Alliance between the Hegemony, the Confederation, the Palatian Alliance, and nine separate Far Rim nation states. The ratification of the agreement faced significant opposition by both the Confederation Senate and the Hegemonic Council. The Senate was wary of the economic burdens it would impose and the requirements it held for the Confederation to commit he vast bulk of its armed forces to the Hegemony front. The Hegemonic Council objected to the provisions requiring full sharing of all science and technical data, an obligation that flowed almost entirely in one direction as a result of the Hegemony's generally greater tech levels.

The name came to refer to the alliance itself, though such usage was not specified in the document and was entirely colloquial.

Excerpt from "Fighting the Highborn,"
a History and Tactical Manual for Combat Against
the Highborn, by Andromeda Lafarge.

The Highborn were created to help mankind, to pull the empire back from the abyss. Instead, they hastened the decline, and brought the Cataclysm into being more quickly than the previous decline would have done.

They were created to be teachers, but they longed to become tyrants. They were conceived as mentors, but they took the role of conquerors. They were brought into being to save humanity, yet they came to see themselves as gods.

The Highborn appear to be human, indeed, save for their size and the lack of any discernible physical imperfections, they look just like men and women. Whether they are, in fact humans whose evolution has been enhanced by artificial means, or they are indeed a new species, is a matter of conjecture and debate among scientists. This volume will not concern itself with such questions, for they are irrelevant to its purpose. The guiding principal of this work, the purpose for which it has been written and updated, is a simple one. The Highborn seek to rule over normal humans, totally and utterly. That makes them the enemy of all men and women who crave freedom and self-determination, all those who would not be slaves crawling before manufactured gods. If you are of this mind, read on, for this book is dedicated to one purpose, and one only.

The complete eradication of the Highborn.

Strata of the Hegemony

The Hegemony is an interstellar polity located far closer to the center of what had once been the old empire than Rimward nations such as the Confederation. The Rim nations and the Hegemony were unaware of each other's existence until the White Fleet arrived at Planet Zero and established contact.

Relatively little is known of the Hegemony, save that their technology appears to be significantly more advanced than the Confederation's in most areas, though still behind that of the old empire.

The culture of the Hegemony is based almost exclusively on genetics, with an individual's status being entirely dependent on an established method of evaluating genetic "quality." Generations of selective breeding have produced a caste of "Masters," who occupy an elite position above all others. There are several descending tiers below the Master class, all of which are categorized as "Inferiors."

The Hegemony's culture likely developed as a result of its location much closer to the center of hostilities during the Cataclysm. Many surviving inhabitants of the inward systems suffered from horrific mutations and damage to genetic materials, placing a premium on any bloodlines lacking such effects.

The Rimward nations find the Hegemony's society to be almost alien in nature, while its rulers consider the inhabitants of the Confederation and other nations to be just another strain of Inferiors, fit only to obey their commands without question.

Masters

The Masters are the descendants of those few humans

spared genetic damage from the nuclear, chemical, and biological warfare that destroyed the old empire during the series of events known as the Cataclysm. The Masters sit at the top of the Hegemony's societal structure and, in a sense, are its only true full members or citizens.

The Masters' culture is based almost entirely on what they call "genetic purity and quality," and even their leadership and ranking structure is structured solely on genetic rankings. Every master is assigned a number based on his or her place in a population-wide chromosomal analysis. An individual's designation is thus subject to change once per year, to adjust for masters dying and for new adults being added into the database. The top ten thousand individuals in each year's ratings are referred to as "High Masters," and they are paired for breeding matchups far more frequently than the larger number of lower-rated Masters.

Masters reproduce by natural means, through strict genetic pairings based on an extensive study of ideal matches. The central goal of Master society is to steadily improve the human race by breeding the most perfect specimens available and relegating all others to a subservient status. The Masters consider any genetic manipulation or artificial processes like cloning to be grievously sinful, and all such practices are banned in the Hegemony on pain of death to all involved. This belief structure traces from the experiences of the Cataclysm, and the terrible damage inflicted on the populations of imperial worlds by genetically engineered pathogens and cloned and genetically engineered soldiers.

All humans not designated as Masters are referred to as Inferiors, and they serve the Masters in various capacities. All Masters have the power of life and death over Inferiors. It is not a crime for a Master to kill an Inferior who has injured or offended that Master in any way.

Kriegeri

The Kriegeri are the Hegemony's soldiers. They are drawn from the strongest and most physically capable specimens of the populations of Inferiors on Hegemony worlds. Kriegeri are not genetically modified, though in most cases, Master supervisors enforce specific breeding arrangements in selected population groups to increase the quality of future generations of Kriegeri stock.

The Kriegeri are trained from infancy to serve as the Hegemony's soldiers and spaceship crews, and are divided in two categories, red and gray, named for the colors of their uniforms. The "red" Kriegeri serve aboard the Hegemony's ships, under the command of a small number of Master officers. They are surgically modified to increase their resistance to radiation and zero gravity.

The "gray" Kriegeri are the Hegemony's ground soldiers. They are selected from large and physically powerful specimens and are subject to extensive surgical enhancements to increase strength, endurance, and dexterity. They also receive significant artificial implants, including many components of their armor, which becomes a permanent partial exoskeleton of sorts. They are trained and conditioned from childhood to obey orders and to fight. The top several percent of Kriegeri surviving twenty years of service are retired to breeding colonies. Their offspring are Krieger-Edel, a pool of elite specimens serving as mid-level officers and filling a command role between the ruling Masters and the rank and file Kriegeri.

Arbeiter

Arbeiter are the workers and laborers of the Hegemony. They are drawn from populations on the Hegemony's many worlds, and typically either exhibit some level of genetic damage inherited from the original survivors or simply lack genetic ratings sufficient for Master status. Arbeiter are from the same general group as the Kriegeri, though the soldier class includes the very best candidates, and the Arbeiter pool consists of the remnants.

Arbeiter are assigned roles in the Hegemony based on rigid assessments of their genetic status and ability. These positions range from supervisory posts in production facilities and similar establishments to pure physical labor, often working in difficult and hazardous conditions.

Defekts

Defekts are individuals—often populations of entire worlds—exhibiting severe genetic damage. They are typically found on planets that suffered the most extensive bombardments and bacteriological attacks during the Cataclysm.

Defekts have no legal standing in the Hegemony, and they are considered completely expendable. On worlds inhabited by populations of Masters, Kriegeri, and Arbeiters, Defekts are typically assigned to the lowest level, most dangerous labor, and any excess populations are exterminated.

The largest number of Defekts exist on planets on the fringes of Hegemony space, where they are often used for such purposes as mining radioactives and other similarly dangerous operations. Often, the Defekts themselves have no knowledge at all of the Hegemony and regard the Masters as gods or demigods descending from the heavens. On such planets, the Masters often demand ores and other raw materials as offerings, and severely punish any failures or shortfalls. Pliant and obedient populations are provided with rough clothing and low-quality manufactured foodstuffs, enabling them to devote nearly all labor to the gathering of whatever material the Masters demand. Resistant population groups are exterminated, as, frequently, are Defekt populations on worlds without useful resources to exploit.

Hegemony Military Ranks

Commander

Not a permanent rank, but a designation for a high-level officer in command of a large ship or a ground operation.

Decaron

A non-commissioned officer rank, the term defines a trooper commanding ten soldiers, including or not including himself. Decarons are almost always chosen from the best of the base level legionaries, pulled from combat units and put through extensive supplemental training before being returned to take their command positions.

Quinquaron

The lowest rank truly considered an officer. A quinquaron officially commands fifty troopers, though such officers are often assigned as few as twenty and as many as one hundred. Quinquarons can also be posted to executive officer positions, serving as the second-in-command to Hectorons. Such postings are common with officers on the fast track for promotion to Hectoron level themselves.

Hectoron

The commander of approximately one hundred soldiers, or a force equivalence of armored combat vehicles or other assets. As with other ranks, there is considerable latitude in the field, and Hectorons can command larger or smaller forces. The Hectoron is considered, in many ways, the backbone of the Hegemony armed forces.

Quingeneron

An officer commanding a combat force of five hundred soldiers or a comparable-strength force of heavy combat or support assets. In recent decades, the Quingeneron rank has been used more as a stepping stone to Kiloron status. Quingenerons also frequently serve as executive officers under Kilorons.

Kiloron

The commander of one thousand soldiers, or a posting of comparable responsibility. Despite the defined command responsibility, Kilorons often command significant larger forces, with senior officers of the rank sometimes directing combat units as large as twenty to fifty thousand. Kiloron is usually the highest level available to Kriegeri, though a small number have managed to reach Megaron status.

Megaron

The title suggests the command of one million combat soldiers or the equivalent power in tanks and other assets, however, in practice, Megarons exercise overall commands in combat theaters, with force sizes ranging from a few hundred thousand to many millions. Megarons are almost always of the Master class.

Blood on the Stars will Continue with
Attack Plan Alpha
Book 16

Printed in Poland
by Amazon Fulfillment
Poland Sp. z o.o., Wrocław

52652719R00244